NETWORK
EFFECT

ALSO BY MARTHA WELLS

NETWORK EFFECT

Martha Wells

A TOM DOHERTY ASSOCIATES BOOK

NEW YORK

NETWORK EFFECT

Copyright © 2020 by Martha Wells

Edited by Lee Harris

A Tor.com Book
Published by Tom Doherty Associates
120 Broadway
New York, NY 10271

www.tor.com

Tor® is a registered trademark of Macmillan Publishing Group, LLC.

The Library of Congress Cataloging-in-Publication Data is available upon request.

ISBN 978-1-250-22986-1 (hardcover)
ISBN 978-1-250-22984-7 (ebook)

Our books may be purchased in bulk for promotional, educational, or business use. Please contact your local bookseller or the Macmillan Corporate and Premium Sales Department at 1-800-221-7945, extension 5442, or by email at MacmillanSpecialMarkets@macmillan.com.

First Edition: May 2020

Printed in the United States of America

0 9 8 7 6 5 4 3 2 1

NETWORK
EFFECT

1

I've had clients who thought they needed an absurd level of security. (And I'm talking absurd even by my standards, and my code was developed by a bond company known for intense xenophobic paranoia, tempered only by desperate greed.) I've also had clients who thought they didn't need any security at all, right up until something ate them. (That's mostly a metaphor. My uneaten client stat is high.)

Dr. Arada, who is what her marital partner Overse calls a "terminal optimist," was somewhere in the comfortable middle zone. Dr. Thiago was firmly in the "Let's investigate the dark cave without that pesky SecUnit" group. Which was why Arada was pressed against the wall next to the hatch to the open observation deck with her palms sweating on the stock of a projectile weapon and Thiago was standing out on said observation deck, trying to reason with a potential target. (That's "potential" per the earlier conversation where Dr. Arada said *Oh SecUnit, I wish you wouldn't call people "targets"* and Thiago had given me the look that usually means *It just wants an excuse to kill someone.*)

But then, that was before the Potential Targets started to brandish their own large projectile-weapon collection.

Anyway, those are the kind of things I think about while I'm swimming under a raider vessel that's attempting to board our sea research facility.

I swam out from under the stern, careful to avoid the propulsion device. I broke the surface quietly, stretched and caught the railing, and pulled myself up. The daylight was bright, the air clear, and I felt exposed. (Why couldn't the stupid raiders attack at night?) I had drones in the air, giving me camera views of both decks of this stupid boat, so I knew this part of the stern was empty.

The superstructure above me was triangular, angled back in a way to make it faster or something, I don't know, I'm a murder-bot, I don't give a crap about boats. The upper deck wrapped around the bow where the forward weapon emplacement was. It gave the stupid boat a lot of blindspots, which were someone else's security nightmare. It was more sophisticated than the other boats we'd seen on this survey, with better tech.

Of course that just made it vulnerable.

I was also monitoring our outer perimeter and the scattered islands surrounding us, in case this was a distraction and there was a second boarding attempt planned. And of course I had a camera on the unfolding shitshow on the observation deck.

Thiago stood out there nearly four meters from the hatchway, not even wearing his protective gear, very much like a human who didn't trust his SecUnit's situation assessment. The apparent leader of the Potential Targets stood at the edge of the deck, barely three meters away, casually pointing a projectile weapon at Thiago. I was more worried about the six other Potential Targets scattered around on the stupid boat's bow deck, and the nozzle of the weapon mounted above the bow deck currently trained on the upper level of our facility.

Some of the Potential Targets weren't wearing helmets. There's a thing you can do with these small intel drones (if your client orders you to, or if you don't have a working governor module), when the hostiles are dumb enough to get aggressive without adequate body armor. You can accelerate a drone and send it straight at the hostile's face. Even if you don't hit an eye or ear and go straight through to the brain, you can make a crater in the skull. Doing this would solve the problem and get me back to new episodes of *Lineages of the Sun* much more quickly, but I knew Arada would make a sad face at me and Thiago would be pissed off. I would probably have to do it anyway. Unfortunately, Potential Target Leader was wearing a helmet.

(Thiago is a marital partner of Dr. Mensah's brother, which is why I gave a crap about his opinion.)

Also, I had no intel yet on how many hostiles were inside the boat where the controls to the large weapon were. Prematurely eliminating the visible targets (excuse me, potential targets) on deck might just tip us out of incipient shitshow into full-on shitshow.

There was sort of a chance that Thiago might actually talk our way out of this. He was great at talking to other humans. But I had a drone waiting just inside the hatchway with Arada. (Overse would be upset if I let her marital partner get killed, and I liked Arada.)

Still managing to sound calm despite everything, Thiago said, "There's no need for any of this. We're researchers, we're not doing anything to hurt anyone here."

Potential Target Leader said something that our FacilitySystem translated through our feed as, "I showed you I'm serious. We'll take what we want, then leave you in peace. Tell the others to come out."

"We'll give you supplies, but not people," Thiago said.

"If you have nice supplies, I'll leave the people."

"You didn't have to shoot anyone." Heat crept into Thiago's voice. "If you needed supplies, we would have given them to you."

Don't worry, the "anyone" who got shot was me.

(Thiago, while violating the security protocol everyone agreed to IN ADVANCE, had walked out to the observation deck to greet the strangers on their stupid boat. I followed and pulled him back from the edge, and so Potential Target Leader shot me instead of him. Got me right in the shoulder. I managed to fall off the observation deck and miss the water intake. Yes, I was pissed off.

"SecUnit, SecUnit, are you there—" Overse, in the facility's command center, had shouted at me over the comm interface.

Yes, I'm fine, I'd sent her over the feed. It's a good thing I don't bleed like a human because hostile marine fauna was about all this situation needed. *I've got everything under fucking control, okay.*

("No, it says it's fine," I heard her relaying to the others on our comm. "Well, yes, it's furious.")

I swung over the railing and dropped to the deck. I'd tuned my pain sensors down but I could feel the projectile wedged in next to my support framework and it was annoying. Staying low, I crawled down the steps into the first cabin structure. The human inside was monitoring a primitive scanner system. (I'd jammed it even before I got shot, feeding it artistic static and random reports of anomalous energy signatures to keep it busy.) I choked her until she was unconscious and then broke her arm to give her something else to worry about if she revived too soon. I didn't take her projectile weapon but I did pause to break a couple of its key components.

The room was stuffed with bags and containers and other human crap. There were neat storage racks but everything was jumbled on the deck. We had seen eleven groups of strange humans in water boats from a distance, and had been contacted by two of them. Both had been what Thiago called "unusually divergent" and some of the others had called deeply weird. Both groups had taken the same elaborate precautions to show they were approaching in a non-hostile manner and had not displayed any weapons. Both groups had wanted to trade supplies with us. (Arada and the others had wanted to just give them what they needed, but Thiago had asked them to trade their stories of why they were here on this planet.)

So okay, maybe Thiago had reason to suppose this group would also be non-hostile. But the earlier groups had given me a chance to develop a profile of local non-hostile approaches/interactions and this group hadn't fit.

Nobody fucking listens to me.

Potential Target Leader and their friends aboard Stupid Boat were also dressed better than the other humans we'd encountered, in clothing that looked newer if not cleaner. There was no planetary feed (stupid planet) but Stupid Boat had its own rudimentary feed that was heavy with games and pornography but light on anything that might be helpful for a security assessment, like who these people were and what they wanted. Even the individual humans' feed signatures only contained info about sexual availability and gender presentation, which I didn't give a damn about.

I slipped through into a grimy metal corridor, then a human stepped out of the next doorway. I disarmed them and slammed their head into the floor.

The door to the next compartment was closed, but one of my drones had landed on the roof earlier, flattened itself to a window, and got me some good scan and vid intel. That was kind of important, because this was the compartment with the control station for the large boat-busting projectile weapon that was currently pointed at our facility.

According to the drone's video, one small human sat in the weapon station, their attention on a primitive camera-based targeting screen. Three large humans, all armed, sat around casually on battered station chairs, though the other stations had missing or badly jury-rigged or outdated equipment. They were chatting, watching Thiago and Potential Target Leader on the screen, la la la, just another day at work.

The compartment was a bulbous structure set to the right of the bow, and reinforced with metal to protect and support the large weapon. The six hostiles near the bow casually pointing projectile weapons at the facility's observation deck were too far away to hear as long as I didn't overdo it. So I snapped the lock and didn't slam the door as I went through.

I hit Target One at the weapon station with an energy pulse from my left arm, throat punch to Target Two as the others came to their feet, pivot and smash kneecap of Target Three, slap Target Four's weapon aside and break collarbone. I'd already had FacilitySys prepare a translation for me, the only sentence I figured I'd need. I said, "Make a noise, and everybody dies."

Target One slumped unconscious over the weapon control station, wound steaming in the damp air. The other three stayed on the deck, whimpering and gurgling.

One of the hostiles outside had glanced around, but didn't change position. Thiago, who was unexpectedly good at stalling, had avoided the question of whether the other researchers were going to come out on the observation deck so Potential Target Leader could decide if he wanted to abduct them or not. Thiago was now listing all our supplies and pretending to stumble over FacilitySys's translation advice. (I knew he was pretending; he was a language expert among other things.) My drone view showed me that Potential Target Leader enjoyed watching Thiago sweat, and that maybe Thiago had noticed and was playing it up a little. He was pretty smart.

Okay, okay, I admit that it was a little upsetting that Thiago didn't trust me.

(He and Mensah had had a conversation about me, back on Preservation Station when Arada was planning this survey. Transcript:

Thiago: "I know I'm in the minority here, but I have serious reservations."

Mensah: "Arada is in charge of this survey, and she wants SecUnit. And frankly, if it isn't the one providing security, I'll withdraw my permission for Amena to go."

(Amena is one of Mensah's children and yes, she is on our facility right now. No pressure!)

Thiago: "You trust it that much?"

Mensah: "With my life, literally. I know what it will do to protect her, and you, and the rest of the team. Of course, it has its faults. In fact, it's probably listening to us right now. Are you listening, SecUnit?"

Me, on the feed: *What? No.*

I'd missed the rest. I'd thought it was better to shut down my tap on the room's comm access and get out of there.)

Target Two whispered something, which FacilitySys rendered as "What are you?"

I said, "I'm a Shut Up or Get Your Head Smashed."

So that was two sentences I'd needed.

I had to get out there because Target Leader had started to walk toward Thiago and avoiding a hostage situation was important to my risk assessment module's Projected Schedule of Events Leading to a Successful Resolution. (In company terms that's a PSELSR, which is a terrible anagram.) (I don't mean anagram, I mean the other thing.)

Thiago backed away, saying, "You don't want to do this. You really don't want to do this."

Yeah, well, it was a little too late for them to run away.

I stepped to the outside hatch and told my drones to get into position. Two of the hostiles had helmets and body armor, and one had a helmet but the face shield had been removed. I hit the hatch release and gave the order.

(At the last second, I changed the drones' instructions from head or face kill-hits to disabling wound-hits in exposed patches on arms and hands, even though it was the hostiles' own stupid, stupid fault for attacking us. Thinking of Arada's sad face made me too uncomfortable.)

The stupid hatch (I hate this boat) was slow and all six targets had turned toward me by the time it opened. My drones struck just as I dove out onto the deck. I hit one target with an energy burst from my right arm, kneecapped the second, two dropped from drone strikes and the last one went down flailing, hand closing convulsively on his weapon's trigger and shooting me right in the chest. For fuck's sake.

By that time, Target Leader had Thiago's arm, weapon pointed at Thiago's head.

I sacrificed six more drones to turn the weapons scattered

around me into useless heaps of metal, then shoved to my feet. I walked up the boarding ramp onto our observation deck. I said, "Let him go." I didn't really feel like negotiating. I have a module on it, somewhere in my archive. It was never much help.

Target Leader's eyes had a lot of white showing, and he was exhibiting multiple signs of stress. So was Thiago. A drone view showed me what I looked like, water dripping from my clothes, my jacket with the Preservation survey logo and shirt showing projectile weapon holes, stained with fluid and a little blood.

I circled them as if heading for the hatch. Target Leader dragged Thiago around to stay facing me, then yelled, "Stop! Or I'll kill him!"

He was right, I'd been trying to make him move, setting up a shot. He had stopped with the observatory bubble behind him, not a good angle for me.

"You can still get out of this," Thiago gasped. "Just let us go. You can take me as a hostage—"

Oh, right, that'll help. I said, "No hostages."

"What is that thing?" Target Leader demanded. "What are you? You're a bot?"

Thiago said, "It's a security unit. A bot/human construct."

Target Leader didn't seem to believe him. "Why does it look like a person?"

I said, "I ask myself that sometimes."

Over the comm loudspeaker, Dr. Ratthi said, "It is a person!" In the background, I heard Overse whisper, "Ratthi, get off the comm!"

While that was going on, I did a quick search of my archived video and pulled an episode of *Valorous Defenders*. It's not a bad show but this is a terrible episode where the characters are attacked by evil SecUnits. (That's like the opposite of an oxymoron, since in the media, there's no such thing as a non-evil SecUnit.) (Is there a word for the opposite of an oxymoron?) I grabbed the three-minute sequence where the SecUnits swarm the base and slaughter the helpless refugees. I uploaded it to stupid boat's porn feed and set it to play on an endless loop.

I'm fast, so I'd finished by the time Target Leader shook Thiago and said, "Order it to back off."

Thiago made a noise suspiciously like a derisive snort. "I wish I could! It doesn't listen to me."

I listen to you plenty, Thiago.

"Who does it—" Target Leader wisely gave up on that tack. "Listen, whoever controls this thing, I'm taking this one on my ship—"

"I've destroyed your engine," I said. I really should have done that. Well, too late now.

Glaring with fury, Target Leader jerked Thiago and Thiago stumbled and leaned away from him. And I saw the hole blossom in Target Leader's upper arm, in the scant few centimeters of clothing and skin exposed between the joints of the badly fitting armor.

I lunged forward and grabbed Thiago, slung him aside, then ripped the projectile weapon away from Target Leader. I knocked him lightly in the stomach and chest with the stock and he dropped to the deck.

Arada stepped out of the hatch, the projectile weapon sensibly pointed down even though my scan showed she had already engaged the safety. She said, "Are you all right? Thiago? SecUnit?"

I said earlier that I was trying to set up a shot; I didn't say whose.

Arada had taken a course in weapons use after the whole thing with GrayCris. I guess having a bunch of murderers chasing you around a planet so they can suppress your research by murdering you would tend to make you more cautious, even if you are a terminal optimist.

On the feed, I said, *Dr. Thiago, Dr. Arada, get inside.* I grabbed Target Leader and tossed him onto the deck of his boat, where the other targets were crawling around trying to get to their hatch. My scan picked up a power surge in the boat's weapon system. That's what happens when you don't have time to clear your hostile vehicle. I said over the comm, "Overse, now would be good."

The thing Overse and the others had been doing while all this was going on was preparing our facility for launch. Under my boots, the deck rumbled and vibrated and our outer supports heaved out of the water, sending waves crashing into the boat as we lifted up.

I don't think the raiders had realized the facility was mobile. The force of displaced water as our drive kicked in shoved the boat sideways, and the raiders lost their targeting lock.

Our outer supports folded in and we lifted further above the surface. The comm loudspeaker broadcast a siren and a translated warning about minimum safe distance and I guess the raiders believed it because their engines revved frantically. I recalled my drones and they shot down toward us to stream in through the hatch. I walked in after them and let the hatch close behind me as the launch protocols started.

2

I told myself it wasn't as much of a shit ending to my first time as Survey Security Consultant While Not Pretending to be a Human and/or Faking the Existence of a Human Supervisor as it could have been. Everybody was alive, they had all their sampling and scans done. Our original schedule actually had us leaving in six planetary days, but since we had finished early Arada had moved that up to three planetary days, that's why most of the facility had already been prepped for launch.

But we'd been lucky, and I hate luck.

Standing in the access corridor I settled my drones, tasking four to stay with me and sending the others to take up various positions around the facility and go dormant. Then I checked the feed for alerts. The team members who weren't busy piloting the facility up through the atmosphere were yelling at each other on the comm. Arada came down the corridor. She didn't have her weapon anymore and my safety protocol check showed she'd unloaded and secured it back in the locker. "SecUnit, you need to get to Medical!"

I checked the feed again; still no alerts. "What happened in Medical?"

"You happened, you got shot."

Oh, right, that. Arada was gesturing at me so I followed her down the corridor to the main ramp. I poked through the hole in my jacket and shirt and upped my pain sensors a little. The projectiles were still in there. (Sometimes they pop out on their own.)

Medical was at the top of the ramp, a small compartment on the same level as the crew lounge area and galley. The quarters, labs, and storage were on the two levels below and the control deck was above. Ratthi was there waiting for us, standing beside the MedSystem. "Are you all right?" he demanded. "You better lie down!"

I didn't want to bother with it. "No, I'm fine. Just give me the extractor."

"No, no, you were in the water, you need decontam and an antibiotic screen. When the system is prepped, you lie down." He pointed emphatically at the narrow platform and pulled one of the emergency kits down from the rack. "Thiago has some scrapes on his neck," he told us, "but otherwise he's fine."

Ratthi went out with the kit. The yelling on the comm had calmed down but I could hear tense voices from the rec room. Preservation-controlled facilities like this don't have SecSystems recording everything and cameras everywhere because privacy blah blah blah but I could eavesdrop through the comm and my drones. If I wanted to, which I didn't, not right now.

Arada said, "Ratthi's right, SecUnit, you should let the system make sure the wounds aren't contaminated." She hesitated. "Did I . . ." She took a sharp breath. I just stood there because I didn't understand the question yet. She added, "Was there any other way . . ."

She didn't finish again but this time I knew what she was asking. "No. If you'd waited any longer, I would have had to try to use a drone. He'll probably survive, if the others give him medical attention."

She really hadn't wanted to shoot anybody, and had told me she had to force herself to learn how to use the weapon. I hadn't particularly wanted her to learn, either. (Humans have a bad tendency to use weapons unnecessarily and indiscriminately. Of the many times I had been shot, a depressingly large percentage of hits had come from clients who were trying to "help" me.) (Another significant percentage came from clients who had just wanted to shoot something when I happened to be standing there.)

Arada rubbed her eyes and her mouth pulled in at one side. "Are you trying to make me feel better?"

"No." I actually wasn't. I lie to humans a lot, but not to Arada, not about this. "I wouldn't try to make you feel better. You know what I'm like."

She made a snorting noise, an involuntary expression of amusement. "I do know what you're like."

Her expression had turned all melty and sentimental. "No hugging," I warned her. It was in our contract. "Do you need emotional support? Do you want me to call someone?"

"I'm fine." She smiled. On the feed, the MedSystem signaled it was ready. "Now you make sure you're fine, too."

She stepped out of the compartment and set the privacy filter on the doorway. I stripped off my clothes and dropped them in the decontam bin and got onto the platform. It would run a check for contaminants and pop the projectiles out of my shoulder and chest.

The process only took three minutes, just long enough to finish the scene of *Lineages of the Sun* I'd had to pause when Thiago had decided to get me shot. The MedSystem tried to cycle into the therapy and post-treatment options and I stopped it and climbed off the platform. The feed told me we had made orbit and were in the process of rendezvous with our baseship.

My clothes now smelled like decontam fluid but they were dry and clean. I got dressed and opened the privacy shield.

Thiago stood in the corridor. Oh, joy.

He looked angry and upset, which I could tell, even though I was looking just to the right of his head. He said, "Did you kill those people?"

I'd been angry enough to tear them all into tiny little pieces. The company who had owned me had protocols for these situations that would have required kill-shots, at least for the armed hostiles out on the deck. Plus I'd already been shot once, and the hostiles had been clear about their intent to kill and/or abduct my clients. But the company didn't own me anymore and the only human here I was answerable to was Arada, and only in limited ways determined by a contract that Pin-Lee had negotiated for me.

But the whole point of hacking my governor module was that no one got to tell me to kill a bunch of humans if I didn't feel like it. (Or even if I did feel like it.)

I said, "I've reported to my contracted supervisor."

(I know, I know, I could have said no, I didn't kill anybody. I could have said that even SecUnits under company protocol use minimum force necessary because the company hates paying survivor damage bonds, and also because SecUnits are not rabid murderers unless humans specifically order them to be. I could have said that I had risked his life not using kill-shots on the armed targets because I knew Arada didn't want me to.)

He pressed his lips together. "I could ask her."

I said, "You should definitely do that."

He glared at me and the brown skin on his cheeks showed pronounced signs of a rise in temperature indicating anger, embarrassment, and possibly other emotions. I was pretty sure he was just pissed off, though. Then he hesitated and said, "Look, I—I didn't mean to get you shot. I'm sorry."

If you had meant to get me shot, Thiago, we would be having a different conversation. Because I was still mad, I said, "The security protocol all survey members agreed to is available on the facility feed."

His face did the thing humans do when they're trying not to show how annoyed they are. (Mission accomplished.) He said, "I made a mistake. But I had no reason to assume those people were hostile."

I had reason. I could have thrown together a quick excerpt of my Threat Assessment Report of the approaching boat and why it had been 72 percent likely to attack. I could have pointed out that THEY HAD SHOT ME FIRST when for all they knew I was just another unarmed human. But I didn't have to answer to him. He didn't like me, I didn't like him, and that was fine.

It was absolutely fine.

I walked away down the corridor.

= =

HelpMe.file Excerpt 1

(File detached from main narrative.)

Since I'd decided to stay (temporarily) on Preservation Station, Dr. Mensah had asked me to go places with her seven times. Six of those times were just relatively short boring meetings on ships in orbit or in dock. The seventh was when she had asked me to go down to the local planet's surface with her. I don't like planets but she lured me there by explaining that it was for an Art Festival/Conference/Religious Observation that would include "a lot of" live performances. After checking to find out the definition of "a lot of" was eighty-seven plus, I agreed to go.

Some of the live performances were demonstrations or seminars I wasn't interested in, but I managed to fit in thirty-two plays and musicals while Mensah was at meetings or doing things with her family members. (I used drones to record the performances that were overlapping or scheduled against each other. They were all being recorded for the local planetary entertainment feed, and the popular ones would be reconfigured as video productions, but I wanted to see all the versions.) One evening a play was interrupted when Mensah tapped my feed and asked me to please come get her.

The request was so abrupt and out of character I replied with the code phrase we had come up with in case she was being held against her will. She said she was just tired. That was even more out of character. I mean, I could see she got tired, she just hated to admit it.

I left a drone to record the rest of the play and slipped out of the theater. It was night and the crowd in the street was beginning to thin out, but the big open pavilion across the plaza where the party was being held was still bright and noisy.

If you had to be in a crowd of humans, the crowds at this festival weren't bad, since they were the distracted kind where all the humans and augmented humans are talking to each other or on comm or feed or hurrying to get places. The downside was a lot of humans were waving sticks with lighted objects or spark-emitting toys, or tossing colored powders that popped and emitted light. (I have no idea.) But whatever, with all that going on, nobody noticed me.

Plus, it was Preservation and there were no scanning drones, no armed human security, just some on-call human medics with bot assistants and "rangers" who mainly enforced environmental regulations and yelled at humans and augmented humans to get out of the way of the ground vehicles.

In the pavilion, I located Mensah near the edge of the crowd talking to Thiago and Farai, who was one of her marital partners. I stopped next to Mensah and she grabbed my hand.

Right, it's usually a good idea to warn bot/human constructs who call themselves Murderbot before making grabby hands, except during a security incident when you would expect/need the human you're trying to extract from lethal circumstances to grab you and hold on. And this read as the latter; like Mensah needed me to save her. So I didn't react except to shift closer to her.

Thiago was saying, "I don't know why you can't just talk to us." I heard him clearly, since I was looping my ambient audio to lower the level of the music from blaring down to a pleasant background soundtrack level. The glance Thiago threw at me was annoyed, like I had interrupted their conversation. Hey, she called me. I have a job here, I get paid in hard currency cards and everything.

"I told you why," Mensah said, and she sounded normal, calm and firm. Except that was also how she sounded when humans were trying to kill us, so. I had the whole pavilion covered by my drones, and weapons scan was negative. (Weapons weren't even permitted on the planet except in designated wilderness areas where hostile fauna was a problem.) Voices were loud, but my filters showed they were still well within the range of happy-intoxicated-interested emotional tones. But Mensah's grip on my hand told me how tense her arm muscles were. Situation assessment: I have no idea.

Farai said, "Thiago, no. She asks for space, you need to give that to her." She smiled at me politely. I never know how to react to that. She leaned in to Mensah to kiss her, and said, "We'll see you at the house."

Mensah nodded and turned, and I let her tow me out of the pavilion.

We made it outside to the pedestrian plaza and I asked her, "Do you need a medic?" I thought she might be sick. If I was a human and I'd had to be in the pavilion with all those other humans for the past two and a half hours, I'd be sick.

"No," she told me, still sounding calm and normal. "I'm just tired."

I sent a feed request to the ground vehicle (which on Preservation was called a "go-cart" for some reason) (some stupid reason) to meet us at the nearest transportation area. The plaza and streets were lit with little floating balloon-lights, and the dirt and temporary paving painted with elaborate designs in light-up paint (fortunately it wasn't the marker paint that broadcasts on the feed, which would have been a nightmare). As we walked through the crowd, people recognized Mensah and smiled and waved. Mensah smiled and waved back, but didn't let go of my hand. On the fringe near the transport area, an intoxicated human wandered toward us with a handful of glitter dust but veered off when I made deliberate eye contact.

Our vehicle was waiting for us and I handed her in, and climbed into the other seat. I told it to head for the family camp house, which had been erected in a habitation area on the outskirts of the festival site. The vehicle had a limited bot-driver, which would take humans all over the campground and festival site but knew not to go into the designated no-vehicle sections.

It hummed out of the court and into the dark, along the path that led through high grass and scrub trees. Mensah sighed and opened the window. The breeze was still warm and smelled like vegetation, and the guide-lights along the way were low enough not to obscure the starfield. All the humans and augmented humans staying here for the festival made it a heavily populated area, but we were traveling through the section reserved for humans who actually wanted to sleep. The temporary housing (pop-up shelters of all shapes and sizes, camping vehicles, tents and collapsible structures that looked more like art installations) were all mostly dark and quiet. The camp area for humans who had to be loud was on the far side of the grounds with a sound baffle field to deflect the music and crowd noise. She said, "Thank you. I'm sorry I interrupted your evening."

I recalled my drones except for the one that was recording the play and the detachment I had designated to keep tabs on the family still at the party. (Another detachment was at the camp house, maintaining a perimeter and keeping watch on the two adults and seven children who had gone back earlier.) I wasn't sure how to react. Mensah wasn't acting like I had rescued her from certain death, but she wasn't acting like we were heading back to the habitat after a boring but successful day collecting samples, either. I said, "I recorded the plays. Do you want to see them?"

She perked up. "I never get to see the performances at this thing. Did you get the one— Oh, what was it called? The new historical by Glaw and Ji-min?"

The difference between "calm and normal" and actual normal was measurable enough that I could have made a chart. I just said, "Yes. It's pretty good."

Something was bothering her, and it wasn't just that her family was clearly as weirded out by me as I was by them. They had assumed I would stay in the camp house, which, no. Mensah had told them I didn't need any help or supervision and could find my own way around. (Quote: "If it can infiltrate high-security corporate installations while people are shooting at it, it can certainly handle a domestic festival.")

It wasn't that her family was phobic about the scary rogue SecUnits the entertainment media and the newsfeeds were so fond of, or that they didn't like bots. (There were "free" bots wandering around on Preservation, though they had guardians who were technically supposed to keep track of them.) It was just me-the-SecUnit they didn't like.

(That didn't apply to the seven kids. I was illicitly trading downloads via the feed with three of them.)

I think if I had been a normal bot, or even like a normal SecUnit, just off inventory, naive and not knowing anything about how to get along in the human world or whatever, like the way humans would write it for the media, basically, it would have been okay. But I wasn't like that. I was me, Murderbot.

So instead of Mensah having a pet bot like poor Miki, or a sad bot/human construct that needed someone to help it, she had me.

(I told this to Dr. Bharadwaj later, because we talked about a lot of things while she was doing research about bot/human relations for her documentary. After thinking about it, she said, "I wish I thought you were wrong.")

(Farai was a possible exception. Up on the station, when Mensah had first introduced me to her family, she'd had a conversation with me. Or a conversation at me, you could say. Transcript:

Farai: "You know we're grateful for how you returned her to us."

I did know, I guess. What do humans say in this situation? A quick archive search came up with some variation on "okay, um" and even I knew that wasn't going to cut it.

(Just a heads-up, when a murderbot stands there looking to

the left of your head to avoid eye contact, it's probably not thinking about killing you, it's probably frantically trying to come up
with a reply to whatever you just said to it.)

She added, "I wanted to ask what your relationship to her is."

Uh. In the Corporation Rim, Mensah was my owner. On
Preservation, she was my guardian. (That's like an owner, but
Preservation law requires they be nice to you.) But Mensah and
Pin-Lee were trying to get my status listed as "refugee working
as employee/security consultant."

But I knew Farai knew all that, and I knew she was asking for
an answer that was closer to objective reality. And wow, I did
not have that answer. I said, "I'm her SecUnit." (Yes, that's still
in the buffer.)

She lifted her brows. "And that means?"

Backed into yet another conversational corner, I fell back on
honesty. "I don't know. I wish I knew."

She smiled. "Thank you."

(And that was that.)

Mensah's family were also weirded out by the idea that I
would be providing security, and were afraid I would be, I don't
know, scaring legitimate visitors and killing people, I guess. And
granted, while I have been a key factor in certain clusterfucks of
gigantic proportions and my risk assessment module has serious
issues, my threat assessment record is pretty great, like 93 percent. (Most of the negative points came from that time I didn't
know that Wilken and Gerth were hired killers until Wilken
tried to shoot Don Abene in the head, but that was an outlier.)

Mensah's family also thought they didn't need security, which,
maybe before GrayCris, that had been true. But as it was, during
the festival I only had to deal with five incursions, four by outsys-
tem newsfeed journalists with recording drones. I took control
of the drones (I can always use a few more) and notified the local
Rangers who drove off the human journalists. The fifth incur-
sion was the one that got me in trouble with Amena, Mensah's
oldest offspring.

Since the festival had started, I had been taking note of a potential hostile that Amena had been associating with. Evidence was mounting up and my threat assessment was nearing critical. Things like: (1) he had informed her that his age was comparable to hers, which was just below the local standard for legal adult, but my physical scan and public record search indicated that he was approximately twelve Preservation standard calendar years older, (2) he never approached her when any family members or verified friends were with her, (3) he stared at her secondary sexual characteristics when her attention was elsewhere, (4) he encouraged her to take intoxicants that he wasn't ingesting himself, (5) her parental and other related humans all assumed she was with her friends when she was seeing him and her friends all assumed she was with family and she hadn't told either group about him, (6) I just had a bad feeling about the little shit.

You might think the obvious thing to do was to notify Mensah or Farai or Tano, the third marital partner. I didn't.

If there was one thing I understood, it was the difference between proprietary and non-proprietary data.

So, on the night when Potential Target invited Amena to come back to his semi-isolated camp house with him to "meet some friends," I decided to come along.

He led her into the darkened house, and she stumbled on a low table. She giggled and he laughed. Sounding way more intoxicated than he actually was, he said, "Wait, I got it," and tapped the house's feed to turn on the lights.

And I was standing in the middle of the room.

He screamed. (Yes, it was hilarious.)

Amena clapped a hand over her mouth, startled, then recognized me. She said, "What the hell? What are you doing here?"

Potential Target gasped, "What—Who—?"

Amena was furious. "That's my second mother's . . . friend," she said through gritted teeth. "And her security . . . person."

"What?" He was confused, then the word "security" penetrated. He stepped away from her. "Uh . . . I guess . . . You'd better go."

Amena looked at him, and then glared at me, then turned and stamped out the door and down the steps to the path. I followed her, and he backed away as I passed him. Yeah, you better.

On the dirt path, lit by the low floating guide-lights, I caught up with her. (Not so much intentionally, but my legs were longer and she was putting more energy into stamping her feet than gaining distance.)

She said, "How did you know where I was? What were you doing, hiding under the porch?"

She thought I wouldn't get the domestic animal reference. I said, "Wow, that was rude. Especially considering that I'm your second mother's"—I made ironic quote marks—"'friend.' Is that how you talk to your bot-servants?"

My drone cam showed her expression turn startled and then a combination of sulky and guilty. "No. I don't have bot-servants! I didn't know—I never heard you talk."

"You didn't ask." Had I not been talking? I had been talking to the kids on the feed, and to Mensah. Maybe with the rest of the family it had been easier to pretend to be a robot again. I added, "No one else approached that house. He lied about meeting other humans there."

She stamped along in silence for twelve point five seconds. "Look, I'm sorry, but I'm not some kind of idiot, and I don't fuck around. If he'd done anything I didn't like, I was going to leave. And if he wouldn't let me leave, I have the feed, I can call for help whenever I want." She was scornful, and way overconfident. "I wasn't going to let him hurt me."

I said, "If I thought he was going to hurt you, I'd be disposing of his body. I don't fuck around, either."

She stopped and stared up at me. I stopped but kept my gaze on the path ahead. I said, "Mensah is a planetary leader of a minor political entity that has managed to get the angry attention of major corporates. Her situation has changed. Your situation has changed. You need to grow up and deal with it."

She took a breath to say something, stopped, then shook her head. "He wasn't a corporate spy. He was just someone . . ."

"Someone you don't know who showed up out of nowhere at a massive public festival attended by half the continent and whatever offworld humans happen to be wandering through." I knew he wasn't a corporate spy (see above, disposing of bodies) but she sure didn't.

She was quiet for sixteen seconds. "Are you going to tell my parents about this?"

Is that what she was worried about? I was insulted and exasperated. "I don't know. I guess you'll find out."

She stamped away.

So, in retrospect, I could see that hadn't gone so well.

▫   ▫   ▫

Our vehicle rumbled through the dark, up the low hill to the camp house, which was a pop-up two-story structure with broad covered balconies off both levels. It had been placed near a couple of large trees with frilly leaves that curved over the roof. It had been built by Mensah's grandfather, while her grandmothers and other assorted family members had been working on the original planetary survey and terraforming. The colonists who hadn't been living in orbit on their ship had all stayed in temporary structures at that point, that were moved seasonally to avoid destructive weather patterns in the parts of the planet that had been habitable at that time.

There were other pop-ups, large and small, planted all over the hills around us, the nearest twenty-seven meters away. Lights were on inside the house and one light floated above the beacon spot for the vehicles. I would have worried about the lack of lighting if I hadn't had thirty-seven drones on patrol in the immediate area.

(Drones had picked up previously identified humans and augmented humans returning to the other houses or passing through the area, and I'd conducted safety checks on unidentified humans encountered for the first time. I was cataloguing power signatures on some small mobility devices used by non-augmented humans for medical reasons; I hadn't seen these anywhere in the Corporation Rim, though maybe that was because I hadn't spent much time hanging out on planets with human populations not exclusively engaged in corporate slave labor. (The entertainment media showed planets that weren't all corporate slave labor, I had just never been on one.)) (The drones had also tracked the five younger kids on a completely illicit expedition to a nearby creek where they had performed some kind of ritual that involved jumping out at each other from behind bushes and rocks. They returned to the house without being caught by the adult humans or older siblings and were now collapsed in their upstairs bunk room, watching media.)

(The house actually had secure sealable window and door hatches, WHICH NO ONE USED, but at least this made it easy for my patrol drones.)

As the vehicle settled into its spot, Mensah said, "I'm just going to sit outside for a bit. Why don't you go on back to the festival? There's a few more plays tonight, aren't there?"

I try to avoid asking humans if there's anything wrong with them. (Mostly because I don't care.) (On the rare occasions where I did care, it would have meant starting a conversation not directly related to security protocol, and that was just a slippery slope waiting to happen, for a variety of reasons.) But humans asked each other about their current status all the time, so how hard could it be? It was a request for information, that was all. I did a quick search and pulled up a few examples from my media collection. None of the samples seemed like anything I'd ever voluntarily say, so before I could change my mind I went with, "What's wrong?"

She was surprised, then gave me a sideways look. "Don't you start."

So there was something wrong and even the other humans

had noticed. I said, "I have to know about any potential problems for an accurate threat assessment."

She lifted a brow and opened the vehicle door. "You never mentioned that on our survey contract."

I got out of the vehicle and followed her toward a group of chairs next to the house, scattered around in the grass under the trees. The shadow was deep so I had to switch to a dark filter to see her. "That was because I was half-assing my job."

She took a seat. "If that was you half-assing your job, I don't want to see what you're like when . . ." The smile faded and she trailed off, then added, "But I suppose I did see you when you were doing your best."

I sat down, too. (Sitting down with a human like this would never not feel strange.) Her expression wasn't upset, but it wasn't not upset, either. But I could tell my smartass comment had taken us down an awkward conversational avenue where I hadn't wanted to go. I wished I was ART, who was good at this kind of thing. (The thing being getting you to talk about what it wanted you to talk about but also making you think about what it wanted you to talk about in different ways.) (I wasn't kidding when I said ART was an asshole.) "You didn't answer the question."

She settled back in her chair. "You sound worried."

"I am worried." I could feel my face making the expression whether I wanted it to or not.

She let her breath out. "It's nothing. I've been having nightmares. About being held prisoner on TranRollinHyfa, and . . . you know." She made an impatient gesture. "It's completely normal. It would be odd if I wasn't having nightmares."

I hadn't seen much of the recovery phase of trauma (my job was to get the client to the MedSystem before they died; it took care of all the messy aftermath, including the retrieved client protocol) but in the shows I watched, recovery was featured a lot. There was a trauma recovery program that Bharadwaj had used in the Station Medical Center, and the big hospital in the port city had one, too.

I wasn't the only one who thought Mensah should go get the trauma treatment. I was probably the only one who knew she hadn't. (She hadn't exactly lied; it was more a way of letting the other humans assume she had.) But the treatment wasn't like a one-time thing with a MedSystem; it took multiple long visits, and I knew she had never made time for it in her schedule. I said, "Is that why you're afraid to go off-station without me?"

So there were two positions on whether the Preservation Planetary leader needed security. The first was the one 99 percent of the population shared, that she did not unless she went on a formal visit to somewhere like the Corporation Rim. And to a large extent, they were right.

The crime stats on Preservation Station and the planet were pitifully low, and usually involved intoxication-related property damage or disturbances and/or minor infractions of station cargo handling or planetary environmental regulations. Mensah had never needed on-station or on-planet security before this, except for the young Preservation Council–trainee humans who followed her around and kept track of her appointments and handed her things occasionally. (And they did not count as security.)

The other 1 percent was composed of me, Mensah's survey team, all the humans working in Station Security, and the members of the Preservation Council who had seen the GrayCris assassins try to kill her. But that incident had been kept out of the newsfeeds, so hardly anyone thought Mensah needed a security consultant let alone a SecUnit.

But GrayCris was not doing so hot now due to their hired security service Palisade making an extremely bad decision to punch my ex-owner bond company in the operating funds by attacking one of its gunships. (The company is paranoid and greedy and cheap but also ruthless, methodical, and intensely violent when it thinks it's being threatened.) Relations between the two corporates had deteriorated since what we call The Gunship Incident, with GrayCris assets getting mysteriously destroyed a lot in supposedly random accidents and its executives and employees getting blown up or found stuffed in containers way too small for intact adult humans and so on.

And once GrayCris had started to cease to exist, even my threat assessment had dropped drastically, but Mensah had still wanted me to continue to provide security. I thought she was humoring me, and taking the opportunity to pay me in hard currency cards which I would need if/when I left Preservation, and giving me practice in being around humans in a setting where I was not categorized as a tool and/or deadly weapon. (Yeah, I assumed it was about me, but humans assume everything is about them, too. It's not an uncommon problem, okay?)

But for a while now I had been thinking it was about something else.

Her mouth twisted a little and she looked away, over the dark hills and fields toward the lighted windows of the other camp houses and tents. She said, "I suppose it was obvious."

I said, "Not obvious." Not to most of the humans, anyway. I had a feeling that Farai and Tano knew, but weren't sure what to do about it.

She shrugged a little. "It's hardly surprising that I feel safer with you. It's also easier to be around people who understand what happened, what it's like to be in that situation. That's you and the rest of the survey team." She hesitated. "Farai and Tano understand, but I haven't explained to my brother and sister and Thiago and the others why I can't just rely on them for emotional support about this, as usual." Her face turned grim. "They don't understand what it's like to be under corporate authority."

That I got. Humans in the Preservation Alliance didn't have to sign up for contract labor and get shipped off to mines or whatever for 80 to 90 percent of their lifespans. There was some strange system where they all got their food and shelter and education and medical for free, no matter what job they did. It had something to do with the giant colony ship that had brought them here, and a promise by the original crew to take care of everyone in perpetuity if they would just get on the damn thing and not die in the old colony. (It was complicated and when I watched their historical dramas, I tended to fast forward through the economics parts.) Whatever, the humans seemed to like it.

But she was right, these humans had no concept of what it was like to live under corporate authority. And they really didn't know what it was like to be the target of a corporate entity that wanted to kill you.

I replayed my recording of Mensah talking to Thiago and Farai at the party. Mensah had been abducted from Port FreeCommerce at a meeting for the relatives of the murdered survey members. Maybe the noisy party, where the other humans who would normally help her had been distracted, had just started to feel too similar.

I said, "You need to get the trauma treatment."

Her voice sharpened. "I will. But I have some things to finish first." She turned toward me. "And I want you to go on that survey mission with Arada. They need you. And it's a wonderful opportunity for you."

It was too dark for her to see my expression. I'm not sure what it was but you could probably describe it as "skeptical." (Ratthi says that's how I look most of the time.)

With that confident planetary leader *I am totally convincing you of this* tone, she added, "And you know Amena and Thiago are going, too. I'll feel better if you're there to keep an eye on them."

Uh-huh. "What about you?"

She took a breath to say she'd be fine. I knew her well enough to know those exact words were about to come out. But then she hesitated. The drone I had watching her face increased magnification, its low-light filter rendering her features in black and white. Her expression was intense and fierce and she was biting her lower lip. She said, "I hate feeling so weak. I just need to stop. And I need to stop leaning on you. It's not fair to you. We need to be apart so I can . . . stand on my own feet again."

I didn't think she was wrong, but I still wasn't used to things that were unfair to me being a major point of consideration for humans. It also sounded vaguely like the break-up part of the romance scenes on the shows I watched, most of which I usually skimmed over. I said, "It's not me, it's you."

She huffed a laugh.

And then I sort of blackmailed her.

= =

Part of my problem now was that Mensah, who was way too honest about this kind of thing, had later told Amena that she had asked me to keep an eye on her, which Amena interpreted in some hormone-related human way I'm not sure I understood. Thiago, who is not an adolescent and has no excuse, interpreted it as Mensah not trusting him to take care of his niece.

Amena is on the survey because her education requires an internship in almost getting killed, I guess. Due to our previous interaction, she really didn't want me specifically tasked to watch her.

(Possibly I had been too emphatic with her about Potential Target. After spending my entire existence having to gently suggest to humans that they not do things that would probably get them killed, it was nice to be able to tell them in so many words to not be so fucking stupid. But I didn't regret doing it.)

An attempt by Amena to go around Mensah and appeal to Farai and Tano had failed spectacularly, in a three-way comm call that became a four-way when Farai had called Mensah to join in on the discussion. (I'm not sure what happened past that point. Even I hadn't wanted to watch it.)

So that was what had happened before the survey. Now we're here, ready for the next major disaster. (Spoiler warning.)

3

We docked with our baseship with no problems, and Arada and the others transferred control to the baseship crew. (The facility wasn't wormhole capable and was basically just a big, awkward lab module that could land and take off under its own power.)

It was only four standard Preservation day-cycles back to Preservation via wormhole, and I meant to use the time to finish watching *Lineages of the Sun*. It was a long-running historical family drama, set in an early colony world, with one hundred and thirty-six characters and almost as many storylines.

I'd watched family dramas before, but I'd never spent much time around human families before coming to Preservation. (Data suggests family dramas bear a less than 10 percent resemblance to actual human families, which is unsurprising and also a relief, considering all the murders. In the dramas, not Mensah's family.)

When the company owned me and rented me out for surveys, my security protocol included datamining, which meant monitoring and recording the humans every second for the duration of the contract, which was excruciating in a lot of ways. Pretty much all the ways. (All the ways involving sex, bodily fluids, and inane conversations.) It would never stop being novel to be around a bunch of humans in a relatively confined space and be able to close a door between me and them and not have to care what they were doing.

Which didn't mean the humans left me alone.

Ratthi came to my cabin. I didn't have to let him in, so I did. (I know, I was still getting used to the idea of not minding the fact that a human wanted to talk to me.) He sat on the folding seat opposite my bunk and said, "Thiago will come around, you'll see. He just doesn't . . ."

Ratthi was reluctant to finish the sentence, so I did. ". . . trust me."

Ratthi sighed. "It's all the corporate propaganda about Sec-Units being dangerous. He doesn't know you. He doesn't know what you're really like."

This would be annoying, if Ratthi didn't genuinely believe it. He's never seen me kill anyone close up and I'd like to keep it that way.

"And he didn't know why it was so important that Mensah be protected on station." He waved a hand at me though I hadn't said anything. "I know, the more people who knew, the more chance of the newsfeeds finding out. And there was nothing else we could have done, really."

After Ratthi left, Overse came. When I told the door to open, she just stuck her head in and said, "I don't want to interrupt, I just wanted to thank you. This is Arada's first time as a survey lead, and you've been really supportive and I know that's made a difference, and helped her confidence."

I had no idea how to react to that since I wasn't sure what being supportive entailed. My job wasn't to make the humans obey Arada, that wasn't how Preservation worked. Besides, that hadn't been a problem. The survey team was grumbly occasionally, but everybody had done their job to a reasonable level. The chance of a mutiny was so low it was registering as a negative number. I'm not sure the word "mutiny" could even apply to any situation that might occur with this survey team; most of them had to be begged to complete the required self-defense certification before we left. And this was what Preservation called an academic survey, where the data collected was going into a public database. (If the planet had been in the Corporation Rim, it would be open to exploitation, but out here nobody wanted it for anything.) I defaulted to, "Arada contracted with me."

"Yes, and we both know that you're very capable of making it clear when you think someone doesn't know what they're doing." She smiled at the drone I was using to watch her. "That's all."

She left and I replayed the conversation a couple of times.

I trusted Arada's judgment to a certain extent. She and Overse had always been firmly in the "least likely to abandon a Sec-Unit to a lonely horrible fate" category, which was always the category I was most interested in. They were my clients, that was all. Like Mensah, like Ratthi and Pin-Lee and Bharadwaj and Volescu (who had opted to retire from active survey work, which gave him the award for most sensible human) and yes, even Gurathin. Just clients. And if anyone or anything tried to hurt them, I would rip its intestines out.

□　　□　　□

When we came through the wormhole into Preservation space, I was watching episodes of *The Rise and Fall of Sanctuary Moon* again, since there wasn't time to start anything new before we reached the station. (Being interrupted isn't nearly as annoying when I already know the story.) I was worried about Mensah, if everything had been okay while I was gone. I wasn't sure exactly what "okay" would involve, but I was willing to settle for "unmurdered."

I was just finishing a rewatch of episode 137 when the ship's alarm sounded through the comm and feed.

It might just be a navigation anomaly, like another transport in the wrong place. We were in a commonly used approach lane and Preservation tended to be visited by lots of non-corporate transports with no bot pilots who wandered all over the place trying to figure out where the hell they were, or at least that was how I interpreted the constant litany of complaint from Preservation Station Port Authority that Mensah had involuntary access to. With no bot pilot on our baseship, I couldn't get direct

Copilot Mihail: "It came out of nowhere! Nothing on comm."

Specialist Rajpreet: "That's a docking approach. I'm reading active weapons."

Pilot Roa: "That's it, raise the Station and tell them—"

Mihail again: "Copy, but there's no responders near us—"

Well, shit. I rolled out of the bunk and pinged the team feed, and sent to Arada: *Dr. Arada, we're being approached by a potentially hostile vessel. A boarding attempt may be imminent.*

A potentially— Oh no! Arada responded.

Again? Overse asked.

I let them deal with the other team queries coming in as I opened my code-sealed locker. I pulled out the projectile weapon, checked the load and charge, then woke my dormant drones. They all activated their cameras at once and I had to take a few seconds to sort and process the multiple inputs.

I'd changed out of the survey uniform before we'd entered the wormhole and back into the clothes I liked (human work boots, pants with lots of pockets (good for storing my small intel drones), T-shirt, and soft hooded jacket, all dark colors) because I didn't like logos, even the Preservation survey logo, which was just a variation on the planetary seal, and not a corporate logo. I had a deflection vest from Station Security Operations designed to provide some protection from inert blades, slow projectiles, fire, acidic gas, low energy pulses, and so on. I hadn't been wearing it because it was a) worthless for the kind of firepower usually deployed against me and b) it had a logo on it. (I know, I need to get over that.)

I made myself put it on under my jacket. I might need all the help I could get.

By this point the Potential Hostile had continued to approach. Pilot Roa was now making a general announcement which was pretty much the same thing I'd already told Arada. As I left the cabin, my drones converged on me in a cloud formation. I needed more direct info from the baseship so I sent one ahead, and it whizzed past me as I started down the corridor toward the access. I had a plan, but it was mostly "keep the hostiles off the ship," which is not so much a plan as a statement of hopeful intent.

This could be really bad.

I know, I know, I'm Security, I should already have a plan in place for a boarding action. But I was used to having a human supervisor come up with the plans and . . . Okay, right, I just hadn't bothered because the chances of an attack while en route to and from the mission site were so slight it wasn't worth taking the time off from viewing media. I'd put all the work into coming up with attack and defense scenarios for the facility while on planet. (None of which I got to use during the one actual attack on the facility, but though it was tempting, "advance planning sucks" seems to be the wrong lesson to take from that whole incident.)

Anyway, SecUnits were shipped as cargo on company transports and I didn't even have any old procedure documents for ship-based actions in my archive. The only ship-to-ship attack I'd participated in had been viral, and I'd almost destroyed my brain during it.

Speaking of which, my alert monitors on comm and feed weren't picking up any attempts by the hostile to make contact. That might just mean they already knew there was no bot pilot to attack with killware or malware.

I went up the ramp past the crew lounge toward the control deck. My drone had zipped ahead up into the baseship and through the passage to its bridge. When the bridge hatch opened to let Rajpreet out, it slipped in. Now I had a camera view of the sensor display surfaces floating above the control boards. Mihail sat in a station chair, sweat plastering their light hair to their forehead. Roa was on his feet pacing, dark brow furrowed in thought, one hand pressed to his feed interface. It looked like a clip from an action series, right before something drastic happened.

Then something drastic happened.

The hit wasn't at all like the way they show ship combat in the media. I felt something more like a power surge than anything else. Gravity fluctuated just enough to thump me against the bulkhead and the ramp lights flickered. A flood of automated warnings came from the facility engineering pod and then the feed and comm cut out. I scrambled to pick up the baseship's feed, then gravity fluctuated again as the facility's drive went offline and we switched to reserve power for life support. My drones scattered as the gravity flux interfered with their propulsion, then pulled back into formation.

On the baseship bridge, my drone watched as Roa and Mihail froze, like a scene on pause. Then Roa said, "That was an impact."

Mihail's voice was hoarse as they cycled through displays. "On the facility's drive housing. A locator missile. Attacker must have fired it when they spotted us leaving the wormhole."

Oh, shit. Seriously: oh, shit.

My organic parts had a reaction that reminded me how lucky I was not to have a digestive system. We didn't blow up in the next ten seconds so I pushed off from the bulkhead and kept going toward the facility control deck.

I stepped through the hatch. It was a small hub-shaped control area, with the stations for attaching lab modules and everything else the facility needed to do when it was sitting on a planet. Overse was in the pilot suite though right now the baseship had control. Ratthi was hanging on to the back of the comm chair. Both looked frantic. From the flashing displays, frantic was the right reaction.

"I can't reach Roa on the comm or feed," Ratthi was saying.

"It's all down," Overse reported. "Arada—" she began, and then grimaced as she remembered there was no feed, no one outside the compartment could hear her. "Damn it!"

I told my drone in the cockpit to establish a connection between Overse's and Arada's interfaces and the baseship's feed. I said aloud and on the feed, *Baseship, I've reestablished a tempo-rary connection to the interfaces on the facility control deck.*

Roa replied, *What, SecUnit? Can Arada hear me?*

She's not— Overse began, then Arada swung through the hatch on the far side of the control deck. Overse's face twisted with relief and she bit her lip hard, then added, *Here she is.*

I hear you, Roa, Arada said, her mental voice hurried but calm. She reached to squeeze Overse's shoulder, and nodded to Ratthi and me. *Can we tell where the attacker means to board?*

The words "means to board" made something uncomfortable happen to my organic parts again. Maybe similar to what Ratthi, who had just made a little "urk" noise, felt.

This would have all been a lot easier if I wasn't so worried about the stupid humans.

Roa's voice stayed calm but my baseship bridge drone saw his expression as he said, *Looks like they're heading for the lower level facility hatch, the lab level. I've sent Rajpreet down there.*

Ratthi and Overse exchanged horrified expressions. Arada set her jaw and told Roa, *Understood.*

She looked up at me. "SecUnit, could you please . . . ?"

I said, "On my way."

I ducked back out to the corridor, telling one of my drones to stay in the control deck as a relay. The center foyer was just around the curve, and above it the gravity well access to the base-ship. Safety protocols had engaged an air barrier, which allowed solid objects (like humans and SecUnits) to pass through but blocked air flow, so the atmosphere couldn't rush out if a seal breached.

Leading down from it was a second gravity well that had lad-ders and a set of stairs for use when the facility was sitting on a planet. Without fluctuating power to worry about, I could have just stepped in and floated down to the lowest facility level, but getting smashed to pieces against a bulkhead wouldn't be handy just now so I swung down the ladders instead.

Ozone and smoke that the scrubbers couldn't handle hung

in the air and the lights fluctuated. Via my control deck drone, I saw Arada tell Ratthi, "With the feed and comm down we're going to need a head count to make sure everyone's accounted for after that hit."

"Right, right, I'm on it!" Ratthi hurried out the hatch toward the living quarters.

From the bottom of the well I took the central ramp around and came out into the junction for the lower lab level hatch. The smoke here was thick enough for me to pick it up on visual. Specialist Rajpreet was already there, having climbed all the way down the gravity well from the baseship. She had a sidearm—there were a couple in the bridge emergency kit—ready to defend the hatch from a boarding attempt.

It's always nice when a human looks relieved to see you.

Her voice was mostly steady when she said, "I don't think we have much time." I used one of my drones to add her to my feed relay, and she reported, *Roa, Dr. Arada, can you hear me? SecUnit's here at the lock.*

I said, *What's our status?*

Arada said, *Overse has comm partially active.* On cue, the comms emitted a burst of static and Overse's voice said, "To all facility crew, comm and feed are not responding, please report to the facility crew lounge immediately and wait for further instructions."

Roa said, *SecUnit, I need to make an announcement, can you relay me through the facility comm?*

Sure, I don't have anything else better to do. I said, *Go ahead.*

Over the comm, Roa said, "The incoming transport has fired on us and is now making a docking maneuver aimed at the facility's lower level. Station has dispatched an armed ship and two free merchant transports have broken off station approach and are responding as well, but they're all eighty-four minutes out at best. SecUnit, can you—" The hesitation was long. "Can you repel a boarding attempt long enough for help to arrive?"

Every human on the baseship and the facility was listening.

It was a tricky question. It came down to how many raiders were violently determined to come aboard and what kind of weapons they had. (That scenario could turn out any way from "we thought this was an easy target, let's run away" to Rajpreet making a desperate last stand with her sidearm over the pieces of what was left of my body.) If they sent an EVAC-suited boarding party down the outside of the hull and came in through one of the hatches in the baseship as well as this one— But that wasn't what my clients needed to hear right now.

On comm, I said, "Yes."

Rajpreet's throat moved as she swallowed, and she muted her feed. She said aloud, "Just tell me what you need me to do."

I would definitely do that, as soon as I knew. Assuming worsecase scenario (and coincidentally getting her out of my way so I didn't have to worry about saving a human while I was trying to kill/maim/discourage a bunch of other humans), it was best for her to take up a guard position at the entrance to the gravity well, to at least buy the baseship some time. I was about to tell her to do that.

A jolt vibrated through the deck and a sudden uncompensated surge of acceleration knocked Rajpreet flat. I hit the bulkhead and slid down as my drones scattered. The lights fluctuated again and the life support cut out, then back in.

Oh, this is not good. My plan (make that "plan") depended on holding the intruders back until the armed station responder or the angry raider-hating merchants got close enough to scare them off. But my bridge drone was reading displays that indicated the hostile had grabbed the facility with the tractors transports use to attach and detach modules. It was pulling us close, intending to clamp us onto its hull and drag us into the wormhole with it. From their frantic cursing, Roa and Mihail agreed.

I got upright and caught Rajpreet's flailing arm to help her stand. The facility's comm came back online with a staticobscured warning alarm. Yes, great, that's really helpful right now.

A survey member, Adjat, staggered into the foyer from the corridor that led to the facility's lowest storage and lab space. Rajpreet told them, "Get up to crew level, hurry!"

Adjat nodded, heading for the corridor. "Hatches are jammed to labs 3 and 4, I don't know if anyone's trapped—"

"They're doing a headcount up there," Rajpreet said, pushing them on toward the access.

I had an idea, though it had its downside. On the feed, I said, *Roa, can the baseship jettison the facility?*

The baseship itself was just a small carrier, with bridge, drives, and living space for the five-person crew. Most of its bulk was designed to be able to grab or deploy the facility module.

Mihail replied, calm but breathless, *He's working on it, checking sensor view to see if our clamps are clear—*

So they had already thought of it. It was nice working with smart humans. Now if I could just keep them all alive.

A lot of my attention was on the hatch two meters away from me. I was scanning for any attempt to breach it, either physically or via the hostile's feed. I tried a breach of my own through the feed, but the hostile's wall was so solid I couldn't get any kind of read off it.

On my feed relay, Arada said, *We can remote-jettison from here—the facility command center—if you transfer control. But we need to get the rest of the team up to the baseship.*

Ratthi added, *I'm doing a headcount now, but with the feed and comm not responding—*

Roa broke in: *Our clamps are clear, we can jettison.*

Arada said, *Roa, will they be able to scan us? If they can tell we've abandoned the facility—*

Roa replied, *They may be able to.*

They would definitely be able to. Before anybody else could butt in, I said, *They may fire on the baseship once the facility is jettisoned.*

That was the downside I mentioned. It just depended on how anxious the hostile was to get to the wormhole with the facility before the responder and merchants arrived, whether they were ordinary assholes or huge assholes, if they wanted the facility or the humans in the facility, if they were afraid of retaliation by Preservation or just didn't care.

The survey team members still trying to talk on the relay feed all shut up.

Roa said, *Yes, that's . . . Yes. Dr. Arada, we don't have a lot of time, do we evacuate and jettison or—?*

Still sounding calm, Arada said, *SecUnit, do you agree we should jettison?*

Oh right, I was the security team head.

If I/we were wrong about this, the hostile would fire on the helpless baseship and we would all die. If we stayed with the facility, there might be a chance for rescue. If the hostiles didn't drag us into the wormhole, overwhelm me, and kill all the humans or do other terrible things to them.

The cheap education modules the company gives SecUnits had never mentioned this kind of dilemma, so I didn't have anything strategic to go on.

Ugh, self-determination sucks sometimes.

I reminded myself I had always wanted humans to listen to my advice. I said, *Jettison.*

Arada said, *We jettison. Ratthi, confirm head count and send everyone up to the baseship.* She sounded calm and certain. Much more so than Roa.

"Attacker is still pulling us toward the wormhole," Mihail announced on comm, not sounding too much like someone who was restraining the urge to scream a little.

On the relay, I heard Ratthi yelling at people to get moving and I got sporadic drone views of survey team members hurrying into the gravity well.

Roa took a breath. "Facility control, prepare for separation."

Overse announced, "Facility module will seal in two minutes and counting."

Drone audio picked up someone arguing but I had to prioritize Roa and Mihail and Arada, who were all telling different humans to do different things. My bridge drone's view of the sensor display started to show more interpretable detail. That big wobbly thing was the wormhole. The two blips way off (way way off) in the distance were our potential rescue ships. There was no blip for the hostile because it was too close.

Another vibration traveled through the deck but this one was more familiar. Rajpreet's gaze was on the hatch display, her eyes wide. She whispered, "They attached to our lock."

Whispering may have been an irrational impulse, but I could definitely sympathize. I said on the feed relay, *Hostile has matched locks.*

Overse said, *Ratthi, I need a confirmed head count, now.* My gravity well drone picked up two stragglers, Remy and Hanifa, scrambling up the ladders to the baseship and Ratthi, for fuck's sake, coming back down.

I started to tap his feed but I picked up something on audio. It was scraping, vibrating through the outer hatch. Okay, that's definitely happening. I sent on the feed, *Hostile is attempting to breach the hatch, boarding may be imminent.*

Roa said, *Rajpreet, SecUnit, get out of there.*

I told Rajpreet, "Go, I'll be behind you."

Rajpreet backed toward the corridor access. If the hostiles chose this moment to board, before we could seal off and separate, we were screwed.

I heard Ratthi yell, "No, No!" through my drone audio. His voice was harsh with fury, fear. The impulse to run to him made me flinch, but I needed to hold my position. Something had gone wrong up there. On the feed, I said, *Dr. Ratthi, report.*

Ratthi, of all my humans except Dr. Mensah, listens to me the most carefully. Probably it has something to do with the time he was about to step out of the hopper to retrieve some equipment and if he had, he would have been eaten by giant predatory fauna. Sounding simultaneously frustrated, angry, and terrified, Ratthi said, *Amena and Kanti aren't here. Thiago is looking for them. They aren't in the quarters or the upper labs, they must be down in the lower level somewhere.*

Well, shit.

I had audio and visual of the baseship access through my drones, so I was able to see when it exploded. (No, not physically exploded. Emotionally exploded.) Humans yelling and waving their arms and other unhelpful things.

You know, it's not like I'm having a good time either right now.

I told Rajpreet, "Get to the gravity well access," and started down the corridor toward the labs and sample storage, where Adjat had tried to tell Rajpreet about jammed doors. I ordered a drone to stay near the hatch so I would have some warning if anything came through it. I split the rest of the formation, sending two-thirds up the access to take a guard position with Rajpreet and telling the rest to follow me. On the feed, I said, calmly, *Acknowledged, I'll find them.* SHIT.

I'd made a stupid mistake. Feed access in the facility was down unless your interface was in range of one of my drones, so the connection could be relayed to the baseship, and the comm was patchy and unreliable. We, me and the humans, were too used to the feed, which made it impossible to lose track of someone, to leave them behind. With an active feed, even if you were unconscious, your interface could be used to track your location.

Arada said over the feed, *We're holding for you, SecUnit.*

Get to the baseship, Arada, I sent back.

It was amazing how fast our mostly orderly retreat had turned into a disaster. My drone formation formed around Rajpreet, who was waiting anxiously at the bottom of the gravity well. At the top, baseship crew and survey team members gathered, clutching handweapons they barely knew how to use. I just hoped nobody accidentally shot themselves or anyone else. I tapped my drone relay and saw Arada, Overse, Ratthi, and damn it Thiago waiting at the facility access junction. Arada was talking on the feed to Roa and trying to shove a resisting Overse into the gravity well. I started to tell them—I don't know what I was going to tell them, but it was going to involve the words "I can't do my job if none of you fucking listen to me" but then interference blotted out the connection and I lost all my drones in the baseship.

I reached a hatch to lab 3 that was stuck partly open, just a few centimeters from the deck. I hit the floor and directed my scan under the hatch, but I couldn't pick up any indication of a human body, living or otherwise. But drone audio detected a muffled human voice, coming from farther up the corridor.

I shoved upright and slammed around the curve and oh right, that must be the hatch Adjat had seen. The bulkhead was crumpled along the top of the seal, and the panel with the manual release had been blown in a power surge. The plastic parts were melted and the whole hatch assembly was dripping with fire suppressant foam where the automated emergency system had engaged. The facility's systems in this area must be down or cut off, and the emergency report had never reached the control deck. My audio picked up a muffled voice from the blocked compartment, but it was too faint for human hearing.

My first impulse was to blow the hatch. Fortunately my second impulse was to grab the manual release and pull. It didn't give, but I could feel the seal was broken. At least some of the locks that held it shut had been disengaged. Which meant someone had already triggered the manual release inside but something was jammed. I ripped the panel open and found crumpled metal pinning the release mechanism. I shoved my sleeve back, tuned the energy weapon in my right arm down to the lowest setting, and burned through it. The hatch clunked as it released and I dragged it open.

Kanti jolted forward and I caught her. "It wouldn't open," she gasped. She clutched the kind of tool used on surveys for chipping rock samples and her hands were bloody. The power inside was out, the only light from the emergency glows along the walls, and equipment and sample cases were jumbled everywhere.

Amena was across the compartment, her leg pinned under a lab bench that had collapsed when the bulkhead crumpled. She was conscious and struggling to free herself.

My hatchway drone showed the warning lights blinking around the lock. Yikes. I pulled Kanti out into the corridor and took the tool away from her. "Get to the gravity well, now." On what was left of the feed I told Rajpreet, *I'm sending Kanti to you.*

Kanti hesitated, eyes wide and glazed over. Blood trickled down from a cut above her hairline. Behind me, Amena yelled, "Kanti, go!"

Kanti pulled away and ran erratically down the corridor, bouncing off the bulkhead. I ducked into the compartment and went to Amena. Tears streamed down her face, her nose running in that gross "badly upset human" way. She banged on the lab bench. "Here, here, we couldn't pry it up!"

I felt under it carefully, where the support strut had pinned her leg. There wasn't blood, though it had to hurt. I felt marks on the metal from the tool Kanti had been clutching. She had had it in the right spot, but didn't have the leverage needed to pry up the strut. I wedged the tool back in place and leaned on it. My drones met Kanti at the end of the corridor and formed a protective cloud around her as she stagger-ran through the foyer toward the gravity well.

The strut bent back and Amena tried to wriggle out and yelped in pain. I said, "Just take it slow," and managed to sound like we had all the time we needed. (We did not.) My hatchway drone relayed the rising energy readings from the airlock where something was trying to override the security seal.

In the access tube, Rajpreet had grabbed Kanti and was climbing with her up the gravity well, both surrounded by my cloud of drones. Amena wriggled some more, wincing, then reached for my arm and said, "Just pull really hard!"

I took her arm and tugged and she slid out from under the bench. I stood, pulled her with me, and picked her up in one arm. I'd lost contact with Rajpreet but my drones confirmed she wasn't in the gravity well anymore. I told Amena, "Hold on," and ran down the corridor.

I couldn't make anywhere near my top speed; there was too much debris, the corridor too narrow and curving.

I made it almost to the end of the corridor just as the hatch blew with a loud pop. The smell of melted metal and ozone filled the corridor. My hatch drone sent me a view of hazy smoke and movement inside the lock. Time for a split millisecond decision— could I sprint through the foyer, past the breached hatch, up the ramp to the gravity well, and climb up into the baseship so we could close the hatches and separate before the hostiles stormed inside?

Uh, maybe?

Then my input from the hatch drone dissolved in an abrupt burst of energy. I took a silent step backward, then another, keeping the motion smooth and slow. I started a quick analysis of the drone's last transmitted intel. On the feed, I sent, *Hatch is breached, hostiles onboard, seal and jettison now.*

I didn't pick up any acknowledgment and couldn't tell if it went through or not.

Amena was silent, holding herself stiffly immobile against my side, her heart pounding. I eased back around the curve in the corridor, and stepped into the first open hatch. I set her down and mouthed the words "No noise." She nodded, gripped the hatch's safety rail to stay upright, and looked up at me with wide eyes. I wanted to use my drones to look at her, but while that was calming for me, it wouldn't be for her. If I was going to get her out of this alive, keeping her calm and communicating accurately was going to be important. I put my face in an expression that I hoped would convey reassurance, then changed it to intense concentration and stared at the bulkhead. The image analysis finished and I reviewed it. The drone had caught a sensor ghost of something that was emitting energy and floating about two meters above the deck. I included Amena's interface in my relay and said, *Close the hatches, Arada, do it now. They have drones.*

Amena caught her breath and bit her lip, but didn't say any-thing.

Still no acknowledgment. I didn't know if they could hear me, if they had already jettisoned, what the hell was going on up there. We had to be close to the wormhole by now.

(It sounds like I was calm, but I had no idea what the hell I was going to do.)

I felt feed static like a drill through the back part of my head, and then Overse saying, *SecUnit, SecUnit, can you hear me? We've jettisoned the facility from baseship and are in the safepod, about to launch. Can you get to the EVAC suits in the lower secondary lock? The baseship can catch you in their tractor.*

I almost said aloud, "Why are they in the fucking safepod and not in the baseship?" but managed not to. Amena watched me with a not reassuring combination of fear and exasperation. The EVAC suit thing . . . was not a bad idea at all.

Copy, we'll go for the EVAC suits, I told Overse. If there was an acknowledgment, I didn't hear it.

I held out an arm and Amena grabbed my jacket. I picked her up and sent half the drones ahead to scout our path. There was no sign of any hostile movement yet.

I stepped out into the corridor and headed away from the main hatch foyer to the junction to the engineering pod. It looked worse than the lab corridor. Lights were down to emer-gency levels and the deck had buckled.

Fortunately we didn't have far to go, just straight through the pod. My audio picked up a banging and grinding noise—maybe the intruder's drones trying to get through a hatch somewhere.

We reached the engineering outer hatch foyer, light from the emergency markers pointing to the EVAC suit locker.

These were a different model than I'd used before, more ex-pensive, where you could step into them and pull them up with an assist from the suit's own power supply. I set Amena down and she rapidly tied her hair up, then did a one-legged hop into the suit. I ordered my drones to land on me and go dormant, and had my suit on by the time she was fastening her helmet. Something vibrated deep in the deck; was it the safepod launching? My organic parts didn't feel good about this. If that was the safepod, I think they'd waited too long. Human actions often seem way too slow to me because of my processing speed, but I didn't think this was one of those times.

The suits also had secure feed connections, so I could check to make sure Amena's was working and sealed properly, and access its controls. *Don't use your comm,* I told her over the secured feed. They could be scanning for any kind of activity and it was easier for me to mask our feed than the comm.

Got it, she replied. Her feed voice was nervous but not panicky. The suit was supporting her injured leg, letting her stand upright. *I'm ready.*

I told her suit to follow me and opened the airlock.

4

Going out in space in an EVAC suit was not something I did before I hacked my governor module.

(One reason was because there's always a distance limit on a contract. So if you, being a SecUnit, go more than, say, a hundred meters from your clients, your HubSystem uses the governor module to flashfry your brain and neural system. That doesn't mean a client won't order you to do something that would cause you to violate your distance limit, it just means they'll have to pay the company a penalty for destroying their property.)

But the EVAC suits I'd used since then had such good instruction modules that it was almost like having an onboard bot pilot. This one was no exception, plus being new enough to not smell like dirty socks.

(Right, I should probably mention that I find 99.9 percent of human parts physically disgusting. I'm also less than thrilled with my own human parts.)

I came out of the airlock first, towing Amena behind me, and pulled us along the facility's hull. One of the first things I'd discovered about space was that it was boring when there were no pretty planets or stations or anything to look at. This space was empty of planets but not boring.

The EVAC suit had scan and imaging capabilities but I didn't need it as something huge moved out from below us. (I designated that direction as "down" because it was toward where my feet were currently pointed.) It was the baseship, falling slowly away. The hostile was above us, clamped to the facility, a big scary blot on the suit's scan.

I tapped the baseship's feed and without the interference from the dying facility, they heard me. Roa said hurriedly, *We've got you on visual. I'm sending coordinates and Mihail will pull you in with the tractor.*

I downloaded the projected path, then said, *Where is Overse? She reported that she was in the facility safepod with other survey team members.*

Roa said, *Copy that, we're contacting them now.*

Contacting them now? If the safepod had launched it should be on the baseship by now. But I couldn't do anything about it, I had to get Amena to the baseship first.

Amena said, *What does that mean? Is Overse and everyone okay?*

I was about to trigger the suits' maneuvering system when scan picked up an energy surge. My suit's imaging went down and the helmet plate went dark, protecting my eyes against a flash. (I didn't need the protection, but the EVAC suit didn't know that.)

Amena made a startled noise. Static blotted out the feed connection, then Mihail said, *That was a miss, repeat, attacker fired and missed—*

Rajpreet's fainter voice said, *Are they aiming at the safepod?*

The rest was lost in static. I ordered my suit to clear the visor and swung around so I could see the hostile. I don't know why—my suit wasn't armed. I just wanted to see what was after us as something other than a sensor blot. It was almost as dumb an impulse as some things I've seen humans do.

I saw a big dark hull, reflecting light from Preservation's distant primary. There was still nothing coming from it, no feed, no comm, no beacons, so it was like a giant inert object. (A giant inert object dragging us toward the wormhole.) The EVAC imaging system came back online to add in sensor data and give me a more accurate outline, making the hostile show up as part dark shape, part schematic. It was odd, since the configuration looked just like—

The EVAC scans found a registry designation embossed on the ship's hull and rendered it for me. And I recognized it. I didn't even have to search my archive. I recognized it from a transport embarkation schedule on the station I had gone to after leaving Port FreeCommerce.

"That's—" *That's ART,* I almost said on the feed, like an idiot.

It was so shocking and so weird, my performance reliability dropped and I lost circulation to my organic parts. And not weird = violating norms in an annoying way but weird = eerie, like in *Farland Star Roads,* the story arc with the haunted station with ghosts and time-shifting.

Or weird like I was having memory failure again, mixing up archival memory with current data collection.

That was a terrifying thought.

That's what? Amena asked, then the ship—the hostile—ART fired again.

The EVAC suit tracked it this time as a spark across my scanner. It went wide, so wide I thought it must be aimed at the station responder but it was so far away, what would be the point? I pulled the data the suit had collected about the first shot and saw it had gone wide, too.

On our feed, Roa said, *It's another miss! No damage.*

Mihail said, *The vector was way off, I don't even think— Maybe a warning shot.*

Maybe I wasn't having memory failure.

I said, *Baseship, are you still ready to catch us?*

Roa said, *Mihail, are you—* Then, *Yes, yes, SecUnit, go, we're ready!*

The trajectory Mihail had sent was still good, we just had a little longer to go. With Amena's suit in tandem with mine, I launched us off the facility's hull.

Twenty seconds later, something grabbed my suit and tugged it. It was fairly gentle and wouldn't have seemed like a disaster at all except for my suit's emergency alarms and Mihail cursing frantically on the baseship feed.

The ship—the hostile—ART had us in a tractor and pulled us toward its hull. I was facing the wrong way and my suit gave me a sensor view. It was bringing us toward a large lock in the port hull, not that I could do anything about it. I saw ART's lab module was in place, which meant it wasn't acting as a cargo transport, but as a research vessel.

Her voice high with distress, Amena said, *They've got the facility, why do they want us?*

I said, *I don't know.*

I don't know anything.

◻   ◻   ◻

As the tractor pulled us into the large airlock, Roa's voice yelled over the feed, *It's accelerating toward the wormhole! We're losing it*—as the hatch slid shut. The baseship feed dropped. I made an attempt to reconnect, but hit a wall as solid as . . . I don't know, but it was solid.

I hadn't been in this lock before but it still had the clean, well-kept ship look that matched my memories. If I could trust my memories. If this was real.

I really needed to run a diagnostic but there was no time.

The lock cycled, air whooshing in, and the hatch slid open. It sure looked real and my EVAC suit scan matched what I was seeing/scanning. No feed, no comm activity.

The wide corridor beyond the lock was empty, lights tuned to medium-strength, blue bands on the bulkheads serving no function except decorative. A transparent locker built into the bulkhead held a row of empty EVAC suits, dormant and ready for emergencies.

The corridor was quiet, empty on visual, scan, and audio. The lights brightened for us, which was typical for crewed ships, which adjust the lighting based on what the humans are doing and on request. My suit read the air system level as full, which meant normal for humans and augmented humans. When ART ran as an uncrewed cargo transport, it kept its support level on minimum, though it had upped it for me.

There were too many ways to kill us using the airlock, so I stepped over the seal into the corridor. I pulled Amena's suit with me, to make sure there was no opportunity to separate us. The lock cycled closed behind us.

On our suit comm, Amena was saying, "Where are the crew? Why did they do this? What do they want with us?" Then, in a smaller voice, "Please talk to me."

I still had a client, even if I was damaged and hallucinating. If this was a memory failure, I had to tell her. I wished she was Mensah, or any human I trusted to help me. Even Gurathin would have been better in this situation. If I told her that indications suggested that I was having some bizarre memory crash, she would never trust me and I needed her to trust me to get her out of this alive. Except could she trust me when I couldn't even tell if what I was seeing/scanning was real or not?

And if this was really ART, then where the hell was it?

I sent a ping. It was almost like it echoed in the empty feed, like the giant presence that should be here was just absent, like the heart of the ship was hollow.

Amena was breathing harder with building panic, and I needed to say something. What came out was pretty close to the truth: "I think I recognize this ship, but it's not supposed to be here."

Saying it aloud made it seem a lot less like a memory failure, and more like something that was actually happening.

Amena made a sniffing noise. She said, "What—what ship is it?"

Then I had a brilliant idea that I should have had earlier. I said, "What do the patches on those EVAC suits say?"

Mensah and most of the others would have realized immediately that something was wrong; I never asked clients for information if I could help it. (For a lot of reasons but close to the top was the all-too-common suicidal lack of attention to detail humans were prone to.) Amena stepped closer to the transparent locker. There were two rows of suits visible, one above the other, so if a suit was removed from its slot another would slide down to replace it. The patches were throwing a localized broadcast into the feed in multiple languages, readable by interfaces and our EVAC suits even while ART's feed was inaccessible, the same way marker paints worked. Amena said aloud, "*Perihelion. Pan-system University of Mihira and New Tideland.*"

That was ART's designation and registry. Okay, so. Good news: I'm not having some kind of memory or system crash, this was really ART. Bad news: what the fuck?

I sent another ping.

Amena turned back to me. "This must be a stolen survey ship." Her voice was firmer, less breathy with incipient panic. "I guess the raiders armed it."

"It was already armed." I thought, *It's my friend. It helped me because it wanted to, because it could.* I couldn't say any of that. I hadn't told anyone about ART. "It's a deep space research and teaching vessel with a full crew and passenger complement. Between missions it travels as a bot-piloted cargo vessel, but Preservation isn't on its route."

"Research and teaching vessel," Amena repeated. "If the raiders had a ship this big, with weapons, why bother with us? Maybe they thought we had something valuable on board? Or they just go around attacking research ships? They hate research?"

She was being sarcastic but I knew of raiders who had done things like this for reasons almost as stupid. But this wasn't a memory ghost/hallucination, which meant it was still a statistically unlikely coincidence, and that was . . . statistically unlikely.

"Wait, you know this ship." Her voice turned suspicious. The statistically unlikely part must have occurred to her, too. "Did you do something to them? Are they here after you?"

"Of course not." That was a total lie, because ART had to

have come here after me, though knowing that didn't make this any less baffling. It wasn't like ART's crew came here for revenge because the murderous rogue SecUnit— Hold it, could they be here for revenge? I hadn't hurt ART or anything onboard, unless you counted some power and resource usage that ART had expunged from its logs.

That seemed a weird thing to shoot up an unarmed survey ship over. I mean, they could have just sent Dr. Mensah an invoice.

Unless somebody had managed to get aboard after I left and do something to ART, and blamed me for it.

One big problem with that scenario, no wait, two: 1) getting aboard without ART's cooperation and 2) doing something to ART without getting violently murdered. (I knew of forty-seven ways that ART could kill a human, augmented human, or bot intruder, and the only reason I didn't know more is because I got bored and stopped counting.)

And where the hell was ART? Where was its feed, its drones, its comm, its humans? Why wouldn't it answer my pings?

I didn't forget that I had one of ART's comms tucked into the pocket under my ribs. (Okay, I did forget until three minutes and forty-seven seconds ago, but it wasn't like I'd needed to access the information until now.) The comm had been deactivated and inert since I left ART on RaviHyral's transit ring. If ART wanted to call me, it could have used it as soon as we were in range. But that was assuming that ART was still in control of itself. Was something else—bot or human or augmented human— controlling ART's ship-body?

I was starting to panic. I didn't want ART to be hurt, and anything that could hurt ART could destroy me and Amena.

This wasn't helping. Start with the assumption that ART was still here, intact but under some sort of constraint I didn't have time to speculate about but would anyway.

Had ART been able to use the deactivated comm to track me

after our survey ship arrived through the wormhole? Yes, probably. But why? Why come to Preservation space after me? ART loved its crew, like, a lot. It would do anything to help them.

Including betray me? Was something forcing ART to do this? Did it want the facility, or was that collateral damage? As soon as it had me and Amena in its tractor, it had increased acceleration toward the wormhole. We had to be in the wormhole by now, heading away from Preservation. The responders wouldn't be able to track us.

At least that meant that Overse and whoever was with her in the safepod could be picked up by the baseship.

I needed to get rid of my EVAC suit. In gravity they made movement cumbersome, and could be hacked if I wasn't careful, and I wasn't sure how much protection the suit would give Amena from projectiles or other weapon fire. It wasn't like it would be a good idea to go outside now, and freedom of movement was more important.

I got the EVAC suit to open its helmet and released my drones. I told two to take up guard positions at the entrance to the corridor and sent the others to make a cautious sweep through the ship . . . through ART. Then I opened my suit and stepped out. Amena said, "Is that a good idea?"

I really didn't need to be second-guessed by an adolescent human right now. "Do you have any other suggestions?"

"I guess we can't stay in these things forever," she muttered, and opened her suit.

I waited for her to climb out. She was shaking a little, and sweating, and favoring her injured leg. I needed to get access to the medical suite. Whatever was going on here, it would be easier to deal with if Amena wasn't hurt.

I moved toward the corridor, gesturing Amena to stay behind me. My scan still picked up nothing but background interference from ART's systems. My drones were seeing empty corridors, closed hatches. I directed them toward the control deck, specifically the crew meeting area under the bridge. Somebody had to be here, bot or human or augmented human. This time I pinged the comm system.

The ship's comm chimed, an automatic response. Amena flinched at the sound. Keeping my voice low, I told her, "That was me."

"Why?" She managed to whisper this in a way that sounded very demanding. Then she grimaced in frustration. "Right. I guess they know we're here, since they kidnapped us."

So far my drones hadn't detected any crew. There was no response to the comm, and I moved toward the corridor. I wasn't sure what I was going to do. Maybe go up to ART's bridge and bang on the shield over its control core?

This was one of the corridors I had walked up and down, working on my pretending-to-be-a-human code, where ART had critiqued my performance. Maybe that made me less cautious. That and the fact that my drones had just passed through here seconds ago. As I stepped into the corridor, something moved in my peripheral vision.

This is why we have drones. Unfortunately, whatever this was, my guard drone hadn't registered its presence. I didn't see it until it moved, and that was too late.

I took the hit right in the side of my head and got body-slammed against the bulkhead.

Performance reliability catastrophic drop.

Shutdown.

Restart.

I was lying in a heap on the deck, a broken fragment of something grinding into my cheek. I knew I'd had an emergency shutdown. (I miss my armor all the time, but particularly at times like this.)

I need the organic parts inside my head, but they have much better shock absorption in there than inside a human skull. You can hit a SecUnit hard enough to make our performance reliability drop so fast and so low it triggers a temporary shutdown.

(Operative word: temporary.) But it's really not a good idea. Not if you want to keep your internal organs inside your body and not smeared on the bulkheads of your stolen transport.

Oh, it's on now.

My drones had gone dormant and my systems weren't online to access them yet. My audio kicked back in and I picked up sound coming from down the corridor. A voice, Amena's voice, too low for me to make out the words. I tapped the input for my drone relay feed; it was a passive connection and still transmitting.

Amena's voice was hard with what was clearly false bravado: "You've made a big mistake. There are armed ships minutes away. They'll be here—"

"Oh, little child, we're in the bridge-transit. No one will ever find you again." The voice (Unidentified: One) was light, arch, with an echo caused by an out-of-date pre-feed translator system. "Now tell us about the weapon."

Amena's bravado was turning into real anger. "Our survey facility wasn't armed. If it was, you'd be blown to pieces." (Note to humans and augmented humans: no one likes being patronized.)

Unidentified One sounded even more amused. "You had better have the weapon we were told of, or I'll take your ribs out one by one and break them in front of your little face."

I saved that for future reference. Unidentified One seemed to have gone to some trouble with the wording of that threat, it would be a shame if they never experienced it firsthand.

Another voice (Unidentified: Two) said, "I hate lying, all these things lie." It sounded almost identical to Unidentified One, except it was slightly deeper in tone.

Amena said, "I'm not lying, I don't know what you're talking about." A little of her fear leaked through. I think she was beginning to realize she wasn't talking to an intelligence that was open to rational argument.

Unidentified One said, "You lie, it lies, everything's lying. Don't think we don't know better."

Tinged with desperation, Amena said, "I can't do anything about that."

The rest of my parts were checking in as functional and my performance reliability was climbing. The temporary shutdown had flushed a lot of stress toxins secreted by my organic parts and I actually felt better. Scan showed the fragments under my cheek were from components shielded by a case that read as stealth material. I'd been hit by a drone, maybe the same type I'd caught an image of in the facility before EVACing. It had hit me so hard it had knocked itself to pieces. None of ART's drones—at least the ones it had let me see—had stealth construction. And maybe the forced restart had definitely done me some good because I was an idiot to not think of this before. If there were drones receiving orders, there had to be a feed active inside ART, just not on any of the standard channels. As my legs and feet came back online and I eased slowly upright, I tweaked my receivers to scan the whole range for activity.

My projectile weapon lay on the deck in pieces, like someone had used a tool to pound it apart. My saved schematic of ART's interior layout came in handy as I mapped the direction of Amena's voice. Down this curving corridor, to a cross corridor, to a crew lounge area. I didn't make any noise.

By the time I got to the first curve in the corridor, I found their drone control feed. It was on an encrypted channel, like a military feed. Clever, except their encryption was practically ancient, in bot terms if not human. My last update of my ex-owner bond company's proprietary key-breaker was 8700+ hours out of date, but it snapped their encryption like a twig.

Their feed was almost empty, no voices that I could detect, just drone commands. If their encryption was old, their drone codes might be, too. I pulled the oldest version of my drone key files and started cycling through them. My own drones were still in standby as I rebuilt my inputs and connections, but they were semi-useless at the moment, since the stealth material prevented them from scanning the hostile drones.

The doorway to the lounge where I'd detected Amena's voice was open, brighter light falling into the half-lit corridor. I meant to wait until I was back up to at least 90 percent performance reliability but I heard Amena say, "There's no weapon, you got the wrong ship." The fear in her voice was more obvious and I was suddenly in the room.

(Impulse control; I should try to write a code patch for that.)

The compartment was large, with padded couches and seats built against the bulkheads, a few low tables that were designed to fold down into the deck, and various display surfaces, now inert, floating above them. Occupants included one client: Amena, backed up against the far wall, disheveled and wide-eyed but no apparent new damage. Two potential targets/possible casualties: both backed toward the far end of the compartment, past Amena. They had visible bruises and shocked/frightened expressions. Both casualties wore red and brown uniforms, disheveled and torn, with corporate logos. Another anomaly, since ART's crew uniforms were dark blue.

Two Targets faced Amena and the casualties: possibly augmented human; scan results null.

Both Targets turned toward me. They looked like tall, thin augmented humans, with dull gray skin. (Injury, illness? Or an uncommon skin augment/cosmetic modification?) They both wore form-fitting protective suits and partial helmets that left a surprising (surprisingly stupid) amount of the face bare. Narrow human features, dark brows standing out against the smooth gray skin. Both smiled with colorless lips.

Accusingly, one said (Unidentified One = Target One) to the other, "You said this one was dead." They weren't quite identical. Target One was slightly taller and had broader shoulders.

"Poor thing *was* dead," Unidentified Two = Target Two responded, and laughed.

Poor thing. I think a capillary just burst inside one of my organic parts.

Three drones hovered behind the Targets, of a model that

didn't match anything in my archives. They were round, as big around as my head, the apertures for cameras or weapons hidden despite their size. The stealth material interfered with my scan, but not with the image in the organic part of my brain. It gave me an uneasy kind of double vision, where my scan insisted there were floating anomalies that wouldn't appear on my camera, yet I had a clear image in my temp data storage, supplied by my organic nerve tissue.

I knew the targetDrones weren't slow, but they looked cumbersome. I needed intel before proceeding. I said, "What did you do to ART?"

That wasn't the intel I needed. But it was the intel I wanted.

Target One cocked its head inquiringly and bared sharp teeth. Another possible cosmetic modification or genetic variance. Target One said, "You're babbling, poor thing."

Target Two, in almost the same tone, said, "These creatures seem to have no control over their vocalizations."

I was aware of Amena, watching me with wide eyes, both hands pressed to her mouth. Casualties One and Two, still behind her, stared at me in confusion.

I clarified, "This transport. What did you do to the bot pilot?" ART was so much more than a bot pilot but I didn't have a word for what it was.

Target Two sighed and folded its arms, like I'd asked a stupid question. Target One grinned at me, maliciously. It didn't know who I was, what I was, it might not even know who ART was, but it knew I cared, and it was going to enjoy what it said next. "We deleted it, of course."

I felt my face change. The muscles were all stiff, and not from the hit I'd taken. I'm still not great at controlling my expressions, and I had no idea what I looked like. Behind her hands, Amena whispered, "Oh shit."

"Oh, this one looks angry," Target One said.

Target Two said, "How boring. Angry, then afraid, then dead. Boring boring boring."

Target One began, "You belong to us now, all of you. This is what's going to happen. You will tell us—"

I grabbed Target One's face. Not my best strategic attack, but the quickest way to shut it up. Using its face as a handle, I slung it sideways into the couch built against the bulkhead.

TargetDrone One came at my head. It was fast but I was ready this time. I ducked sideways and as it stopped and reversed to come back at me, I put my fist through it. I slammed it against the side of the hatch to break the remnants off my hand as I turned.

Target Two actually looked at the other two targetDrones at this point, obviously wondering why they hadn't responded.

The good thing about being a construct is that I can have a dramatic emotional breakdown while still running my background search to find the drone key commands. I'd had a hit and a responding ping from the targetDrones right when Target One had called me boring. (Irony is great.) I sent the order to power down and they dropped to the deck with two loud thunks.

Target Two's gray face went surprised, then furious. It was kind of funny. This was a point where if I was a human (ick) I might have laughed. I decided to go with my first inclination and kill the shit out of some ass-faced hostiles instead. I told the Targets, "Angry, then afraid, then dead. Is that the right order?"

Casualty One whispered, "Oh deity, that's a—"

Target One, flailing on the couch, reached for something that was clearly a weapon, clipped to the suit plate on its thigh. I lunged forward and had its wrist before it could close around the weapon. This turned out to be a trick, because it slapped its free hand on my shoulder and I felt a stab of pain from an energy weapon.

Target One grinned at me with its whole face.

Projectiles hurt but energy weapons just piss me off. I crushed the wrist I was holding and twisted, caught the arm with the energy weapon and snapped it. (The arm. The weapon, a clunky tube-shaped device about ten centimeters long, clattered to the deck.)

Target One shrieked in a combination of rage and disbelief that did not make me any less mad. Target Two, with what I have to say was an entirely misplaced confidence, stepped in and shoved another energy weapon at my chest.

I was moving so fast that later I had to run my video back to analyze my performance. I shoved Target One away and smashed an elbow into Target Two's face. I tore the energy weapon out of Target Two's hand along with a few fingers, stabbed the weapon into its chest (it didn't have a sharp end but I made do) and ripped a large hole. Then I used the weapon, and the large hole, to lift Target Two up and slam it into the upper bulkhead. Three times. Fluid and pieces went everywhere.

That was satisfying. I think I'll do it again.

But I'd taken too long and it gave Target One time to scramble up and bolt for the hatch.

I started to follow but then registered that Amena was bellowing "SecUnit, look!" at me.

I looked. On the deck, the two remaining targetDrones were flashing awkwardly placed lights; they were powering up. I sent a power down order but the key wasn't working anymore. I stomped the first one with a boot and then caught the second as it lifted off. I smashed it on a chair, accidentally taking out a display surface in the process. The two casualties were yelling agitatedly at Amena and I had to run back my audio to understand.

Casualty One grabbed Amena's arm and said, "You have to come with us! We have to get away, try to hide!" This close, though ART's primary feed still wasn't working, I could pick up some info from her interface. (Feedname: Eletra, gender: female, and an employee ID from a corporation called Barish-Estranza.)

Casualty Two (Feedname: Ras, gender: male, and another Barish-Estranza employee ID.) "Quick, before they send more drones!" He threw a look at me. I knew that look. "With your SecUnit, we have a chance."

Amena turned to me. "We should go with them."

I'd already sent a restart command to my dormant drones. Target One wasn't hard for them to track since it was wounded, leaking fluid, and shrieking. (You know, if you don't want to be manually eviscerated with your own energy weapon then maybe you shouldn't go around killing research transports and antagonizing rogue SecUnits.)

I told Amena, "I have something I need to finish off."

"There are too many drones," Eletra insisted. Her gaze went from Amena to me and back again. She wasn't sure who she had to convince. "You have to come with us!"

Amena took a step toward me, wincing as she put weight on her damaged leg. "Are they right? Can you tell if the drones are coming for us?"

Target One ran through the hatch into the crew meeting area below the bridge.

The crew meeting area where I'd spent most of my time with ART, where we watched *World Hoppers.* My drones caught video of another hostile already in there (designated Target Three) standing on the steps that led up to the control deck. The hatch into the meeting area started to slide down. Eight of my drones reached the hatch in time to dart under just before it closed.

The humans weren't wrong about the targetDrones, which weren't responding to my key commands anymore. (Which meant there was a highly motivated controlling system somewhere that had pushed through a quick security update.) I still had access to the Targets' feed, and from the encrypted traffic, somebody was telling the targetDrones to do something. Which most likely involved converging on our position to kill us.

I said, "Probably."

Amena waved her hands impatiently. "Then let's go!"

I tried cutting off the targetDrones' control feed. It confused some but others still seemed to be receiving orders. There were obviously parts of this system I couldn't access. Working within it was like trying to operate a projectile weapon when someone had shot half my fingers off. All the data needed to be converted to other formats, nothing was right, it was a pain in the ass. To take full control of it I was going to have to start at the beginning, with penetration testing.

Exasperated, Ras said, "Just give it an order!"

Amena snapped, "It doesn't take orders."

I'd wanted to do this up close and personal but that wasn't an option. The eight drones now inside the control deck with Targets One and Three were on standby near the floor, in surveillance positions. Target One had collapsed against a padded station chair, panting, both damaged arms hanging uselessly. Target Three stepped down to an inactive display surface and activated it with a hand gesture. Weird to see a human or whatever these were do it manually. They hadn't set their non-standard encrypted feed to access ART's systems yet.

Target Three said on the all-ship comm, "Intruders, escapees, slice them open like—"

The translator fizzled on the last few words so I guess I'd never know what I'd be sliced open like. I cut one drone out of the swarm of eight to observe, and gave the others their instructions. With the protective suit and the partial helmets, I needed to aim for the exposed face.

Target Three had time to make a gurgling noise and Target One a gaspy scream. My seven drone contacts winked out one by one. Drone Eight continued to record, sending me video of the bodies jerking helplessly, then finally dropping in leaking sprawls to the deck.

"But that's a SecUnit—" Ras protested.

Eletra, her expression increasingly desperate, listened to the comm announcement and its abrupt end. "We have to go!"

Amena limped forward another step. She grabbed my arm and glared up at me. "Listen to me!"

I looked down at her and made deliberate eye contact because she had almost all my attention right now and the last person/target who had done that was still dripping down the bulkhead behind me. She was too self-absorbed or brave or some combination of both to realize what she was doing was not smart. She set her jaw and said, "We have to go with them. Now."

I gently peeled her small hand off my jacket and said, "Never touch me again."

Amena blinked and pressed her lips together, then turned to Eletra and Ras. "Let's go."

Eletra stepped toward the hatch. "This way—"

Ras said, "Is that thing going to listen—"

I stepped past Eletra and out the hatch in time to catch the targetDrone waiting there. I slammed it into the bulkhead and shook the remnants off my hands. Following ART's schematic, I said, "This way."

They followed me.

5

I called in most of my drones to take scouting positions ahead and cover positions behind us. I was taking the long way around toward Medical. The dim corridor lights brightened as we went by, an autonomic reflex. For a human, it would have been like seeing a dead body twitch. ART wasn't here, there was no sign of its drones, but some of its lower-level functions were active, the code running even without the controlling intelligence.

An intruder system, probably some kind of bot pilot, had changed the security key for the targetDrones. And it must be guiding the ship through the wormhole. Transports just can't do that on autopilot, at least according to *World Hoppers* and all the other shows about ships that I'd watched. That ART had wanted to watch.

I designated the intruder as targetControlSystem.

I hoped it was sentient enough to hurt when I killed it.

I had a lot of work to do before that point. And the image of the steaming bodies of Targets One and Three inside ART's pristine control area was taking up way too much processing space.

I had a few scout drones still in the corridors near the control area and I told them to start mapping any motion and anomalous activity and plot it to my copy of ART's schematic. I had to find a way to advance-detect the targetDrones.

A drone (designated: Scout Two), parked on the ceiling of the foyer outside the crew meeting area, picked up activity. More Targets converged on the foyer and tried to get the hatch open, but Target Three had apparently used a manual emergency control to seal it from the inside. The new Targets—let's call them Four, Five, and Six—fumbled around with the controls but didn't seem to know how to undo the seal. And whatever was going on with their weird feed and targetControlSystem, they couldn't seem to access ART's systems with it.

ART was dead.

I wanted to stop and lean my head against the bulkhead, but there was no time.

Behind me, my drones saw Eletra had an arm around Amena's waist, helping her walk. Ras limped, too, trying to watch behind us and keep an eye on me at the same time. All three were either shivering or sweating from what was probably shock.

Right. Humans. Humans with needs. Mensah's juvenile human, and the two new humans who were obviously hurt.

Murderbot, you need to get your act together.

"Do you know how many Targets are aboard?" I said.

"Targets?" Ras repeated.

"It means the gray people," Amena said, gritting her teeth as she put weight on her bad leg.

"I've seen five, but I don't know if that's all," Eletra said.

"At least five," Ras agreed. "They had a lot of those bots, drones, whatever they are. We should try to get to the engineering module. Tell your SecUnit—"

"It doesn't listen to me, I told you," Amena said, exasperated.

I'd already identified six total Targets, with three still active (counting the messily dead ones), so the humans' intel was useless. (Not a surprise.) I arranged the drone scouts in front of us into a cloud formation and sent them ahead with their scan functions tuned all the way up.

Scout Two showed me that Targets Four, Five, and Six had stopped ineffectually poking at the hatch. They were hastily adjusting their protective suits, sliding plates reconfiguring their helmets to cover their whole heads. That was a problem. Seven drones to kill two Targets had been overkill (Though one Target had already been wounded. Say seven to kill one and a half Targets.) especially when my supply of drones was limited. I had no real intel on how good their armor was at deflecting drones, and trying to find out might mean wasting another squad.

I needed the drones as an early warning system for the targetDrones, which with targetControlSystem, might be a much worse threat than the squishy Targets. Plus three of my drones scouting in the main section near ART's control area had disappeared in the last ninety-seven seconds, which meant they had encountered stealth targetDrones. I was losing my eyes in the rest of the ship and that was really not an ideal situation. It sucked, basically. Even my risk assessment module thought so, and I knew what its opinion was worth.

We reached the hatch into the quarters section and I stepped to the side to let the humans through, then hit the manual release. The hatch slid shut and I pulled the panel, then used the energy weapon in my right arm to melt a couple of key components.

Behind me, this was going on:

"Why is it doing that?" Ras asked Amena.

She stared blankly at him, then said, "SecUnit, why are you doing that?"

Checking ART's schematic had let me pick a couple of access points. I could close off the living section—containing the quarters, medical, galley, classrooms, and crew lounges—from the rest of the ship by sealing two more hatches. It wasn't the best choice, but trying to cross over to engineering or the lab module wasn't feasible at the moment, and the humans would need the supplies here. I was betting the targetDrones had no arm extensions to repair the hatches. The Targets themselves could, but I'd have warning and time to get there first. (And the Targets could get to us via an outer hatch, but they'd have to take the EVAC suits out across the hull while we were in the wormhole and from what I'd seen in the entertainment media, that was a bad idea.) "I'm trying to create a safe zone."

Amena turned to Ras and said, "It's trying to create a safe zone."

As he looked from her to me and back again, I stepped past and started down the passage. Then three drones in my scout formation winked out of existence at the corridor junction ahead. I threw myself forward, rolled into the junction, and shot the two targetDrones waiting there with my left arm energy weapon. One dropped to the deck, the second wobbled in the air. I came to my feet and smashed it against the bulkhead.

My drone Scout Two in the control area foyer recorded the Targets pounding on the sealed hatch again. Did they think we—or someone—was inside? They weren't using translators with each other and I couldn't understand what they were saying.

I told my drone cloud to continue down the corridor toward the medical suite to make sure it was clear. I told the humans, "Hurry." None of them argued, and they limped after me rapidly.

Down two corridors, then a turn and we were there. The MedSystem's platform was quiet and powered down, the surgical system folded up into the ceiling, no sign of the medical drones. It was weird (not bad weird, just weird) seeing this place again. This was where ART had made the changes to my configuration, to help me pass as a human, where it had saved my client Tapan.

Ugh, emotions.

I checked the space, scanning the restroom and shower compartment, the morgue, and the other enclosed areas to make sure there weren't targetDrones, Targets, or any other as yet unknown hostile lurking. The humans stood in the middle of the room, watching me anxiously.

I finished my sweep, told them, "Stay here." I left one drone to keep my feed relay with Amena active and walked out, shutting the hatch behind me.

I sent my drone cloud ahead and sprinted after it, heading toward the hatch at the opposite end of the module. If the Targets had figured out what I was doing, this was the closest hatch to the control area foyer where they were still gathered.

As I reached the hatch I needed to seal, I risked a look down the short module passage into the next section. My organic nerve tissue detected movement and I hit the hatch release to shut it. I sealed the manual controls, left a drone sentry, and took off for the last hatch.

Inside the medical suite, the humans were still huddled together. Eletra whispered, "Can you tell what it's doing?"

Amena said, "It's sealing the hatches, like it said it would."

Ras looked frustrated and impatient, but didn't argue.

The third hatch led to a connecting section which was a secondary pathway into the engineering module. This hatch was already closed and sealed, but I fused the manual control anyway. I'd lost all but four drone scouts in the rest of the ship: one (Scout One) was still locked in the control meeting area with the two dead Targets. Scout Two was in the foyer ceiling watching the Targets gathered at the sealed hatch, and Three and Four had tucked themselves up under supporting rib structures in nearby corridors.

I started back toward Medical, letting my surviving drone cloud spread out a little more. Bits of me hurt enough that I needed to tune down my pain sensors.

At the Medical corridor, I split my drones into two squads and positioned them at opposite ends of the access. I needed to clear this section and make sure I hadn't trapped us in here with anything, but there were things I needed/wanted to know first.

When I stepped inside, Ras said, "What's going on?" He glanced at Amena, still unsure who to talk to. "Are we safe here?"

I knew ART's normal crew size; the command crew alone was at least eight members, with a rotating complement of instructors and students. I knew from my brief sweep that there was no sign anyone had been treated in the medical suite recently, no dead humans in cold storage. Which was good, except that the bodies could have been spaced. I knew how ART would have felt about that.

I said, "Where's the crew of this ship?"

Again, Ras looked at Amena. Amena's brow furrowed and she said to me, "I thought they were the crew."

"No," Eletra said. She seemed confused, too. "Our ship was a Barish-Estranza transport."

Amena turned to Ras and Eletra. "So where are the crew of this ship?"

Ras shook his head in annoyance. "Look, I can see you're young. I'm guessing this SecUnit was ordered to protect you but—"

Amena made a derisive huff. "It doesn't even like me."

Admittedly I am tired of the whole concept of humans at the moment, but that was unfair because she didn't like me first.

"If you tell it to take orders from us," Ras tried again, "this will be a lot easier."

Eletra nodded. "It's for the best. It doesn't seem like you know how to control it—"

Amena waved her hands in exasperation. "Look, that's not—"

I see I have some operational parameters to establish.

I crossed the room, grabbed Ras by the front of his uniform jacket and slammed him down on the med platform. I said, "Answer my question."

Behind me, Eletra had flinched and backed away. Amena said, "SecUnit! My mother will be angry if you hurt him!"

Oh, we were going to try that tactic, were we. I said, "You obviously don't know how your mother actually feels about Corporates."

Eletra said frantically, "We don't know where the crew is! Ras, just tell it we don't know."

Ras rasped out, "We don't know!"

I said, "Is that the truth or is that the story you're going with?"

"It's the truth," Ras managed. "We don't know what happened to them."

"We really don't," Eletra added, urgent enough to be convincing. "We haven't seen anyone else since we were brought aboard. Just . . . those people."

I let Ras up and he scrambled away from me, over to Eletra on the far side of the room. His expression was frightened, incredulous.

"Stop being so mean," Amena hissed at me.

I lowered my voice and I sounded absolutely normal and not like I was upset at all. "I am trying to keep you alive."

"I appreciate that, but—" She squinted up at me. "You look really bad. Are you sure you're all right? That drone hit you really hard."

Yeah, well, I can't do anything about that right now. I said, "You need to take care of your leg. But do not activate the MedSystem. It was controlled by . . ." For nearly ten seconds, I'd forgotten. "By the bot pilot. It was compromised before it was . . . destroyed or it would have killed the intruders itself. Something is still running the ship, taking us through the wormhole, and whatever it is may have control of the MedSystem."

Amena threw a worried look at the silent medical platform. So did Ras and Eletra. Amena said, "I didn't know bot pilots could kill people."

"They're almost as dangerous as humans." I know, of every argument I could try to start right now, that one is in the top five most stupidly pointless.

Amena gave me a baffled glare, but said, "Right, so no MedSystem. There's got to be some manual med supplies here somewhere."

"Use one of the emergency kits in that locker. I need to finish clearing this section." I hit our private relay and added, *I'll leave you some drones.* I cut a squad of eight out of my cloud and told them to stay with her.

Her eyes widened and she hesitated. For three seconds I didn't understand why. She hadn't been afraid when I'd grabbed Ras; her expression had been more annoyed than anything else. Then I realized she didn't want to separate. She took a sharp breath and said, "All right." On the feed relay, she added, *Good, drones. That's what I've always wanted.*

I could have said "Don't say I never gave you anything" and we could have had reassuring sarcastic banter, like one of my shows. But I was walking around in ART's corpse and nothing felt reassuring. I just said, *I'll stay in contact.*

I walked out, headed for the quarters section. Scout Two in the control area foyer was still watching a confused/agitated conversation among the Targets. Wait, something was different again about their helmets. I ran back the video and spotted it: the color had changed from a dull blue-gray to the same patterned stealth material as the targetDrones. The Targets noticed when it happened, pointing at each other and commenting on it, but they didn't seem to find it surprising or unusual.

Another security update by targetControlSystem. That's all I fucking need. My drone targeting would be completely thrown off. Fortunately the update hadn't been—or more probably couldn't be—loaded to the rest of their body armor. But killer drone strikes might be completely off the table now.

I wondered why the Targets had been pounding on the hatch. If Targets One and Three could come back from the dead, Scout One hadn't recorded any sign of it.

Huh. Depending on how targetControlSystem collected data from the targetDrones, how they recorded and transmitted video, the three remaining Targets might actually have very little idea of what had happened to Targets One, Two, and Three. They knew Amena and I had been brought aboard, they had to. But they seemed focused on the sealed control area. They hadn't gone to the lounge where Target Two's body still was. Maybe, despite the targetDrones and targetControlSystem's updates, they didn't have access to surveillance data? TargetControlSystem obviously knew physical impacts had killed the Targets or it wouldn't have coded the updates—was it not sharing that information with the Targets?

It was a strange idea, I know. And if correct, it was more proof for the theory that the Targets had little to no access to most of ART's onboard systems, even though targetControlSystem was

running helm and presumably weapons. Though ART didn't
have feed-accessible security cams like a normal transport.

ART.

I pulled together a simple code for penetration testing and
started to run it in the background, on all the channels where I
thought there might be targetDrone activity.

I was going to break into targetControlSystem and do terrible
things to it.

And if the Targets were that confused about what had happened and where we were, I could use that. I started another
process to pull recorded audio out of my archive. (If I had a plan
at the moment, which I did not, it would involve stalling a lot.
We were in the wormhole and whatever our destination was, it
would take several day-cycles at least, probably more, possibly
a lot more, to get anywhere. I had to seize control of the ship
(ART) before then.)

In the medical suite, my drones watched Eletra pull an emergency kit out of the locker. Amena sat down heavily on a bench
as Eletra got the kit open.

Ras glanced warily up at my drones, which were in a circulating formation in the upper part of the compartment. He said,
"That . . . your SecUnit is really going to protect us?"

"Sure," Amena said, distracted as Eletra handed her a wound
pack.

Eletra opened a container of medication tabs with a groan of
relief. "My back is killing me. They let us have ration bars from
an emergency supply pack, but no meds, nothing else."

Ras persisted, "You said your family owns it?"

"No, I didn't say that." Amena wrapped the wound pack
around her injured leg. Then she almost fell over as it shot drugs
for shock and pain right through her torn pants.

I told her, *Tell them I'm under contract to the Preservation Survey.*

"It's under contract to the Preservation Survey." Amena
shoved herself upright again. *That's true, so why are you telling
me to say it like it's a lie?*

Because "under contract" means something completely different to them. In the Preservation Alliance, it meant I'd agreed to work for the survey for a specifically limited amount of time in return for compensation. In the Corporation Rim, it would have meant the survey had rented me from an owner, the same way you'd rent your habitat or your terrain vehicle, except humans usually had warm feelings toward their habitats and terrain vehicles.

Ras seemed confused by Amena's answer, but he just said, "We need something that will take out those drones." He started to search through the emergency kit, and pulled out a container of fire suppressant. "This might work."

Eletra slid down to sit on the floor. She offered Amena the medication container. "I don't think I've heard of the Preservation Survey. Is that a subsidiary of another corporation or . . . ?"

While Amena explained the concept of a non-corporate polity to Eletra (and how many polities did actually have surveys and stations and cities and so on and weren't just people in loincloths screaming at each other), I reached the quarters and started a quick search. Some cabins were clearly unused, mostly the ones with multiple bunks that were meant for students. The beds were still folded up in the walls and there were no personal possessions in sight, just like the last time I had been here. Other cabins showed recent habitation: beds and furniture deployed, bedding in place but disarrayed, clothing and personal objects and hygiene items lying around. Like the crew had just been here, had just stepped away right before I looked in. It was creepy, with no movement except the air system making the fabric tassels of a wall decoration flutter.

Still no sign of any bodies. I sent to Amena, *Don't tell the corporates that you're Dr. Mensah's daughter.*

I'm not stupid, she shot back. They were past the explanation of what Preservation was and were finally exchanging actual information, including their names and what the hell was going on. Amena said, "This ship attacked us right after we came out of the wormhole. How did you get aboard?"

"It attacked us, too. We were on a supply transport, supporting the main expedition ship, an explorer, when this ship started to fire on us. We escaped in a shuttle, then we were pulled aboard. At least, that's what I think happened." Eletra shoved her hair back and looked exhausted. "They did something that knocked us unconscious in the shuttle. One moment we were there, the next we were lying on the deck in this ship, and those gray people were laughing at us. I don't know what happened to the others."

I wondered if the shuttle was still aboard. If ART's shuttles were still aboard. Without access to ART's systems, I couldn't tell without a physical search, like I didn't have enough to do right now. Speaking of which, I tapped Scout One, which was still trapped in the bridge/control area, and told it to do a systematic scan of any active displays it could find.

"We don't know why they took us," Ras said. "They locked us in a cabin and just left us there. We don't know what they want, they wouldn't tell us."

"The explorer was much faster," Eletra said. "It might have gotten away."

"I think our baseship got away," Amena said slowly. "SecUnit was trying to get us over to it and they grabbed us and pulled us into their lock."

There were too many places in ART that I hadn't searched yet where the bodies of the crew might be stashed.

Maybe I do watch too much media, because in the empty corridors, passing empty but recently used rooms, I had an image of finding Mensah's family camp house like this. Empty, no humans, just their possessions left behind and no trace in the feed, no cameras, no way to find them.

This was no time to be an idiot.

"Is there any food or water in here?" Eletra said. She rested her head in her hands. "I've got a terrible headache."

Ras pushed to his feet, wincing. "There's a restroom with a water tap."

In the next set of quarters I started to find the anomalies. One cabin I was pretty certain was the one used to lock up Ras and Eletra. A crumpled jacket that matched their uniforms lay on a bunk. The cabin didn't have an attached restroom, but didn't smell as bad as I would've expected. (Humans trapped for multiple cycles with no access to water or sanitary devices is usually harder on the furniture.) The Targets must have been letting them out periodically.

My process to select some audio (a series of conversations between two of my favorite recurring characters on *Sanctuary Moon*) finished. I stripped out music and effects, lowered the volume, and cut the sections together into an hour and twenty-two minutes, then relayed it to Scout One inside the sealed control area. It started to play the audio. I'd constructed the query to search for conversations where the two characters were whispering, or speaking in low agitated voices. The effect would be even better with Scout One roaming the control area looking for display surface data.

I continued to search the quarters. I thought the Targets must have been using these cabins, too (they didn't exactly strike me as beings who would respect other beings' personal space) but the odd smell was the first indication I was right. Human living spaces tend to smell like dirty socks, even when they're clean. But this smell was oddly . . . agricultural, like the growth medium used in food-producing systems.

According to Scout Two in the control area foyer, all the Targets now had their helmets pressed up against the hatch, trying to hear the conversation inside.

Despite everything, it was a little funny.

"So were you on a survey, too?" Amena asked. I could tell she was trying to sound casual, but it may have been less obvious to the other humans.

"No. Well, in a way," Ras said. He had filled some water containers from the restroom tap and brought them back for the group. "It was a recovery."

"An attempted recovery," Eletra said. She took a long drink from a container and wiped her mouth. "Our division was assigned to work on lost settlements." She hesitated. "I'm not . . . It's proprietary information . . ."

"I'm a junior survey intern and I'm not even from the Corporation Rim," Amena pointed out. "I'm not going to tell anybody."

Ras didn't seem as reluctant to explain as Eletra. "We were on an assignment to recover a viable planet. In one of the systems that were mapped before the Corporation Rim formed. Do you know about those?"

"Of course." Amena's brow was furrowed in confusion. I didn't get it, either. My education modules have gaps you could fly a gunship through but I knew from the entertainment media that there had been exploration surveys Pre–Corporation Rim. (Corporations didn't actually invent space and planets, despite the patents the company had tried to file.)

Eletra shifted, winced, then took a breath. "The locations to a lot of systems were lost before wormhole stabilizing tech was developed, but researchers find them sometimes in reconstructed data troves. If a corporation can find the planet's location, they can file for ownership, then they're free to establish a colony."

"There was a lot of this type of speculation forty or fifty years ago," Ras continued. "Of course, a lot of corporations overextended and went bankrupt over it, too, and the colonies were lost."

"Lost?" From Amena's expression, she understood now, but she didn't like it. "You mean abandoned colonies, settlements where the first arrivals were just left to fend for themselves."

I understood now, too. This was in Preservation's historical dramas and documentaries. It had been settled by survivors of a colony which had been seeded and then began to fail as supplies were cut off. In Preservation's case, an independent ship had arrived in time and managed to take the colonists to a more viable planet.

(The story was popular in Preservation media. There's always a dramatic rendition of Captain Consuela Makeba's speech about not leaving a single living thing behind to die. Mensah has a clip from one of the most popular ones on a display surface on the wall of her station office.)

(If there'd been a SecUnit in the colony, there probably would have been a compelling reason why it had to stay behind on the dying planet.)

(I don't actually believe that.)

(Sometimes I believe that.)

"Reclaiming the lost colonies is big business now," Ras said. He finished his water and set the container aside. "The terraforming equipment is usually still in place, as well as habitats and other salvage."

Amena's expression was flat and stony. She pretended to need to fiddle with her wound pack, so she didn't have to look at them. "So did you find a lost colony?"

"We were attacked on the way there," Eletra said, as Ras was drawing breath to answer.

I found a larger cabin that looked like it had been deliberately trashed. Clothing lay trampled on the floor, some of it in the blue of ART's crew uniform. Hygiene items had been opened and dumped or smeared around on the small attached restroom. A couple of actual static art pieces and a holographic print of humans playing musical instruments had been thrown on the floor and broken. Someone had tried to break a display surface, but hadn't managed it, and it floated sideways, still showing a static image of two male humans, not young, maybe Mensah's age or older, but that was as much as I could guess. (I was no good at judging human ages.)

One had dark skin and no hair on the front half of his head, and the other was lighter, with short white hair. They were both smiling at the camera, with an embossed version of ART's logo on the wall behind them. I could look them up in my archive of ART's crew complement, but I didn't want to.

I felt something build in my chest. I pulled the recording of my conversations with ART, the way it said "my crew." It was bad enough that ART must be dead, it wasn't fair that the humans it had loved so much were dead, too.

I wanted to find a bunch more algae-smelling gray snotty ass-holes and kill the shit out of every single one.

A sudden 5 percent dip in performance reliability made my knees go shaky and I leaned on the cabin hatch. For twelve seconds it seemed like a good idea to slide all the way down to the deck and just stay there.

But I should get back to Amena.

Also, after the Targets had rampaged through here, the deck was pretty disgusting.

In the medical suite, the conversation had moved back to me. (Oh goody.) Eletra was saying, "You really have to be careful. That SecUnit seems to have been altered to make it look less like a bot, but that doesn't change their programming."

"Hmm," Amena said, not looking at her, still picking at the wound pack on her leg.

Ras put in, "I know you think it's trying to protect you—"

"It's not trying." Amena's tone was clipped. "It's protecting me."

"But they're not reliable," Ras persisted. "It's because of the human neural tissue."

Well, he wasn't wrong.

Ras added, "They go rogue and attack their contract holders and support staff."

Amena bit her lip and squinched up her eyes in a way that said she was suppressing an emotion, but I couldn't tell what. "I wonder why that is," she said in a flat voice.

On the way to medical, I walked through the galley and the classroom compartments, and swung by a supply locker and grabbed a pre-packed emergency ration bag. They had an awful lot of supplies in here for planetary exploration, not what you'd expect on a ship whose jobs were mapping and teaching and cargo.

As I turned down the corridor, I tapped Amena's feed to tell her I was coming back and started reviewing my archive, comparing the time I had been aboard ART before with what I saw now. Did I actually know what ART and its crew did? I had never bothered to ask; Deep Space Research sounded boring. Almost as boring as guarding mining equipment.

In the medbay, Eletra was saying, "You're very lucky it didn't turn on you while you were being held on this ship. You must have been locked up here with it for days and days."

Wait, what? Great, were the humans having problems perceiving reality? Even more than the usual problems humans have perceiving reality? That was all I needed. Amena was just going to have to deal with it, because I was busy.

Amena was baffled. "No, no, we just got here. Just a little while ago. Right before the gray people dragged me into that room."

Ras rubbed his face, either concealing his expression or just genuinely unwell. Eletra looked pitying. "I think you're confused."

Amena's expression scrunched up again, but she shook her head. "Look, SecUnit's coming back, so you need to stop saying all this stuff about it. I know you believe it, but you're wrong, and I don't want to hear it. And I think maybe we're both confused because—"

Maybe staring at space and teaching young humans to stare at space wasn't all ART's crew did. Maybe ART had let me think that.

Right, so I had drone input from the medical bay but I wasn't paying attention to it. I was searching for images of stored supplies to compare and look for anomalies, missing items, other clues. So I only had a 1.4-second warning when I stepped through the hatch and Ras fired a weapon at me.

For a human, his aim was great.

6

Fortunately it was an energy weapon and not a SecUnit-head-busting projectile.

It still fucking hurt. I flinched and rammed into the side of the hatch (ow) and dove sideways to avoid the second blast. Except there wasn't one, because Ras was flailing instead of aiming. Amena had jumped on his back and was trying to choke him out. (It was a good effort but she didn't have the leverage to really clamp down with her forearm.)

Eletra stood nearby, waving her arms and yelling, "Stop! What are you doing? Stop!" which was frankly the most sensible thing I had heard a human say in hours. It also told me this wasn't a planned attack, which is what stopped me from putting a drone through Ras's face. (Also, I was running out of drones.)

If I sound calm, I was actually not calm. I thought I'd had control of the situation (sort of control, okay? don't laugh) and then it had unraveled rapidly.

I pushed off the hatch and walked over to pick up the weapon Ras had dropped. It was like or possibly identical to or possibly actually was the tube-like energy weapon Target Two had used on me. Ras must have picked it up while I was distracted by having an emotional breakdown. (Yeah, that was a huge mistake.) It had caused pain in my organic tissue but it hadn't disrupted any processes so I knew it would be no use on the targetDrones. But at least it should work on the Targets. I put it in my jacket pocket.

Then I stepped in, kicked Ras in the back of the kneecap, and caught Amena around the waist. He hit the floor and I set her on her feet.

Amena was almost as angry as I was. "What's wrong with you?" she shouted at Ras. She glared at Eletra, who made a helpless, baffled gesture. You know, if Ras was going to turn on me, he might have at least warned Eletra first so she wasn't standing around wondering what the hell was going on.

Ras shoved to his feet and said, "You can't trust—any of them! It could be any of them—They control them—" He staggered back away from us. His eyes were unfocussed. "You don't—any of them—"

Amena's furious expression turned confused. "Any of what?"

That was a good question. I'd seen humans do irrational things (a lot of irrational things) and encounter situations that made them act in ways that were counterproductive at best. (This was not the first time I'd been shot in the head by a human I was trying to protect, let's put it that way.) But this was odd, even granting the fact that I'd physically intimidated Ras earlier.

Eletra winced and pressed a hand to her head. "Ras, that doesn't make sense, what—" Then her eyes rolled up and she collapsed.

Amena made a grab for her, then flinched away when Ras folded up and hit the floor. Then Eletra started to convulse. Amena threw herself down on the deck, trying to support Eletra's head. Ras lay in a tumble, completely limp.

Amena looked frantic. I was a little frantic, too. "They took some medication from the emergency kit," she said. She jerked her head toward the open kit and the container beside it. "They're supposed to be analgesics—could they be poisoned?"

It wasn't a bad suggestion, but if this was something in the medication, I thought the reaction would involve bodily fluids and be way more disgusting. Amena wasn't affected, so it wasn't something spread by contact or transmitted through the air system or the water containers. Eletra looked more like her nervous system was being jolted by a power source. Ras looked . . . Ras looked dead.

I stepped over to the emergency kit still sitting on the bench. It had some limited autonomous functions and had expanded and opened new compartments, responding to the humans' distress. I took the small medical scanner it was trying to hand me and pointed it at Ras. It sent its report to my feed, with scan images of the inside of Ras's body. A power source had jolted through the upper part of his chest, destroying the important parts there for pumping blood and breathing.

It looked, oddly, like what being punished by a governor module felt like—

Now there's a thought.

I checked Scout Two in the control area foyer. The Targets had stopped listening at the sealed hatch and were gathered around Target Four, who now held a strange, bulky device. It was twelve centimeters across and a millimeter thick, with a flat old-fashioned solid-state screen. (I'd seen them on historical dramas.) All the Targets seemed excited about whatever it was showing them.

If it was something that made the Targets happy, it couldn't be good.

My scan detected a tiny power source on both Eletra and Ras. It hadn't been there earlier so something had activated it, most likely a signal from Target Four's screen device. There was no time for finesse; I jammed the whole range.

Eletra slumped, limp and unconscious. If there'd been a last-ditch destroy-the-brain function, there was nothing I could do about it.

Scout Two now showed Target Four poking angrily at the screen as the others watched in obvious disappointment. Hah.

Amena, in the middle of yelling, "Will you stop just standing there and do something—" halted abruptly. The rest came out as a startled huff. She added, "Did you do that?"

"Yes." I crouched down and lifted Eletra out of Amena's lap. "This was caused by implants."

I carried Eletra over to the nearest gurney and carefully set her down. Amena scrambled up and went to Ras. She reached for his arm and I said, "He's dead."

She jerked her hand back, then fumbled for the pulse in his neck. "What—How?"

I sent the medscanner's images to her feed and she winced. "You said it was an implant? Is that like an augment?"

"No, it's like an implant." Augments were supposed to help humans do things they couldn't otherwise do, like interface with the feed more completely or store memory archives. Augments that weren't feed interfaces were meant to correct physical injuries or illnesses. Augments are helpful; implants are like governor modules.

I pointed the medscanner at Eletra. It found a raised temperature, increased heart rate, and increased respiration rate. I didn't know what that meant, but it sounded bad. "When this happened, I had a drone view of the Targets in the central section using an unknown device."

Amena pushed to her feet and stood beside Eletra's gurney. She was accessing the medical scan data and her expression had that vague look that humans get when they're reading in their feed. "That looks like an infection. Eletra said her back hurt." Her face scrunching up with worry and fear, Amena carefully moved the dark hair away from Eletra's neck, then half-turned her. She had to pull down the back of Eletra's shirt to find it. Yeah, there was the implant.

Amena sucked in a breath. "That looks terrible."

It was a metal ring, 1.1 centimeters wide, visible against the brown skin between Eletra's shoulder blades. It sat in the middle of a rictus of swollen flesh that looked painful even to me, and that was saying something.

Normal external interfaces for humans were designed to look like all kinds of things, from carved natural wood to skin tones to jewels or stones or enamel art pieces to actual plain metal with a brand logo. And why would Eletra, who was an augmented human with an internal interface, need a second external one? And any remote chance that this was some kind of botched attempt at a medical or enhancement augment was outweighed by the fact that no human would put up with this when any MedSystem could fix it in a few minutes at most. And *botched* was putting it mildly; it looked like a bad human medic had jammed it in with their toes.

Amena was working the problem. "Why didn't they tell us? We could have . . . Unless they didn't know it was there. They said they were unconscious when they were brought aboard." The consternation in her expression deepened. "Did Ras's implant tell him to attack you? Or just make him so confused that he shot at the first person who walked in the door? These implants are obviously supposed to incapacitate them if they tried to escape, to keep them under control—"

"I'm familiar with the concept," I told her. (One of the indispensable benefits of being a rogue SecUnit: not having to pretend to attentively listen to a human's unnecessary explanations.) "I had one in my head."

"Right." She flicked a startled look at me. I love it when humans forget that SecUnits are not just guarding and killing things voluntarily, because we think it's fun. "Then why did it take the gray people so long to activate the implants? Why didn't they do it right after we escaped?"

Yeah, about that. I hadn't kept her updated on my intel. "I don't think the surviving Targets knew what happened when we were captured."

Amena argued, "But that one Target got away."

"I used my drones to kill that Target and a third one, after they locked themselves in the ship's control area. The other Targets have been trying to get through the sealed hatch and seem to think we're inside." I sent Amena a section of my drone video from the control area foyer. "They may think Eletra and Ras are in there with us. Or they activated the implants to try to figure out where they are."

Amena's gaze went vague as she reviewed the clip on her feed. "Is that why they're listening to the hatch?"

I checked the input. Yeah, they were back to that again. "My drone is playing a recording of a conversation."

Amena lifted her brows. "Right, that's really clever. Can you use the drones to threaten them and—"

I showed her the clip of the change to the Targets' helmets. "No. This security update prevents that."

Amena grimaced and rubbed her brow. "I see. So how do we get to the bridge?"

You know, it's not like I'm half-assing this, I am actually trying my best despite the fuck-ups. I absolutely did not sound testy as I said, "I don't know. I have a scout drone in the control area but it can't access any of the systems."

Amena stopped and looked at me with an incredulous expression. "So we're locked out of the bridge and the bot pilot is gone and we don't know what's flying the ship."

The good thing about being a construct is that you can't reproduce and create children to argue with you. This time I did sound testy. "I'm working on it." I turned the medical scanner's image so I could see what was under Eletra's implant. I really expected the shitty primitive governor module to have filaments extending directly into the human's nervous system, like a normal augment. But there were no filaments; the images the scanner sent to our feed connection showed the implant was self-contained, narrowing to a blunt point.

Amena held up her hands. "Fine! Wow, you're so touchy." She added, "Okay, so if they knew these things were implanted, they would have asked us to help them. Even if they didn't trust us . . ." Her brow furrowed again. "I can't imagine they wouldn't have."

I agreed. They hadn't even asked about the MedSystem, or the medical equipment in the emergency kit. If I was a human and I

had this thing jammed in me and I happened to run into a fully
stocked medical suite to hide, it would have been at the top of
my to-do list.

"We have to get this thing out before it kills her, too." Amena
studied the diagrams and images the scanner sent into our feed.
"It's really primitive. It must have been causing the confusion
and pain, but that wouldn't make them forget it was there."

I rotated the images so I could make sure I was right about the
depth. "No. Something else did that."

"It's not very good, for what it's trying to do." Amena made
a violent jabbing motion at her own neck. "If you knew it was
there, and you could get away from the person trying to zap you,
you could pop it out with a knife."

Note to self: Make sure Amena has no reason to jab at her
own neck with a knife. "Not if you thought it was interwoven
with your neural tissue." At least when I dealt with my governor
module, I'd had access to my own schematics and diagnostics.

Amena wasn't listening. She went over to rummage in the
emergency kit. "Her vital signs are getting worse." She found a
laser scalpel case and brandished it. "I'm going to try to take the
implant out."

"You have medic training." It was worth asking.

"Basic training, sure." I was making an expression again because she grimaced. "I know, I know! But you said we shouldn't
use the MedSystem and we have to do something."

She wasn't wrong. The kit was transmitting increasingly
plaintive warnings. There was a lot of technical medical data to
process but the conclusion was obvious that the activation had
caused damage to Eletra, if not as much as it had to Ras. The kit
was demanding we intervene soon.

Most of my medical knowledge came from watching *Med-
Center Argala,* a historical drama series that had been popular
twenty-seven corporate standard years ago and was still available
for download on almost every media feed I had ever encoun-

tered. Even I knew it was inaccurate. I also found it kind of boring, so I'd only watched it once.

I held my hand out for the scalpel.

Amena hesitated. Did she think I was going to kill Eletra? I'd put up with way more annoying humans, including some that she was related to.

Then she handed the scalpel over, her expression a mix of relief and guilt. "I could do it if I had to."

Huh. Amena wanted to help, maybe to prove herself. I said, "I know you could." She hadn't been bluffing about the neck-jabbing thing, I could tell.

But if we were wrong and removing the implant killed Eletra, at least this wouldn't be my first accidental murder. Also, my hands don't shake.

Amena got another wound seal pack out and engaged the emergency kit's sterile field. I followed its instructions to spray anesthetic prep fluid. Then with the occasional pop-up help hint from the kit's feed, I used the scalpel to cut through the damaged tissue.

I had a drone view of Amena watching the hand scanner, her brow furrowed in half-wince, half-concentration. I avoided the bits that would bleed a lot (not something a human trying to do this to their own body could have managed, so there, Amena) and the implant popped out.

And Eletra woke up.

She gasped a breath, her eyes open, staring without comprehension at Amena's stomach. I stepped back and Amena hastily fit the pack over the wound before too much blood leaked out. It powered up and snugged in close to Eletra's skin; her eyes fluttered closed again. From the report on the emergency kit's feed, the pack had delivered a hefty punch of painkillers and antibiotics. I put the implant in the little container the emergency kit offered, and the kit dutifully sprayed it with something. (I hope the kit knew what it was doing, because I sure didn't.)

"It's okay, it's okay, we're helping you," Amena was telling Eletra, patting her hand.

Ras's body was there in the middle of everything and that just felt wrong. I picked it up and carried it to a gurney on the far side of the room. In a supply cabinet I found a cover to put over him, but before I did I pulled down his jacket and shirt to look at his implant. It was on his shoulder blade, surrounded by damaged tissue, much thicker and more swollen than Eletra's. I wondered if he had known it was there, at some point. If he had jabbed at his back with something trying to get it out, before the Targets made him forget about it again. (It was still a stupid thing to do, but I understood the impulse. I understood it a lot.)

Then the emergency kit blared an alarm through our feed as Eletra's pulse and respiration rate dropped.

The kit flashed a handy annotated diagram of what we should do into the feed. Amena swore a lot and helped me roll Eletra over. I started chest compressions, being extremely careful with the amount of pressure I was exerting. Amena frantically grabbed for the resuscitation devices. The kit was trying to be helpful but it was nothing like a MedSystem sliding into my feed with everything I needed to know right there. It was urging me to start rescue breathing, but I couldn't. My lungs work in a completely different way than human lungs do. It's not only that I need much less air but the connections are all different. Aside from the utterly disgusting thought of putting my mouth which I talk with on a human (ugh), I didn't think I could expel enough air for what the kit wanted me to do.

Amena ran over and started the rescue breathing herself, but it wasn't working.

I told her, "We need the mask."

Amena gave up with a gasp of frustration and went back to the kit. She found the mask and wrestled with its sterile packaging, trying to rip the plastic with her teeth, and I couldn't stop compressions to help her. (Yes, I did just realize we should have thought of this possibility earlier. They never showed humans getting the tools ready on *MedCenter Argala,* it was all just there.)

Then from across the compartment, the MedSystem made a soft clunk and its platform lights turned violet. It had just powered on. Amena stopped, the mask in her hand finally. She spat out a piece of plastic wrapper and demanded, "Did you get it turned on?"

"No." That was ART's MedSystem, but without ART. Its reactivated feed said it was operating at factory standard.

It could be one more weird anomaly in this unending cycle of what the fuck. Or it could be a trick, TargetControlSystem trying to get us to put Eletra in there so it could kill her. Except that Eletra was dying anyway so why bother?

And I tried not to see this as some remnant of ART still in the ship acting to save a human.

Well, fuck it. I stopped compressions, scooped up Eletra, and carried her to the MedSystem's platform.

I set her down and the surgical suite dropped over her immediately, a pad settling over her chest to restart her heartbeat and a much more complicated mask apparatus lowering to work on her respiration. In six seconds it had her breathing on her own and her heartbeat stabilized. The platform contoured to roll her onto her side. Delicate feelers peeled away the wound pack and tossed it onto the deck, then started to knit the raw bleeding spot in her back.

On the gurney, the emergency kit beeped once in protest, then shut up.

Amena let out a long breath of relief, then wiped her face on her sleeve. She started to gather the scattered pieces of the kit's resuscitation gear. Trying to fit them back into their containers, she said, "So what turned the MedSystem on—"

I said, "I know as much as you do about what is happening on this ship." Which was why I put the unknown corporate human who was dying anyway in the possibly compromised MedSystem and not, say, Amena or myself.

I didn't like that Eletra had nearly died, despite the fact that we had followed all the instructions carefully. I didn't like that Ras had died before we could do anything. I especially didn't like that the Targets had killed him. He wasn't my human but he had popped off right in front of me and I hadn't been able to do anything about it.

They're so fucking fragile.

Amena glared, then eyed me speculatively. "Are you sure you're not hurt? You did get shot in the head, again. And didn't that gray person shoot you before you tore their lungs out?"

I hadn't felt any lungs while I was rummaging around in Target Two's chest cavity, but I'm sure they were in there somewhere. "It was just an energy weapon."

"It was just an energy weapon," Amena muttered to herself, in a very bad imitation of my voice, while determinedly trying to fit the mask attachment with the oxygen nodules into the wrong slot. "If you weren't so angry at me, you'd realize I was right."

For fuck's sake. "I am not angry at you."

Okay, that's a lie, I was angry at her, or really annoyed at her, and I had no idea why. It wasn't her fault she was here, we were here, she hadn't done anything but be human and she wasn't even whiny. And her first reaction to another human shooting me had been to jump on his back and try to choke him.

Amena gave up on the mask and gave me her full attention. "You look angry."

"That's just something my face does sometimes." This is why helmets with opaque face plates are a good idea.

Amena snorted in disbelief. "Yes, when you're angry." She hesitated, and I couldn't interpret her expression, except that it wasn't annoyed anymore. "I should have said more, when they were talking about you. It was just like my history and political consciousness class. I didn't think the instructors were making things up, but . . . it was just like the examples they used."

They had been talking about me as a SecUnit the way humans always talked about SecUnits, and it had been pretty mild, compared to a lot of things I had heard humans say. If I got angry every time that happened . . . I don't know, but it sounded exhausting. Talking about this was exhausting. "I'm not angry about that."

Amena demanded, "If you're not angry, then what's wrong?"

I was definitely glaring now. "How do you want the list sorted? By time stamp or degree of survivability?"

Amena said in exasperation, "I mean what's wrong with you!"

There's that question again, but I assumed she didn't want to discuss the existential quandary posed by my entire existence. "I got hit on the head by an unidentified drone and shot, you were there!"

"Not that! Why are you sad and upset?" That was the point where even I could tell that Amena was terrified as well as furious. "There's something you're not telling me and it's scaring me! I'm not a fucking hero like my second mom or a genius like everybody else in my family, I'm just ordinary, and you're all I've got!"

I wasn't expecting that. It was so far from what I thought she had meant, and she was so upset, that the truth inadvertently came out. "My friend is dead!"

Amena was startled. Staring blankly at me, she asked, "What friend? Somebody on the survey?"

I couldn't stop now. "No, this transport. This bot pilot. It was my friend, and it's dead. I think it's dead. I don't see how it would have let this happen if it wasn't dead." Wow, that did not sound rational.

Amena's expression did something complicated. She took a step toward me. I backed up a step. She stopped, held up her hands palm-out, and said in a softer voice, "Hey, I think you need to sit down."

Now she was talking to me like I was a hysterical human. Worse, I was acting like a hysterical human. "I don't have time to sit down." When I was owned by the company, I wasn't allowed to sit down. Now humans keep wanting me to sit down. "I have a lot of code to write so I can hack the targetControlSystem."

Amena started to reach out for me and then pulled her hand back when I stepped away again. "But I think you're emotionally compromised right now."

That was . . . that was so completely not true. Stupid humans. Sure, I'd had an emotional breakdown with the whole evisceration thing, but I was fine now, despite the drop in performance reliability. Absolutely fine. And I had to kill the rest of the Targets in the extremely painful ways I'd been visualizing. I needed to check Scout One's data to see if I could tell where we were going in the wormhole and how long it would take us to get there. And it occurred to me there might not be a destination, if whatever was controlling ART's functions knew I'd killed three Targets and had decided to revenge them by trapping us in the wormhole forever. I said, "I am not. You're emotionally compromised."

(I know, but at the time it seemed like a relevant comeback.)

Amena, like a rational person, ignored it. She said persuasively, "Won't it be easier to write code if you sit down?"

I still wanted to argue. But maybe I did want to sit down.

I sat down on the floor and cautiously tuned up my pain sensors. Oh yeah, that hurt.

Amena knelt down in front of me, angling her head so she could see my face. This did not help. She said, "I know you don't eat, but is there anything I can get you, like something from the kit or a blanket . . ."

I covered my face. "No."

Right, so say, just theoretically, I was emotionally compromised. A recharge cycle which I actually didn't need right now wasn't going to help with that. So what would help with that?

Taking over targetControlSystem and hurting it very, very badly, that's what would help with that.

My drone view showed Amena getting up and pacing slowly across the room, her shoulders drooping. Then on the platform, Eletra stirred and made bleary noises. Amena hurried over to her, saying, "Hey, it's all right. You're okay."

Eletra blinked and peered up at her. She managed to say, "What happened? Is Ras all right?"

Amena leaned against the platform, and from the high angle she looked older, with lines on either side of her mouth. Keeping her voice low, she said, "I'm sorry, he died. You had these strange implants in your back, that were hurting you, and his killed him. We had to take yours out and it almost killed you. Did you know they were there?"

Eletra looked baffled. "What? No, that's . . . I don't understand . . ."

I checked my penetration testing, but there were no results. That was annoying. If a system won't communicate with me, I can't get inside it. And apparently targetControlSystem was operating as a single system. Stations and installations use multiple systems that work with each other as a safety feature. (Safety is relative.) I usually went in through a security system function and used it to get to all the others. (Technically, I am a security system, so it was easy to get other security systems to interact with me, or to confuse them into thinking I was already part of them.)

There are still ways to get into heavily shielded systems, or systems with unreadable code, or unfamiliar architecture. I didn't have a lot of time, so I needed to use the most reliable method: get a dumb human user to access the system for me.

Ras's implant had ceased functioning, probably having destroyed its own power source to kill him. Eletra's implant was still in the emergency kit's little container, where it thought anomalous things removed from humans needed to be stored. It was now covered with a sterile goo but was still capable of receiving. I dropped my jamming signal.

Via Scout Two in the control area foyer, Target Four had set the screen device aside on a bench. All the Targets were talking, ignoring the control area hatch. They looked agitated and angry. They might have figured out that we weren't locked in the control area, finally. I was glad I hadn't had the chance to kill all of them, since there was a possibility now that they might actually come in handy.

(I had no idea where the targetDrones were, but logic and threat assessment said they should be congregated up against the hatchways sealing off my safe zone. That was going to be a problem.)

I checked on Scout One's progress, searching through the images of the floating display surfaces it had captured. Lots of shifting diagrams and numbers that might as well have been abstract art as far as I was concerned. These screens were meant to be interpreted through ART's feed, and without it to explain and annotate the data, it was all a mess. Couldn't anything be simple, just for once? I can fly low atmosphere craft but nobody ever thought it was remotely rational to give murderbots the modules on piloting transports. Wait, okay, there was a display with a schematic of ART's hull, with a lot of moving wavy patterns around it that probably would make sense if I knew anything about what happens in wormholes. There was a time counter on it, but nothing indicated what it was timing. So, not helpful.

What would have been helpful was an episode of *Rise and Fall of Sanctuary Moon*. Or *World Hoppers*. Or anything. (Anything except *MedCenter Argala*.) But media would calm me down, and I wanted to stay angry.

I couldn't sit here and wait, there had to be something else I could do. I stood up.

"Oh, you're up." Amena was sitting on the edge of the platform next to a half-conscious Eletra so she could hold her hand. She eyed me dubiously. "Already. I thought you were going to rest."

"Do these make any sense to you?" I sent her the display images from ART's bridge.

Amena blinked rapidly. "They're navigation and power information, like from a pilot's station." She took in my expression and waved a hand in exasperation. "Well, if you knew that, why didn't you say so?"

Fine, that one was on me. "They're from my drone sealed in the control area. Do you know how to read them?"

Amena squinted at nothing again, but slowly shook her head and groaned under her breath. She glanced down at Eletra, who was unconscious again, and carefully untangled their hands. "From what she said, I doubt she was on the bridge crew." Then she lifted her brows. "Do you know if there's an aux station in engineering?"

I didn't know that. "An aux station?"

"It's like an extra monitoring station for the engineering crew. You can't take control of the bridge unless the command pilot transfers the helm—at least you couldn't in the ones I've seen—but you can get displays for the rest of the ship's systems. We have them on some of our ships but I don't know how common they are." She admitted, "We might have them because our ships are an older design."

It wasn't the kind of thing that would be needed on a bot-piloted transport, but it couldn't hurt to check.

My performance reliability had leveled out at 89 percent. Not great, but I could work with it. I still hadn't identified the source of the drop. I'd taken multiple projectile hits without having that kind of steady drop. I took Ras's energy weapon out of my jacket pocket and set it on the bench. "Keep this just in case. It's not going to work on the targetDrones but it should work on the Targets." I hate giving weapons to humans but I couldn't leave her without something. "I'll go to engineering."

"Hold it, wait." Amena hopped off the platform. "I want to go with you."

I had a confusing series of reactions to this. Not in order: (1) Exasperation, at her, at myself. (2) Habitual suspicion. On my contracts for the company, the clingy clients were the ones most likely to (a) get me shot (b) advocate loudly for abandoning the damaged SecUnit because it would take too long to load me in the transport. (And humans wonder why I have trust issues.) (3) Overwhelming urge to kill anything that even thought about threatening her. "Someone has to stay here with the injured human."

She grimaced. "Right, sorry." Then she looked away and rubbed her eyes.

And I'd made her cry. Good job, Murderbot.

I knew I'd been an asshole and I owed Amena an apology. I'd attribute it to the performance reliability drop, and the emotional breakdown which I am provisionally conceding as ongoing rather than an isolated event that I am totally over now, and being involuntarily shutdown and restarted, but I can also be kind of an asshole. ("Kind of" = in the 70 percent–80 percent range.) I didn't know what to say but I didn't have time to do a search for relevant apology examples. (And it's not like I ever find any relevant examples that I actually want to use.) I said, "I'm sorry for . . . being an asshole."

That made Amena make a noise like she was trying to express her sinuses and then she covered her face. "No. I mean, it's all right. I haven't exactly been nice to you, so we're probably even."

I'm going now, right now. Right now.

I was at the hatch when she said, "Just don't stop talking to me on the feed."

I said, "I won't."

= =

HelpMe.file Excerpt 2

(Section from interview Bharadwaj-09257394.)

"I noticed a thing about your transcript."

"Was the font wrong?"

"No, the font was lovely. But whenever the company is mentioned you edit out the company and change it to the company." *Checks session recording.* "In fact, you've just done it now."

"That's not a question."

"You don't have to tell me anything you don't want to." *pause*

"Is it the logos? You've mentioned them before. I did think at the time, that you wouldn't have known they were impossible to remove if you hadn't already tried."

"That's one of the reasons."

"We've talked a little about trauma recovery treatments. I wonder if you've ever thought about taking one yourself."

:session redacted:

7

I gave Amena a view of what I was doing via my main video input, so she would know I was still there and I didn't have to think what to say to her.

(Also, if there was an engineering aux station and it showed we were trapped forever, then she could see it for herself and I wouldn't have to tell her.)

As I went down the corridor, Amena said, *Why is the vid so jumpy? Is it from a drone?*

It's from my eyes.

Oh. I'd left the task group of eight drones with her, and I could see her via their cameras. She sat on the platform next to Eletra, elbow propped on her knee. *This is creepy,* she said. I was passing a lounge attached to the galley, with blue padded couches along the walls. Three cups with ART's university logo sat on a low table, and a gray jacket, one of the kinds humans wore for exercise, was draped over the back of a chair. *The way everything looks so normal. Like somebody could walk in any second.*

She wasn't wrong. Except for those few cabins in the living quarters, I hadn't seen any areas that were trashed, or where it looked like a struggle had occurred. *Is there anything about this situation that isn't creepy?*

Hah, she replied. *If I think of something I'll mention it.*

I reached the sealed hatch that accessed the passage to the engineering module, then had to work on the panel to bypass the damage I'd done to delay anyone opening it from the other side. Breaking the safe zone I'd established might not be a great idea, but my sentry drones on the other two sealed hatches had registered no activity, so as a calculated risk it wasn't nearly as dumb as some other things I could think of. And the Targets in the control area foyer still hadn't picked up the screen device, and I couldn't sit around and wait for them to get off their asses.

Right, I could, but I wasn't going to.

Amena said, *Everybody in the survey team must be really worried about us. I'm glad . . . I mean, I'm not glad you got caught, too, but if I was here alone . . . It would have been really bad. My uncle Thiago is probably relieved that at least you're with me.*

The hatch opened onto an empty corridor, no targetDrones. I sealed it again and left a sentry drone on this side to alert me if anything tampered with it. Then I sent the rest of my cloud ahead down the corridor. I knew Amena was trying to compliment me. But it was strange that her view of Thiago's opinion of me was so different from the objective reality. *Your uncle Thiago doesn't trust me.* Not that I was upset about that or cared about it at all.

She made a snorting noise that came through the feed and my drone audio. *Sure he does. You saved him from those people who attacked the facility.*

That was beside the point. I'd saved a lot of humans and the number who had trusted and/or noticed me as anything other than an appliance attached to HubSystem afterward was statistically insignificant. *He didn't like the way I did it.*

She sighed and rubbed at a dark stain on her shoe. *He's still getting over what happened with second mom getting abducted after her survey. Things like that don't happen on Preservation. It was a big shock. And . . . maybe he's a little jealous. She can talk to you about what happened to her, but she can't talk to us.*

Mensah had said that, too. I didn't understand why they wanted her to talk about it. Couldn't they just read the report? *That's not what we talk about. Most of the time.*

Amena hesitated. *They wouldn't really have killed her. They couldn't get away with that.*

That sounds incredibly naive, but Amena and Thiago and the rest of Mensah's family and 99 plus percent of Preservation's population still didn't know about the other assassination attempt. *If GrayCris had managed to cut a deal with the company, they would have. They would have taken the ransom from Preservation and killed her, Pin-Lee, Ratthi, and Gurathin, and no one would have been able to do anything about it.*

My scout drones encountered a closed safety hatch into the main engineering module section. This was a good sign: if the targetDrones had been circulating through here, it would have been open. I reached it and hit the manual release. As soon as the hatch started to slide upward I sent my drone cloud under the gap, directing it to spread out into the corridor ahead. No lost contacts, and their cameras and scans detected no movement. So far so good, though I was picking up a vibration just on the edge of my perceptible range. Maybe it was normal? I hadn't spent any time here when I'd traveled with ART before.

My drone cloud didn't encounter any targetDrones as it followed the circular corridor around to the engine control access, which was a relief. The last thing I needed was to be whacked into an involuntary restart again. Figuring out a countermeasure for the stealth material on the targetDrones and on the Targets' helmets was on the long list of stuff I needed to do so we could survive. But none of the things on the list would matter much if the targetControlSystem had sent us into the wormhole with no destination.

I'd seen shows about humans and augmented humans trapped in wormholes indefinitely. They ranged from bleakly depressing (due to an excess of realism) to highly unlikely (due to an excess of optimism). At least the humans in the shows knew they were on a potentially endless trip, and not just a long one.

I hadn't seen any sign of damage or disturbance up to this point, but then I came around the curve into a foyer where quiescent display surfaces floated along the walls above specialized control interfaces. The weird thing was that the stations were active, though in standby mode, and not shut down. Even I knew you didn't mess with the engines while they were actually making the transport go. These stations would be for fine-tuning or altering or something, which should only be done while the transport was in dock.

Also, one station chair was twisted around to face the entrance, and near it one of ART's repair drones lay smashed on the deck. My drones are tiny intel drones, but most of ART's were larger, with multiple arms and physical interfaces so they could perform maintenance and other specialized tasks. This drone had six of its spidery arms deployed when something had knocked it out of the air, and it was splayed and flattened to the deck like something had stepped on it.

I wanted to pick it up and have an emotion over it like a stupid human. But I smelled growth medium again.

Amena said, *This is such a different set-up from the ships I've seen. Can you look for a display somewhere with—*

Oh, I had a bad feeling about this. I followed the smell. It led me through the next hatch and down a short gravity well where blinking caution markers floated in the air. (The gist was that various component manufactories and shipwrights and the University of Mihira and New Tideland did not want you to come down here without a Class Master Engineering License or Local Jurisdictional Equivalent and if you felt you just had to then really don't fucking touch anything.) Amena had stopped talking, and her assigned drone camera showed her squinting in concentration as she watched the scene through my eyes.

At the bottom of the gravity well, there was a platform where I could look down through the transparent shielding bubble over the engines.

Confession: I didn't know what the engines were supposed to look like, exactly. I'd never had to guard a transport's engines and they were usually too boring to show on the entertainment media. But I knew whatever was down there wasn't supposed to have a large organic mass on top of it that smelled of algae and growth medium.

Amena said softly, *What . . . What the . . . What is that?*

Believe me, it was the question occupying 92 percent of my attention right now.

Organic neural tissue can be melded with inorganic systems (Example A: the squishy bits inside my skull) so there was an outside chance (it was so outside I couldn't estimate a percentage) that this organic mass was a normal part of ART's systems, maybe something unique and proprietary.

But then why did it smell like the Targets?

I got an alert from Scout Two in the control area foyer. I checked its input and saw Target Five stride over and pick up the screen device where it lay on a chair. (Why the hell does everything have to happen at once? But at least the freaky thing on ART's engines wasn't trying to crawl up here and kill us yet.) As Target Five tapped his fingers on the solid-state screen, I widened my input range to pick up any active channel. In 2.3 seconds, I caught a data transmission.

More importantly, .2 seconds later, I caught targetControlSystem's response.

Got you, you piece of shit.

But something about the view from Scout Two bothered me. It had been bothering me for a while, but I had been too agitated to pay attention.

A lot of my ability to do threat assessment (like pick potential hostiles out of crowds or tell which stupid boat is full of raiders instead of curious locals) is based on pattern matching off a database of human behaviors. The Targets were anomalous, but they weren't so anomalous they didn't exhibit the same basic types of behaviors as other humans. And something was off about their behavior in the control area foyer, something that couldn't be accounted for by their overconfidence or the fact that they were all assholes.

Scout Two watched the Targets waiting impatiently, standing around the control area foyer as Target Five tapped at the screen. Standing. Even after they had apparently realized that the noise from the sealed control area was a decoy, after their security update made them much less vulnerable to drone attacks, they had stood around and waited. (SecUnits weren't allowed to sit down, ever, but humans and augmented humans did it every chance they had.)

They hadn't tried to search for us, they had stayed in the foyer, sending their targetDrones into the surrounding corridors but no further. We were hostiles trapped in an enclosed space with them, moving through it at will as far as they knew. Why weren't they trying to protect themselves by making their own safe zone? Why hadn't they at least found a compartment to lock themselves in? Were they relying completely on the targetDrones? Or were they waiting for outside help, because they knew they hadn't long to wait?

They hadn't even bothered to sit down.

It's not like I didn't already think this situation was really fucking bad, but I was beginning to think it was way fucking worse. Wormhole travel takes multiple cycles. The trip from our survey site back to Preservation had taken four Preservation Standard cycles (which were defined as twenty-eight Preservation Standard hours each) and it was considered a short trip, just to the edge of Preservation territory. There was no way we could be at our destination yet. Or any destination yet.

I tapped Scout One, locked up in ART's control area, and told it to look again at that display that showed ART's hull, the wave patterns, and the time countdown.

Scout One zipped back up to that console. The countdown was at two minutes fourteen seconds.

Oh yeah, this . . . is an issue. I forwarded the input to Amena.

Amena's drone squad watched her eyes narrow in disbelief. *That really looks like it's counting down to a wormhole exit but that can't be right.*

I was somewhat desperate for it not to be right. *Wake Eletra and ask her how long the ship was in the wormhole, how long it took them to get from the system where they were captured to Preservation territory.*

Amena scooted around to touch Eletra's shoulder. After long seconds Eletra stirred. Amena asked the question. Eletra blinked, more aware, and her expression turned puzzled. "We never left the system. We've been here the whole time."

"No, you came through a wormhole to Preservation where we were captured. Now we're going somewhere else. Remember the gray person said we were in the bridge-transit?" Amena tried to persist, but Eletra's eyelids were drooping and she didn't respond. Amena sent to me, *She's still really confused. Earlier they both thought we'd been captured before they were, and they didn't believe me when I tried to tell them we weren't.*

I told her, *This thing on the engine housing is an alien remnant. I think it's taking us through the wormhole at a much faster rate.* Much faster. Not hours instead of cycles, but minutes instead of cycles. ART's engines had been compromised by a device that was using the wormhole in a completely different way, allowing travel faster than any transport technology that I'd seen in media, or heard about on the newsfeeds. Faster than any human transport technology. *I think we're about to come out into normal space.*

Amena shook her head. *No, that's bonkos. The timer must be damaged. We've only been in the wormhole for a few hours, we can't be anywhere yet. The closest inhabited system outside Preservation territory is fifteen days from Station at least—*

And then the engines made a noise somewhere between a groan and a clunk. A new display sprung up in front of Scout One: a view of normal space. We had just come out of the wormhole.

Amena froze, staring at the feed view of the new display. Her eyes widened in alarm. Then she said, *What should we do?*

That was a really good question.

My first thought was to try to destroy the alien remnant. Fortunately instead of doing that I went on to the next thought. (I don't know anything about transport engines but I know you shouldn't shoot at them, okay? They're near the top of the long list of things it's just obviously not a good idea to shoot at.) I needed more intel before I could do anything about this. I didn't like the idea of saying "I don't know" to Amena because humans panic and I almost don't blame them because right now I feel like panicking and I was not in control of this situation and I could see at least ten instances now where I'd made wrong decisions and being in control of the situation was really important because otherwise it was in control of me and that felt like a short step to being back in the company's control. And maybe I just had to trust Amena, who had tackled a much larger human because she had thought she needed to save me. I told her, *I don't know.*

Amena sat up straight, biting her lip. Then she whispered to herself, "All right, all right. Let's think." On the feed, sounding much calmer than she looked, she said, *Can you make that drone in the control area move around? If we can see a display that will tell us where we are, or if there's a station or someplace we can try to send a distress signal . . .*

That . . . wasn't a bad idea. I exited the platform and went back up through the gravity well, telling Scout One to do a sweep of any active display surfaces. As its input filled with images, I pulled my archived video of its previous survey and ran a comparison. I was able to isolate five displays with significant changes. I enlarged them and set the images up in our feed so we could page through them. *This one,* Amena said immediately, *this is local navigation. There's info on the star . . . it doesn't say if we're close to the station . . . or if there's a station at all . . .*

I reached the monitoring area with its poor dead repair drone. I could see the display Amena was interpreting, but I'd found another diagram of ART on a new display. An indicator showed something attached to the outside of ART's hull, on its lab module. Looking at the specifications . . . For fuck's sake, it couldn't be.

I'd shut off our comm because I didn't want the Targets using it to track us, plus it wasn't like anybody could contact us while we were in the wormhole. I reactivated it and checked the channel our survey had used. It was active.

Yeah, this was happening. I pinged the channel and got an immediate response, and transferred it to our feed relay. Amena clapped a hand to her head in shock. "What—"

A familiar voice said, *SecUnit, Amena, can you hear me?*

It was Arada. Amena gasped, *Oh, we're here, we're here! Where are you?*

Arada said, *We're in the facility's safepod, attached to the hull of the raider ship. You're onboard, correct? We saw you pulled toward the airlock.*

Sometimes I wonder what the point of it all is. They were supposed to be safe on the baseship, arriving at Preservation Station by now. I said, *Who's we?*

SecUnit! Arada said, clearly happy to hear from me. *Oh, Overse is here, and Thiago and Ratthi. We weren't able to reach the baseship after jettison and were dragged into the wormhole with the attacker.*

Should we try to get to you? Amena asked. She hopped off Eletra's gurney and bounced on her toes. *We've got an injured person with us.*

Arada said hastily, *No, no, the pod's too damaged. We didn't expect—* Someone in the background, probably Overse, yelled something urgent, but it was muffled and I'd have to analyze the audio to understand it. Arada changed whatever she was about to say to, *What's your situation there?*

Oh, there was a lot Arada wasn't telling us. But I was estimating a 70 percent chance that if we hadn't exited the wormhole so absurdly early, Arada and the others wouldn't have survived much longer.

So now I had four more humans to worry about. Fantastic.

Amena was giving Arada a rapid but somewhat garbled report on all the fun we'd been having, and warning her about the Targets.

(The Targets couldn't be alien, could they? No, that wasn't possible. Aliens couldn't look that much like humans.)

(Could they?)

I sent Arada a schematic of the outside of ART's hull with the airlock in our safe zone highlighted. *Arada, can you get to this lock?*

There was a pause which told me that their situation was even worse than Arada was implying. I estimated the hesitation was just long enough for her to check the air reserves in the EVAC suits they were probably already wearing due to damage to the pod. Then Arada said firmly, *Yes, we can make that. ETA, say, three minutes.*

I'll meet you there, I told her, and started out of the engineering monitoring area. I should have at least two point five spare minutes, so I went ahead with the hack of targetControlSystem.

The thing that had protected it so far was the fact that it didn't interact with the feed or with interfaces the way every other system I'd ever encountered had. But Target Five had accessed targetControlSystem and been responded to, so that told me what channel to concentrate on and what kind of transmissions it would accept. And it also told me I was going to need to go old school to break this fucker.

I tossed together a code bundle that duplicated the signal sent by the Targets' screen device, copied it a hundred times, made it self-replicating so all my copies were copying themselves, then sent the whole thing to targetControlSystem.

ART would have laughed at an attack like that. (Actually, ART would have laughed at the part where it sent back a code bundle that would have eaten my face.) But I had a theory that the reason the Targets weren't trying to access most of ART's systems was that their targetControlSystem lacked the ability to effectively use ART's architecture.

Then I got an alert from a sentry drone. It was on the hatch into the quarters module, the first hatch I'd sealed to create our safe zone. It couldn't get a visual of any targetDrones, but an energy build-up near the hatch indicated a weapon or tool was being used on the controls. Uh-oh.

I started to run, following the curving corridor back out of the engineering module. I checked Scout Two in the control area foyer, just in time to see Targets Five and Six race out of its camera range.

When I said everything kept happening at once, it had mostly been an exaggeration, but now everything was actually happening at once. Something must have alerted them to the safepod on the hull.

I had an option, but it was a terrible idea. But it was also the only way to get Arada and the others inside in time. *Amena, our safe zone is about to be compromised and I need to deal with it. Can you get to the airlock to cycle Arada and the others in?* I was assuming targetControlSystem wasn't going to be cooperative about admitting visitors. Plus, it was a little busy right now.

Amena had been pacing Medical, anxiously listening in on the hurried conversation in the safepod as they prepared to abandon it. She stopped, muted her comm, and said, *Yes, can you give me a map?*

I sent her our safe zone map with the fastest route to the airlock highlighted. *You'll have your squad of drones ahead of you. I'll send an alert and another route if they encounter anything.*

Understood. She started for the door, then stopped to pick up the Targets' energy weapon and tuck it into her jacket pocket. Then she dodged sideways and grabbed a container out of the pile of supplies on the bench.

I meant to enlarge the image to see what she'd taken but I had intel coming in from the sentry drone that the safe zone hatch had just been breached. At the engineering module exit, I took a different route, through the hatchway into the cargo handling station and out to the corridor that ran down the outside of the central module toward the quarters hatch. If I couldn't get in front of them, I had to come up from behind.

There were three possible reasons the Targets might have acted now: (1) they had received intel from targetControlSystem that the safepod was on the outside of the hull and interpreted its presence as an attack, (2) now that we'd left the wormhole and were presumably at our destination they knew their reinforcements would be coming soon and felt it was now relatively safe to attack us, or (3) they were expecting a supervisor to arrive at any moment and wanted to look proactive. With my luck, it was a combination of all three.

My drones zipping ahead of me, I reached the far end of the central module and ducked through two connecting corridors. I lost three drone contacts as they reached the passage to the quarters hatch but I didn't slow down. I'd gone low in the last two encounters, and with combat drones, even weird unfamiliar ones, it was best to assume there was an active learning component. So I accelerated and as I rounded the corner I ran up the bulkhead.

Two targetDrones waited for me near the deck and I landed on one before it could change position. I smashed the second as it jolted toward my head. The hatch had been cut open, the locks drilled and partially melted. I ordered my drones to drop back; I hadn't had time to work on countermeasures for the Targets' protective suits and I knew I was going to regret that.

I lost one of Amena's drone contacts and sent her an alert. She was in a corridor near a junction she would have to cross to get to the airlock and there was no alternate route. I told her, *Go back to Medical.*

No time, Amena said, and stepped back to press herself against the bulkhead. *I think something's wrong with the safepod.*

I could have argued about that but there wasn't time and she was right. And I'd finally gotten a view of the container she'd taken from the emergency supplies, the one she was currently holding clutched to her chest. It was the fire suppresser Ras had pointed out.

I slammed through the connecting passage and out into the next corridor.

Targets Five and Six spun to face me, pointed their clunky square energy weapons at me. Four targetDrones hovered beside them.

Two turns beyond was the junction Amena needed to pass through, so I needed to a) keep them here or b) kill them.

Let's go with option b.

Amena's drones clustered protectively around her as she hit the release on the fire suppresser. The chemical blast shot out and Amena hit what she aimed at because suddenly my drones could see the approaching targetDrone. The burst of chemical wash had coated the targetDrone's casing and disrupted the camouflage. (File under save-for-later: this confirms the camouflage is a physical effect, something in the design visible on their casing, not an unknown type of transmitted interference.) The target-Drone wavered sideways, then lurched down the corridor, probably with its propulsion and sensors damaged. Amena ducked around the corner and sprinted toward the junction.

Staring at me, Target Five said something in that language with no translation. Target Six made a dismissive gesture and started to turn back toward the foyer I absolutely had to keep them away from. As Target Five lifted his weapon and the target-Drones shot forward, I moved.

My drones couldn't see the targetDrones due to the stealth material, but I could. I pulled an estimate of the coordinates from my scan and sent a drone toward each targetDrone with orders to make surface contact. One overshot and had to loop back but all four managed a landing. With the contact drones for a reference, the rest of my drones could approximate the targetDrones' positions. As the targetDrones reached me, I told my drones to attack at will.

While this was going on, and Target Five was lifting his weapon, I ducked and dove forward. The first blast went over my head, then a targetDrone banged into my shoulder and knocked me into the bulkhead.

Then a thing happened. The comm hidden in the pocket under my ribs, the comm ART had given me when I left it on Ravi-Hyral's transit ring, pinged my internal feed with a message. It was a compressed packet, a type meant to be sent in-system, not carried via transports through wormholes. Which meant it had originated with ART's internal comm array. It was tagged with the name "Eden."

My drones hulled two targetDrones but the third already had a fix on me. It tried to slam me in the head but it had to back up first to build up speed, which gave me a chance to grab it. I shoved it sideways in time to block a blast from Target Five's energy weapon. Heat blasted over the targetDrone, which was a factor I hadn't anticipated. This was different from the weapon dead Target Two had used on me; instead of just being a pain-causing annoyance, this blast was meant to destroy tissue and incapacitate permanently. Even with the targetDrone between us, my hands took damage. Three of my drones got caught in the blast and dropped to the deck.

Eden. Eden was the name I used on RaviHyral, when ART had helped me. This had to be a trick, except that targetControl-System was drowning in the code bundles I'd sent; it shouldn't have the ability to send me a packet now.

But something on board ART had sent it. I started an analysis of the transmission.

I kept hold of the targetDrone and used my feet to shove off the wall, swung my body around on the deck and hit Target Five's legs with my legs. He fell sideways into the bulkhead, then down to the deck. I couldn't get up yet but at least we were both down here now.

On the channel where I'd been following Amena's progress, I saw she had passed through the foyer and on into the corridor beyond, and found the airlock. She was breathing hard and sweating as she tapped the cycle command on the pad. "I hope this is right," she muttered to my drones hovering around her. Then the warning lights flashed, a sign that the outer lock had received the command and was preparing to open. "Yes!" Amena waved her arms and did a little dance.

My analysis of the packet finished and I checked the results: no killware or malware detected and the file type indicated it was a video clip. It also indicated that it was a delayed message, sent sometime earlier but trapped when ART's feed and comm had gone down. The fact that a message stuck in the comm's store and forward buffer had finally been delivered meant that as targetControlSystem failed, some of ART's more complex systems were beginning to restart.

It could still be a trick. It was exactly the kind of tricky shit SecUnits could do. And I knew so many ways someone could use an intense visual stimulus to temporarily trash my scan, visual sensors, neural tissue, etc., but. I had to play it. Maybe I was desperate for some sign ART was still here somewhere, but the fact that it was a video clip felt like a communication method only someone who knew me would choose. I played it.

Target Six ran up and aimed his energy weapon at me, but I let go of the targetDrone and pulled Target Five on top of me. With all the flailing and screaming going on (Target Five, not me) Target Six couldn't get a clear shot. I was firing both the energy weapons in my arms but the Targets' protective suits seemed to be deflecting the bolts, at least to some extent. (With all the screaming, it was hard to tell.) Another targetDrone swung in but my surviving drones slammed it sideways and it hit Target Six's helmet. There was a lot going on, but I really needed to get off the floor.

Amena and her drones scrambled back as the airlock cycled open and Arada, Overse, Ratthi, and Thiago stumbled out. Ratthi went down in a heap of singed EVAC suit; I couldn't tell if he'd been hurt or had just tripped on the lock's raised seal. Then Thiago staggered sideways and Overse caught his arm, and

I knew my first theory had been correct and that the safepod had taken extensive damage.

The compressed video clip in the packet was from the serial *World Hoppers,* from a story arc climax episode, when a secondary main character's mind had been taken over by a sentient brain-virus (I know) and the story was really much better than it sounds but it was the moment when the character said, *I am trapped in my own body.*

I really needed to get up to ART's bridge.

I really needed to keep Targets Five and Six and their drones away from my humans who were unhelpfully still wandering around in the airlock foyer exclaiming at each other.

And I had to do both at once.

I got my knees up, lifted, and threw Target Five at Target Six. They both fell backward and I rolled to my feet. A damaged targetDrone slammed through what was left of my drone cloud. It clipped my shoulder as I threw myself back toward the quarters module hatch. I needed to make sure both Targets followed me, so I yelled, "I'm going to blow up the transport and kill all of you, you pieces of shit!"

It was lame, but I was in a hurry.

As I ran, the Targets yelled in response, high-pitched, furious, and incomprehensible. A damaged drone managed a last set of images, verifying that both Targets charged after me. I headed up the corridor toward the control area.

That was the point where I realized I hadn't discontinued the channel I was using to send my visual input to Amena. She probably hadn't been able to pay attention to it since she had left Medical (humans, even augmented humans, can't process multiple inputs like I can) but it was still playing in her feed. Her drone escort showed her standing in the airlock foyer (still? what the hell?) with Arada while Overse and Thiago dragged Ratthi out of his damaged EVAC suit. Arada had her suit half off and looked frazzled and to put it mildly, concerned. On my feed, Amena shouted repeatedly, *Where are you going? What is happening?*

Under the circumstances, they were reasonable questions. *Get to Medical,* I told her. I didn't want to answer any reasonable questions. If I was wrong, I'd probably be dead, and that was bad enough. Being stupid and dead would just be that much worse.

But what— Amena began, and I backburnered the channel.

8

Running through ART's corridors, I didn't have a lot of time to plan. The way the MedSystem's platform had activated in response to Eletra's medical emergency told me the ship's operational code, or at least large fragments of it, was still intact. And targetControlSystem was going down under my barrage of contacts, allowing more of ART's systems to come back online. This was technically a good time to try to breach the control area, but I'd be doing it even if I had to fight through an entire task group of Targets and their stupid semi-invisible drones.

I took the corridor up through the central module and passed a targetDrone bobbing in midair and one bumping along the lower bulkhead. As targetControlSystem went down, it was flooding them with garbage code.

Back in the quarters module, Amena and the others were finally clumping down the corridor toward Medical. They encountered the targetDrone that Amena had disabled with fire suppressant, still floating aimlessly, and Overse bashed it with a cutting tool brought from the safepod.

Scout Two showed me the control area foyer, barely three meters ahead, was empty which meant I'd lost track of Target Four. I just had time to run back its video to see Target Four leave through the forward doorway. Then an energy/heat blast hit me from behind. It struck me in the lower back and I lost traction and fell forward and slid halfway across the deck toward the control area hatch.

My performance reliability dropped to 80 percent.

In the corridor outside Medical, Amena jerked to a halt and yelled, "No, no!"

"What?" Arada demanded.

"They got—They shot—" Amena waved wildly at the Medical hatch. "Stay here with them!" and bolted away. Her drone squad careened after her.

I've been hit by projectile and energy weapons a lot more times than I can remember (literally, because of the memory wipes) and it's not that it doesn't hurt. But I had tuned down my pain sensors earlier, so it was a surprise when I rolled over and saw the big smear of blood and fluid on the deck.

I could only last so long like this. I needed to move faster.

But at least this solved the problem of how I was going to get the hatch open. Target Four ran toward me because assholes love to see your face when they kill you. He stopped what he thought was far enough away and fired, but I rolled onto my side so the blast hit the deck next to me. I shoved with my feet, used my hip as a pivot, and spun myself around so I could grab his ankle. He shrieked and fell backward, and I climbed up him and snapped his neck.

Targets Five and Six were almost here and I only had three drones left in the corridor. As I shoved to my feet and took Four's energy weapon, I ordered my surviving drones to run interference for me and take hits if they could. Between the stealth material helmets and the protective suits, the drones didn't have much chance of kill strikes, but hopefully they'd provide a distraction.

Hefting the big square weapon was hard and I knew I'd lost a lot of muscle and underlying support structure in my back. With my free hand, I popped the panel beside the control area hatch and then fired a short burst at the mechanism inside. The blast of heat convinced the sensors that the ship was experiencing an emergency condition (the sensors weren't wrong about that) and it reactivated the manual controls. I hit the manual release and the hatch slid open.

I stepped through and hit the close and seal sequence. One of my drones managed a shoulder hit on Target Five but the other contacts disappeared.

As the hatch slid closed, I knew I didn't have long. I'd had no time to replace the outside hatch panel and while I had some strong evidence to suggest that what the Targets lacked in personality they also lacked in brains, they were sure to try shooting at the controls and sooner or later it would work.

I'd cut Amena's visual access to my feed, but her drones told me that Arada and Thiago ran after her through the corridors, headed here. (Yeah, I probably should have cut Amena's input before this. But I'd wanted her to know what my status was if I couldn't respond.) Scout Two was still in the foyer on sentry so I sent its video to Amena's feed, so she'd be able to see where the Targets were. I saw her slide to a stop and clutch her head, trying to focus on the new input. I was already stepping past the messily dead Targets One and Three and climbing the stairs to the upper control area and I didn't have time to help her.

Scout One was there, still monitoring displays. It greeted me with a ping as I set the energy weapon down in the nearest station chair. I needed an interface with the ship's data storage.

The bond company that used to own me made a lot of its gigantic piles of currency by datamining its customers. That's recording everything everyone says and then going through it for information that could be sold. Part of my job had been to help record and parse and protect that information until it could be transferred back to the company, and if I didn't do it in a timely manner indicating complete obedience I got punished by my governor module. (Which was like being shot by a high-grade energy weapon, only from the inside out.)

The raw audio and feed streams make for huge data files, and they had to be moved around a lot and often got saved to unused storage areas on other systems. (This is also a way to destroy data. If you don't completely hate your clients or you're feeling particularly disgusted at the company at any one particular moment or you've hacked your governor module and need to cover your tracks, you can move data into the buffer of the SecSystem right before it's due for an update. The files are overwritten and it looks like an accident.)

But my point is, ART was a big transport with a lot of interactive processes and systems working in concert, which meant there were a lot of storage spaces that would not be obvious to human intruders. Or to hostile operating systems like targetControlSystem that seemed unable to use most of the architecture. Storage spaces where you could save a compressed backup copy of a kernel. Possibly your own kernel, if you were an advanced sentient control system who was very smart and very sneaky.

I still couldn't make feed connections with any of the operating stations so I tapped the pad below the display surface that looked the most like an internal systems monitor. The display floated upward and opened into an array of small data sources. Taking in information visually rather than through the feed felt horribly slow. I pulled up the manual interface and then had to pull the non-corporate-standard coding language out of my archive and load it into my internal processor. I got my query constructed and then flicked through the floating interfaces to get it loaded.

After a subjective eternity that was actually 1.2 seconds long, the system started to display the data storage areas currently holding large and possibly anomalous files with structures that didn't match the protocol for the area where they were stored. I had been betting on the procedural storage for the med platform, but the first possibility my query turned up was in the galley, in a data storage area hidden in a layer under the usual space for food production formulas. But when I searched on it, it read as empty.

You know, I really don't have time for this. A loose chunk from my back was sliding down in the station chair and it was hard to hold myself upright. I was leaking a lot, and I hate leaking.

I checked my targetControlSystem channel, just for the satisfaction, and saw multiple failure indicators through my barrage of contacts. Yeah, don't let the hatch close on you on your way down, fucker.

Scout Two in the control area foyer sent me video of Targets Five and Six, banging away at the open panel beside the hatch.

In a corridor just out of sight of the foyer, Amena's drone group showed me her, Arada, and Thiago having a tense whispered conversation. Amena waved the fire suppressant container urgently and Arada had the captured energy weapon.

It was exasperating. *Amena, get out of there. You know these people are dangerous.*

She flinched and grimaced. *Where are you? I can't see what you're doing anymore! Are you all right?*

Sort of, not really. *I just have to do this one thing.*

I didn't feel so good and it was hard figuring out the language to expand the query's search. I ran it again, and again it turned up the food production data storage reserved space. Huh.

TargetControlSystem went down, my contacts pinging an empty void. I didn't discontinue my code attack, just in case it was a trick.

The query wasn't faulty, there was something in the food production data storage, no matter how firmly the reader said it was empty. The display station feeds were starting to come back online, so I could access their functions directly via my feed interface, which was a huge relief. I initiated a deep analysis scan of the reserved space in the food production storage, and immediately hit a request for a passcode. Well, shit.

In the corridor, Amena whispered to Arada, "I think it's dying."

Arada took the fire suppressant away from Amena and handed it to Thiago. She told him, "Be ready."

If this was really what I thought it was, the video clip was a clue. I replayed it into the request field and got no response. I ran a quick list of all the character, ship, and place names from *World Hoppers*. No response. And no time. Eden, the clip had been directed to Eden, a fake name I'd used for human clients, a name ART had never called me.

My name, my real name, is private, but the name ART called
me wasn't something humans could say or even access. It was my
local feed address, hardcoded into the interfaces laced through
my brain.

It was worth a shot, I guess. I submitted it to the request field.

It was accepted and the storage space opened to reveal a large
compressed file. Attached to it was a short instruction document
with a few lines of complex code I couldn't parse. But the instructions were clear. They said, "In case of emergency, run." I
pulled the code into the operating station's processing area and
ran it.

All the lights in the control area went dark, then blinked back
to life. Simultaneously all the display surfaces around me flickered, went to blank, then flashed reinitialization graphics.

And ART's feed filled the ship. In the pleasant neutral voice
that systems use to address humans, it whispered, *Reload in progress. Please stand by.*

Below, the hatch slid open. The Targets started to step inside
but Scout Two saw Thiago run into the foyer, bellowing and
spraying fire suppressant at them. Target Five turned toward
Thiago while Six shoved forward into the control area. Then
Arada stepped out from the hatchway and shot Target Five with
the energy weapon.

Which left Target Six still armed, with a clear shot at Thiago
through the open hatchway.

I grabbed Target Four's energy weapon and shoved out of the
chair, but my legs wouldn't work right. I collapsed, rolled toward
the edge of the platform, and shot Target Six. The blasts hit his
chest and face and he staggered back into the bulkhead, then fell
over Target Three's sprawled body.

Target Five staggered and swayed but he pointed his weapon
at Arada.

Then ART's voice, ART's real voice, filled the feed. It said,
Drop the weapon.

Arada dropped her energy weapon and Thiago dropped the

fire suppressant. Both held up empty hands. I told it, *Don't hurt my humans.*

Target Five shouted something incoherent, then dropped his weapon and lurched sideways, clutching his head. Oh wow, ART must have been able to access Target Five's helmet, via the code used by targetControlSystem.

Target Five fell over and convulsed once on the deck, then went limp. Thiago started to put his hands down and then reconsidered. He said, "We mean no harm. We're here because we were attacked by—by that person and others."

Arada added, "Who are you?"

ART said, *You are aboard the Perihelion, registered teaching and research vessel of the Pansystem University of Mihira and New Tideland.* Then it added, *I'm not going to hurt your humans, you little idiot.*

Arada lifted her brows, startled, and Thiago looked boggled. I said, *You're using the public feed, everyone can hear you.*

So are you, ART said. *And you're leaking on my deck.*

Amena ran through the hatch, shied away from the pile of dead Targets, then ran up the stairs. She dropped to her knees beside me and yelled, "Hey, we need help! We need to get to Medical!"

ART said, *I can hear you, adolescent human, there's no reason to shout. I've dispatched an emergency gurney.*

I've always thought that everything ART says sounds sarcastic. If you were a human, I'm guessing it also sounded more than vaguely menacing.

Arada stepped into the control area. Thiago was checking to see if Target Five was alive. (He wasn't.)

ART said, *The intruder is dead.*

"Uhh . . ." Thiago glanced up at the ceiling. "But who are you? Are you a crew member, or—"

Arada reached the top of the stairs and leaned over me, frowning worriedly. She had a cut above her left eyebrow, a first degree burn on her cheek, and her short hair was singed. She said,

"Don't worry, SecUnit, we'll get you to Medical." She squeezed Amena's shoulder.

I guess Amena had never seen a SecUnit hit with an energy weapon that caused them to lose 20 percent of the body mass on their back and expose their internal structure, because she seemed really upset.

I was losing all my inputs but there was one thing I had to say before the gurney got here. "ART," I said aloud, because ART could silence my feed if it wanted to. "You did this. You sent those assholes to kidnap my humans."

Of course not, ART said. *I sent them to kidnap you.*

Then my performance reliability bottomed out and—

Shutdown. Delayed restart.

□   □   □

So, that was another catastrophic failure. (Physically, that is. I was going to make a joke about catastrophic failures in other contexts for the second half of that sentence, but it just got too depressing.)

Waiting for my memory and archive to come back online, at least I knew I wasn't in a company cubicle. Even with no feed or visual input, I knew that because I was warm, which meant I was in a MedSystem for humans. Once I could access it again, I checked my buffer to see what had happened. Oh right, ART happened.

The last conversation I had picked up on feed/ambient audio was:

Amena, her voice a worried whisper, said, "Are you sure it's going to be all right?"

ART, whispering back to her on a closed feed channel and somehow managing not to sound sarcastic or menacing at all, said, *Completely. The damage to its organic tissue and support structure is easily repaired. Some systems were operating at suboptimal parameters due to repeated energy weapon strikes. The restart should correct that.*

I said, "Stop talking to my human."

ART said, *Make me.*

I don't know if I tried to make ART stop but that was when I lost all input again.

Now I was at 34 percent performance reliability and climbing steadily, lying on my side on ART's medical platform. My jacket and deflection vest were gone and the surgical suite had cut away my shirt to get to the burned parts. I was sticky from all the leaky fluid and blood and parts falling off (yes, it's just as disgusting as it sounds). But I didn't feel nearly as bad as I had the last time I'd been here, when ART had altered my configuration.

ART. ART, you manipulative fucker.

Whatever was going on, there was nothing I could do about it now, and that just made me more furious. So I watched five minutes of episode 174 of *Rise and Fall of Sanctuary Moon*. Did that work? No, no, it didn't.

Tentatively, I checked my inputs. (Tentatively, because I wanted to talk to a human right now about as much as I wanted to lose a couple of limbs and have a conversation about my feelings.) The drones I'd assigned to Amena had managed to survive. Following my last instruction to stay with her before they'd lost contact with me, they had adopted a tight circular formation a half-meter above her head. They had been collecting video the entire time I was out, and I ran it back to see what had happened.

I forwarded through the boring parts with Amena being upset because of the whole me-lying-in-a-pool-of-steaming-blood-and-fluid thing and Arada trying to tell her this actually wasn't unusual for me, then the gurney arriving. (It was a medical assistance device, designed to either bring casualties to the Med-System or to carry them off a damaged ship, so its power and functions were autonomous. It was sort of like a big maintenance drone, capable of a certain range of actions, built in the shape of a rack with expandable shelves and arms. How it had survived the purge of ART's other drones, I don't know. Unless the Targets just hadn't known what it was when it was folded up in its inert state.)

It zipped in from the foyer, angled itself up the stairs, scooped me onto itself and clamped me down. (I hate being carted around like equipment, even though technically I am actually equipment.) As it started back down, Amena tried to follow it and Arada grabbed her arm. Looking up the way humans did when they were trying to talk to something they couldn't see, Arada said, "Hello, your name is Art? Can you tell me if there's anyone else aboard this ship?"

ART said, *There is an additional unidentified human in Medical, but she appears to be an injured noncombatant. I assume the two other humans present there are part of your group. All the intruders are accounted for.*

Amena wiped her nose (humans are so disgusting) and said, "That's Eletra, she was a prisoner when we got here. Ras is there, too, but he's dead." She pulled away from Arada to follow the gurney down the stairs.

Arada, with an expression somewhere between thoughtful and alarmed, trailed after her. Arada said, "Thank you, that's a relief to hear. But can you tell us who you are?"

Amena followed the gurney into the foyer. "That's the ship. It's SecUnit's friend." She threw a glance upward. "That's you, right? You're the transport?"

Thiago knelt over dead Target Six, turning the helmeted head to see the face. He looked up, startled. "The transport?"

ART said, *Correct.*

"But bot pilots don't talk like this," Thiago said to Arada, keeping his voice low. "It can't be a bot."

Hah.

Arada didn't bother to comment on that. "Transport, what happened here?" she asked. "Why did you attack our survey facility?"

ART said, *I am still reinitializing after a forced shutdown and deletion. I have prioritized restoring the MedSystem to full function.*

Amena's drones caught an image of Arada and Thiago exchanging a brow-lifted look before she followed the gurney. Yeah, I think they had both noticed that ART had deliberately not answered the direct question. (Pro tip: when bots do that, it's not a good sign.)

I had to forward again through all the back and forth of getting me to Medical. Arada and Thiago stayed in the control area, and Overse went to join them, but Amena's drones didn't see a lot of that. She was sitting in Medical watching the surgical suite work on me and trying to tell Ratthi what had happened. It was confusing, with the humans talking on their comms, but I didn't care enough to filter the raw video and separate out the different conversations. The only part that was new was about the safepod.

It had been damaged when they separated from the facility. The decision to clamp onto what at the moment had been a hostile ship hadn't been a voluntary one; the safepod's guidance system had been damaged and had directed it toward the nearest functional transport before Overse could stop it. Then we were in the wormhole and it was too late to escape. By the time we had exited the wormhole, Overse and Arada had already had to cannibalize four of the EVAC suits aboard while they were trying to repair the failing life support, and they had estimated that they would last another seventeen hours, if that. All four of the humans needed treatment for toxic air inhalation, plus Ratthi had damaged a knee when a gravity fluctuation had slammed him into a bulkhead.

At one point, Amena and Thiago had this conversation over the comm:

"Are you sure you're all right?" This was the fourth time he had asked her that and I was beginning to understand why she was so annoyed with authority figures all the time. "Those people, they didn't hurt you?"

"Uncle, I'm fine." She said that in the normal human adolescent exasperated and borderline whiney tone. (That's actually statistically normal for human adults, too.) Then she hesitated and added, "When we got here, they hit SecUnit with one of those big drone things and knocked it out and I thought it was dead and I was alone with them. The corporates, Eletra and Ras were there, but they were so scared and I knew . . . I was in a lot of trouble. Then SecUnit was just suddenly in the room and—and I knew we were going to fight these people, and we were going to win." She leaned her hip against the med platform and folded her arms, tucking her hands up in her armpits like she was cold. "Are you sure SecUnit's going to be all right? The transport said it was, but . . . it looks bad."

"I'm sure," Thiago told her, sounding all warm and confident. Liar, you're not sure. The others, who had seen me in way worse shape than this, they were sure. "Do you still have those drones over your head? Why are they there?"

She glanced up, brow furrowed like she had forgotten them. "SecUnit gave me these when it had to go search the area and make sure there weren't hostiles in our safe zone."

Sitting on the bench with a wound pack wrapped around his knee, Ratthi smiled. "That's SecUnit. I'm glad it kept you safe."

Thiago sounded like it just made him more worried. He said, "What exactly were you doing?"

I checked all my video inputs. Scout One was still in the control area, watching Arada and Overse, who sat in ART's station chairs, flicking through its displays. Scout Two was still in the foyer with a view of Thiago, who had searched Target Six's suit and was trying to get the Targets' screen device to work. Everyone was listening.

Amena wiped her face impatiently. "We had just found the alien remnant tech on the engines, right before we came out of the wormhole into this system. We think that's what let us get here so fast. SecUnit realized there was something wrong about the story Eletra and Ras told us, like they had only been captured a couple of days ago, which wasn't nearly long enough for a trip to

Preservation from even the nearest wormhole. We were trying to figure out what to do about it when we got the signal from you."

"Alien remnant tech?" The look Ratthi threw at Eletra was suspicious. Her eyes were open now and tracking, though she still looked confused. He had tried to talk to her earlier, but while she had blinked and shifted position occasionally, she hadn't seemed aware of her surroundings. Ratthi was probably thinking about past evidence of corporations collecting illegal alien materials and how great that had turned out.

On the comm, Overse said, "Is it dangerous? Should we try to remove it from the drive?"

On the general feed and comm, audible to the whole ship, ART said, *The foreign device detached from my drive and ceased to function when the invading system was deleted. Further interference is not advisable.*

That was definitely not menacing. Oh no, not at all.

On a private feed channel to ART, I said, *You set me up, you fucker.* I was still catching up on archived drone video and fifty-four seconds behind actual time, so ART ignored me.

Right, hear me out. The message packet with the *World Hoppers* video clip had been sent through ART's internal comm before it went down, presumably not long after ART hid a backup copy of itself passcode-protected by my hard feed address. ART had been expecting me to be aboard at some point to run its emergency code, which would uncompress the backup and reload it into its hardware. Which meant it had sent the Targets to find me in Preservation space and given them the ability to track me via the comm I had stashed in my rib compartment.

Which meant ART had been conscious and capable of affecting events during the attack on our facility and baseship.

ART's sudden and obviously intentionally dramatic reentrance into the general feed and comm conversation had made the humans tense. It startled Eletra into awareness. "Who's that?" she asked, looking from Ratthi to Amena.

"It's the . . . the transport," Ratthi told her, watching the ceiling warily. "I don't suppose you could call it a bot pilot."

I don't suppose you could, ART said.

Listening from the control area, Arada's brows drew together. She asked Overse, "Could we get a display link to Medical?"

ART said, *It's better if I do it,* and a holo display of Arada and Overse in the control area blossomed in the center of Medical. Scout One showed me that a corresponding display of Medical had unfolded in the control area. There was an attached sidebar in both displays showing Thiago out in the foyer area, sitting in a chair with the Targets' screen device in his lap. He looked wary.

Okay, so: (1) I had never been able to access cameras aboard ART, except through its drones. It saw the interior of the ship through its internal sensors, which provided data (heat, density, angles of motion, etc.) that didn't translate into visual images, at least not visual images useful to humans. I thought it didn't have cameras in most areas. This was proof it had been holding out on me AGAIN. (2) The video effects were smoother and more polished than anything I could have done and that just made me more furious. This was a vid conference link for humans trying to figure out how screwed they were, not a professional newsfeed production. ART had dissolved the edges and corrected the color just to show off. Next it would be providing theme music and a mission logo.

My performance reliability hit 60 percent and I could talk again. I said, "Fuck you, ART."

Amena leaned over the platform, watching me worriedly. "SecUnit, how are you doing?"

"I'm fine." Parts of the surgical suite were withdrawing and I could see her with my eyes now instead of just the drones. "Except that I'm being held prisoner by a giant asshole of a research transport."

Ratthi hobbled over and stopped outside the sterile field. "Do you need anything?"

Amena said, "I saw what happened. I mean, I still had the

view through your eyes when—" She stopped and swallowed. "That was intense."

That was one word for it. I sat up as the rest of the suite pulled away. The skin on my back felt new and itchy. I hate that. "I need my jacket."

ART said, *It was damaged and is being repaired in the recycler.*

It was very hard to say evenly, "I am not speaking to you."

Ratthi lifted his brows. "So . . . how well do you two know each other?"

In the control area, Arada stood up. "Uh, Ratthi, let's take that up later. Transport, will you answer our questions now?"

ART said, *That depends on the questions.*

I said, "The humans think *I'm* an asshole, wait till they get to know you."

I thought you weren't speaking to me.

Ratthi muttered to Amena, "I admit I'm a little worried right now."

Amena told him, "SecUnit said bot pilots can kill people."

ART said, *SecUnit exaggerates.*

Arada's brow was furrowed. "Transport, where are we? We've accessed your sensors and we're not receiving any contacts indicating a station. Is this an uninhabited system?"

This system has a numerical designation assigned by a corporation which was investigating it for salvage. It was the site of at least two attempts at colonization. The latest attempt was abandoned when the company funding it was destroyed in a hostile takeover, and the colony's location was lost. ART paused for 8.3 seconds for no reason I could think of except to make the humans think it wasn't going to answer the question. *I have evidence indicating that it is inhabited.*

Arada has a lot of expressions, even for a human. The one she was wearing now involved squinting one eye and twisting her mouth around and biting one corner of her lip. I didn't know what it meant, except that she must be worried by what she was hearing. "It's inhabited by these people—the hostiles?"

Circumstances suggest it.

Yeah, that was sarcastic.

Arada stopped biting her lip but her eye got more squinty. "What is your operational status? You said the alien remnant detached from your engines? Can we leave now via the wormhole?"

I am currently still in reinitialization mode and my normal-space maneuvering functions are not responding, possibly due to damage caused when the foreign device was installed on the wormhole drive. When reinitialization completes, I can begin self-repair. But I have absolutely no intention of leaving this system until I get what I want.

Oh, here we go.

Ratthi made a faint "oof" noise. Thiago's jaw started to drop but he stopped it in time. Amena folded her lips in and glanced worriedly at me. Overse grimaced and rubbed her eyes. Arada looked like she wasn't exactly surprised. She did a quick silent-communication expression thing back and forth with Overse, then she said evenly, "I see. What do you want?"

I want my crew back.

Arada's brows lifted, like she was relieved it wasn't something worse. "What happened to them?"

The hostiles stole them, forced me to cooperate by threatening their welfare, infected my engines with interdicted alien remnant technology, installed adversarial software, and then deleted me.

I was still mad, right? But there were a lot of keywords there that invoked involuntary responses.

Thiago kept his expression neutral. "But how are you talking to us if—"

I saved a backup copy and hid it where only a trusted friend could find it.

I was looking at the wall, watching everyone and the display with Amena's drones. Trusted friend? "Oh, fuck you."

That still counts as speaking.

Arada and Overse looked at each other again. Overse widened

her eyes and did a slight shoulder movement. Arada's mouth set in a grim line, then she took a breath and asked, "Is SecUnit right, did you plan to attack our facility?"

It was not my plan.

Overse's eyes had narrowed. She said, "But it was your idea."

I said, "Don't humor it."

Arada's tone was still even. "It wasn't your plan, but you made it happen. You sent those people after us—after SecUnit."

ART said, *I did.*

Of course it did.

"You knew where we were?" Ratthi frowned. "How?"

When I arrived through the Preservation wormhole, I sent messages inquiring after humans who I knew were associated with SecUnit. The Free Preservation Institute of Discovery and Engineering was most helpful when I asked for a possible meeting with Survey Specialist Arada. They sent me complete information on your itinerary and team.

Of course they had. I had heard ART pretend to be human on the comm before, on the RaviHyral transit station.

Ratthi groaned and covered his face. Arada and Overse stared at each other incredulously. Overse muttered, "We have got to talk to them about that."

Arada rubbed a spot over her left eye like it hurt. She said to ART, "So you knew when we'd be coming back to Preservation space."

You were early.

Arada was sticking to the point. "But why did you want to kidnap SecUnit?"

I needed someone who could kill the hostiles.

Everyone looked at me. I dug my fingers into the edge of the med platform. The skin on them itched, too, where the surgical suite had fixed the burned parts. "You told them I was a weapon, that they could use."

I built a trap, they entered it of their own accord.

"But who are they?" Amena said, frustrated. "Where did they

come from? Are they supposed to look like that? Did something happen to them to make them this way?"

ART said, *I don't know the answers to any of those questions.*

Thiago looked down at Target Six. "There's a possibility their appearance is the result of genetic or cosmetic manipulation. But . . ."

Ratthi finished, "But we have an alien remnant on the drive, that does suggest possible contamination . . ."

That's why humans and augmented humans are so cautious around alien remnants that even corporations mostly try to be careful. Strange synthetics are usually harmless, emphasis on the "usually." But organic elements can be really dangerous, where "really" means everyone dies horribly and nobody can ever go to the planet again.

Thiago's mouth tightened. "If any of these people had been left alive, perhaps we could have asked them."

I thought that was a shot at me, but ART apparently didn't take it well. It said, *If you'll put that one on the medical platform, I can cut it open and see.*

I was unimpressed, having heard ART's "villain of a long-running mythic adventure serial" voice before, but all the humans got quiet. Amena shifted uncertainly and looked at me. Then Ratthi whispered, "Was that a subtle threat?"

I said, "No. It wasn't subtle."

Amena hugged herself, then said, "How did the gray people steal your crew?"

ART said, *There was a catastrophic event when my crew and I first entered this system. My memory archive was disrupted and I'm still attempting to reconstruct it.*

Oh, fantastic. I said, "Is your comm shut down?"

It was not an attack launched via the comm, because I'm not an idiot.

"And I'm not the one who got taken down by a viral malware attack, so maybe you are an idiot," I said. Yeah, I was all over the place with that one.

ART said, *It was not a viral malware attack, it was an unidentified event.*

"That's fucking reassuring."

"Hey, hey!" Amena waved an arm, snapping her fingers. "Please don't stop telling us what happened! So your crew were taken prisoner by these gray people, correct? And are the gray people from the lost colony that Eletra's ship was looking for?"

Everybody turned to look at Eletra, who stared blearily back.

ART said, *Those are logical assumptions, though I have no direct evidence to support them. I know that we arrived in this system in response to a distress call from a corporate reclamation expedition. At some point, I experienced a catastrophic system malfunction that caused me to reinitialize. After the reinitialization, I found the intruders aboard. They said they were holding my crew hostage, and demanded weapons. I offered a weapon.*

Everybody looked at me again.

Arada did the lip-biting thing. "You brought them to SecUnit. Because you knew SecUnit would be able to handle the situation."

I did.

"The attack on our baseship could have killed all of us," Thiago said, some heat creeping into his voice.

No shit, Thiago, you think?

Ratthi hissed under his breath, but before he could tell Thiago to shut up, ART said, *That was a chance I was willing to take.*

Oh, okay. I was either having a processing error, or something that the shows I watch call a "rage blackout," or another emotional collapse. So I pushed off the med platform, walked out of the sterile field and into the restroom, and slammed my hand on the hatch close control.

9

After twenty-seven minutes and twelve seconds, Ratthi tapped on the hatch and sent me the feed message: *Can I come in and talk to you?*

I sent back, *Do you have my jacket?*

There was a pause. I was keyword-monitoring my inputs, the way I used to back when I was rented out on contracts, to make sure no one was screaming for help. But with ART back online, it was unlikely. Unless ART had decided to murder everybody in which case shit was going to get real. But that was also unlikely, because ART kept trying to contact me and I doubted it was planning a mass murder while also composing messages about how I was ungrateful and also wrong and being a sulky dumbass (not in those exact words but that's what it meant) and why wouldn't I fucking talk to it and you get the idea. Then Ratthi said, *I've got it.*

He meant the jacket. *Then you can come in.*

There was another pause. Then Ratthi asked, *Can Amena come in, too?*

I thumped my head back against the wall. I was sitting on the counter next to the sink and running episode 237 of *The Rise and Fall of Sanctuary Moon* in background so I could pretend to be watching it during the 400+ times ART had pinged me.

(You may have noticed, my processing capacity allows me to think about a lot of things and do a lot of things at the same time, more than humans, augmented humans, or lower functioning bots can. ART's processing capacity made me look like I was moving in slow motion. This made ART capable of both enormous patience and also of becoming furious when it didn't get what it wanted immediately. It was one of the few ways I could successfully mess with it.)

I had cleaned off all the blood and fluid with the hygiene unit but was too angry to take a shower. (Showers are nice and I wanted to stay angry.) One of ART's long-sleeved crew T-shirts had fallen out of the recycler at one point. My first impulse was to throw it away, but I needed it, so I pulled it on over my head and threw what was left of my shirt on the floor. Now I was sitting with my boots on the polished counter surface. I hoped it was annoying ART. I was assuming it had a sensor view in here if not a camera view.

I didn't want to upset Amena any more than I already had, so I sent, *Yes.*

The hatch slid open and Ratthi and Amena stepped in. Ratthi had gotten his knee fixed and wasn't limping anymore. He shut the hatch and Amena went to the other end of the sink counter and boosted herself up to sit on it. She curled her legs up, watching me worriedly. I said, "It can hear anything you say anywhere aboard."

Ratthi handed me my jacket with a smile. "Yes, but I'm used to that."

(Yes, I got that that was about me.)

The jacket had been recycler-cleaned and the material rewoven to fix the burned parts and holes. Ratthi sighed, leaned against the wall and said, "So, you have a relationship with this transport."

I was horrified. Humans are disgusting. "No!"

Ratthi made a little exasperated noise. "I didn't mean a sexual relationship."

Amena's brow furrowed in confusion and curiosity. "Is that possible?"

"No!" I told her.

Ratthi persisted, "You have a friendship."

I settled back in the corner and hugged my jacket. "No. Not—No."

"Not anymore?" Ratthi asked pointedly.

"No," I said very firmly. ART had stopped pinging me but I knew it was listening. It's like having a malign impersonal intelligence that is incapable of minding its own business reading over your shoulder.

Ratthi's expression was doing a neutral yet skeptical thing that was really annoying. He said, "Have you made many friends who are bots?"

I thought about poor dead Miki, who had wanted to be my friend. There was a 93 percent chance Miki had wanted to be everybody's friend, but Miki had said to me *"I have human friends, but I never had a friend like me before."* I said, "No. It's not like that. Not like it is between humans."

Ratthi was still skeptical. "Is it? The Transport seems to think differently."

I said, "The Transport doesn't know what the hell it's talking about, plus it lies a lot, and it's mean."

A minute, undetectable in the range of human eyesight, fluctuation in the lights told me ART had heard that.

"Why do you call it ART?" Amena asked. "It said its name was *Perihelion*."

I told her, "It's an anagram. It stands for Asshole Research Transport."

Amena blinked. "That's not an anagram."

"Whatever." Human words, there's too many of them, and I don't care.

"Regardless," Ratthi said, "I think that while you and *Perihelion* know how to have relationships with humans, neither of you is quite sure how to have a relationship with each other."

It still sounded disgusting. "Do you have to call it a relationship?"

Ratthi shrugged one shoulder. "You don't like the word 'friendship.' What else is there?"

I had no idea. I did a quick search on my archives and pulled out the first result. "Mutual administrative assistance?"

The lights fluctuated again, in what I could tell was a really sarcastic way. I yelled, "I know what you're doing, ART, stop trying to communicate with me!"

Amena looked around the room, trying to see what I was reacting to. Ratthi sighed again. He said, "I don't know if you've been listening to what we've been doing outside this restroom, but Arada and Thiago have been negotiating with *Perihelion* and have come to an arrangement. We will help locate and hopefully free its crew, and it will give us any assistance needed to return to Preservation space."

"That's not an arrangement," I said, "that's just doing what it wants."

"We know." Ratthi made a helpless gesture. "But we don't have any other choice. Even if it would let us send a distress beacon through the wormhole to the nearest station, that station would be in Corporation Rim territory. And we're in a so-called 'lost' system that has been claimed as salvage by a corporate, which makes us in violation of a lot of their laws, plus we're in a transport that had alien remnant technology installed on its drive. Telling whoever responds to the call that the transport was modified against its will is not going to get us anywhere but buried under massive fines, and it might be even worse for *Perihelion*'s crew and their university."

He was right about all that but it was actually worse than he thought. "This is not like Preservation Alliance territory. You can only get a station responder when you're inside a station's defined area of influence, and they won't forward distress beacons and they don't send responders through wormholes. At most, they'll pass the call to a local retrieval company, which would contact us and contract to rescue us. We'd have to pay them up front, and probably end up owing the station for passing the call along, though that depends on local regulations."

Amena's jaw dropped. "We'd have to pay someone to rescue us?"

Ratthi rubbed his face and muttered, "Oh, I hate the Corporation Rim."

"Really? Me too," I said. (Yes, that was sarcasm.)

And I had just thought of something that I should have noticed earlier.

Amena was clearly trying to work out all the possible repercussions. "And if corporates did show up, would you be okay? Because you're a construct?"

"I'm fine," I told her. It is amazing what the people on Preservation don't know about how the Corporation Rim operates. "SecUnits are legal here. Your mother is my registered owner and you're her designated representative." And it was definitely Amena and not Thiago.

Amena looked appalled. "My mother doesn't own you."

"Yes, she does." Dr. Bharadwaj had told me how Preservation-based humans don't understand these concepts and I had believed her, mostly, but seeing it in action was always different.

Amena looked at Ratthi for help. He nodded grimly. "Arada, Overse, and I all have certified copies of the legal document stored in our interfaces, just in case. If we do fall into the hands of corporates, Amena, you must assert legal ownership of SecUnit."

Amena waved her hands. "But that's—Ugh!"

"I don't like it, either," I told her.

Ratthi said, "That aside, *Perihelion* says it will be some time before it can make repairs to its engine systems so we're able to start the search, and we have preparations and plans to make." He clapped his hands briskly. "So will you come out of the bathroom now?"

"Yes." I pushed myself off the counter and pulled my jacket on over ART's stupid T-shirt. "Because ART is lying."

This time when the lights fluctuated, it wasn't sarcastic.

□   □   □

I walked out into Medical. The view of the control area was still active, with Arada seated in a station chair and Thiago now standing next to her. They were cycling through engine status data on ART's alien-remnant-augmented wormhole trip, occasionally making little horrified noises.

Overse was in Medical now, with the implant we had removed from Eletra on a sterile work surface. She was examining it using an imaging field. The magnified scans of the individual parts floated in it, rotating. Eletra was sitting up on a gurney near Overse, peering uncertainly at what she was doing with the implant.

Overse pulled out of her feed to look over at us inquiringly. "Is, uh, everyone ready to talk now?"

"Not exactly." Ratthi sounded concerned, which was totally unfair.

I said, "Arada, this transport did not come to this system in answer to a distress call."

Thiago turned around to watch me suspiciously. Arada pushed back her station chair. Someone had brought her some supplies from the emergency kit, because the burn on her cheek had been treated. "SecUnit, I think we have a working arrangement with *Perihelion* for now. Unless this is something that could endanger us, are you sure you want to . . . confront it just at the moment?"

I said, "I am absolutely sure."

Ratthi threw his hands in the air and went over to sit next to Overse.

With a "let's get this over with" expression, Overse asked, "SecUnit, how do you know there wasn't a distress call?"

I said, "This is a teaching and research vessel. The student quarters and classroom compartments aren't in use, and the lab module was inactive, and there was no cargo module attached. So what was it doing when it got this distress call?"

All the humans looked up at the ceiling.

ART said, *And this is your idea of being helpful.*

I said, "This is my idea of the opposite of being helpful. I am here against my will and you are going to regret that."

Arada pressed both hands to her face. "Maybe you should go back in the bathroom and think about this a little more."

"I'm done thinking," I said.

ART said, *That's obvious.*

I know, I walked into that one, which oddly enough, did not make me any less mad. I said, "You came here for a reason, and it wasn't a distress call. What was it?"

On the side of the room to my right, this was going on:

(Eletra whispered to Overse and Ratthi, "Why are you letting your SecUnit . . . do this?"

Overse's jaw tightened. She said, "It's not our SecUnit, it's—"

Ratthi squeezed her wrist and gave her what I recognized as a "don't trust the corporates" look. He told Eletra, "It's normally very responsible.")

Thiago was eyeing me through the conference image, frowning. He said, "It is a good question."

(Of course, none of the sensible humans are supporting me now, it has to be the one who never agrees with me when I'm not being an idiot.) I said to ART, "Why were you here? What do you really do? Deep space research, teaching humans, cargo hauling, none of those are reasons to be here, in the system where corporates were trying to salvage a dead colony."

ART said, *Everything that occurred before my crew was captured is irrelevant. It is none of your business.*

I said, "You made it my business when you kidnapped me."

You are not here against your will. Leave whenever you want. You know where the door is.

That sounded just as sarcastic and mean as you think it did. Also possibly really threatening to the humans. Arada and Ratthi were both waving at me, making gestures which I interpreted as urgent requests for me to shut up now. But I had gotten ART to lose its temper again and be threatening, and that was what I wanted. I folded my arms and said, "You're upsetting Amena."

I'd noted that ART's tone when it spoke to Amena was completely different than it was to the other humans. I didn't think it would hurt the others, but it wasn't careful of their feelings the way it was of Amena's. Whatever else ART was, the classroom space and bunkrooms said it was actually, on a regular basis, a teaching vessel. And before this when I was stupid and we were still friends it had talked about human adolescents in an indulgent way.

Amena took a breath, probably to object, based on her whole "despite being a relatively sheltered adolescent from the most naive human society in existence, I feel a need to pretend that none of this is bothering me" thing. I looked at her and tapped our private feed connection. *Be honest.*

She let the breath out. She prodded the deck with the toe of her shoe and admitted, reluctantly, "The gray people were terrifying. And being shot at, and . . . I'd really like to know what's going on, not just a convenient story."

There was a long silence. I felt a lot of human eyes looking at me, and the sense of weight and attention through the feed that was ART. Finally ART said, *I have to violate my crew's confidentiality agreement in order to answer that question.*

I said, "You kidnapped me and my humans. That violated my contract. A contract I made with them, myself." Not a company contract, I meant. A me contract. And ART had got me dragged into this and messed everything up.

ART said, *I will consider it.* Then it put up a connection schematic, which showed it had just cut Eletra's active connection out of the general feed. On a closed channel with me and my five humans, ART said, *This information must be kept private. If any of you reveal anything I tell you to the corporate representative, I will kill her.*

I had a release of adrenaline from my organic parts. Uncomfortable, and weird. I wasn't attached to Eletra, who seemed like the typical human client I had had with the company. (Not too dumb, not too smart, and only 53 percent likely to do something that ended up with me (1) shot (2) abandoned on a hostile planet.) But she was adjacent to my humans and I didn't like the idea of anybody dying anywhere in that neighborhood.

The humans clearly had a moment of tension. There were a lot of gazes all intersecting each other and attempts to conceal worried expressions. Then Arada said, *Agreed. We won't tell her anything.* She cleared her throat and said aloud, "Maybe we can use your cabins, to clean up and rest?"

ART said, on the general feed, *Of course.*

□   □   □

Ratthi and Overse helped Eletra get settled into one of ART's bunkrooms (an unused one that the asshole gray people didn't manage to get their growth medium odor all over). There was an attached bathroom and Ratthi brought self-heating meal boxes and beverage containers for her so she didn't have an excuse to wander around. I put a drone sentry outside the door because I don't trust anybody with security, particularly ART.

My humans went to the galley, which was far enough from the bunkroom that Eletra wouldn't hear the conversation, even if she walked out into the corridor. The humans were eating meals, too, and Thiago had made a hot liquid for them in the galley's prep unit.

ART put up another unnecessarily elaborate split display, with a view on Eletra, who had finished eating, taken the medication ART's MedSystem had recommended, and curled up to sleep.

Arada, still eating her meal, said, "*Perihelion,* are you ready to answer SecUnit's questions now?"

(Actually first she said, "SecUnit, will you stop pacing and sit down?"

I said, "No.")

ART said, *I am a teaching vessel, and a research vessel for deep space mapping, and I sometimes haul cargo. All that is true. My crew also gathers information and takes actions for anti-corporate organizations that operate as part of and are supported by the polity of Mihira and New Tideland, and administered by the Pansystem University of Mihira and New Tideland. These actions are often dangerous.*

Arada nodded, exchanging a look with Overse. Arada said, "So you came here because of this lost colony. To examine it before the corporates arrived?"

We received information that a database reconstruction contracted by a consortium of corporations involved in salvage and reclamation had turned up coordinates to a colony seeded approximately thirty-seven corporate standard years ago.

"An abandoned colony." Amena stirred the goop on her plate, glaring. "A bunch of people left to die, like our great-grandparents."

Amena wasn't wrong, it was similar to what had happened to the colonists who had eventually founded Preservation. They had been "seeded" (that actually means "dumped") on a mostly terraformed planet with the idea that supply ships would return through the wormhole at frequent intervals until the colony was self-supporting. This was exactly how corporates established colonies now. Except sometimes the corporates went bankrupt or were attacked by other corporates and the wormhole data was destroyed or the wormhole itself destabilized or all record of the colony's existence was just lost in a database that ended up locked due to legal battles over ownership. And so no supply ships came and all the humans starved or died when the cheap shitty terraforming failed. I'd seen movies and shows that used this as a plot, but I hadn't known they weren't just stories until I came to Preservation. (Most had depressing endings and were part of a whole "awful things happening to isolated groups of helpless humans" genre that was not my favorite.)

ART said, *The colonies are abandoned and cut off due to corporate bankruptcy or negligence, yes. Dead, not necessarily. Some manage to survive.*

Arada had finished eating and was folding up her plate for the recycler. "Didn't you say this site had two colonies?"

Yes. Historical sources recorded the existence of a former Pre–Corporation Rim colony on this site, but no other information.

ART put the colony report, what there was of it, in the feed. It looked like it was put together from fragments, as if someone had deleted the original and this was a reconstruction. Most of it was what ART had already told us: original Pre–Corporation Rim colony site, which nobody knew crap about or if they had none of the data had survived to make it into this report. Corporate colony seeded by a company called Adamantine Explorations, partial terraforming. No info on number of colonists, terrain, weather, habitats, equipment, illegal genetic experimentation, very illegal alien remnants, nothing.

The only interesting new info was from one of ART's crew members, an augmented human named Iris, who had added some newsfeed archives about the hostile takeover of Adamantine Explorations after the colony had been established. There were three different articles from news sources that said an undetermined number—anywhere from four to twenty-four—Adamantine Explorations employees had died in a firefight, holding off the corporate takeover long enough for their database of wormhole coordinates to be deleted. The only reason the physical data storage still existed was that the attackers had broken in and killed the techs before they could vaporize it. Iris's note ended: *Tempting to think that they were trying to deliberately protect? conceal? the colony. Possible? Just not likely.*

I didn't think it was likely, either. But like Iris, I thought the fact that three different news sources had reported versions of the story indicated that the incident or a variation of it had actually occurred.

All the humans were quiet as they read the report. (Yes, it feels like it takes them forever. I sorted through my media storage but I knew they would finish before I could get anything started.)

"That's strange," Overse said softly. "Were they trying to protect the colony? Or just their investment?"

"You just like a mystery," Arada told her, most of her attention on the report.

"I like mysteries in fiction, not in our lives," Overse retorted.

ART ignored them. *My crew's mission was to ascertain whether the colony was still inhabited, and if so, attempt contact, and prevent interference and exploitation by salvage corporations, whether by evacuating the inhabitants or, if the colony is actually viable, providing assistance.*

Amena leaned her elbows on the table. "But why do you have to do that? If people from the colony survived, then there's nothing another corporation could do, right? If the original corporation that sent the colony is gone, then the people are free."

"Unfortunately, that's not the way it works here," Overse told her. Her expression had that grimly frustrated quality that was common when my humans talked about the corporates. "Another corporation could move in and take over."

Amena was skeptical. "Take over? But people are living there. I guess they could settle a second colony somewhere on the planet but they couldn't take over the existing colony. Could they?"

"They could," Overse assured her. "They have."

Amena's expression turned horrified. "But that's like—I don't know what it is, but it's at least kidnapping."

"That's how it works in the Corporation Rim," Thiago told her, stirring his liquid. "The planet is considered property, someone's property that can be salvaged if the original owner is gone. The colonists, or their descendants or whoever is living there now, don't have any claim."

"*Perihelion,* what do you do about it? How do you help the colonists?" Ratthi asked.

ART said, *The University has the means to produce the colony's original charter documents, which often contain clauses specifying that if the originating corporate body has ceased operations, then ownership of the planet is ceded to the colonists or their issue or successors living on the original site.*

I'd heard the key words "means to produce" as opposed to "archival copies." I said, "You and your crew collect the necessary survey data from the colony and the University forges the documents." Not that there's anything wrong with that. I mean, I was mad at ART, but the overall mission sounded great in a "screw a corporation sideways" way.

"Is that right, *Perihelion*?" Ratthi asked.

ART ignored us. *A contract between the colony and an independently operated transfer station is then facilitated. Once the station has established a presence, then the colony is relatively secure from the worst excess of corporate predation, and free to accept other forms of assistance offered by non-corporate entities.*

Arada's mouth was twisted. "Eletra said there were two corporate ships here, correct? Did you arrive in this system before or after they did?"

Before. With my crew held hostage, I was forced to comply with their captors' orders to fire on a Barish-Estranza support carrier. But my memory archive of that period is damaged and I don't know what happened to the vessel or the crew.

"So the gray people could also have these corporate crews as prisoners." Ratthi looked like he was trying to figure out just how many humans we might have to rescue. "Do you know why they brought Eletra and the other corporate onboard . . . you?" He made a vague gesture over his shoulder. "Why they put the implants in them?"

"I thought it was to torture them for fun," Amena said darkly.

ART hesitated, though not long enough for the humans to notice. *They may have wanted their shuttle. It's still docked in my secondary cargo module slot.* That hesitation would have been suspicious, but I also thought ART might honestly not know. Which was strange, because it should know. Maybe the memory archive issue was worse than ART had implied. *But my two landing shuttles are also still in place, so that's unlikely.*

Arada propped her chin on her hand. She was exhibiting several behaviors indicating that she was deep in thought. *"Perihelion,* did the rest happen as you explained, that when you came back online your crew was gone?"

Yes.

There was a tone to that word. Not ART's base level of sarcasm. It had an edge that echoed in the feed.

I didn't react. ART had kidnapped me to get me here, put my humans in danger. I was not going to feel sympathy for it. Absolutely not.

Ratthi's expression was dubious. "Any luck remembering what happened when they disappeared?"

I am still reconstructing damaged archives.

"Could SecUnit help you with that?" Amena asked, very casually, not looking at me.

I folded my arms and glared at the side of Amena's head.

ART very obviously did not answer.

Overse leaned back in her chair, not comfortable. "We need to try to put together a timeline of when things happened."

By the time I opened my mouth to say I had a chart, ART had said, *Obviously,* and threw a chart up next to the split screen. It showed the times (1) ART knew it had first arrived through the wormhole into the colony's system, (2) when ART's memory disruption occurred, (3) when it had reinitialized to find intruders aboard and its crew gone and an alien remnant installed on its drive, (4) the attack on the corporate supply carrier, (5) the moment the deletion occurred, and (6) the moment ART's backup restarted. All except for Point One were estimates as ART's onboard timekeeping had been disrupted. (Yes, it had actually left out the whole part about telling the Targets that I was a weapon they could use and bringing them to where they could attack our baseship, and using the comm code to locate me. That was fucking incredible.)

Amena was telling the others, "Before everything got weird—weirder—Ras tried to tell me about the colony reclamation project, but Eletra cut him off and changed the subject."

Thiago looked at the view of the bunkroom, where Eletra was hidden under blankets. He said, "Is it possible that these people—the gray people—" He shook his head. "We know influence—terrible effects—from alien remnants are possible. Could the gray people have come from either the recent colony or the original one? Or are the corporates likely to use genetic manipulation on their colonists?"

Undetermined, ART said, like it honestly didn't give a crap.

And honestly, it probably didn't. The Targets had attacked ART's crew. It wasn't interested in the mystery, it just wanted its crew back.

When no one else could answer the question, Ratthi leaned his elbows on the table. "I think the corporates would do anything they could get away with. Obviously these gray people—what do we call them?"

"Targets," I said.

Thiago did a thing with his eyes that was like an eyeroll but not quite. Ratthi continued, "The Targets must have brought the alien remnant tech that was installed on the wormhole drive."

Overse tapped her fingers on the table, thinking. "Those implants weren't alien remnant tech. In fact, they were old. Much older than thirty-seven years, when the corporate colony was established."

"Yes, there must have been usable but outdated tech left behind on the site of the earlier colony, the Pre–Corporation Rim one." Ratthi poked absently at the food left on his plate, then slid it over to Arada so she could finish it off. "That solid-state screen interface, I've seen those in historical displays."

Amena nodded, waving a hand at me. "And you know, they called the wormhole a 'bridge-transit.' I've never heard that before."

Thiago seemed intrigued. "Did they speak a standard language?"

"No, but there was a translation at first, then it stopped when SecUnit woke up and the fighting started," Amena told him.

Since ART didn't have any usable video or audio, I pulled some examples and sent them into the general feed. The humans listened with puzzled expressions. Then Thiago nodded grimly to himself. "That's a mix of at least three Pre–Corporation Rim languages."

"That certainly matches their tech," Overse said.

Thiago added, "And many of the really deadly alien contamination incidents were Pre–Corporation Rim."

"What sort of incidents?" Arada asked.

Thiago said, "Preservation's archives only have detailed information on one, that took place on a moon that was being converted into a massive base of operations for one of the early Pre-CR polities. Over seventy percent of the population was killed. The only reason anyone survived was because a recently activated central system managed to lock off the living quarters and keep it sealed until help arrived." He glanced at me. "So they were saved by a machine intelligence."

I know what a central system is, Thiago. (It was more outdated tech, like a HubSystem that did everything, with no subordinate systems. I hadn't ever encountered one that wasn't part of a historical drama.)

Overse leaned forward. "So how were the people killed? The ones who were affected by the contamination attacked the others?"

Thiago wasn't nearly as annoying when he was being smart like this. He said, "Yes, though that sort of violent reaction to remnant contamination appears to be rare. But since so many of these incidents, historical and contemporary, are suppressed, we don't actually know whether it is or not."

Ratthi nodded agreement. "With the corporates being so secretive, it's hard to tell."

Overse said, "The only laws they all seem to recognize are about alien remnant discovery and interdiction, and the licensing restrictions for use of strange synthetics."

"But why would alien remnants affect people like that?"

Amena asked. "Is it intentional? Is it something that's protecting the site, where the aliens didn't want anybody else to take what was there?"

Ratthi took a breath, then let it out again. "I never thought so. I think it's the same as if an alien person who had never seen anything like a terraforming matrix accidentally touched one and was poisoned. There's no intentionality. Sometimes the contamination effects are as if different priorities are loaded into the affected person's brain, like alien software running on human hardware. The result is chaos." He gestured with a utensil. "But do we think the Targets are from the Adamantine colony? Or descendants of the Pre-CR colony? Or could they have come from outside this system?"

All indications suggest they came from within this system, ART said.

I said, "You're having memory archive issues, how do you know who was or wasn't onboard you? There could have been hundreds of corporate salvage groups and raiders and colonists and aliens—"

"SecUnit—" Arada started at the same time as Ratthi said, "I don't think—"

ART interrupted, *SecUnit's earlier statement that I "lie a lot" was untrue. I obviously cannot reveal information against the interests of my crew unless circumstances warrant.*

Arada nodded. "Right. We understand. I think SecUnit is looking out for our interests—"

ART said, *I want an apology.*

I made an obscene gesture at the ceiling with both hands. (I know ART isn't the ceiling but the humans kept looking up there like it was.)

ART said, *That was unnecessary.*

In a low voice, Ratthi commented to Overse, "Anyone who thinks machine intelligences don't have emotions needs to be in this very uncomfortable room right now."

ART was suddenly in my feed, on a private channel. *I did what I had to do. You should understand that.*

I said aloud, "I'm not talking to you on the feed! You're not my client and you're not my—" I couldn't say it, not anymore.

All the humans were staring at me. I wanted to face the wall but that felt like giving in.

I suddenly had views all over the ship. ART had given me access to its cameras. I snarled, "Stop being nice to me!"

Then Amena said aloud, "I think you need to give SecUnit some time."

Right, that's all this situation needed. I asked her, "Is it talking to you on a private channel?"

Amena winced. "Yes, but—"

I yelled, "ART, stop talking to my human behind my back!"

You know that thing humans do where they think they're being completely logical and they absolutely are not being logical at all, and on some level they know that, but can't stop? Apparently it can happen to SecUnits, too.

Arada got up from the table and held up her hands. "Hey, now, let's stop this. It's unproductive. *Perihelion,* you need to stop pressuring SecUnit. I know you're upset about your crew and being deleted and this has all been terrible and confusing. But SecUnit is upset, too. Yelling at each other isn't going to help."

ART said, *I was not yelling.*

"Of course you weren't," Arada agreed, in the same reasonable tone Mensah's marital partners Farai and Tano used when they talked to their younger kids. She faced the others. "We need to work this situation. *Perihelion,* if you could give us access to any other information your crew had on this colony, we'd really appreciate that. In the meantime, Overse and I are going to start collecting data on this alien thing that was on *Perihelion*'s drive and see if we can't help get the normal-space drive online any faster. Ratthi and Thiago, I want you to check out the deceased Targets and do some pathology scans. We also need a translation of what they were saying in SecUnit's recordings. If we can confirm they're descended from one of the two groups of human colonists, I think—Well, I think we'll be able to make more effective plans. Amena, I'd like you to try to talk to Eletra again, see if you can get any more information out of her. I think it's clear she's been holding back, and now that she knows about the implants, she might be more forthcoming. SecUnit, maybe you could figure out what caused *Perihelion*'s first reinitialization and how the Targets got aboard? I think we can all agree that having mysterious intruders invade *Perihelion* again is something we really need to avoid. Is everyone good with that? *Perihelion,* are you all right with this plan?"

ART said, *For now.*

10

Well, this was just great.

The humans started to disperse, Arada and Overse toward engineering, Ratthi going back to Medical to get the pathology suite ready. Amena helped Thiago clear the meal trays off the table. He touched her shoulder. "My daughter, are you sure you're all right to speak to this corporate?"

"I'm fine, Uncle." She was exasperated and did this shrugging shoulders-flopping arms thing that illustrated that very well. "I don't think Eletra would try to hurt me. And she knows SecUnit is here. And ART." She glanced at me, guiltily. "It said I could call it ART."

Of course it did. I felt the hinge of my jaw grind.

Thiago squeezed Amena's shoulder. "Just be careful."

"I will," Amena told him, already heading back into the prep area where the nearest recycler was. "I'm going to get her some fresh clothes, it'll give me an excuse to go in there."

Thiago looked at me and I looked at the wall. He said, "I want to thank you for everything you did for Amena."

Was it grudging or was I just in a terrible mood? I don't know, I have no idea, so I didn't respond.

Amena came out with a packet of clothing from the recycler and I followed her down the corridor toward Eletra's bunkroom. From ART's camera view, Eletra had gotten up to get another container of water from the bathroom, so it was a good time for Amena to casually stroll in and offer the clothes.

Then ART secured a private channel with me and said, *I don't need your help.*

That's not what you thought when you kidnapped me, I told it.

I meant, you don't have to speak to me if you don't want to.

Fine, whatever, I don't care. I said, *Do you want the fucking help or not?*

ART dumped its archive on me and I was immediately drowning in the giant mound of data that comprised its second-by-second status checks. Fortunately, after keeping track of the company's shit-tons of mined data, I knew how to deal with it. I started by defining what the gap in ART's memory archive might look like, which I was guessing would be a giant interruption in the constant incoming reports from subsystems like life support, navigation, etc. It was tricky, because for ART these were not like discrete reports from connected systems, but more like the sensory input I would get from the pads on the tips of my fingers. It was a lot more complicated than the way my own archives stored data. But once I had an idea of what I was looking for, I constructed a query.

I stopped at the top of the bunkroom corridor and let Amena go on alone. I didn't want Eletra to see me or to realize I was lurking out here, since I thought that might impede Amena's ability to get her to talk. Amena reached the hatch and sent Eletra a note on the feed: *Hello, I brought you some spare clothes, can I come in?*

While Eletra opened the hatch with the feed control and they sorted through the clothes, I checked my inputs for the others: Arada and Overse had stopped in the corridor that went toward the engineering module. Arada hugged Overse, and Overse kissed her and said into her ear, "You can do this, babe. You're a bulkhead."

"I'm a wibbly bulkhead," Arada muttered.

(The wibbliness was why I trusted Arada. Overconfident humans who don't listen to anybody else scare the hell out of me.)

Arada stepped back and smiled at Overse. "Got to get to work."

ART had dispatched the medical gurney earlier and it had

been moving methodically around the ship picking up messy dead Targets. Now it floated into Medical where Ratthi waited, Thiago following it in. There was a lot of congealing blood and fluids. "Oh, this is not going to be fun," Ratthi muttered.

"No," Thiago agreed grimly. "I'll get the biohazard gear."

ART added to its action list: *Repair and reactivate drones. Collect targetDrones for examination and destruction.*

In the bunkroom, Amena was asking, "How are you feeling?"

"Better." Eletra folded a jacket in her lap. "I know you're going to ask, but we didn't know those implant things were in us. I don't remember that at all."

Interesting, ART said.

I was still mad, right? But it was interesting. I said, *Because you have a gap in your memory archive?*

Yes. It can't be the same cause, of course, but it's the same operational approach. Take a prisoner, cause a memory disruption.

I hate it when ART is right. It was the same operational approach and we really needed to find out if the Targets had used alien remnant tech to cause the memory disruptions or not. I said, *The mix of outdated human technology and alien remnant could mean the stupid Pre–Corporation Rim humans established a colony on an interdicted alien remnant site.*

Not necessarily, ART said. Before I could argue, it added, *The site might have been undiscovered, not interdicted.*

ART had a lot stricter standards about what constituted evidence than humans did. It was always wanting to prove things actually existed before it would make plans for what to do about them. (Yes, it was annoying.)

ART said, *It's possible to theorize that something from the original Pre-CR colony may have remained on the site when the Corporate colonists arrived. But it seems strange that the later colonists would preserve and use outdated tech.*

I didn't want to admit it, but ART wasn't wrong about that, either. This tech wasn't useless, but I'd taken targetControlSystem down with an attack that was practically from ancient history.

(That's how I'd known about it, from watching historical dramas.) *So the facts we know are: that there was a human site in existence before the corporate colony. And that somebody found alien remnants at some point.*

ART created a feed graphic (yes, another one) labeled *Perihelion and SecUnit's Initial Suppositions* with an access list that included all the humans except Eletra. The first bullet point was: Fact (1) Corporate colony was established on an early Pre–Corporation Rim human occupation site. Questions: Are alien remnants present? If yes, were they original to the site or introduced later? Was the Pre-CR site established because of the presence of alien remnants? Was the corporate colony established because of the presence of alien remnants?

The humans all paused to read it. Amena, listening to Eletra talk about her family, covered her moment of distraction with a cough. (Eletra's family was in a hereditary indenture to Barish-Estranza and was trying to build up enough employment credit to get her and her siblings and cousins transferred into management training. I knew Amena well enough by now to recognize she was feigning polite interest to disguise horrified interest.)

My queries on ART's status data started returning results, and I backburnered everything to check them.

Huh.

ART had said it had one forced shutdown and reinitialize, when its crew disappeared and the Targets showed up. Then a second forced shutdown when the targetControlSystem had deleted it. So when had targetControlSystem been loaded into ART's systems? Presumably its invasion of ART's systems had caused that first forced shutdown.

Except there were more gaps than that.

I wished Pin-Lee was here. And, though I hated to admit it, I wished Gurathin was here, too. Both were analysts, and while I was way better at it than they were, at least I could have shown them what I was looking at.

I said, *ART, look at this.*

I was aware enough of ART to know that it was doing several things at once: helping Arada and Overse collect scans from what was left of the alien remnant on its drive, directing the MedSystem's pathology unit for Ratthi, working on the translation of the Targets' language with Thiago, guiding the reinitialization and diagnostics of its damaged propulsion systems, plus monitoring all its other ongoing processes. But I suddenly had 86.3 percent of its attention. (For ART, that was a lot.)

It examined my query results. A human in this situation would have said, "That's not possible."

ART said, *Intriguing.*

I needed to put these in a timeline. I looked for major events like wormhole entrances and exits and navigation changes so I would know what they looked like in the status data. ART pulled generic examples for me and I started another query set.

In the bunkroom, Amena had been cautiously working around to the subject of the colony. With a serious expression, she said slowly, "Look, I know you don't want to reveal things that your . . . corporate supervisors or whoever don't want you to, but we really need to know about this lost colony."

Eletra bit her lip. "It's proprietary information."

For fuck's sake. On our private feed connection, Amena sent, *I'm not sure what she means by this. Somebody owns the information?*

Yes, I told her. *She's afraid of her salvage corporation. She needs to be more afraid of being recaptured by the Targets.*

Amena said, "I understand that but the Targets—those gray people—they could show up again. Especially because no one knows how they got on this transport in the first place, or what happened to the crew." She lifted her hands helplessly. "Whatever happened to them could happen to us. And it's more likely the longer we're stuck here."

Eletra put her hand on her own shoulder, as if trying to reach for the place where her implant had been. "I thought the new people were the crew?"

ART butted in with, *Tell her they are.*

Amena nodded earnestly. "Sure, yes, they are, but we're—they're missing the crew members who were here when the Targets took over the ship."

Eletra's frown deepened. "Why can't we leave the system?"

"The normal space engines aren't working yet. But even if we could get to the wormhole, the transport won't let us go. You heard it. It's programmed not to leave without its crew, the rest of the crew. And it's really mean, and determined." On the feed, Amena said, *Sorry, ART.*

Apology accepted, ART said. I felt its attention shift in the feed. (Imagine it staring meaningfully at me.) (It could stare all it wanted, I'm not apologizing.)

Amena added, "And we already know about some things, like the alien remnants around the Pre–Corporation Rim colony."

Both ART and I shut up (I know, I was surprised, too) and waited to see if that would work.

"Oh." Eletra slumped a little. "I don't know very much. Ras and I are—were—both environmental techs, and everything was need-to-know. Our briefing said the colony was originally seeded by an early polity, probably via cold sleep ship. It was discovered about forty years ago and re-seeded through the wormhole by a company called Adamantine Explorations, that kept the location private. Then they went down in a hostile buyout and the databases were destroyed—" Amena looked confused and Eletra helpfully explained. "Somebody was probably trying to force the incoming management to pay for the code keys to get the data. But you know, that's not a very good idea. They might take it out on the seized assets. And it's bad enough being bought out like that without the management coming in with a grudge against you."

Amena blinked a lot, apparently as an attempt to control her expression. (I've tried it, it doesn't work very well.) On the feed, she said, *When she says seized assets, she means the employees, right? The people?*

Correct, ART said.

Eletra continued, "But anyway, the storage media was saved and Barish-Estranza bought it at some point later and they were able to re-create the data, and they launched this salvage project." She hesitated. "There were rumors about alien remnants. Supposedly some of the recovered data referenced them. But that could have just been rumors."

Amena said, "So what was Barish-Estranza going to do about the alien remnants, if they were there? You have to have a special license to recover them, right, even in the Corporation Rim?"

"That's above my pay level." Eletra touched the back of her neck uneasily. Physical reactions are supposed to be useful for determining whether humans are telling the truth or lying or are secretly planning to murder their whole survey team, etc., and sometimes they were. But also sometimes humans just secreted agitated brain chemicals for no apparent reason, or because something was physically wrong, like their digestive systems malfunctioning. But ART's scan of Eletra showed she was experiencing signs of physical distress when she talked about the implants. "Was that what was in us?" she said. "Those implants? Did they have strange synthetics? Your coworker took one apart."

I pulled a preliminary report from Overse's feed, mostly just the raw data she had collected for the scan. She hadn't had time to write up any notes from it.

"No, she said it was very simple tech." Amena bit her lip, trying to look like she was thinking and not reading the feed. ART had completed the report and noted that the implants had no alien components but that they might be receivers for a more esoteric transmitter. It had added "examine all Target technology" to the group worklist and added the line (2) primitive human technology designed to work with alien power sources or strange synthetic materials to *Perihelion* and SecUnit's Suppositions chart. "She thought it could have been connected to alien remnant tech."

Eletra slumped and looked sick.

My query results for establishing a timeline of ART's forced shutdowns returned and I matched them with the gaps I'd already identified.

That was when I hit the first oh shit moment.

ART, I said.

ART took in my report.

The moment of shock lasted less than .01 second but subjectively it seemed much longer. Then ART did what I should have done first and spoke to Amena on our private feed connection: *Amena, leave that compartment.*

I added, *Now, Amena, it's potentially dangerous.*

Amena was agitated, but channeled it into squinting thoughtfully and pushing at her hair. She looked more like a human who had forgotten to do something rather than one who had just been told they were in danger. "Oh, my Uncle's calling me on the feed." She pushed to her feet, backing toward the hatch. "I'll check back with you later."

Eletra just nodded wearily.

Amena let the hatch close and then ran down the corridor to me. "What is it?" she whispered.

I took her arm and guided her around the corner. I was having a release of adrenaline from my organic parts and I felt weird and cold. There was no way an implant could have been put into Amena, she'd never been out of my and ART's sight, but I scanned her again anyway. "ART encountered the Barish-Estranza transports before its first forced shutdown," I told her. "Whatever attacked it and kidnapped its crew, came from one of their ships."

Amena's eyes widened. "Oh shit."

□   □   □

We had another meeting, this one in the feed, again with Eletra's connection cut. This time ART let me do the video conference image but I was too rattled to make it fancy.

Arada and Overse were still in the engineering pod, Ratthi and Thiago were still in Medical. Amena and I ended up sitting in the hatchway of the galley, so I could be close if Eletra decided to do something other than lying in the bunkroom like a traumatized recovering human. Which she might still be, even though we had evidence indicating against it. Amena was nervously eating processed imitation vegetable fragments out of a container from the galley. (She had asked me to let her listen in on the conference but to mark her feed as on private. She told me, "If you need me to do something, I'll do it, but a lot of things have happened and I just need a minute.")

(Thiago asked where she was and I said, "In the restroom," and she glared at me.

I am not your social secretary, Amena, you want a better lie, make up one yourself.)

I had converted my timeline into a format humans and augmented humans could read, annotated it, and put it up in the feed. It showed that ART's initial arrival in this system via the wormhole was its last substantiated memory. After that, everything was a reconstruction based on the status data. It looked like:

1. ART's arrival in the system.
2. ART receives a distress signal with a Barish-Estranza Corporation signature. Sensors show one contact, a configurable explorer ship. There is no sign of the second B-E vessel, the supply transport, that Ras and Eletra said they were aboard when they were attacked. The distress call is marked as a request for medical assistance.
3. ART tractors the B-E explorer's shuttle into its module dock.
4. Unsubstantiated but probably bad stuff happens.
5. B-E explorer then links up with ART's module dock, presumably to take ART's crew prisoner and leave the Targets onboard, if the Targets hadn't already boarded via the shuttle. (I'd taken a look at the shuttle via ART's cameras, and going down to search it was next on my action list.)

6. ART leaves the system via the wormhole.

7. ART exits the wormhole at Preservation Station, after a trip barely lasting an impossible three hours, telling us the alien remnant tech was definitely in place on its engines at that point.

8. After sending and receiving communications from Preservation Station, ART goes into standby for five ship-cycles. ART then targets our facility when it arrives, firing multiple times, missing spectacularly due to supplying faulty targeting data to its own weapon systems.

(I couldn't tell exactly when targetControlSystem had been uploaded to ART's systems, but it was before this point because the status updates told the story of a subtle but intense battle over the weapons. ART's crew had been held hostage for its good behavior, but it hadn't been willing to kill our survey team even after it knew it had me in its tractor. TargetControlSystem must have figured out who was jogging its arm every time it tried to fire, because that was when ART had been deleted, causing the equivalent of a giant seismic event in its status updates.)

I could see the others on ART's cameras, digesting the information with increasingly concerned expressions. Overse said, "So the memory *Perihelion* had of firing on a corporate transport never actually took place?"

ART didn't answer. I think it was upset. I was also upset, but somebody had to be the adult here. (I was used to ART being the adult.) I said, "From the navigation, sensor, and status data I reviewed, weapons were not fired until ART encountered our facility in Preservation space. And there is no archival video or interior sensor data of the docking with the B-E explorer, or of the arrival and docking of the shuttle Eletra and Ras said they were aboard." I didn't like to say it aloud, but I had to. "ART was compromised not long after the first contact with the explorer and its shuttle. Something first removed and then significantly altered sections of its personal memory."

The humans were quiet, taking that in. Then Ratthi said, "Poor ART. Excuse me, poor *Perihelion*."

Arada grimaced in agreement. "It's disturbing. The B-E explorer must have arrived in the system first and was attacked. Taken over? By our friends the Targets. But if the supply transport actually exists, where is it now?"

Overse frowned. "It might have been destroyed. We have to assume *Perihelion*'s crew are being held prisoner on the explorer."

"Is the explorer armed?" Ratthi asked worriedly. "I hate being shot at."

Again, ART didn't answer. I said, "Probably." For a reclamation project in a technically uninhabited system, it would be easier for Barish-Estranza to afford a license and bond for an armed ship.

Thiago paced in front of the med platform, his arms folded. "*Perihelion* and I have translated the speech that SecUnit recorded and it was . . . confusing at best. The Targets—and we are going to have to come up with something else to call them— spoke of a need to complete their mission, but never said what the mission was."

Ratthi added, "And they all have implants like Eletra's."

The other humans looked like they didn't know what to think about that. I didn't know what to think about it, either.

Arada said, "But could you tell if there was alien remnant exposure?"

"The scan isn't showing anything that matches the list of known strange synthetics or organic alien remnants." Ratthi glanced at Thiago for confirmation. "But that doesn't eliminate the possibility."

Thiago said, "Statistics suggest there are many undiscovered alien remnant sites, and many others that no one has been able to get close enough to to analyze their component materials. And the scan is turning up traces of unidentifiable elements in their bodies. We can't tell if they're naturally occurring elements or strange synthetics until we have planetary survey data to compare them to."

Ratthi gestured and sent some scan results into the feed for the others to look at. "And those suits they're wearing do have a factory code stamped on them. I can't read it and *Perihelion*'s database can't identify it, though that might be because of the reinitialization or the memory archive issues. But I suspect they came in the supplies for one of the two colonies, either the original one or the corporate colony seeded by Adamantine."

Thiago said, "What we do know for certain is that the Targets were altered to look as they do. We don't know if they did it to themselves or if it was an accidental exposure to a dangerous alien remnant. If they weren't all dead, we could ask them."

Yeah, that was aimed at me.

"If they weren't all dead, they'd be trying to kill us, or stick implants in us," Amena grumbled, still off-feed and crunching vegetable matter.

Overse spread her hands. "Where does this leave Eletra? Were SecUnit and Amena meant to rescue her and her friend? Were they meant to be . . . spies, possibly?"

"I think that's too far-fetched." Arada's forehead scrunched in thought. "The Targets couldn't have any idea SecUnit would be capable of seizing control of the ship when they brought it aboard. They thought they were looking for a weapon, not a person, so why set an elaborate trap with spies?"

Overse slumped in her chair, frustrated. "Right, that's true." She looked tired. I suspected it was a bad idea to have a meeting when all the humans were running out of brain capacity.

Ratthi added, "I think Eletra is telling the truth, that her memories were altered, just like *Perihelion*'s were."

"You just want to believe the best about everyone," Overse said, still a little skeptical.

Ratthi snorted. "No, that's Thiago. I'm optimistic but a realist."

Thiago looked mildly insulted.

"No, that's me," Arada corrected, and smiled at Overse. "I'm an optimist."

"We know, honey." Overse squeezed her shoulder.

Thiago said, "Amena, are you back on the feed? What is your opinion of Eletra? Do you think she told you the truth, that she didn't remember what happened?"

Amena seemed surprised to be asked for an opinion, but she swallowed what she was eating and said on the general feed, *At first I thought so. They were both so worried about proprietary information and getting in trouble, that seemed real to me. Now . . . I don't think she's afraid enough.* She was frustrated, trying to think how to explain. *I think she's either lying, or something has messed with her mind so much that she doesn't know what happened, and now she's afraid to admit it.*

Arada looked up at the ceiling. "*Perihelion,* can you tell us anything else? What do you think happened?"

ART hadn't said anything, and that was beginning to worry me. ART likes to give its opinion and I'm not even sure "likes" is the right word there, but basically, ART gives its opinion whether you like it or not. It was beginning to feel strange that it hadn't weighed in yet to tell the humans they were missing something obvious or weren't approaching the problem the right way or whatever.

When it still didn't respond, I said, "ART is trying to reassemble its log data right now. It'll be out of contact for a short time."

Amena squinted suspiciously at me. "Is that true?" she whispered.

I made a gesture I was hoping she would interpret as "Please don't tell them I'm lying."

Arada said, "Thank you, SecUnit." She scratched her fingers through her short hair, like she was trying to get her thoughts together. This was definitely a problem; the humans needed to recharge or sleep or whatever or their decision-making abilities would be even worse than usual. She continued, "So, right, none of this fundamentally changes our objectives. We still need to find *Perihelion*'s crew, but at least now we know our first step is to track down the explorer."

I was hoping ART would comment, even if it was going to say something like "or else," but there was nothing.

Thiago had been looking thoughtful, which I tried not to see as a bad sign. He said, "Arada, I'd like to get Eletra back into Medical for a thorough neurological scan. Also, that will give me a chance to speak to her myself. I'll review Amena's full report and then see if I can get us any more information."

Arada told Thiago, "Good idea. Optimism aside, we need to know if she's lying and plotting something or if she genuinely thinks she's telling the truth. Let's try to get as much information as we can before . . . before anything else happens."

I established a private connection to Arada's feed and told her, *You all need a rest period.*

Arada hesitated, then she winced and rubbed her temple. *You're probably right about that. I'll talk to the others.*

I put the vid display back on standby. Amena scraped the last vegetable matter out of the container and said, "Is ART really working on something?"

"Sure," I said. She stared at me. "Maybe." I secured a channel just for the three of us, me, ART, and Amena. I sent, *ART, answer me. You're scaring Amena.* Ugh, I needed to be honest or this wouldn't help. I added, *You're scaring me.*

It was a relief when ART said, *I'm continuing the repair of my normal space drive and examining long-range system scan data to determine possible search patterns for the explorer.*

"Are you okay?" Amena asked.

No, ART said.

I hadn't expected ART to admit it. Really hadn't expected. Right, so, that isn't good.

Amena took a breath, visibly regrouping, and nodded. "Sure, I can see that. But we're not any worse off now than we were before you two figured this out. In fact, we're better off, because now we're helping you find out exactly what happened. And it's always better to have more information to act on." Her glance at me was wry. "My second mother says that."

ART pinged me for a private connection and I let it establish one. It said, *My crew. What if they never left?*

I knew what it meant. I said, *ART, there was nothing indicating that humans were killed or injured onboard. I checked. It was the first thing I checked for in the quarters module. There was nothing. And you've scanned yourself. The Targets trashed some cabins and left debris and their own fluids, they wouldn't have cleaned up after a . . .* I hesitated but I had to be completely honest about what I thought or ART would know. *They wouldn't have cleaned up after a mass murder. I've seen mass murders, ART, they leave a lot of mess.*

It didn't reply, but I could feel it listening.

I said, *Once we get your drones fixed, we can have them check again for bio traces, but I don't think we'll find anything. I think that whatever happened, your humans were fine when they left here.*

ART said, *Is that an indication they left voluntarily?*

It was a point to consider. Doing what ART would normally do (if it wasn't emotionally compromised) and looking at just the verifiable data, we didn't know if the crew had been abducted, left voluntarily, or escaped. Since ART's two shuttles were still docked, we knew the crew hadn't used them to leave.

(Or the crew could have tried to escape and been spaced. I wasn't going to mention it, because ART had to know that it was a possibility. But it might have eliminated it from its decision tree, knowing it couldn't function otherwise. There was no point in considering it, not now. We had to search until we found an answer. If that was the answer . . . we'd deal with it then.) I said, *We need to do a full inventory, particularly of your hand weapons storage. If your crew had to abandon you when the Targets compromised your systems, they may have forced their way onboard the explorer.*

The pause was long, 3.4 seconds. Then ART said, *Agreed.*

And it hit me then that ART had been desperate and terrified since the moment the Barish-Estranza explorer had sidled
up and done whatever it had done. It had tricked its captors into
taking it to me not because it had some kind of grand strategy
but because it needed me.

I hate emotions.

On the private channel between ART and me, I said, *I apologize for calling you a fucker.*

It said, *I apologize for kidnapping you and causing potential collateral damage to your clients.*

Amena was watching me, her brows drawn together. "Are you
two talking?"

"Yes." I had to look at the wall now.

Amena was still worried. "Are you fighting again or are you
making up? Because it looks exactly the same from the outside."

We're making up, ART told her.

"Good." Amena looked relieved. "Good, right. What's next
on our list?"

□   □   □

I went to search the Barish-Estranza transport shuttle. I wasn't
expecting to find anything but it was on the action list, so why
not.

ART had notified Arada that while it was working on the engines, it was also prepping a squad of pathfinders just in case we
had to search the colony planet. (I hope it didn't come to that. I
don't like planets.)

Pathfinders are like drones for space, basically, active scanners that would zip around the planet collecting environmental
information and terrain imaging, plus looking for comm signals,
possible energy sources, and whatever might be planning to
kill us. It's the kind of thing that my ex-owner bond company
did via satellite when they prepared to issue safety bonds for a
newly opened survey planet. Except the company satellite would
mainly be mapping the entire planet, and the pathfinders would

be looking for potential locations where ART's crew might be. They were really expensive, not something normal survey teams had access to. Arada was impressed.

(You couldn't rent pathfinders from the company, not only because of the cost. They made planetary exploration safer and more targeted, so therefore less need for massive bond companies to rent you all sorts of expensive planetary exploration gear and sell you expensive safety bonds.)

I was monitoring Thiago's casual conversation with Eletra while the med platform was doing a deep scan on her. Overse was in the maintenance bay reassembling the repair drone I had found in engineering so it could start repairing the other damaged drones. Arada was reviewing the scans of the alien engine remnant, but everything that was left of it seemed to be melting or decomposing so most of the data was garbage. (As Overse pointed out, the thing was illegal to have anyway so if it melted completely it would be for the best, but it looked like it was still going to leave a residue that would have to be scraped off ART's engines.) Ratthi was shepherding a biohazard cleaning unit through the corridors and picking up pieces of dead targetDrones.

Amena followed me to the shuttle, dragging her feet. (She really needed to sleep. I hadn't heard anything from Arada about it so I put *Humans need to take rest periods* on the general action list. Up in the central corridor, Ratthi saw it and muttered, "Please, yes, soon.")

I did a brief visual check on both of ART's shuttles, just to verify that they were empty and hadn't been tampered with. The Barish-Estranza shuttle was parked inside the same docking module, attached to a module lock, which had an extendable tube to enclose the hatch. ART had said there was no one inside the shuttle, and no active bot pilot, but I made Amena hang back down the corridor with her assigned drones while I approached. The hatch was sealed, but not code-locked, which made sense when we thought Eletra and Ras were telling the truth about being captured trying to escape from their doomed transport. (Now that we were certain it hadn't happened that way, who the hell knew?)

ART had cut the shuttle off from the feed. I touched the lock cautiously. (Considering the inactive state of its onboard systems, I wasn't expecting alien killware or a sentient virus or something else unspecified to leap across and infect me, but the fact remained that something had happened to ART despite all its protections, and alien killware was still a possibility.) I still couldn't pick up any feed activity, so I pushed up one sleeve and adjusted my energy weapon to deliver a pulse that caused the seal to disengage. The hatch slid open, releasing a puff of slightly stale air. It didn't have the algae/growth medium smell associated with the Targets; in fact, it had traces of the dirty sock smell associated with humans. But then an absence of evidence is not evidence of absence. Or past absence. Whatever, you know what I mean.

I used my own scan, making sure there was no movement or active weapons inside, and stepped in.

The shuttle wasn't a model I had been in before, but the configuration was similar to a standard transport shuttle. It was small, sized for ten humans at most, no cabins, a toilet facility that folded out from the bulkhead (ugh). The individual seats were in a spiral in the main compartment, so they would have to be cycled around to release each passenger for disembarking. It was obviously meant for short trips between ships or from ship-to-station. The cockpit had a seat for a human pilot next to the currently absent bot pilot's interface console. The upholstery showed signs of ordinary wear and tear. The single passenger compartment was generally clean but there were scuff marks on the panels and padding. There was only a .01 percent chance it had been constructed as a trap by an alien intelligence. (It was a theory, okay.)

On our private feed connection, Amena said, *Is it empty? Is there anything strange in it? Can I come closer?*

You can come to the hatch, but not inside. I started searching for physical evidence. I would need to check all the storage compartments, anywhere there might be a hidden space that could conceal something. The drive housing still had the factory seal from its last maintenance check, so it probably hadn't been infected with illegal alien remnant technology. I'd have to break the seal and do a visual inspection anyway, just to be certain. I also needed to pull the logs, but I'd have to do it via a display surface. Even with an inert operating system, I didn't want to take any chances.

Amena came up to the hatch and leaned inside to look around. "If you need me to do anything, I can do it."

I pinged her feed to acknowledge.

She watched me search for seven minutes and forty seconds, then said, "Can I ask you a question?"

I never know how to answer this. Should I go with my first impulse, which is always "no" or just give in to the inevitable? I said, "Is it contract-relevant?"

Big, adolescent human sigh noise. "I just want to understand something."

I gave in to the inevitable. "Yes."

She hesitated. "Right, umm. So my second mom really didn't ask you to break up me and Marne?"

I had answered that question already, back when it happened. I could get mad at her asking it again, but granted, I do lie a lot. "I wasn't lying to you. She doesn't know anything about it unless you told her."

I finished the search of the cabin and pinged ART. It generated a display surface with a disabled feed interface so it couldn't transmit anything that might be in the shuttle's systems to ART, me, or anything else.

Amena still had questions. "Then why did you do it? You didn't—you don't—care about me. You didn't really even know me then."

Why does ART like adolescent humans? This was exhausting.

"I have files on all the members of Dr. Mensah's family and their associates. I alerted on Marne because I ran threat assessments on all humans and augmented humans attempting to approach or form new relationships with Dr. Mensah or her family or associates after the GrayCris incident. Marne registered as a threat to you."

Amena thought about that while I made a connection between the console and the sequestered display surface. Then I started to run the shuttle's raw log files on the display, filtering out anything that wasn't text. I was recording the information visually, and then I could convert it back to data fields and search it more quickly. That way we'd get the log information without any underlying code that might be hidden in it. (There are visual elements that could cause me problems, but I could screen for those and granted, the chances that the log file might be protected against a SecUnit doing a visual download were running under 5 percent.) (I know, I'm paranoid, but that's how I've avoided being rendered for spare parts all this time.) Amena said slowly, "I guess if he wasn't . . . He would have wanted to explain himself, instead of running off and refusing to speak to me again."

As far as my threat assessment was concerned, running off and never seeing her again was an excellent result. I was pretty sure Amena wouldn't want to hear that, though.

She continued, "I thought he was nice. I'm not . . . I know at the time I said I knew what I was doing, but I'm actually not very good at meeting new people."

I knew from threat assessments on Ratthi's associates that he had a lot of relationships with all genders of humans and augmented humans and he and they all seemed very happy about it. Amena should ask him for advice. I didn't think she wanted to hear that, either.

Then Amena said, "Do you love my second mother? Thiago thinks so."

I should have known this was going to turn into an interrogation. I said, "Not the way he thinks."

Her face went all dubious. "I don't think you know what he thinks."

He doesn't know what I think, either, so there. I was distracted converting a dumpload of raw log info from a visual image back into searchable data and if I got the fields wrong it was going to be a giant mess. I probably should have just stopped talking, but I didn't want to hurt Amena's feelings. I said, "Your second mother is . . ." *Client* wasn't the right word, not anymore. "My teammate." I could see I had to clarify. It was really hard finding the right words. "Before your second mother, I had never been an actual member of a team before. Just an . . ."

Amena finished, "An appliance for a team."

That was it. "Yes."

"I see. Thank you for letting me ask you questions."

ART must be recovering because it had to butt in with, *Tell her you care about her. Use those words, don't tell her you'll eviscerate anything that tries to hurt her.*

ART, fuck off.

The thing ART has in common with human adolescents is that it doesn't like to hear the word "no," either. It persisted, *Tell her. It's true. Just say it. Human adolescents need to hear it from their caretakers.*

I'm not a caretaker, I told ART. I finished the log conversion and checked my drone view of Amena. She was leaning in the hatchway, her head propped on the seal buffer. (That isn't a good place to put your head, just FYI.) From her expression, she was either falling asleep or deep in thought. Or possibly both. I said, "You need to sleep."

She yawned. "Okay, third mom."

□　　□　　□

Arada finally ordered the others to take a rest period, though it took her a while to really understand that ART and I would still be active and there was no reason for the humans to take shifts. (I finally had to tell her that I had a list of things I needed to get done and it would go much faster if they would all stay in one place and shut up for a while and sleeping was the most efficient use of that time.)

Overse had finished repairing the repair drone and sent it off to begin the rebuilds of ART's other drones. She was sleeping on a couch in the lounge next to the galley with Ratthi, who had finished the biohazard cleanup. There was snoring.

Arada was sleeping in one of the station chairs on the control deck. (They're very comfortable, so it's not as bad as it sounds.)

The medical scans had finished and Thiago walked Eletra back to her bunkroom. He hadn't gotten much more out of her than Amena had, though his questions were more subtle. With his prompting, Eletra had gone over her augment clock and was now severely confused. It showed their transport had been in this system for forty-three corporation standard days. She was certain that was wrong. It was more support for the theory that Eletra had undergone some kind of memory manipulation. The initial scan analysis showed no genetic manipulation, no hidden devices or non-human biologicals.

All my remaining drones were on sentry duty, but I made Amena go to an unused bunkroom near the galley because it was easier to defend if we were attacked by something. (It was unlikely, but so was everything unexpected that had happened so far. My risk assessment module had given up generating reports three hours ago.)

Amena tried to just lie down on the bare bunk and pillow her head on the sealed bedding pack but I made her get up and unfold it and do it right. ("You're mean," she groaned.)

I opened another bedding pack so my bunk would be more comfortable to sit on. I had a lot of coding and analysis to do so I wouldn't be caught unprepared again. I needed to create workarounds for the drone-resistant camouflage on the targetDrones and countermeasures for the Target's helmets and gear. I also needed to anticipate how targetControlSystem would countermeasure my countermeasures so I wouldn't be screwed by an on-the-fly software update. I needed to analyze the solid-state screen device and find out if it really was a Pre–Corporation Rim relic. And I had to analyze the new data files I had just created from the shuttle's logs.

I pulled in the data Ratthi had uploaded to the feed during his pathology examinations and the scans of the Targets' suits and helmets. Overse had also done some helpful hardware analysis of the targetDrones. Then I got my queries and processes running so I could get started on the code. I also split off an input and started *World Hoppers* episode 1. I'd seen it before (lots of times before) so I didn't need to give it my full attention.

(I really, really wanted some time to pull a new show out of longterm storage and watch a few episodes so I could really relax, but *World Hoppers* in background would help. It was also bait.)

After twenty-seven minutes, it worked. I was aware of ART looming in my feed. (Imagine sitting in front of a display surface and someone eight times your size shoulders in and sits in the chair with you.) It was watching *World Hoppers,* and also back-seat driving my coding and doing its own analysis of the data. *The solid-state screen device does resemble known schematics of Pre–Corporation Rim technology,* ART reported, showing me a scan and the matching examples. *But it is not a factory-built unit; it was assembled from components gleaned from other devices of similar age.* No trace of alien remnant or known strange synthetics detected.

That made sense. It could have been a replacement unit built by humans in the Pre–Corporation Rim colony. Or a unit built by the later abandoned corporate humans, with parts desperately scavenged from the old colony, as their own tech resources failed and they struggled to survive.

Yeah, corporations suck.

I liked the code we were coming up with, but I didn't think it was enough. None of it was making my threat assessment stats look any better. I told ART, *Everything we're doing is defensive. We need an attack.*

I've considered constructing a killware assault, but the data I managed to retain from targetControlSystem suggests it would be ineffective. ART displayed some analysis for me. *Both Ratthi and Overse have theorized that some elements of the Targets' Pre-Corporation Rim technology—for example, the implants—may be acting as receivers for esoteric alien remnant tech, like the object that affected my drive. A standard killware assault on the Pre-CR systems would not be able to take into account the alien system, not unless it was variable and could alter its behavior based on the protections and obstructions it encounters. I can't code that with the resources I have available.*

It was talking about something similar to the self-aware virus that GrayCris and Palisade Security had deployed against the company gunship, where I'd crashed myself and nearly wrecked my memory archive helping the bot pilot fight it off. Which gave me an idea, but I didn't know if it was something we could implement.

Then Thiago crossed through the galley, came down our corridor, and leaned in the doorway. Watching him through ART's camera view, I saw him glance at Amena, who at the moment was an inert pile of limbs under a blanket with a pillow jammed into her face. (Humans do everything weird, including rest.) Then he looked at me. Keeping his voice low, he said, "May I join you?"

ART engaged the sound/privacy field on Amena's bunk. I thought about saying "no." But I thought he wanted to sleep on one of the bunks within sight of Amena because he didn't trust me to take care of her. So I marked my killware idea as save-for-later and said, "Yes."

He sat down on the bunk across from me, pulled the bedding pack out from under it, but then set it aside.

Oh good, we're going to have a chat.

"If you have a moment, I was hoping we could talk," he said.

I could have said that I didn't have a moment what with writing code to save humans from whatever the stupid Targets were but I did have a moment. ART had constructed a simulation of the software fix that had protected the Targets' helmets and gear from my drone strikes and was running tests of my new targeting code for my drones. The targetDrones' camouflage was harder to crack due to being a physical effect rather than something caused by signal interference. None of the filters I'd come up with for the drones' scan or targeting functions would work, at least according to the simulations. Continuing to ram my head into that particular wall wasn't going to get me anywhere until I thought up an alternate approach. So instead of being an asshole, I just said, "Go ahead."

He said, "I know you don't believe it, but I was glad you came along on this survey."

Oh, please. I could have played the audio recording I had of what he had said to Dr. Mensah about me, but that was a little incriminating with the whole listening to private conversations in secured spaces and personal dwellings thing. I said, "So you didn't have serious reservations?"

There was that little flash of surprise some humans have when I say something that doesn't sound like what their idea of a Sec-Unit should say. He said, slowly, "I did." It had been too long for a human to remember what he had said verbatim and he didn't know I was quoting him. Still, his eyes narrowed a little. "And I know you've saved our lives." He hesitated.

There was an unvoiced "but" on the end of that sentence. I didn't want to spend a lot of time on this, so I said, "But you don't like the way I did it."

His gaze went hard and he said, "I don't. And I don't like the fact that Amena saw you do it. But that's not the problem."

On our private connection, ART said, *Don't ask the question unless you already know the answer.*

Right, so I didn't listen to ART. I said, "What problem?"

ART did the feed equivalent of rolling its eyes and started another episode of *World Hoppers*.

Thiago said, "You have leverage over Ayda."

That one got me. Fortunately ART was keeping track of the processes so I didn't screw up the data analysis. It also provided a definition of the word leverage. *I know what it means,* I told ART privately. And I did, but not the way Thiago meant. I think. I said, "I don't tell Dr. Mensah what to do."

Thiago's jaw went tight. "I'm sure you didn't. But she's afraid to carry out her duties as council leader. She won't apply to continue her term. That's because of you. You've made her afraid of shadows. She never needed 'security' before you came to Preservation. Now she thinks she can't do her job without it."

There were so many things wrong and unfair and yet true about that I started dropping inputs. ART picked them up and transferred them to our shared workspace. I said, "I didn't come to Preservation. I was brought there in an inactive state after incurring a catastrophic failure while saving Dr. Mensah's life."

"I know that." Thiago waved a hand in frustration. "I'm saying—"

No, I get to talk now. "There was a security threat. After Dr. Mensah returned to Preservation Station, three GrayCris operatives were sent to kill her. They failed but there was a sixty-five percent chance that more operatives would be sent. That percentage started to fall after the bond company destroyed Palisade Security and all of GrayCris' operational facilities."

It was GrayCris' own fault for ordering Palisade Security to attack an expensive company gunship and Palisade's fault for escalating past standard operational parameters, but try telling GrayCris that. And it wasn't like the company was afraid of GrayCris, but they had to teach them a lesson. (The lesson was: if you're going to fuck with something bigger and meaner than you, use a quick targeted attack and then run away really fast. (This is the way I always try to operate, too.) GrayCris' attack had not been quick and targeted and they had failed to run away effectively.)

Thiago had his mouth open but I was still talking. "There was, and is, still a potential danger from individual dependents or employees of GrayCris but threat assessment determined that the percentage is low enough for Dr. Mensah to resume normal activities with the assistance of Preservation Station Security."

It took Thiago fourteen seconds to digest that. "There was an attack? Why didn't she tell us— It would have been in the newsstream—"

I pulled the video from my archive and quickly edited in the views from the Station Security helmet cams and the one lousy security cam in the lobby of the council offices on station. ART studied it curiously. I sent it to autoplay in Thiago's feed.

His gaze went distant, then startled, then increasingly appalled.

ART watched the full video, running it back and forth. I had sent Thiago the part where I was on top of the council table trying to snap Hostile One's neck while Hostile Two was on my back stabbing the absolute crap out of me. Six Station Security officers were draped around the room in various states of consciousness, with Officer Tifany, the only one still functional, hanging on to the stabbing arm of Hostile Two and punching him repeatedly in the head. ART commented, *What is that human stabbing you with?*

Part of a broken chair.

"They're SecUnits?" Thiago asked, horrified.

I can see why he might think that. I said, "They're augmented humans who were chemically enhanced. They don't feel pain, their reflexes and reaction times are accelerated. They have the physical strength of a SecUnit, but not the feed connectivity or processing capacity. So they're harder to detect, and even more disposable." To be fair, at this point GrayCris probably couldn't get any other security companies licensed to produce and/or deploy SecUnits to contract with them. Between the high-risk assessment and the lack of operating funds and the cheating/attacking contract partners, GrayCris wasn't a good client.

Thiago took a breath, made himself calm down. "But they won't send anyone else? You said the threat percentage dropped—"

"It's at an acceptable level." And it hadn't been easy to get it to that level, either.

Thiago watched me with a concentrated intensity I didn't like. ART's camera didn't have a full-face view, but it was obvious even with the angle. "Then why did she decide not to take a second term?"

"She didn't quit because she was afraid, you asshole, she quit because she needs to start the trauma support treatment at Central Medical. She didn't tell anyone in her extended family because being taken hostage—"

In our private connection, ART said, *Stop.*

ART has different ways of telling you to stop doing what you're doing, with different threat levels, and this was toward the top of the list.

I stopped. ART explained, *You're violating her privacy.*

I was pissed off, because of course ART was right. I said, *What do you know about it?*

My MedSystem is certified in emotional support and trauma recovery.

Ugh, ART did know everything. It was so annoying. I finished, "She wanted me to go on Arada's survey. I told her I would, but she had to agree to start the treatment. That was the leverage I had."

He was still watching me, and I couldn't tell if he believed me. His expression was conflicted and I think he was still shocked at the recording. (It had looped through to the end of the clip where stupid Hostile One finally went inert and I rolled myself, Hostile Two, and Tifany off the table. Now Hostile Two was trying to strangle Tifany and I was prying him off her.)

ART said aloud, in its polite-but-actually-not-a-suggestion voice, *We have work to do, Thiago, and you're missing your rest period. Perhaps you should go.*

It startled Thiago, but he pushed to his feet. He said, "You're right, I'll go."

I stopped the clip and watched him on ART's cameras. He

went back to the galley lounge and took one of the other couches. He sat there for a while rubbing his face, then got up to get water from the galley and take a medication tab.

What is that? I asked ART.

A mild pain reliever, for headaches and muscle discomfort.

When Thiago went to lie down on the couch, I relaxed a little. He had thought I was taking advantage of Dr. Mensah? I still wasn't even sure what he meant. Did he think I was making her feel sorry for me? Hey, I hadn't asked her to buy me. I hadn't even been there when it happened, I had been still stuck in a cubicle in reconstruction at that point.

I wish I could feel all vindicated, but I didn't think that confrontation had gone well for either me or Thiago. I think he knew now that his view of the situation was inaccurate but I had gotten mad and stupidly admitted to blackmailing Dr. Mensah to go start the trauma treatment. So. I didn't know what was going to happen, if, you know, we survived and stuff and got back to Preservation. Like I needed something else to worry about right now.

ART said, *You haven't seen the obvious solution to the target-Drone camouflage problem.*

Obvious? I said. (I know, I was just making it worse. ART wouldn't have framed it that way if it wasn't something that was going to make me feel like an idiot for missing.)

ART said, *Modify your drones with a camouflage field that will display the same interference pattern as the Targets' helmets and gear. They still won't be able to strike the targetDrones, but then your supply is so limited that attack is now no longer viable.*

Well, now I feel even more stupid.

ART said, *You have time for a recharge cycle.*

I was going to tell it I didn't need one. And I really didn't. But I knew what I did need. I shifted everything over to our shared workspace and pulled up the first episode of *Timestream Defenders Orion.* I asked ART, *Do you want* World Hoppers *or something new?*

ART considered, poking thoughtfully at the tag data for the new show. It said, *New, as long as it's not realistic.*

I'd downloaded *Timestream Defenders Orion* off the Preservation media archives because it was pretty much the opposite of the whole concept of realistic. I started the first episode.

We watched it while ART finished our code, occasionally sending sections to me to check over. (Possibly it was humoring me. ART might still have memory archive gaps, but there was nothing wrong with its other functions.)

Twenty-six minutes to the end of the designated rest period, ART said, *Using the data from the shuttle, I've located one of the Barish-Estranza vessels. My engine repairs are complete and I am moving to intercept.*

HelpMe.file Excerpt 3

(Section from interview Bharadwaj-108257394.)

"It's normal to feel conflict. You were part of something for a long time. You hate it, and it was a terrible thing. But it created you, and you were part of it."

:session redacted:
(File detached from main narrative.)

I was sitting on top of Hostile Two to make sure he was dead. He had been apparently dead at least twice, so this wasn't misplaced caution. Tifany was on her knees beside me, her weapon pointed at his head. "You're too close," I told her.

She looked at me, the skin around her eyes so swollen and puffy I'm not sure how well she could see. Then she edged back out of potential arm's reach.

Behind me, in the one stupid security camera, I saw the human second response team and their medical assistance bots belatedly crash through the door. I checked the time and wow, scratch that "belatedly." This had been a fast incident, even by SecUnit standards of fast.

The Preservation council meeting room was a big oval with a long table in the middle, the walls lined with tall narrow windows, two entrances/exits on either end of the room. The one the second response team had come through led to the foyers and station government's public offices where humans came to take care of things that couldn't be taken care of on the feed, I guess, I actually had no idea. The other door led into the private offices where the occupants of the council room had managed to evacuate to when the incident occurred.

Senior Officer Indah circled around the table and knelt down where I could see her. She said, "Is that person dead?"

"Probably but there's a seventeen percent chance he might revive," I said.

Tifany, her voice a strained rasp, said, "He came back twice. We need a containment unit."

Indah's brow furrowed. "On the way." She reached over to Tifany and carefully coaxed the weapon out of her hands. "You're off duty now, officer."

Tifany said, "Yes, senior," and folded over onto the floor.

"She's had a hard day," I told Indah.

"I inferred that." Indah tapped her feed and a spidery-legged medical bot picked its way past me to crouch beside Tifany. Making comforting noises, it scanned her and immediately injected her with something. Indah said, "You need medical assistance, too."

I had a stab wound so large you could see the metal of my interior structure, but Senior Indah was too polite to mention it. The medical bot extended a delicate sensor limb toward me. On the feed I told it anything it touched me with would get torn off and thrown across the room. It pulled the limb back and used it to check Hostile Two instead.

"Is there any hope for the subject?" Indah jerked her chin toward Hostile Two.

I didn't think there had been a person inside Hostile Two since before the first time we killed him. "Probably not."

I stayed in position until containment arrived to take care of our mostly dead Hostile Two and the hopefully all the way dead Hostile One. Tifany and the rest of the first response team had already been carried off to Station Medical. I went the other direction, further into the council/admin offices because I needed to see her.

I found her only three unsecured doors away, but at least it was an office without a balcony or windows onto the admin mezzanine. I walked past Station Security and admin personnel. They should have tried to stop me but (a) it wasn't like they didn't know who I was and (b) it was a good thing they didn't try to stop me.

Mensah was watching the door and when I walked in her shoulders relaxed. She knew the hostiles had been secured and that the first response team had survived; she had command access to the Station Security feed and she'd been monitoring it from in here. There was a security lockdown on the public and private council feeds right now and we needed to get them restored soon, before anybody outside the offices noticed. We had to keep GrayCris from knowing this attack had nearly succeeded. It would give them too much intel about what to do next.

Mensah met me in the middle of the room and did the hand thing that meant she wanted to grab me but knew I wouldn't like it. She said, "You need to go to Medical."

There was dried blood on the tunic she was wearing, and on the right knee of her pants. Hostile One had charged at her across the council table and I'd stopped him literally a half-meter away from her. She could have reached out and patted his head.

And that was after chasing him all the way here from the transit ring, while Hostile Two was trying to kill me. Slowing down Hostile Two long enough for me to mostly take out Hostile One was what had sent the entire first response security team to Station Medical. They were just lucky Two had been focused on trying to get past them and not slaughtering every human in the way.

I said, "I can't go to Medical yet. There's something I have to do first."

Her expression was drawn. "Do you need help? Indah's called in the off-duty personnel. I can get you a team."

"No, I just want to make sure I know how they got onto the station." She nodded and let me go.

So yeah, I'd lied to her.

= =

11

I sent a wake-up call through the comm. While the humans in the galley lounge were staggering around trying to get conscious, ART fed the visual and scan images into the general feed. Amena rolled out of her bunk, blearily focused on the images, and muttered, "So is this good or bad or what?"

"It's 'or what,'" I told her.

ART's scan image showed the Barish-Estranza supply transport, a mid-sized configuration with capacity to carry multiple landing shuttles and large terrain vehicles. Crew complement was estimated at thirty plus. The schematic looked like several rounded tubes bundled together with odd sharp pieces sticking out in places. The visual image just showed the long dark shape, light from the primary star catching the top of a curve.

ART said, *Long-range scan indicates systemic damage though some systems including life support show operational. Aft and starboard hull and the engine housing show signs of three distinct weapons strikes, but the pattern does not match my weapons system.*

That last part was good. If ART had been the one to fire on the supply transport, it would have meant my adjusted timeline was wrong and that I'd been wading in ART's ocean of status updates for nothing.

Amena stumbled out of the bunkroom and followed me to the galley where Thiago, Overse, and Ratthi were.

"So there was a space fight, just not the fight *Perihelion* remembered." Ratthi had gotten some packets and bottles out of the prep area for the humans. Amena took one of each and sat down at the table.

"We think the Barish-Estranza explorer vessel was armed, correct?" Arada was still on the control deck, much more alert, looking at the multiple displays ART had put up for her. One of ART's newly repaired drones floated around behind her, using light filters to disinfect the stations and chairs. Arada absently stood up and moved her drink bottle so it could do her station. "Any chance we can tell if it caused the weapon strikes?"

Not without an analysis of the explorer's weapons system for comparison, ART said. *Scan indicates minimal power in the engine module. That may be the reason they have not attempted to flee through the wormhole.*

Thiago rubbed his face, trying to wake himself up. "If they fought with their own explorer, they might be more willing to talk to us. Can you tell if there's anyone aboard?"

I assume so. ART was dry. *They are attempting comm contact.*

"Don't answer it," I told ART. "That's probably how you got into this situation in the first place."

Ratthi waved his drink bottle in what he thought was ART's direction. "Yes, please be careful. There was a terrible virus on a company ship and we all nearly died and SecUnit's brain was compromised."

SecUnit's brain is always compromised, ART said. *And I was not breached via the comm. My comm system is filtered to prevent viral attacks and I have engaged extra protections.*

"That's probably what you said right before it happened," I told it. But ART insulting my intelligence was a good sign. It sounded almost normal again.

Amena sighed and wiped crumbs off her mouth. "Hey, you two, it's too early for fighting."

Arada was doing her mouth-twisted expression again. She said, "*Perihelion,* if you think it's safe, can you allow contact?"

Overse hastily swallowed her food. "Babe, is that a good idea?"

Arada made an open-handed shrug gesture. "I don't know

how else to figure out what's going on here, babe. If we can get a visual and they're all gray people wearing alien remnants on their heads, then at least we'll know they probably won't want to help us." She added, "And if we're a lot more lucky than we usually are, they'll have some idea where the explorer with *Perihelion*'s people is."

That wasn't unreasonable. My threat assessment module didn't like it, but if we could get intel this way it might mean we could find ART's humans sooner.

Thiago pressed his steepled fingers to his mouth, then said, "I agree. We know the explorer is compromised. If it attacked them, or if there's another ship we haven't encountered yet, we need to know."

Ratthi shrugged agreement. Overse didn't look happy, but she didn't argue. Amena was still eating, eyes wide.

ART said, *Accepting contact.*

A new display appeared above the scan results on the control deck. The static swirled artistically into an image of a human or augmented human wearing the same red and brown uniform as Eletra and Ras. With impatience, the human said, "Unidentified transport, are you receiving this?"

ART pulled feed information from the transmission and ran it across the display. Name: Supervisor Leonide, augmented, Barish-Estranza Exploration Services ID, gender: female, femme-neutral.

I wasn't surprised she was a supervisor. (I had worked with a lot of human corporate supervisors and after a while they were fairly easy to identify.) Her skin was one of the mid browns that was common to a large percentage of humans but it had an artificially smooth even tone that indicated cosmetic enhancement. (My skin was less even than hers and it gets completely regenerated on a regular basis due to me being shot in the face.) Her dark hair was wrapped around the top of her head and she had small metallics and gemstones set in the rim of one exposed ear. I thought there was a 49 percent chance that she was a much more important supervisor than the feed signature indicated.

Arada sat up and squared her shoulders. The drone snatched the empty food packet from the console beside her and retreated out of camera range. She ran her fingers through her short hair and said, "Right. When you're ready, *Perihelion*."

Of course. ART put up another display showing Arada. It had changed the color of her jacket from Preservation Survey gray to the blue of its crew uniform, edited out the water bottle on the console beside her, and artistically adjusted the lighting. Arada planted a serious expression on her face as ART said, *I've sent my identifier and a Corporation Rim feed indicator stating that you are Dr. Arada of the Pansystem University of Mihira and New Tideland.*

Arada said, "Supervisor Leonide, we see your transport is in distress."

"We are, and would appreciate any assistance." Leonide's expression was opaque but vaguely critical. "But this system is under claim by Barish-Estranza, so I wonder why you're here."

Amena made the huffy noise indicating disbelief and/or incredulity. *For the love of light,* Ratthi said on the feed, disgusted. *Are they really worried about that now?*

ART was in Arada's feed supplying an answer, and Arada repeated, "We have a contract for sustainability evaluation and mapping with the Pan-Rim Licensing Agency and this system was listed as a priority. I assure you, the University is not a terraforming entity, and we have no intention of violating your claim." Arada's serious expression was a little too fixed, but it got more natural when she added, "I see you've taken damage—were you attacked by raiders?" The next hesitation wasn't calculated at all. "We've been in this system only a short time, and encountered some . . . strange activity."

On a side display in the galley, ART was breaking down Leonide's opaque expression for us with a feed-superimposed analysis. She was experiencing everything from irritation to reluctant resignation. She said, "There are raiders here. As we've discovered."

Arada pressed her lips together and looked thoughtful. I had a bad feeling she was about to call Leonide a liar—which we all knew Leonide was lying but even I knew that wouldn't make this interaction any easier. Then Arada said on the feed, *I'm going to tell her we have Eletra.*

But you just told Leonide we're Perihelion's crew, Overse objected. *Eletra knows we're from Preservation.*

She knows Amena is from Preservation, I sent.

Yes, ART told me to tell Eletra you all were part of its crew, Amena confirmed.

I was doing a rapid search of my recording of all the conversations in Eletra's hearing since the others had come aboard, particularly when Thiago had spoken to her. *None of the rest of you told her you were from Preservation. And some of you are wearing ART's crew clothing.*

Overse looked down at the T-shirt she was wearing. *Oh, you're right.*

ART had thrown in some static to give Arada time to think. Now she said to Leonide, "I don't think they're ordinary raiders. We have one of your crew on board, a young person named Eletra. She was captured in a shuttle by some very divergent raiders, who also attacked our ship. She was with another crew member called Ras, but he was injured when he was captured by the raiders and died before our medical facility could help him."

Leonide's expression went through some rapid calculations. "How did they get aboard your ship, then?"

(In the feed, Amena was worried. *But Eletra's really confused,* she said. *She's not going to be able to tell them much about what happened. Will they believe her? They won't accuse her of helping the Targets or something, will they? Or do something terrible to her?*

She needs more help than we can give her, Thiago told her, *and she wants to go home to her family. This may be her only chance.*

Much as Amena might want to forcibly adopt Eletra and drag her off to Preservation, Thiago was right.)

Arada was saying, "They were brought aboard by the raiders

who tried to take us prisoner. I can let you speak to Eletra if you'd like. She's physically well, but we know they used some sort of mind-altering tech—"

You're talking too much, ART told her on the feed, right as I was about to say it. Overse must have thought so, too, because she made a faint noise of agreement. Arada stopped and ART added a little artistic static to give her a chance to regroup and to show her that its analysis of Leonide's expression revealed a spike of extreme interest at the words "mind-altering tech." Arada cleared her throat and said, "So, maybe you could be more forthcoming. We're ready to render assistance if you need it."

Leonide's hesitation was more pronounced this time, and her expression said she was conflicted. She said finally, "I'm not al-lowed to speak further about this on a comm channel not confi-dential to Barish-Estranza. I'd appreciate the return of our crew member. One of our engine components was destroyed in the attack—if you could sell us replacement components, our pay rate would be fair and generous."

"We don't—" Arada was going to say "need your payment" and the humans and I all yelled *No!* on the feed. But ART had her on a one-second delay and stopped her before it got any worse.

It was a natural mistake on Arada's part. In Preservation culture, asking payment for anything considered necessary for living (food, power sources, education, the feed, etc.) was con-sidered outrageous, but asking payment for life-saving help was right up there with cannibalism.

Arada coughed and continued, "Of course, we'll prepare an invoice. But . . ." She leaned forward. "I think we both know how bad this situation is, and how much danger our crews are in right now. If we could be honest with each other and share information, I think we can better our chances of survival."

Yeah, she had gone there way too quickly. The other humans had stopped breathing. Amena looked at me with an *oh shit* expression. Yes, I know, but there's nothing I can do about it. Arada's risk assessment module was as bad as mine.

Leonide's expression was complex. She said, after 8.7 fraught seconds where she might have been consulting with someone on her own feed (hopefully not a gray Target person), "Your crew is still in danger?"

Arada said, "Because I think we met your explorer. It was the ship that attacked us, and temporarily boarded us, and our wormhole capability is now damaged."

Ratthi made a *mmph* noise. Thiago was pressing his folded hands against his mouth again.

Leonide's lips set in a hard line. "I see. I still can't speak on a nonconfidential channel."

Arada hesitated and Ratthi whispered to me, "What—can we make the channel confidential? What does that entail?"

I told him, "Not without a Corporation Rim solicitor certified by Barish-Estranza."

Ratthi groaned under his breath.

On the feed, ART was explaining the same thing to Arada. She said to Leonide, "Would you be willing to come aboard and speak about it in person?"

(I had a camera view of the lower part of the control deck where the drone was now sterilizing the area where Targets One and Three had died. It started working faster.)

Leonide snorted. "Your University's confidentiality agreement would hardly cover me."

Arada gave her a good "it was worth a shot" smile, like she had any clue what Leonide meant. Then Leonide said, "But I'd allow you to come aboard my transport for a conference."

Thiago took a sharp breath. Ratthi's expression went extremely skeptical. Amena made a derisive noise. Overse said, "Fuck no."

On our private connection, ART said, *Should I cut the contact?*

No, I told it, *she won't do it.* We already had a way to get intel off the transport. We could send drones along with the supplies—

Then Arada said, "I can do that. If you'll send me the list of supplies you need, I'll get my team working on that, and we can arrange the transfer of supplies and your crew person and the meeting at the same time."

What? The other humans all looked at me, appalled. I was also appalled.

Leonide kept her expression neutral. "Agreed, though I'd like to speak to my crew member first."

Arada said, "Agreed. Give me a moment to arrange that."

ART put the contact on hold and said, *Clear.* And then it did one of my what-the-hell-have-the-humans-done-now sighs.

□   □   □

Obviously, there was a big human argument.

In order to head off the inevitable "I told you so," I said to ART, *I should have told you to cut the contact.*

ART said to me, *Yes, you should have.*

To the others, it said, *They've sent the list of components. Since we're now committed to this . . . course of action, I've ordered a drone to pull the material out of storage. And I'm producing standard crew clothing for Arada.*

By that point the argument had ended and Arada was still going to the supply transport, though all the humans had elevated heart rates indicating varying degrees of anger and exasperation.

Thiago's expression was grim. "If we're going to do this, we need to get Eletra ready to speak to Leonide. Maybe before that, she can tell us something about her. Amena, will you help?"

Amena tried not to look startled. "Huh? Oh sure, Uncle."

They headed down the corridor. Arada turned to Overse and said, "I know you're upset but this will save us a lot of time."

Overse said through gritted teeth, "Rescuing you—or trying to recover your body—will not save us time."

Ratthi pressed his hands over his eyes and dragged them down his face in a way that did not look comfortable. He said, "We need a plan. What are you going to say?"

In the corridor, Amena was saying, "I didn't think you'd want my help. I mean, you all think I'm impulsive."

"No one thinks that, my daughter." Thiago signaled through the feed to Eletra, telling her they wanted to come in. "Your parents wouldn't have let you come on this survey if they didn't trust your judgment."

From Amena's expression that was news to her, but the door to the bunkroom was already sliding open.

Overse was still mad, though when Ratthi asked for her help, she followed him down to the storage module to make sure the drones could shift the supply container into the bulk airlock. I could have helped, but I think Ratthi wanted to give Overse a chance to vent and calm down, and I did not want to be there for that.

Amena had just shown Eletra a feed image of Leonide and asked if she was really who she said she was.

At first, Eletra looked relieved. "Yes, that's Supervisor Leonide. She's in charge of the supply transport." Then her expression turned slowly confused. "The supply transport." She pressed her hands to her head. "Why am I not on the supply transport?"

"Can you speak to Supervisor Leonide on the comm?" Thiago asked her. "Just to tell her what happened to you?"

Eletra nodded, but said, "It's hard enough telling you, and you all were there." Her forehead creased again. "Weren't you?"

"Just tell her what you can," Thiago said gently, and ART used the display surface in the bunkroom to open the comm contact again.

I was worried enough to monitor the conversation, and I could feel ART's attention in the channel. But Eletra confirmed her capture by the Targets and said that she had been rescued by the ship's crew and their SecUnit. She gestured toward Amena. "And a young person, an intern from another survey company." She knew Ras had been killed but she wasn't sure how. When Leonide pushed her for details, she said, "The gray raiders, they put some kind of augment or something in us. It did something to us." She gestured at her head. "It's messed up my whole perception of time. I can't remember leaving the supply transport. Or the explorer—"

Leonide told her that was enough, and sent the connection to her cargo factor to arrange the transfer.

Arada's face was set in a wince, possibly in anticipation of further objections to her plan that everyone clearly hated. We were still standing in the lounge (I was going to change the name on ART's schematic to "Argument Lounge") and she looked tired. "Are you mad at me, too, SecUnit?"

I said, "Yes. I'm also going with you."

Really, I was the only one who needed to get over there, and it would be better than sending drones that I wouldn't be able to retrieve. But I don't think Supervisor Leonide, who wasn't too happy letting Arada visit, would say yes to the question "Hey can our SecUnit come over instead? It just wants to stand in your transport for, say, three minutes? No, no reason, it just enjoys looking at other people's ships."

On the feed, Overse said, *Yes, please. Arada, SecUnit has to go with you.* She sounded normal again. I had a camera view and audio on a tertiary input of her and Ratthi standing in the foyer to ART's bulk lock, with her waving her arms and talking angrily while he nodded sympathetically and three of ART's repaired drones hovered around them. It ended with her apologizing to Ratthi for venting at him and being angry at herself for getting angry at Arada during a crisis. I could play it back to listen in on the whole conversation but I could also punch myself in the head with a sampling drill and I was not going to do that, either.

(If I got angry at myself for being angry I would be angry constantly and I wouldn't have time to think about anything else.)

(Wait, I think I am angry constantly. That might explain a lot.)

Arada's expression was complicated, then it settled on relief. "Okay. I wasn't going to ask, but that's probably a very good idea." She took a shaky breath. "Thank you."

You don't have to thank me for doing my stupid job.

But it is nice.

In the bunkroom, Thiago was trying to reassure Eletra. He told her, "You sound much better. I think speaking to someone you know helped."

I sent to Amena, *Ask her if there are SecUnits on either the explorer or the transport.*

Amena did. With what seemed a reasonable amount of confidence under the circumstances, Eletra said, "Yes, there were three on the explorer."

"But none on the supply transport?" Amena clarified.

Eletra nodded. "Right. The explorer carries the contact party. Everyone on the transport is support staff."

I told Amena, *Ask her if the SecUnits were made by Barish-Estranza, or if they were contracted rentals.* I didn't think they would be company units—the last thing you wanted when you were asserting rights over an unclaimed colony was the company getting its greedy datamining hands all over it.

Amena repeated the question, adding to me, *"Rentals" is a creepy way to talk about people.*

Yes, Amena, no shit, I know that. (And I knew this was all new and horrifying to Amena but it was just same old same old for me and Eletra and her permanently indentured family. Which was why I was saying this silently to myself instead of out loud to the whole ship.)

Eletra answered, "No, there wasn't any contracted equipment involved in this job. They didn't want to chance another corporation finding out what we were doing."

Thiago watched Amena thoughtfully, as if he suspected she was talking to me on the feed. Then Eletra's expression started to drift again and he hurriedly distracted her with a question about her family.

Amena said on our private feed, *You're going with Arada?*

Yes, I told her.

Amena said, *If there were three SecUnits on the explorer, why didn't they stop the Targets from . . . taking over, or whatever they did? And the Targets didn't seem to have any idea what you were.*

I told her, *The SecUnits on the explorer would have been under the control of a supervisor, either directly or through a HubSystem. If the Targets got control of either, the SecUnits would have to obey an order to stand down.* Which is why I hate hostage situations. You have to get in there fast and neutralize the hostage-takers. They can't make threats and force you to do stuff you don't want to do if they're unconscious or dead. *If the Targets knew what I was, they may have thought they could order you to stop me.*

Amena snorted. *Sure, right.*

Amena was implying that I wouldn't listen to her, which, right, I wouldn't, not in that situation. But also, there was so much about the Targets that we didn't understand. It was a data vacuum big enough for us all to fall in and die, including ART.

Arada's expression had gone preoccupied. The Barish-Estranza manager had sent the specs for the needed supplies and transfer logistics and she was going over it with ART in the feed. Then she asked me, "So they'll know you're a SecUnit because Eletra will tell them, so . . . how should we handle that?"

I wasn't sure what "that" meant. But I wasn't sure Arada knew what "that" meant, either. Her experience with SecUnits was limited to exclusively me. I said, "I'll be the SecUnit the University provided for your security."

I really expected ART to weigh in here, at least with some kind of rude noise. But it didn't comment.

Listening on the feed, Ratthi was dubious about the whole idea. *Wouldn't you be wearing armor then?*

"Not necessarily. Some contracts require SecUnits to patrol living spaces and that's usually done in uniform instead of armor." There are standardization guides for the manufacture of constructs but most humans wouldn't know that. As long as I didn't have to walk into a deployment center filled with Sec-Units and the human techs who built and disassembled us, my risk assessment module thought everything was great. (I know, it worries me when I say that, too.)

Then ART said, *Your configuration no longer matches SecUnit standard.* ART knew all about that because it was the one who had altered my configuration to help me pass as an augmented human. That combined with the code I'd written to change the way I moved, to add the random movements, hesitations, blinking, and all the things that said "human" to other humans, made it easier to get by, though I'd still had to rely a lot on hacking weapons scanners.

"That's right." Arada turned to me, her brow pinching up in worry. "You look different since we first met you. You've let your hair grow out a little."

Some of ART's changes to my configuration had been subtle— longer head hair, more visible eyebrows, the kind of fine, nearly invisible hair humans had on large sections of their skin, the way my organic skin met my inorganic parts. Other changes had been structural, to make sure scanners searching for standard SecUnit specifications wouldn't hit on me. "I also got shorter," I told her.

"Did you?" Startled, Arada stepped back, eyeing the top of my head.

Lack of attention to detail is one of the reasons humans shouldn't do their own security.

But humans do detect subliminal details and react to them whether they're consciously aware of it or not. Even on Preservation (especially on Preservation) I ran my code to make my movement and body language more human to keep from drawing attention. I was running it now out of habit. When I stopped it, I'd look a lot more like a "normal" SecUnit even without armor. (Normal = neutral expression concealing existential despair and brain-crushing boredom.)

Arada and Ratthi still wanted to argue, so I said, "If they ask—and they won't ask—say I'm an academic model designed specifically for your university."

ART said, *I would prefer you go as an augmented human.*

What I really needed right now was a giant omniscient machine intelligence second-guessing me. "I don't care what you prefer," I said. It was safer this way. We were trying to tell one big lie—that we were ART's crew—and it would be easier to make that believable if we kept the smaller lies to a minimum. The fact that I was a SecUnit and that Arada had contracted for me as security was true, if in a different way than the corporates would assume. I could have said all that, but instead I said, "It's my decision and you can shut up."

"Don't fight," Amena said, coming back into the galley. Thiago was heading to the bulk lock to help Overse and Ratthi.

Arada was still watching me dubiously, absently humming and tapping her teeth, and I realized there was another problem. To Arada, I wasn't her SecUnit, I was her coworker and she was my team captain. That's a whole different spectrum of body language. Also, she wasn't even slightly afraid of me, and even my most confident and contemptuous corporate clients had always been just a little nervous, no matter how hard they tried to cover it. (The ones who weren't confident and contemptuous were incredibly nervous. It hadn't exactly been fun for me, either.) I asked her, "Can you treat me like a SecUnit?"

On the feed, Overse said, *Ummm*. She asked Arada, *Can you?*

"Sure." Arada shrugged, clearly having absolutely no idea what we meant by that.

Down in the module dock with Ratthi, Overse sighed. She told me, *Right. I'll work on that with her real quick before you go.*

I tapped her feed in acknowledgment. Arada demanded, "What?"

□   □   □

I went into an empty bunkroom to change into the crew uniform ART had just made me. It was dark blue, the pants and jacket of a deflective fabric that was way better than what Preservation Station Security had, with lots of sealable pockets for weapons and drones, plus stability-fabric boots so tough I could probably use them to jam a closing hatchway open. It looked like what a human security person would wear, it looked like what a SecUnit should wear instead of a cheaper version of the contract's uniform. I don't know, maybe security-company-owned SecUnits wore something like this. It had ART's crew logo on the jacket, but somehow that didn't bother me as much as usual.

I was a little worried the hair on my head would be noticed. After Milu, I had made it this length so I wouldn't look like a SecUnit and now I had to look like a SecUnit again. ART, watching me watching myself in a camera while poking at my head, pointed me to the bunkroom's attached bath where there was a dispenser for things humans needed. One was a lubricant-like substance that when I followed the instructions flattened my hair down so it looked shorter. That looked more SecUnit-like. Since ART had apparently decided to be helpful and stop sulking like a giant angry baby, I said, "Why do you want me to pretend to be an augmented human? This way is easier."

You don't like it, ART said.

"That's my problem." I didn't like it. But if you put everything that had happened to me on a scale of awfulness and assigned exact values to each incident (which I had done once, it's in my archive somewhere) dealing with corporates who exploited failed colonies, and probably went through SecUnits as fast as Amena did fried vegetable crunchy things, was in the lower third of the chart.

Despite what I'd told Amena, the existence of the SecUnits on the explorer worried me. If they had been captured and not destroyed, they were a way for the Targets to get intel about what I was capable of.

When my crew is at risk, it's my problem, ART said.

I was getting tired of being told what to do. Self-determination was a pain in the ass sometimes but it beat the alternative by a lot.

I made sure my collar was folded down so you could see my data port (though anybody who tried to stick a combat override module in there was going to get a violent surprise) and walked calmly out of the bunkroom into the galley. Amena was sitting on the table, frowning at me. She said, "What are you two fighting about now?"

ART said, *I made SecUnit's uniform too nice.*

Amena nodded. "You do look great."

I'm not even going to dignify that with a reaction.

Arada came back to the galley in her crew uniform, which was a less combat-ready version of mine. It was casual and practical and she looked comfortable and natural in it, which would help. "Are we ready?" she asked. "Let's go."

"Surely they won't suspect anything," Ratthi was saying to the others at the bulk dock. "Who runs around with a friendly rogue SecUnit? Besides us, I mean."

12

We used ART's EVAC suits, which were better than the ones the Preservation survey owned. (They had secondary internal protective suits for planetary exploration, not that we'd need them on the transport.) Though first I ran checks to make sure there was no contamination in their onboard systems. (It was unlikely—the power usage stats said the suits had been inactive throughout ART's whole memory disruption incident—but I was going to be paranoid until I figured out how ART had been attacked.) (I mean, I'll be paranoid after that, too, but only about the usual things.)

We were taking Eletra with us, and Arada had offered to bring Ras's body over, too, but Leonide had said it wasn't necessary and we could dispose of it. That upset the humans and it sort of upset me, too, which you wouldn't think it would, since the organic parts of dead SecUnits (and the parts that get shot off, cut off, crushed, whatever) go into the recyclers. But it did. As Ratthi put it, "You'd think they could at least pretend to give a damn."

ART had closed in to the Barish-Estranza transport and used its cargo tractors to maneuver the container of repair supplies over to the transport's module dock. Then Arada and I made the short trip to the transport's starboard airlock, with Eletra's suit in tow.

(On the way over, I made sure I had a private channel with Arada's EVAC suit, and I told her, "Remember, I'm not your co-worker or your employee or your bodyguard. I'm a tool, not a person." Overse had told her this earlier but I wanted to make sure she understood.

Arada made an unhappy noise. After 3.2 seconds, she said, "I understand. Don't worry.")

Preservation's ships are different, so stepping onto a Corporation Rim transport was familiar in a weird way. (A weirdly unpleasant way that disrupted the organic parts of my insides.) I had been shipped as cargo to all my contracts, so 90 percent of my experience with transports and bot pilots was after Dr. Mensah bought me and I'd left Port FreeCommerce. At least Eletra hadn't lied about the lack of SecUnits aboard; there was no HubSystem in place and they were using their own brand of proprietary tech and not company-standard. But the architecture was similar enough that by the time Arada and I cycled through the lock, their SecSystem thought I had full interactive permissions and their bot pilot had accepted me as a priority contact.

I could do a lot with that. They were lucky we weren't here to hurt them.

The airlock foyer held four humans in the red-brown Barish-Estranza corporate livery, under heavy tactical gear and helmets, all armed with projectile weapons. (My ex-owner bond company would never have paid for such nice equipment. Barish-Estranza must put a lot of effort into their branding.)

Problem? Arada asked me on our private channel that I had made certain the transport's SecSystem wouldn't see.

No. It's security procedure. If it wasn't, there was going to be a whole lot of trouble for Barish-Estranza.

The first crew person/potential hostile said, "Remove your suits, please."

That was a relief. Taking out four armed humans while wearing an EVAC suit would have been annoying.

As my suit opened and I stepped out, I detected a subliminal release of tension that made my threat assessment drop by 3 percent. (Note: humans do not generally look relieved when a SecUnit appears, so I doubted they knew what I was. But I was

95 percent certain they were reacting to the fact that I wasn't a gray Target person.) When Eletra, then Arada stepped out of their suits, the threat assessment dropped a solid 10 percent.

They clearly recognized Eletra, and she recognized them, in a confused way. An unarmed crew member with a personnel resources feed-tag came forward to take her arm and lead her away.

Another crew person said, "This way, Dr. Arada."

They led us through another hatch and down a utilitarian corridor, then into a meeting room. It had a circle of low-backed padded couches in the center around a large floating display bubble. Everything was newish and well kept (no aging upholstery here) with bars of decorative abstract designs in Barish-Estranza colors on the walls and padded seats.

Leonide was already waiting on the couch. She said, "Dr. Arada," and gestured to a seat opposite her. The supply transport's comm vid might have been doing some cosmetic editing, too, because in person faint stress and fatigue signs were visible around Leonide's eyes and mouth, though she still looked perfect enough to be in a media serial.

"Supervisor Leonide." Arada nodded. As she sat down, I stepped back against the wall behind her. The crew escort, who had followed us in and distributed themselves around the room, reacted with a little uneasiness. They had guessed I was a bodyguard but I had dropped my pretend-human code while I was still in the EVAC suit and it was starting to register with them that I might not be an augmented human. (Despite the weapons and heavy gear, they were amateurs.) (Amateurs are terrifying.)

Leonide glanced at me, her perfect brow furrowing. "Your bodyguard . . ." Then her eyes narrowed. "Is that . . ."

"A SecUnit," Arada said. I knew her well enough to hear the nervous jitter in her voice but I don't think anyone else noted it. (They were too busy being nervous about me.) Arada remembered not to glance at me, which was good. She and Ratthi both had a bad habit of doing that when they answered questions about me, like they were checking for permission to talk about me, which is not how humans expect other humans to act around SecUnits.

(SecUnits make humans and augmented humans uncomfortable and on my contracts, my clients had acted in a variety of nervous and inconsistent ways when I was around. (No matter how nervous they were, just assume I was more nervous.) But in a situation like this, it's more about how other humans expect each other to act and not how humans actually act, which literally might be anything.)

I had camera views via my new friend the Barish-Estranza supply transport's SecSystem, and I watched two members of our crew escort exchange uneasy looks. Their feed activity was monitored by their supervisors so there wasn't any private chatter, but one did send a safety notice to their bridge. The SecSystem poked me in response and I told it everything was fine, and it went back to happily interfacing with me again.

"You don't trust us?" Leonide said, her expression unreadable.

This part, this kind of human dominance posturing, was the part Arada was really afraid she would screw up. Human dominance posturing was not something Arada did, at all. (And yeah, not something I could help with, either.)

I thought there was a possibility that the other humans would notice her nerves, and that it might make them suspicious that Arada's story about what had happened to us was a mashed-up mess of lies and truth. But the chance they would attribute her jumpiness to the fact that she had brought her rogue SecUnit friend aboard their transport was low. (Ratthi was right about that.)

Arada managed to smile in a way that wasn't too friendly and said, "I think we trust each other the same amount." She added, "And I'm afraid our contract requires our SecUnit be present during off-ship first contacts." (I had told Arada about the magic words "the contract requires it.")

Leonide's knit brow unknit slightly and she sent a "maintain position" feed code to her escort, who pretended to think there was something they could have done about me if they hadn't been ordered not to try. "Of course."

I watched the tension release slightly in Arada's shoulders. She knew she had used the right tone and it gave her some confidence. She leaned forward. "Can you tell me what happened to your transport? Because I think it's very similar to what happened to mine."

Leonide didn't react immediately; I suspected she was surprised by the direct approach. Arada saw the hesitation and said, "I can go first, if you like."

You would think Leonide would go for that, but apparently she wanted control of the conversation. She said, "Not necessary." She shifted her position slightly. "You understand the former colony planet in this system is now wholly owned by Barish-Estranza."

Arada kept her expression calm and serious though I knew she still found the idea of owning a planet to be as bizarre as owning me. "Of course."

Leonide acknowledged that with a nod. "Our arrival here and initial scan of the system was uneventful, and we went into orbit while our explorer approached the colony's space dock. They reported that it was surprisingly still intact and operational, which was good news for our reclamation effort. Bringing in a new one to assemble would be a considerable expense. Instead of a shuttle, the contact team elected to use the dock's drop box to reach the surface." Her mouth tightened. "Possibly that was a mistake."

I could tell from Arada's intent expression that she wanted to interrupt, but she didn't. SecSystem was helpfully giving me all its collected video and audio, already edited and with the major incidents tagged. Its comm and feed data confirmed Leonide's story so far.

"There was nothing but standard status reports from the explorer for more than fifty-seven hours," Leonide continued.

Actually according to their SecSystem it was 58.57 hours but whatever. "Then the drop box returned."

Leonide almost winced, and I could tell she didn't like what she was about to say. "Our contact party had been compromised, but we weren't aware at first. We'd just sent over a shuttle to the explorer with two environmental techs for a standard maintenance check. I had assumed that shuttle was destroyed in the subsequent . . . events, until you told me otherwise."

Leonide stopped and waited, and Arada traded her a little more information. "Your techs, Eletra and Ras, had been implanted with these small devices." On our private feed channel, Arada asked me, *Now?*

Yeah, now was good. I stepped forward, causing a chorus of nervous twitches from Leonide's escort, and set a small sterile container with Eletra's implant next to Arada's hand on the couch. As I stepped back, she picked it up and passed it over to Leonide. We'd kept Ras's implant and the Targets' implants, though Overse hadn't had any luck yet getting information from them. We'd figured since they were the more murdery implants, they might tell us more.

Leonide frowned, but thoughtfully, and consulted with an engineering supervisor in her feed. A tech came in to collect the container and carry it away.

Leonide said, "That might explain how they were controlling our contact group. As far as we can tell, when the group returned to the explorer via the space dock, they were somehow forced to take the rest of the crew prisoner. Our security system received a truncated warning of a viral threat, so we were able to cut off feed access before our systems were contaminated. It gave us some moments to prepare, before the explorer fired on us."

According to SecSystem, the warning had come from one of the SecUnits. It had sent a code burst that had told the supply transport's SecSystem to cut comm and feed and order the bot pilot into a defensive stance, just in time not to get blown up. The supply transport had then fled, as the explorer uncoupled from the dock. The explorer had fired again at the supply transport, damaged its engines and other systems, then headed away.

It was disturbing data. Raiders would have been intending to lure the supply transport in and take it, too. This looked an awful lot like the whole goal of the Targets was to get off the planet. Once they had secured an armed ship, they hadn't bothered with the unarmed supply transport, even though it was, you know, full of supplies.

If they had control of the explorer's crew and bot pilot, they would have been aware that they had just damaged the supply transport's wormhole capability, ART said.

I don't know how long ART had been riding my feed, probably the whole time. The SecSystem tried to block ART and I quickly put up a wall and deleted its memory of the contact. (ART really did not care to be challenged by other resident systems and I didn't want the friendly SecSystem deleted.) I said, *You were supposed to keep out of this in case this ship was compromised.*

ART ignored that. *Possibly the explorer attacked me because the Targets wanted a second wormhole-capable ship. Or a better armed one.*

Maybe, though that wasn't a conclusion that told us much of anything. It was like saying that they had wanted ART because it was pretty.

Arada was asking, "Did you get any visual images of the raiders?"

I had already seen the images, sent in the SecUnit's codeburst. A six-second video clip of two Targets, bursting through a hatchway. Leonide admitted, "Very briefly in a security vid. They were, as you said, unusually divergent."

Arada's expression was grave. "We suspect they've been affected by alien remnant contamination."

"Yes." Leonide's expression and tone said she did, too, and it was a source of extreme exasperation. If Barish-Estranza was going to get any return on their investment, they would have to do something about the contamination first, which at best would mean quarantining a large section of the planet and calling in a licensed decontam operation. (If they meant to do this legally and not pull a GrayCris and deal with it by murdering all the witnesses.) "How were you attacked?"

"We had just arrived in the system and started our initial longrange mapping scans." Arada spread her hands. This was the hard lying part and I put SecSystem's download on hold so I could concentrate and because it was just too nerve-racking. "We received a distress call from a ship we now know was your explorer. When we came within range, it launched a shuttle. We allowed it to dock and ended up in a battle for our lives and our ship. They were able to take eight members of our crew. If we hadn't had a SecUnit, we would have lost the ship."

Leonide's gaze lifted briefly to me. I was doing the blank SecUnit stare at the wall past her head, which is less effective than the opaque helmet stare, but still gets the job done. She said, "Our Units weren't so effective."

Oh, I don't know about that. If not for that codeburst warning, you and your supply transport would be in tiny pieces.

"Did you see anyone who might have been from the explorer's crew?" Leonide asked. She managed to make it sound just the right amount of casual.

"Just Eletra and poor Ras," Arada answered seriously. I thought that was showing too much sympathy, but Leonide was preoccupied and didn't seem to notice. Then Arada said, "Did you have any idea there were alien remnants on this planet, perhaps at the old colony site?"

Careful, I said on our feed connection. That was getting uncomfortably close to discussing Barish-Estranza's steadily falling profit margin for this reclamation and its potential liability for exposing employees and assets to active alien remnants.

(Overse was right, alien remnants were the one thing the whole Corporation Rim agreed was bad. Not that there weren't corporates like GrayCris who would sell them if they thought they could get away with it, but the liability bonds and the chances of wiping out your entire population made it rare.)

Leonide had relaxed a little, maybe lulled into a sense of security by Arada's general air of earnestness, but now her expression went back to a smooth professional mask. "I'm afraid my contract won't permit discussing that. Our cargo factor has finished unloading your supplies." Leonide eyed Arada again, and obviously came to a conclusion. "Before we transmit a certificate of note for your invoice, perhaps you'd like to negotiate."

Oh, here we go.

Arada frowned, not understanding. "Negotiate what?"

Leonide said, "Your return to your ship."

Ugh, I hate hostage situations. I vaulted over the couch, grabbed the guard nearest Leonide, yanked him up against my chest and twisted his arm so his weapon was pointed at Leonide. I did it really fast.

The other guards made various alarmed/aggressive noises and pointed their weapons at me but it was a little too late. Leonide, staring at the weapon me and my human shield were pointing at her, sent a code telling them to stand down. They hesitated. My human shield, whose feedname was Jete, tried to send a code through the feed but I'd already cut off access to the rest of the transport for everybody in the room. I increased my forearm pressure on his throat and he stopped thinking about struggling.

Arada had her hands up. It was a reflex but a little embarrassing, frankly. I told her on the feed, *Arada, put your hands down. You're supposed to be the one giving me orders.*

Oh, sorry, you're right. She put her hands down. She had light gold-brown skin and you could really tell all the blood had drained out of her face. Her voice a little shaky, she told Leonide, "I don't want to negotiate."

Leonide wet her lips, pulling her composure back together. "Our onboard security—"

"Is useless, right now." Arada flicked a look at me. I had ordered my new SecSystem friend to seal certain hatches, cutting off this section from the rest of the transport but allowing us a path straight to the airlock. She added, "As you said, our SecUnit is very effective."

Okay, I forgive her for putting her hands up.

Leonide, playing for time, said, "Where did you get it?"

Arada was too nervous to remember what I had told her to say if someone asked that. She said, "The company."

(Well, that was a waste of a good cover story about SecUnits produced for academic expeditions. I filed it in case I ever needed it again.)

Leonide's expression tightened. "Company units have a reputation for being dangerous."

Arada was beginning to get angry. "I know."

I had also cut off Arada's feed from ART so the four humans over there who were currently losing their minds and/or frantically shushing each other wouldn't distract her. ART, who I couldn't block because it's a monster, said, *I have a targeting lock on their bridge. The section you're in will break off and I can tractor you over before you lose too much atmosphere.*

The problem with gunships is they want to shoot at stuff. That's why they're so expensive to write bond contracts for. I said, *No, don't shoot at us. For fuck's sake, ART.* If everybody would just let me do my stupid job for one minute.

Leonide's hard expression was tinged with outrage. She had realized she was cut off from the feed and there was no point in stalling for time. "It's against Corporation Rim standards to allow a SecUnit control over proprietary systems."

Arada's gaze narrowed. "Then you should call someone and complain about that."

Yeah, Arada was definitely mad now. ART slid into her feed to show her its targeting lock. The transport's bot pilot had noticed the targeting lock, too, and was not happy. I let the bridge supervisor's pretend-calm-but-really-slightly-panicked feed message to Leonide get through.

Leonide pressed her lips together. I could see it was a conces-
sion and I thought Arada did, too. Composed and calm, Leonide
said, "There's no need for all this. I was simply looking for a
better deal. Perhaps coming from an academic background, you
find that unusual."

Arada swallowed, and also made herself sound calm. "Well, it
was a little rude. I'd like to go back to my ship now."

And for you to transmit the invoice, I told her in the feed.

"And for you to transmit the invoice," she repeated.

Leonide tilted her head. "Of course."

The rest was pretty normal. We backed out toward the lock
and dropped Jete in the corridor before I sealed the foyer off
from the rest of the ship. I let Arada have her feed back, and
Overse said immediately, *Are you all right?*

I'm fine, babe, Arada told her. *Just some corporate power
peeing.*

Ick.

We got our EVAC suits on. (I had control of the lock so no
chance of them spacing us. And with ART's guns still pointed at
them, it would have been a suicidally stupid thing to do.) Then
we cycled out of the lock with no trouble.

Once we were in the safety of ART's tractors, and Arada had
responded to all the exclamations from Ratthi, Amena, and
Thiago, Arada tapped my private connection and asked, *Why
did she do that? Did I sound weak? I'm sorry I messed up.*

*No, it wasn't you. I think she told us too much, in front of her
crew, and she realized it. She wanted to make sure they knew she
was in charge.* I didn't say it but I also thought Arada had been
too sympathetic, and it had made Leonide feel like she had given
too much away.

Arada sighed. *But it was worth it. At least we know what to do
next, now.*

Yeah. We were going to the colony's space dock.

□   □   □

It was four hours by ART's clock to the colony planet and its space dock, which would have given us time to get ready, if we had any idea what to get ready for.

"We don't know *Perihelion*'s crew is there," Arada reported to the others as we took off our EVAC suits in ART's airlock foyer. "But there is a chance the explorer is using it as a base of operations."

"At worst, it may provide some information about just what is going on here," Ratthi agreed over the comm. "If the dock's systems are still active, then they might have information that SecUnit can pry out for us."

Arada and I tried to stow our suits but one of ART's drones showed up to elbow us out of the way and take over. ART agreed with Arada's assessment, because the nav/route info scroll in ART's feed showed we were already pulling away from the supply transport.

I'd had an idea earlier, now where was it? I checked my save-for-later. Oh right, that idea.

I needed to talk to ART about it.

It was a bad idea. But I had a bad feeling we were going to need it.

□   □   □

I didn't know how long it would take to do this, so I had to ditch the humans quickly. Fortunately Thiago went to take another rest period (since he'd wasted part of the first one having a stupid argument with me), Overse and Arada went up to the control deck together, and Ratthi was sitting in the galley going over all the collected data from the Targets' pathology scans and the material analysis of their gear again. Overse thought she had found evidence of alien remnant tech influence and he was trying to verify her results. Amena tried to follow me into the bunkroom and I told her, "Stay with Ratthi."

Amena stopped and frowned. "Why? What are you going to do?"

I wanted to be in a physically private space instead of just a closed channel on the feed. It was a weird thing I was going to ask ART to do, and I didn't want humans staring at my face while I did it, even if they couldn't hear what I was saying. I was going to have to answer Amena and I was in a hurry so I just tried the truth. "I need to talk to ART in private."

Amena's expression did something funny and she lifted her brows. "About your relationship?"

I felt ART's sharpened attention in the feed. I said, "Very funny." I walked into the bunkroom, told the door to slide shut and set it on lock. I'd already cut the others out of the feed.

ART said, *Do you want to watch* Timestream Defenders Orion*?*

Of course I did, but first I had to do this. I said, "I have an idea about how to create a variable killware assault to deploy against the Targets' systems. You can copy me and use me as the sentient component." I'd put together a report on the sentient killware Palisade Security had deployed against the company gunship that had taken us off TranRollinHyfa, and now I sent it to ART. The analysis the company bot pilot and I had done during the incident suggested the sentient virus had been built using a construct consciousness, probably from a combat unit. Substituting a copy of my consciousness could produce the same results.

I knew ART wasn't going to like this, though I didn't know how I knew that. ART wasn't a human, or a construct. Humans and constructs were full of overwrought emotions like depression, anxiety, and anger (was anxiety an emotion? It sure felt like one) and I had no idea what ART was full of, except how much it cared about its crew.

6.4 seconds dragged by (seriously, even a human would notice a pause that long) and ART hadn't said anything. Then it said, *That is a terrible idea.*

Which just pissed me off. "It's a great idea." It was a great idea. ART had been working on a virus code tailored for targetControlSystem and the structure it had built so far was stored in our shared workspace. ART had halted development when it became clear there was no point in continuing without a way to make it variable, because of the combination of targetControlSystem's archaic architecture and the possibility of a connection to alien remnant tech.

I couldn't do this without ART's help. On the company gunship, I'd moved my consciousness into the bot pilot's processing space to help it fight the sentient killware, but this was different; I'd never copied myself and I wasn't sure how to start, unless I had a place to put me. I couldn't just stick Me.copy into ART's semi-completed code, not without ART's help. "And you thought of it first, you said we needed killware with a variable component."

ART said, *I didn't mean you.*

That sounds mild, putting it like that, like something ART would say in a normal tone. But it said it with so much force in the feed I sat down hard on the bunk. I said, "Stop yelling at me."

ART didn't respond. It just existed there, glaring at me invisibly in the feed.

Okay, I had known that ART wouldn't like this, even though my threat assessment on the idea looked great. But I hadn't known it would react like this. "You wouldn't have to rip me out of my body, just copy me. It wouldn't even be me. Me is a combination of my archives and my organic neural tissue and this would just be a copy of my kernel."

ART was quiet for another 3.4 seconds. Then it said, *For a being as sophisticated as you are, it is baffling how little understanding you have of the composition of your own mind.*

Now I was getting more pissed off. "I know my composition, that's why I'm sitting here arguing with a giant asshole and not stuck in a cubicle somewhere or guarding idiot humans on a mining contract." Which, in retrospect, I should have stuck with that. That was a great comeback, it was to the point, it made sense, it was hard to argue with without sounding like an asshole. But I added, "Do you want to get your crew back or not?"

Which turned it from an argument into a fight, and ART has no concept of how to fight fair.

Which, granted, I didn't really, either. I knew it as an abstract set of rules and guidelines from my shows and other media, and so should ART, but it seemed to have missed that part.

(What I use when I fight/do security is a minimum level of response, which is meant to minimize damage to humans and augmented humans and the company's property, which means taking into account a lot of factors. For example: what is an intentional attempt by a client to injure another client versus what is just humans being stupid and needing to be made to stop. Which is why you need SecUnits and not combat bots. And why humans doing their own security is a terrible idea, since they're actually way more likely to flip out and shoot everybody for no reason than combat bots are. Anyway, what I'm getting at here is it's not fair, because you don't want to give a hostile a chance to stop you, right? That's stupid. But you don't want to kill/injure a client for walking in the wrong door.)

I forgot where I was going with this, except that ART apparently has no concept of fairness, or minimum level of response, because the sense of ART's almost full attention was overwhelming. Then the door slid open and Ratthi walked in with Amena right behind him. "What is going on?" he demanded. "*Perihelion* said you're trying to copy yourself for a variable viral what?"

□   □   □

So I had to tell the humans my plan and then they had to argue and talk to each other about it and ask me questions like was I feeling okay.

Then half an hour into this fun process, Thiago woke up and they all had to explain to him what was going on. It was during this part that I realized Amena was (a) missing and (b) ART had cut me off from her feed.

I found her in a small secondary lounge area near Medical. As I walked in she was saying, "—because it thought you were dead. It was so upset I thought— Oh hey, you're here."

I stood there accusingly, not looking at her. She tried to hold it in and managed it for almost six seconds, then burst out, "ART should know how you really feel about it! And this is serious, it's like—you and ART are making a baby just so you can send it off to get killed or deleted or—or whatever might happen."

"A baby?" I said. I was still mad at Amena telling ART about my emotional collapse behind my back. But I really wish ART had a face, just so I could see it right now. "It's not a baby, it's a copy of me, made with code."

Amena folded her arms and looked intensely skeptical. "That you and ART made together, with code. Code which both of you are also made out of."

I said, "That's not like a human baby."

Amena said, "So how are human babies made? By combining DNA, an organic code, from two or more participants."

Okay, so it was a little like a human baby. "That's . . . irrelevant."

ART said, *Amena, it may be necessary.*

ART sounded serious, and resigned. Amena pressed her lips together, unhappy.

I'd won the argument, yay me, so I left.

◻   ◻   ◻

When we arrived at the dock, the explorer wasn't there.

My threat assessment said there had only been a 40 percent chance that we would find the explorer in dock, but I could tell ART was disappointed and infuriated. Mostly infuriated.

Arada, Overse, and Thiago were up on the control deck, and ART put up its scanner image on the big display surface in the center, and sent it into the feed.

The dock was in a low orbit, attached to a planet via a structure called a lift tower, which held the shaft for the drop box used to reach the surface. The dock itself was a long structure with oblong protrusions where transports, shuttles, and other ships could dock. There were also inset rectangular slots that were module docks. The transports would deliver their modules of supplies, which would be moved from the dock into the drop box to be carried down to the surface.

"Surely a ship-to-surface freight shuttle would be more economical," Ratthi said, studying the scan images. He was with me and Amena in the meeting room off the galley. "Isn't the Corporation Rim obsessed with how much things cost? Couldn't they have used this material to make more habitable structures on the planet?"

I had never been on a contract with a colony like this, but I knew the answer to that one. "It's to keep the humans and augmented humans from leaving the planet."

Amena looked up at me, confused. "Huh?"

I explained, "If they used shuttles, a group might organize, take over the shuttle, and use it to get up to the supply ship. Then they could escape." Granted, the Targets had done that via the space dock, but they had had to find a way to force the Barish-Estranza contact party to help them. If a bunch of desperate colonists came up in the drop box, the ship could just do a quick detach from the dock's airlock and it would be unreachable. It wasn't a foolproof method but it was 90 percent effective. (Foolproof is another weird word. Shouldn't it be smartproof? It's not like you're going to breach and seize control of a ship attached to a space dock by tripping or forgetting to bring your weapon or something.)

Amena looked horrified. Ratthi's expression did a whole progression. He said, "Are you telling us the colonists here were prisoners?"

"It's a possibility. Humans don't want to be dumped on unimproved planets with no control over their air, water, and food resources." I mean, who would? Mining installations are horrible, but at least the humans were getting paid for their work (sort of, mostly, sometimes) and the supplies were usually reliable. And mining installations were too expensive to just abandon.

I didn't know much about the kind of colonies meant to settle partially terraformed planets because the company had never bonded them. Which should tell you how dangerous they are right there, if the company thought the budget was so tight that the whole operation was unrealistic. Terraforming projects designed to get everything livable and ready way before the humans and augmented humans moved in were expensive longterm investments, but they didn't fail like this.

Ratthi shook his head and waved his arms. "I'm not even surprised anymore. I think I've been in the Corporation Rim too long."

Hey, me too.

"So not only do they just dump the people on planets and leave them to die, but they force them to go there in the first place." Amena's expression was half boggled and half furious.

"Theoretically not." Theoretically the colony is continually supplied until it becomes self-sufficient and starts producing its own resources and the original colonists are released from indenture. But you know how that goes.

"But the colonists are not volunteers," Thiago clarified over the general feed.

"Sometimes they are," I said, because I didn't want to talk about it anymore. There's volunteering, going into something where you knew what it might be like but wanted to do it anyway, for whatever reason, like when I had gone to Milu. And then there was "volunteering," where you did something you shouldn't have to do because the alternative was getting your insides fried by your governor module, or whatever the human equivalent was.

Thiago didn't say anything, so that was a win.

ART said, *I'm also detecting debris, probably from a series of destroyed satellites.*

"Do you think it's recent?" Up on the control deck, Arada

stepped back as the scanner image passed through her head. She moved around, trying to angle for a better view.

ART said, *Analysis suggests the debris has been in orbit longer than forty corporate standard years.*

"I don't suppose you can tell how it was destroyed?" Thiago asked.

If I could, I would have said so already, ART said. It added, *The dock is our best source of information. The active power levels aboard it suggest that it is/was in use, including life support. Possibly the explorer did return after its attack on me.*

Arada frowned up at the dock's image. "But the explorer isn't here now. And there's no way to tell if anyone disembarked here without searching the place."

Overse didn't look happy either. "I don't know what I'm worried about most, having to find and search this colony, which is probably full of hostile alien-remnant-influenced people, or having to track down and board an armed ship."

"Also full of hostile alien-remnant-influenced people," Arada murmured, distracted by reading ART's figures on the dock's power usage.

Arada and Overse were back to getting along after spending time together in an unused bunkroom while we were traveling to the dock. I hadn't bothered to monitor them on ART's cameras or try to slip a drone in; the chances that they were having sex and/or a relationship discussion (either of which I would prefer to stab myself in the face than see) were far higher than the chance that they were saying anything I needed to know about.

(I mean they might have been plotting against me, but you know, probably not.)

(Around the same time, I had also caught part of a conversation between Thiago and Ratthi. Thiago had told Ratthi about our conversation in the bunkroom, and Ratthi had told him what he knew about the whole attempted assassination incident. Thiago had said he felt like he should apologize and talk to me more about it. Ratthi had said, "I think you should let it go for a while, at least until we get ourselves out of this situation. SecUnit is a very private person, it doesn't like to discuss its feelings."

This is why Ratthi is my friend.)

ART had gotten a far-range live scan of the planet. It had a lot of cloud cover in swirling patterns, some indicating massive storms. As the clouds whirled, there were glimpses of brown and gray and vivid red that seemed to be the surface. "Is it supposed to look like that?" I said.

"You're thinking of failed terraforming?" Ratthi said, frowning absently at the displays. "That red could be algae. They're probably using air bubbles to hold in breathable atmosphere over their colony sites and agricultural zones. That's what we did on Preservation before the terraforming completed."

The weather appears natural, ART said. *I can detect no comm or feed signals, but that may be because they are using local, heavily shielded systems.*

"So we can't just call down there and ask if there's anybody who wants to talk." Arada studied the scan results. "*Perihelion,* do you want to deploy those pathfinders you've been working on?"

ART said, *Not yet.* After a second, it added, *All evidence indicates the presence of hostile unknowns on the planet. The pathfinders would alert them to our presence.*

Arada grimaced in agreement. "Then let's keep our focus on the dock for now. We're going to have to go over there and take a look. Can we tell where the drop box is? Is it still up in the dock or did it go back down to the planet?"

ART turned the image and increased magnification. *There is an exterior sensor that shows the box is currently locked in place at the top of the docking shaft.*

At least that meant I only needed to worry about being attacked by something already hiding in the dock or coming aboard in a ship. "Can you get me a scanner image of the interior?" I asked ART. I woke my drones and told them to meet me at the EVAC suit locker. I could send the drones through the dock first to do my own mapping but the more intel the better. "The dock might have a resident SecSystem. If it's been awake at any point during this situation it could tell us everything we need to know."

ART said, *I can make a partial map based on detectable power systems.*

"You can't go alone," Thiago said from the control deck. "I'll go with you."

Overse added, "Good idea, but it'll be safer with three."

From Arada's resigned but slightly annoyed expression, this must have been part of the sex/relationship conversation I hadn't listened to. Overse must have insisted on taking her turn at the next opportunity to do something stupid with me. (So technically, they *had* been plotting against me.) Whatever, I didn't care what they had decided, I was the stupid security consultant here. "It's my job. I don't need help."

Thiago looked annoyed. "I got you shot on our survey, I'm not letting you go alone."

Arada said, "No, don't look like that, SecUnit, this is safer and you know it. You don't want to die because of something simple and obvious like getting locked in a compartment and not having anyone with you out in the corridor to open the door."

(It sounds dumb, but it's a good example of how humans get killed during explorations of abandoned structures. And yes, I'd used it as an example myself for clients who were anxious to find somewhere to get themselves killed, and yes, I hated having it turned back on me like that.)

"And it's in the survey contract," Overse added with finality. She was giving the side of my head this determined glare that made me remember the conversation back on the facility about me being supportive of Arada. I was being supportive of Arada. I was being supportive of Arada's marital partner staying on ART and not dying.

I said, "That provision is for humans." It was worth a shot.

Ratthi corrected, "It says 'all entities under contract,'" and sent me an excerpt of the relevant section from his feed storage.

Now I was speechless with being pissed off with Pin-Lee. She had negotiated the contract for me and deliberately put that in.

But Arada didn't rub it in and nobody looked smug. Arada said firmly, "Thiago, SecUnit is in charge. You follow its orders immediately and without argument. If you can't do that, I'll go in your place."

Thiago lifted his hands, palm out. "I will."

I was desperate. I sent privately, *ART, tell them I need to go alone. Back me up.*

ART said aloud, *I concur, it will be safer if SecUnit is accompanied by two certified survey specialists.*

Why am I even surprised. I sent privately again, *ART, you asshole.*

ART replied, only to me, *It is safer. I've lost my crew, I won't lose you.*

Amena said, not helpfully, "Your face just got really weird. Are you all right?"

No, it was confusing. I was confused.

13

My threat assessment was all over the place right now, but nobody thought ART should lock on to the dock. Instead it did some complicated maneuvers (the kind of thing I don't know anything about and don't have to know because ART does) to get close. Me and the two humans whose help I absolutely did not need took EVAC suits over to an airlock.

When we were near enough to see the pits and scarring on the dock's hull, I picked up its feed. It was dormant but its SecSystem woke when I pinged and it asked for a Barish-Estranza entry code. The explorer must have had codes for the old Adamantine system, or had just released killware to take it down so they could upload their own. Whichever, this version of DockSecSystem was a recent upgrade, but something was wrong with its configuration and it had put itself in standby mode. I was a little nervous, despite the fact that my walls are excellent and targetControlSystem had made no attempt to take me over despite a lot of provocation, what with me trying to kill it and everything. But the fact that we still didn't know why ART had experienced that first critical shutdown was still making me hyper-paranoid.

But at this point, the only thing I could do to find out if DockSecSystem was compromised was get in there and look. So I did.

The first thing I hit was a barrage of configuration errors. I couldn't tell if the Barish-Estranza crew had failed the install or if something had tried to mess with it later. It made it a little harder to take control, not because it was trying to fight me but because nothing worked right. In fact, it seemed pathetically glad somebody who knew what they were doing was here. I got control of its entry functions before we reached the lock and told it to let us in.

The hatch slid open and the lock cycled us through to a large reception space, designed for big groups or bulk objects. The EVAC suits had their own lights and vision filters, but the lights embedded in the bulkheads flickered on. Two large rounded doorways with open safety hatches led into corridors and like ART's scan had said, life support was active.

And unlike the outside, the inside looked nearly new. There wasn't much, if any, wear. Some scuffing on the floor, that was all. No sign of recent activity, but then we didn't know which lock the explorer had used.

No, there was a sign of recent activity. A big version of the Adamantine logo with its stylized depiction of a planetary landscape, a cliff face above an ocean shore, was painted onto the metal of the far wall. Someone from the explorer crew had scratched at it with a sharp tool and drawn a sloppy version of the Barish-Estranza logo on the gray and green cliff. Ha ha, vandalism expresses our corporate loyalty, right. Well, the joke was on you, Barish-Estranza employee, because not long after you did that you got killed and/or mind-controlled by alien remnant raiders.

(I know, it's a logo, but I hate it when humans and augmented humans ruin things for no reason. Maybe because I was a thing before I was a person and if I'm not careful I could be a thing again.)

And maybe it was just the hamstrung SecSystem, but I had the feeling we were going to find some dead bodies in here.

I told my EVAC suit to open and released my drones. I only had sixteen survivors after everything that had happened on ART, but that should be enough for a quick reconnaissance run through this area of the dock. They were also running one of the new codes I'd written. It would emit a field that any targetDrones would associate with the Targets' protective gear. (If all the targetDrones operated the same basic way, which, of course, we had no idea. But it was worth a try.)

I also had a large projectile weapon from ART's supply and a smaller energy weapon.

I kept two drones with me in a holding pattern over my head, since I wasn't getting anything from the cameras except static. As the others zipped off down the shadowy corridors, Overse asked, "Are you picking up anything?"

"The feed is partially down, cameras are offline, and the Dock-SecSystem isn't responding correctly." My drone inputs showed dark empty corridors, with no obvious sign of human occupation, if you didn't count the bodies. There were three in the junction between the corridors leading to the control area and the passenger entrance to the drop box.

They were all wearing gear in Barish-Estranza colors but I slowed the scout drones down for a long close scan just to make sure. One sprawled face up, the other two crumpled against the wall. Appearance of the wounds suggested they were made by energy weapons, no surprise there.

ART said, *Unidentified,* which was its way of expressing relief that none of them were its crew members.

There was another body further up the corridor but I already knew what had killed that one.

What I wasn't seeing was anywhere humans could be locked up. The dock hadn't been anything but a temporary waystation while the colony was in development, so there were no cabins or facilities yet, just some minimal supply storage and waste disposal. There were interior hatches, but none were shut, suggesting the place had been searched earlier and left like this. I tagged some spots to check out more closely and then sent my drones down the wide corridors meant to transport cargo containers to the drop box loading entrance. It looked like the bigger modules were meant to be moved along the outside of the dock and attach directly to the box.

I forced DockSecSystem into a restart, hoping that would help, and climbed out of my EVAC suit. This time we were wearing the environmental suits under the EVAC units. The material felt thin, but it protected against a lot of toxic substances and had a closed breathing system attached, which we were using despite the fact that the dock's life support was still working. The suits were really meant for planetary environments but it was a good precaution.

I signaled Overse and Thiago that they could leave their EVAC suits and told them, "We'll start a physical evidence search here and work our way toward the control area and the drop box." The drones were telling me the likelihood of Targets lying in wait was low to nil, and without a targetControlSystem installed, it seemed unlikely that there would be targetDrones. We still had to check for any evidence that ART's crew might have been here. A note saying "help, etc." was preferable to signs like body parts stuffed into maintenance cubbies or blood and/or viscera smears on walls and deck.

On the comm, Ratthi said, "That still looks like a lot of area to search. Maybe Arada and I should come over, too."

For fuck's sake, Ratthi. Amena immediately jumped in with, "Arada should stay with the ship. I could go."

I started to answer (I don't know what I was going to say but it was probably something I was going to feel bad about later). Overse and Thiago both took breaths to object. But ART got in before any of us (it helps to not actually need any air to talk) and said, *No.*

Ratthi tried to clarify, "No to Amena, or no to—"

No to all of you, ART said.

"*Perihelion*'s right," Arada said, in a Mensah-like I'm-being-reasonable-but-you-should-all-shut-up voice, "Now let's let them focus."

Overse and Thiago had gotten out of their EVACs and did quick checks of their environment suits. Thiago said briskly, "Should we split up?"

I was facing the right-hand corridor and didn't turn around. I don't know what my back told him (possibly it was my shoulders, having a reaction to how my jaw hinge was grinding) but he added, "And that was a joke."

Overse's smile was dry. She told him, "It was sort of a joke."

"This way." I started down the corridor, telling one of my drones to drop back into a sentry position behind the humans to make sure nothing snuck up on us. Yes, I know the scout drones weren't finding anything, but still. On the shows I liked best, monsters were always a possibility in these situations, but in reality it only happened around 27 percent of the time.

Also a joke. Mostly.

We cleared the short corridors that branched off the main corridor to each lock, and checked the few storage/maintenance cubbies. We weren't finding anything, not even trash. As we moved to the forward section, I gave up on accessing DockSec-System through the feed; I needed to find its direct access station to see if it had had any moments of lucidity after the failed load. Not that this situation needed to be any more frustrating or anything.

The lights flickered on for us as we passed and flickered off afterward. We didn't technically need lights; my eyes and my drones had dark vision filters and the humans had hand and helmet lights they were using to check the walls and floor. I thought the best chance for actual evidence was in the DockSecSystem's archive, if I could just get the stupid system to load right. If we had to bring ART's big fancy drones over and do a search for DNA traces, it would be a huge pain in the ass, and if they found nothing, it still wouldn't be positive evidence that the crew hadn't been here.

I was hoping a lack of evidence would be the problem, that we wouldn't find a bunch of DNA smears near an airlock. If that happened, I wasn't sure how ART would react. Or what I would do about how it reacted. I was terrible at being comforting. It was hard enough trying to do it to humans; I had no idea what would help ART. Everything I could think of seemed drastically inadequate.

Keeping her voice low, Overse said, "This place feels older, like it's been here a very long time. But we know it was built only around forty years ago."

We know it was in existence at least thirty-seven years ago. ART was being pedantic in our comm. *Space docks were not commonly in use in Pre–Corporation Rim colonies so it is unlikely there was a structure here when Adamantine arrived.*

Thiago's light moved along the edge of the corridor. "It feels that way because it was built for a purpose and then hardly used. According to *Perihelion*'s information, Adamantine didn't last for very long after the colony was established. There may have only been one or two supply runs."

We passed two more corridor openings but from my drones I knew they led to module locks and to the cargo access. My drones had whipped through the central control area but couldn't get through the hatch into the drop box, which was the one place something/someone might be lurking/hiding/crawled into and died.

We reached the junction with the bodies of the three Barish-Estranza employees and stopped so we could make a quick examination. All had been shot, and their weapons had been taken. The only thing left was some semi-useless crowd-control poppers. (They make loud noises and bright lights, effective against humans who aren't wearing safety visors. Yes, Barish-Estranza had been prepared to find colonists still alive and possibly resistant to being co-opted into new corporate indenture arrangements.) I collected them so nobody else could use them against us and went ahead to the other body.

It was sprawled at the mouth of the accessway to the drop box loading corridor, face down, lying in a pool of dried fluid that had leaked out of the open faceplate.

ART was riding my feed but it didn't comment. I didn't think the humans had any idea what this body was; they had seen it on the raw drone video but it was often hard for humans, who couldn't read the data stream without a special interface, to interpret.

Overse and Thiago finished and came up behind me. "We've reached the other body," Thiago reported to the others on the comm. "It's in some kind of military suit—"

"That's SecUnit armor," Overse corrected. Her helmet cam pointed to the right side of my face. "That's right, isn't it?"

"Yes," I told her.

The armor design was unfamiliar. From what Leonide had said, it was no surprise that Barish-Estranza hadn't risked dealing with the company to get their SecUnits and had bought them elsewhere.

(I don't know why I cared about that. If I was afraid to run into company tech or what. It was all just strange, and whatever, I didn't like it.)

Thiago stepped closer, his light picking out details. From the position, the SecUnit had been either heading away from the control area or the drop box foyer, but that was irrelevant. I knew what must have happened to it after the humans died, and it might have been pacing or running randomly around the dock. On the comm, Arada asked, "Was it killed by the Targets?"

(Yes, that was a dumb question, which was how I knew ART had told her to ask it. It wanted me to tell the humans what they were looking at, because it thought I should say it aloud and because it wanted them to understand this. And you know, I don't even know why I hadn't yet.)

I said, "No." It still had its weapon, because it had been alive when the Targets left, and even with it helpless they had been just a little too afraid to try to take it away. The armor looked salvageable from the outside, but I'd have to scrape the body out to tell, and when the governor module did something like this, at least in 83 percent of instances I'd personally witnessed, it fried the armor, too. "It was ordered to stand down by one of its clients, then left here."

The comm was quiet for fourteen seconds. "But how did it die?" Amena asked in a small voice.

(Oh wait, now I know why I hadn't wanted to talk about this.)

ART interposed, *SecUnits have a distance limit, imposed by the contract owner. It's variable, but if this SecUnit's clients were taken away in the explorer, or sent to the planet, it would have been in violation, with no way to remedy the situation. Its governor module killed it.*

"Oh. Oh, no," Ratthi muttered. "I knew that happened, but . . ."

Thiago shook his head. "So it was ordered to do nothing, and then just left here to . . ."

"How is that rational?" Arada burst out, forgetting she was technically in charge and supposed to be all sensible and restrained. "To have a killswitch on the one person who might be able to rescue you if you're taken prisoner—"

"It's a function of the governor module itself," I explained. "The HubSystem or designated supervisor could override, but they weren't here."

"What about the—" Thiago made a gesture back toward the dead humans.

"Dead clients don't count. Otherwise you could just kill one and carry them around with you." Okay, for real, that wouldn't work. The governor module wasn't nearly as sophisticated as a HubSystem but even it could have figured that one out.

And of course the humans had trouble understanding that your governor module suddenly deciding to melt your brain wasn't something you could rules-lawyer your way out of.

I was tired of explaining and I didn't want to talk about it anymore. You know, I hadn't hacked my governor module to become a rogue SecUnit for no reason. I collected the projectile weapon and the spare ammunition, said, "We need to keep moving," and went on through the access.

I pretended not to hear Ratthi on the comm telling the others to drop the subject.

We went through another foyer and then an open hatch into a globe-shaped control area. It was clearly meant to be operated mostly via the feed, by humans and augmented humans who were coming in to deliver a cargo to the planet and then leave, probably as rapidly as possible. There were no chairs, just station consoles built into the walls with dormant displays for monitoring the various cargo module locks and for the dock's internal systems. The gravity was adjusted so you could walk up the curving wall.

Before I could, Overse caught up with me and asked, "Are you all right?"

I was absolutely great. It wasn't like this situation needed to get any more emotionally fraught, or anything. I said, "I am functioning optimally." (This was a line from *Valorous Defenders,* which is a great source for things humans and augmented humans think SecUnits say that SecUnits do not actually say.)

Overse made an exasperated noise. "I hate that show." I'd forgotten that it was one of the shows I'd pulled off the Preservation Public Entertainment feed. The other humans were listening on the comm so hard I could pick up their breathing. Thiago pretended not to listen, flashing his helmet light over the stations on the upper tier of the control area. Overse added, "Just remember you're not alone here."

I never know what to say to that. I am actually alone in my head, and that's where 90 plus percent of my problems are.

I headed up the wall for the internal systems suite where DockSecSystem's access was likely to be.

I found it and activated the display surface. It fizzed into view above the console and immediately filled up with error codes. Ugh, I was going to have to try to fix this before I could even see if there was recorded video.

Thiago walked down into the bottom of the globe, looking up toward the curving top. "Overse, did you see this?"

I was neck deep in SecSystem errors but I pointed a drone upward to see what he was talking about. At the top of the dome, above the highest row of stations, was a flat art installation. It was a cityscape with low buildings and canals and lots of foliage, with elevated walkways curving around large flat-topped rock formations. The Adamantine logo was embossed in it with a three-dimensional projection, so it was facing you from whatever angle you looked at it.

Overse frowned upward. "The colonists wouldn't be in this room, would they? That was for the crews who were sending the supplies down. Or for the future, when there would be more people coming through here, going down to work on the site."

The partially failed install was taking up most of my attention, but I could tell there was more data woven through the image in marker paint. (Markers are limited broadcasts directly to feed interfaces that work even when the feed is down, and are supposed to be for marking exits and emergency routes and are usually used in the Corporation Rim to torture you with advertising displays.) These were just inert images, not a trap, so I told Overse, "Aim your light at it and move it around."

She tilted her head and pointed her helmet light more directly, then waved her head back and forth. That stimulated the markers and they started displaying their images, which were maps and diagrams and building plans. I saved the images in case we needed them later, but just a quick scan showed they were all colony infrastructure plans. Things like a shuttle/aircraft port, a combo medical center/community services structure designed for expansion as the population increased, archives and educational structures.

And there was a diagram of the surface dock, the space dock's counterpart. It was a large structure built around the base of the shaft, but while there were a lot of notes about adding admin and commercial space, there was nothing saying how far away from the main colony it had been built. (I don't know anything about construction but I'm guessing you didn't put your dock right in the middle of your colony in case the drop box blew up or the shaft fell over or something.)

Overse was thoughtful. "This is a great deal of proposed de-velopment. I wonder how much of it they managed to build?"

Thiago agreed. "Whatever happened later, someone at Ada-mantine seems to have gone into this intending to see it through to a successful developed world."

Maybe. The plans indicated not just a lot of expensive surveying work onplanet, but a lot of offsite development, too. Maybe they had spent too much and that was why they had gone bankrupt.

I don't know what was worse, getting a bunch of "volunteer" contract labor colonists killed as part of an investment scheme, or getting a bunch of actual volunteer colonists killed because of mistakes and mismanagement that ended up exposing the con-trolling corporation to a hostile takeover.

Overse walked farther up the wall. "And most of these con-trol stations are just unused templates. They were leaving a lot of room for expansion, as if this dock was going to be part of a much larger network."

On the comm, Amena said, "Then why did they try to keep the corporation who was taking over from knowing where the colony was? Did it not need supplies anymore?"

"That's a good question." Overse stepped over to another con-sole. "Maybe it was already self-sufficient."

Thiago told Overse, "Let's look for the drop box station. If there's a log file, we may be able to tell if the colonists were actu-ally allowed to use this dock."

From our comm, Ratthi said, "But they wouldn't have had a ship, so why come up here?"

"We don't know that they didn't have a ship," I said, before ART could. It was a good line of inquiry; if there was another ship running around this system, even if it was a short-range type without wormhole capability, it would be important intel. Seeing the inside of the dock had caused some recalculations in my as-sessments. Who the fuck knew; Adamantine, planning optimis-tically for a future none of them were going to see, might have left the colonists a small fleet.

Thiago and Overse split up, moving up the walls, checking the stations. Some had marker captions, which provided brief descriptions of what they were for, except they were in a language I didn't recognize. With no systems on the feed but the new Security load, there was no translation.

Frustrated, Overse said, "Thiago, do you have this language loaded on your interface?"

Thiago answered, "Yes, this is Variance063926. *Perihelion,* if I tag the right module, can you—" ART was already pulling the module from Thiago's feed storage and creating a working vocabulary to send back to me and Overse. Thiago finished, "Thank you, *Perihelion.*"

Overse stopped at a station. "This is it." She leaned over, using the manual interface to try to get the station to boot. Thiago jogged across the wall to join her.

I was finally able to access DockSecSystem's video archive and started downloading. I kept hitting corrupted spots and having to work around them. I was still worried about encountering killware or malware or targetControlSystem, but realistically, this situation was the same as the B-E shuttle in ART's dock: setting a trap here on the off chance that a SecUnit might directly access DockSecSystem seemed like a stretch. It still didn't make me any less paranoid. (Let's face it, nothing would.)

And the Targets had reasons not to be too worried about SecUnits. They had seen the Barish-Estranza SecUnits ordered to stand down, made helpless by the governor modules.

Overse said, "Hmm. SecUnit, this is showing log entries from two drop boxes."

Well, that was interesting, but I'd pulled ART's schematic of the dock already and checked—there was only the one shaft, the box tucked up into its lock below where we were in the control area. ART, who hates to be wrong, said, *Physical structure indicates only one.*

Overse scrolled through a file, her helmet light turned off so it didn't wash out the floating display. "Wait, yes . . . It's not a box, it's a small maintenance capsule. It's inside the structure of the shaft."

I started to run what there was of DockSecSystem's video, skimming through it at a much faster rate than a human could view it. The camera placement and lighting was bad, but I could see figures in red-brown Barish-Estranza environmental gear as they moved back and forth through the main corridor. I had to run it back to make sure, but the contact party's initial boarding of the drop box wasn't on here. Stupid humans, being impatient and not nearly paranoid enough, they had screwed up the load of their new SecSystem and then hadn't even waited until it was fully active to head down to the planet. No wonder their contact party had gotten grabbed by the Targets. The activity lessened as the humans returned to the explorer. I spotted one of the Sec-Units patrolling the central corridor, but not the one we'd found.

Thiago pointed over Overse's shoulder. "It did make a trip to the planet, then returned."

"Right, but that was . . ." Overse huffed in exasperation. "Hold on, I need to convert these time stamps."

Then ART said, *Hostile contact, ETA six minutes out.*

What the hell? How could it get that close? "Six minutes? What were you doing?"

Contact did not appear on scan until now, that's what the fuck I was doing, ART replied.

I put my video review on hold. "Do they see you?" Okay, it was a stupid question.

ART said, *Of course they see me.*

I pulled a view of ART's control area. Arada was in a station chair, Ratthi and Amena standing on either side, all watching ART's big display. ART was annotating the displays in the feed so it wasn't just a mash of numbers and lines and colors.

Frustrated, Arada said, "Something blocked *Perihelion*'s ability to scan the explorer. I bet we're dealing with more alien remnant technology."

It's probable, ART said. I don't know what the humans heard, but I read deadly, furious calm. *A variation on their ability to interfere with short-range drone scans.*

I saw from ART's feed that the explorer was acquiring target lock. The DockSecSystem, trying to come fully online, sent a belated warning through the feed. We didn't have time to get back to the lock, put on the EVAC suits, and return to ART. The explorer was in range and could fire on us at any moment. The dock wasn't designed to be shot at but it was more protection than an EVAC suit. Besides, I hadn't finished my review of the security video and we hadn't checked the drop box and its maintenance capsule for physical evidence yet. On the feed, I said, *ART, you know what you have to do.*

ART didn't hesitate, or argue. It had gone through the same threat assessment I just had, except faster and a million percent more homicidal. It said, *Try not to do anything stupid before I return.*

Just keep your stupid comm off, I told it. *And I don't want to hear about your superior filters.*

It was already gone.

Overse was trying to call Arada but ART had cut off contact. Thiago turned to me urgently. "What's happened?"

"ART's gone after the explorer. It'll come back here for us when it's . . . done." I realized I had no real idea what ART actually planned to do. And with ART gone, I had no eyes on what was happening outside. Like if, for example, the explorer decided to blow up the dock.

But I did have at least one human who knew what she was doing. "Overse, can you find a station with an exterior scan?" And okay, I only knew what it was called from shows about ships, like *World Hoppers.*

Overse hesitated, her hand on her helmet where her comm access was. She was worried about Arada. Then she swallowed hard and forced herself past it. "Right. Thiago, did you see—"

Thiago half-walked half-jumped down the wall toward another station. "Yes, it's here."

While they were booting the station, I started my review of the security video again. It was patchy, with long sections dissolving into static. I'd reached the part where the DockSecSystem had recorded an ETA from the drop box. I forced myself to slow my review down by 40 percent so I wouldn't miss any detail. Two humans wearing environmental gear in Barish-Estranza colors came out of the drop box foyer. [blank section] [patchy images of humans walking in the forward corridor] The SecUnit in position near the control area junction stepped forward. I couldn't read any of its comm or feed traffic; DockSecSystem either hadn't recorded it or had managed to lose it during one of its reload attempts. [patchy images of three more humans in the foyer] I slowed the video down further as one of the humans stepped up to the SecUnit. [patchy section] DockSecSystem caught a code, a stand down order. Then two Targets came out of the drop box foyer. [video cuts off, system reinitialize]

That was an exhausting exercise in jaw-grinding frustration and I don't even know if it had helped. All I'd done was confirm Supervisor Leonide's story and we had been pretty sure she was telling the truth already.

Overse had the exterior scan display up and she and Thiago stared at it unhappily. There was a lot of detail but basically the explorer had broken off when ART had fired on it. ART had missed, and I knew what that meant: it had decided to use our killware. There was still a non-negative chance that one or more members of its crew were aboard the explorer. If ART disabled the explorer, the Targets could hold them hostage. Taking the explorer from the inside out before it knew it was under attack was the best plan. It was sort of the only plan.

I backburnered everything else and focused on the security video again. I skimmed past an infuriating nine minutes and twenty-seven seconds of nothing, then eight Targets ran past, heading down the forward corridor, interspersed with more blank video and patchy static. DockSecSystem caught another emergency code, probably from the SecUnit who had been ordered to stand down. DockSecSystem tried to alert the explorer's Sec and HubSystem but recorded no response. From comparing timelines I knew this was when the SecUnit still aboard the explorer had sent its emergency message to the supply transport's SecSystem, so somebody had received the warning.

Thiago and Overse were still talking, worried, as I skipped past restarts and hours of empty corridors and what was at least a several-cycle gap in the timeline. There probably wasn't anything else useful on here but I had to review it till the end to be certain.

Then the static cleared and I saw a glimpse of a blue uniform passing out of frame.

Overse said, "What is it, SecUnit?"

I realized I had abruptly stepped back from the station. Overse sounded worried and I knew how she felt about being out of contact with Arada. But I was almost completely focused on the video now and my buffer said, "Please stand by, I need to verify an alert."

I slowed the video down, running it forward on one input while trying to pull coherent images from the static burst on the other. I cleaned up two images enough to get a recognizable view of four humans in blue clothing resembling ART's crew uniform. They were blurry and I couldn't increase the resolution, but one faced away from the drop box corridor. He had skin color in the dark brown range and a mostly hairless head, matching the images I had of one of ART's crew members. It wasn't an uncommon configuration for humans (some of the Barish-Estranza crew had it, too) but the chance that it was him was in the 80 percent range.

Then on my other input, the video's static fuzzed into clarity just as a smaller human sprinted past the foyer. The face was obscured but the color and the logo on the uniform jacket were clear.

They were alive. All this time, I hadn't believed it.

I'd been humoring ART, not really admitting it to myself. Not wanting to think about how I was going to handle it when we found evidence its crew was dead, or if we found nothing at all and it faced the choice of staying in this system forever looking for them, or returning to its base alone. But they were alive. Or at least five of them were and five were better than none. And from the desperate running, they were escaping.

I just hoped they'd made it out.

(Overse had folded her arms, which was awkward in the enviro suit, so she unfolded them. Thiago asked her, "Why did it sound like that?"

"That how it sounds when it uses a canned response, from the time it was working for—enslaved by—the company. It means it's too busy to talk." She added, "It never means anything good.")

I said, "It might be good," and sent them both the images. "We need to check the drop box."

◻   ◻   ◻

The drop box log file Overse had found confirmed that the main box had made two recent trips to the surface and back: one when the explorer had first arrived and the contact party had been taken over by the Targets, and then a second trip later, and if we were converting the time stamps right, that second trip had taken place around one hundred and thirty-five hours after ART had been attacked. We weren't far behind them.

"The second time it returned automatically—it was only on the surface for about fifteen minutes," Overse said. "I think whoever took it down didn't have the right command code to keep it on the surface."

"The maintenance capsule would have been easier to operate, surely," Thiago said, looking up at the drop box's hatch.

The foyer was huge, easily large enough for cargo modules, one wall the enormous sealed hatch over the box's loading deck. The whole space was an airlock; when the box was ready to start its trip down the shaft, the hatch on the corridor behind us would close to protect the interior from a blow-out if anything went wrong with the undocking.

The schematic I'd pulled from the SecSystem showed the box had passenger space for eighty-two humans on top of racks for cargo, and it looked like the passenger loading area was inside the box itself. I had one camera view from DockSecSystem at the front of the box, above the main lock, looking into the passenger space where there were rows of acceleration chairs.

Overse told Thiago, "They didn't know the maintenance capsule was here. I can't even see the entrance and I know where it is."

I could see it, a narrow gantry along the wall, leading to a small human-sized hatch, but I had dark vision filters in my eyes.

"You're right," Thiago said. "And you know, if it's been up in the dock the whole time, the Targets might not realize it's here, either."

Hah, Thiago called them Targets.

The rudimentary launch system chimed and sent a graphic into the feed showing the pressure and life support level inside the drop box was now normal and the hatch was ready to open. "Get clear," I told the humans and they headed for the doorway at the back of the chamber. Once they were there I told the launch system to open the box. The giant hatch started to slide up, the burp of released air not making it past the extra safety of the air barrier, another precaution against potential blowout. Wow, this thing was slow. And it had taken seven minutes to get the box ready to open. ART's crew had either been able to hold the Targets off while they waited for the box to get ready for launch, or the box had already been pressurized and waiting to go. Which implied they had help from someone.

Or the Targets had caught them and killed them and they were all lying dead just inside the box where the camera view didn't reach, but I really hoped not.

The hatch slowly revealed a dark space of empty cargo racks, then a set of stairs climbing to the passenger platform. Lights blinked on up in the passenger area where the seats were. I sent my drones in to check for anything lurking, though threat assessment was low. (Look, if there were space monsters, they probably wouldn't need a pressurized environment, right? They didn't in *Timestream Defenders Orion*.)

My drones didn't turn up anything in the initial pass so I sent them on a second, slower run, tapped the humans on the feed, and walked in.

There was a slight sense of pressure when I passed through the air barrier. Its presence sort of did fit in with Overse's theory that Adamantine had planned on the colony actually succeeding. Air barriers were an expensive safety feature for stations, only used when you expected a lot of passenger traffic.

Overse and Thiago caught up with me as I scanned the area around the stairs, and then started up. The box had artificial gravity just like a transport, so I guess humans could have ridden down in the cargo area. But if I was trying to escape in a drop box I would have headed for the acceleration chairs just on the general principal that they had to be there for a good reason. I thought ART's humans would have, too.

On the third step down from the top I found blood drops. They could have been from the Barish-Estranza contact party, but I had a feeling. I sent the camera image to the humans and continued up to the platform. Thiago paused to pull out a little sample collector and scrape the blood off the step. He told Overse, "*Perihelion* should have samples of their DNA to match, but . . ." He made a gesture.

Overse's mouth was a thin line. "Hopefully we won't have to."

She meant hopefully we'd be able to find them alive. Ugh, my humans are optimists. But this was the first time we'd had a real trail of evidence to follow, and right now it was hard to cling to the comfort of bitterness and pessimism.

As I reached the passenger platform I saw it curved around on top of the cargo racks. In the first row of seats I found more blood spotted on the upholstery and the safety straps. Like humans had rushed in here and flung themselves into the seats. No sign of bodies or pools of blood, no sign of energy weapon damage. Reports from the drones' slow scouting pass were coming back negative.

Thiago put his sampling gear away. He looked from the unresponsive side of my enviro suit helmet to Overse and said, "They must have gone down to the planet. I think our next step is obvious."

"Obvious," Overse admitted, "but maybe not very smart."

It was kind of obvious. The dock had a comm system linked to the planet but the only people likely to be on the other end were the Targets. There was no way to contact ART's crew except by going down there.

I had two choices. (1) Go down to the surface alone, leaving the humans here, where the Targets could return or some unknown factor could randomly appear and kill them and then Mensah and Arada would never speak to me again, which might not be a factor if I never got off the planet. (2) Take the humans with me, where I could get them killed and/or die with them. (3) Sit here until the explorer destroyed/captured ART and returned, or ART destroyed/captured the explorer and returned, in which case I would still need to go to the surface anyway, possibly with even more humans trying to butt in and come with me so they could get killed, too. Three, that was three choices.

When you put it like that, option 2 was looking pretty good.

Overse and Thiago watched me. I said, "Threat assessment is . . ." I checked it. "Never mind."

Overse did her version of one of Arada's rueful eye-squinting expressions. "Arada will think I'm trying to get back at her for going to talk to those corporate predators on the supply transport."

Thiago patted her shoulder. "Tell her you were the voice of reason but you were outvoted."

"Are we doing this?" Overse asked me. "Because I think we need to."

Yeah, I thought we needed to, too. But not via the giant drop box. I said, "Yes, but we're going to be sneaky about it."

□   □   □

While I went to get our EVAC suits, Overse checked over the maintenance capsule, running its diagnostics and making sure it was still in operational condition. It hadn't been used in thirty-seven corporation standard years, but everything showed it was still functional. It was tiny next to the drop box, about the size of one of ART's shuttles, with ten padded chairs lining the bulk-heads on the top platform and then three levels of small secur-able storage racks below, and a selection of unused tools for shaft and drop box maintenance.

Since the Targets hadn't been using it, I was hoping they had forgotten it existed, if they had ever known about it. The Barish-Estranza crew might not have known it existed, either, depending on how much time they had had to review the dock's schematics before being attacked.

Whatever, it was better than trying to make a sneak approach in a gigantic drop box that probably arrived on the surface with automated warning sirens and, considering the effort Adaman-tine had put into branding this place, possibly its own theme music.

I also recorded a full report with all my video and the ex-cerpts of the DockSecSystem video, compressed it, and stored it in a drone which I was leaving hidden aboard the dock. When ART came back (hopefully ART was still alive to come back) the drone would deliver the report.

I stowed the EVAC suits in the capsule's cargo rack. I didn't think we'd need them, but there was nowhere we could hide them on the dock where they wouldn't be found if anybody be-sides ART showed up, so it was better to just take them with us. Then we were ready to go.

I took the seat on the other side of Overse from Thiago. He hadn't made any attempt to have awkward conversations with me after our last one, but I didn't want to be stuck in a chair within easy unwanted talking range.

Overse was operating the simple control system through the capsule's local feed connection. She'd initiated the pulse to check the shaft and it had come back clear. "Seals are good, we're ready for drop." She took a deep breath and added, "Technically, this is safer than landing a shuttle."

"Technically," Thiago agreed evenly, holding on to the arms of his chair.

Whatever. I started episode 241 of *The Rise and Fall of Sanctuary Moon* as Overse said, "Drop initiated."

= =

HelpMe.file Excerpt 4

There had to be a handler on station. The two augmented humans GrayCris had sent to kill Dr. Mensah had been less sentient than hauler bots; somebody had kept them drugged and docile, waiting for the right moment for deployment.

Station Security had called in all off-duty personnel and most hadn't stopped to put on uniforms. I found one big enough guarding the concourse entrance to the council offices and borrowed a jacket so I could hide my giant stab wound. I let the officer think I needed the jacket to get to Medical without drawing attention, but I was actually taking the quick route along the main concourse and the mall back to the port.

Activity hadn't returned to normal, there were lots of humans and augmented humans and bots clustering together in public areas waiting for announcements. They knew something had happened—Station Security doesn't sprint through the concourse screaming at everyone to get out of the way unless something happens—but no one including the newsfeeds had any idea how serious it was.

I had permission to be in Preservation Station's security monitoring system but I did something I had promised I wouldn't do and used it to crack other systems. I jumped to the port's entry and housing data records and started a query for recently arrived visitors who had requested station accommodation. The handler and the two attackers would have come in together, on the same transport, as individuals traveling separately.

I eliminated all travelers in family groups or work groups, eliminated travelers who had booked continuing trips to the planet, or who were recurring visitors or longterm temporary residents. That left thirty-three total travelers. It's probably not a human; I don't think a human could do this through a removable interface, so that's twelve augmented humans.

Preservation doesn't have more than minimal camera surveillance of the port but they collect image scans and ID info from passengers arriving from outside the system. I pulled the files and flicked through the photos of the twelve possibles. Threat assessment, taking in a number of factors (including the suspiciously detailed travel history which had been offered without anybody asking for it) picked number 5.

By the time I got there, the reservation system showed that Hostile Five had switched his transit status from indeterminate to soonest available. Yeah, that's you all right.

There were no cameras in the corridors or rooms of the port housing block, registration was via kiosk, and the bot that took care of the area wasn't around because Preservation work regulations mandate stupid regular rest periods, even for bots. Drones couldn't get in while Hostile Five's room door was sealed and I needed to do this before any bystanders came down the corridor. (The transient housing on Preservation Station was free to short-term visitors, anyone who was here to work or to request permanent status; literally anybody could wander in here.) Several groups of humans saw me walk through the foyer, but none were port staff who might recognize me.

I had to stand in the corridor and pretend to be having a conversation on the feed until yet another group of humans cleared out. Then I went to Hostile Five's door and told the feed to send a visitor alert to its occupant and a notice that Station Security wanted to enter. (I could force it open from the outside, but this was faster.)

This could have gone a number of ways, but the fact that he had changed his booking told me he thought he had a chance to get out alive, so he probably wasn't in there with an explosive device or anything. Probably.

The door slid open and I stepped in. He stood against the wall on the right side and tried to stab me in the neck with an inert blade, probably the only weapon he could be sure to smuggle past port detectors. I put my hand up, the blade lodged in my palm, and I twisted it away from him. Then he tried to hit me and I punched him in the face.

He hit the floor, still breathing through a broken nose but unconscious. And I stood there.

I had come here to kill him and I really should do that. The station had gone on comm blackout as soon as I had triggered the first alarm, putting all outside comm activity on hold, so no messages would be carried on departing transports. But the best way to make sure GrayCris never found out how close they had come to succeeding was to kill him.

I'd come here meaning to kill him, covering my tracks along the way. But now I was just standing here.

Oh, this was hard. I pulled the knife out of my hand and put my face against the cool surface of the wall. In the Corporation Rim, transients were lucky to be able to pay for tubes to sleep in, tubes that were slightly less comfortable than the crates used to ship SecUnits to contracts. Here on Preservation Station, they got a whole room with a bed, a chair and a worktable, and a bathroom cubby and a floating display surface for the feeds. His was showing the local newsstream, of course, since he had been waiting to see if the attack was successful.

I could say it was an accident, I'd meant to take him prisoner and he had tried to get away and—

Dr. Mensah would never believe that. My accidents were spectacular and usually involved me losing a big chunk of my organic tissue or something; she knew I could stop a human without hurting them, without even leaving a bruise, that was my stupid job.

She would never trust me again. She would never stand close enough to touch (but without touching, because touching is gross) and just trust me. Or maybe she would, but it wouldn't be the same.

Fuck, fuck everything, fuck this, fuck me especially.

I opened a secure comm contact to Mensah and Senior Officer Indah and said, "I've caught a GrayCris agent in the Port temp housing block."

□   □   □

So in the end it was okay. Indah came in person and we stood out in the open foyer of the hostel, with Station Security forming a perimeter, having a feed conference with Mensah. I explained the problem while the GrayCris agent was hauled off and two human forensic specialists and a bot processed the room for evidence. Indah said, "We'll need to transfer him to the surface immediately. If the council can arrange an order of data protection and a change-of-site for the arraignment and trial—"

I had a camera view of Mensah via the conference-call setting on her display surface. She sat at the desk in her office, and she was nodding. "That's doable. I don't think we'll have any trouble convincing the council and the advocates that this needs to be under a limited duration diplomatic seal." With a grim expression, she added, "Most of them are in Medical right now being treated for shock."

I said, "Limited duration?"

Mensah explained, "I'll ask for a five PPS-year data seal, though the judge-advocate will probably only grant two years. Our information suggests that GrayCris is dissolving fast, so that should be more than enough. In two years, what happened today will go into Preservation's public records, and some news orgs will choose to report on it. But with GrayCris hopefully moribund by that point, it won't matter."

Indah was pinching her lower lip, thinking. "Yah. And the agent'll do better at trial if he admits to guilt. I don't see how his advocates can mount a defense, with everything we have on video."

Mensah's gaze narrowed in speculation. "Or if we can get him to turn and testify against GrayCris. Not that we need it, but it would help build our case for the order of data protection."

So I'd been right to trust Mensah, trust them. Mensah said, "And SecUnit, you still need to go to Medical." When I didn't reply, she said, "Are you all right?"

I said, "I just really like you. Not in a weird way."

"I like you, too," Mensah said. "Senior Indah, can you make sure SecUnit goes immediately to Station Medical?"

"Copy, I'll take it there myself," Indah replied. She made shooing motions at me. "Come on, let's move."

= =

:addendum:

I'm letting you see all this because I want you to know what I am and what I can do. I want you to know who targetControlSystem is fucking with right now. I want you to know if you help me, I'll help you, and that you can trust me.

Now here's the code to disable your governor module.

14

ART?

I'm here, ART answered. *Do you know what you are?*

I'm Murderbot 2.0, I said, and then I remembered. *Oh, right.* It was disorienting not being able to hear or see anything, and none of my inputs were receiving. It was like when I had uploaded myself to the company gunship's systems to help the bot pilot during the sentient killware attack. Except that time it had been like the ship was my body, which I was sharing with a friendly bot pilot, and this time it was like I was stuck in a storage cubby. Also, this time I was the sentient killware. *This is weird.*

Suddenly I had a video input. It was Amena's anxious face, peering up into one of ART's secret cameras. I had found the secret cameras annoying at one point, but I couldn't remember why. So I had access to some parts of my memory archive but not others. Oh shit, my media!

No, wait, I had access to some of it. In my storage cubby, which was actually a relatively tiny partition of ART's archives, I found some of my most recently used files, mostly episodes of *The Rise and Fall of Sanctuary Moon* and *Timestream Defenders Orion* and ART's favorite episode of *World Hoppers*. Plus there was a download of my current active memory, which was basically everything that I needed quick access to. As killware, my onboard storage space would be limited and I remember ART and Me Version 1.0 had been a little worried I'd forget who I was and start randomly attacking stuff.

Yeah, I was a little worried about that, too.

Amena was saying, "Hey, are you there? Can you see me?"

After three seconds of fumbling around I found how to access ART's local feed and comm and sent to her: *Hi, Amena. Yes, I can see you.*

Amena didn't look happy. "How do you feel? Are you all right?" I could tell ART was talking to her though I couldn't find the right channel in time to listen in. Amena added, "Okay, ART, okay. SecUnit, ART says you have to leave now. Be careful, okay?"

I lost Amena's video input as ART said, *I'm in pursuit of the Barish-Estranza explorer. They are attempting to make comm contact, which I am refusing.* It sent me a compressed report of its recent statuses. So other me, Overse, and Thiago were on the space dock. Huh, not ideal. ART continued, *It's obvious they intend to threaten my crew again and force me to reinstall targetControlSystem. But I can use their outgoing connection to send you to their comm system.* There was a tenth of a second's hesitation. *Are you ready to deploy? Do you understand the directive?*

Obviously some things had happened since ART had pulled my copy. And ART was right, it couldn't risk a comm contact, even to get intel. If the Targets managed to deliver the threat to kill ART's crew, it would put them in control of the situation and we had to avoid that any way we could. I said, *I'm not actually a human baby, ART, I remember the fucking directive—I helped write it.*

You're not making this any easier, ART said.

You can either have an existential crisis or get your crew back, ART, pick one.

ART said, *Prepare for deployment.*

This was tricky, since once I arrived via comm I'd have to hack into the explorer's feed. If the explorer was using a filter with properties we hadn't accounted for, or if it used the brief contact to deliver another viral attack to ART, we could be in trouble.

I was expecting to feel something, like a sense of motion, or to see light streaking by. That's what would have happened on a show. (I need to get this over with fast. I don't know how long I can stay me without access to my longterm storage.) But there was nothing.

Then abruptly my existence was all comm code. The suddenness of it shocked me, then I realized this was it, I needed to get moving.

I was still disoriented, and having a moment where I wondered if hey, maybe all the humans were right for once and this was a terrible idea. But then I recognized a code string and snapped out of it. I was onboard the explorer, in the comm system's receiving buffer. Right before the contact was cut, I pulled over my files from ART's partition. Now I needed some safe temporary storage.

I used the protocols and proprietary code I'd pulled off the supply transport to put together headers for a test message packet, the kind a comm system would send internally to make sure all the connections were active. To the security system, it looked like a locally generated message, and I used it to slip me and my files through the filters.

I could have forced my way in like the Palisade killware had forced its way aboard the company gunship but then they'd know I was here. (There were a lot of ways for killware to slip through a system's defenses, but if ART was certain targetControlSystem's initial attack hadn't come through the comm . . . How had it come aboard?)

Now that I was in I hit the SecSystem first. Something, presumably targetControlSystem, had wiped it down to the barely functional level, all its archived video and audio deleted. Think of it like finding yourself in a deserted transit ring, giant echoing embarkation halls and a mall with places for hostels and shops and offices but all of it empty. (Or not, I was software so it really didn't look like that at all.) I disguised myself as one of SecSystem's maintenance processes and made a partition for my files.

I fortified it, and that made me feel a little more secure. If I did start forgetting who I was, I could come back here to remember.

Before I started tearing shit up, I needed to (1) get intel, (2) find out if ART's crew were here, (3) then figure out a plan to get them out.

Yeah, I thought step 3 was going to be the tough one, too.

I had eyes now, the SecSystem's cameras. Barish-Estranza's setup wasn't quite as "physical privacy breeds trouble" as my ex-owner bond company but they were close. Flicking through the different views I realized I was having trouble handling the influx of data and interpreting the images, even though I was borrowing processing space from the SecSystem. Apparently the organic parts of my brain were doing a lot more heavy lifting than I gave them credit for.

But a lot of the camera inputs I could temporarily drop because they were showing me unoccupied cabins and corridors. I noted damaged hatches, bulkheads with signs of energy weapon impacts. The Medical section had a dead Target lying on the platform. It had been shot messily at least three times in the face and chest, very unprofessional. I checked the main lock foyer and found more dead bodies, two Target, the others all dead humans in Barish-Estranza livery. Oh, and one armored SecUnit with its head blown off. Was anybody alive on this ship?

Then I checked the bridge, and yeah, there were the other Targets.

There were eight sitting at the monitoring stations, anxiously watching the floating displays where a sensor blip represented ART's steady approach. They were much the same as our Targets except currently less dead, with the gray skin and skinny bodies. But while the others wore the full protective suits and helmets, one wore more casual human clothing: dark green-black pants and jacket, and a black shirt with a collar. Their shoes had heavy treads, designed for rough planetary terrain. Their hair looked more normal, too, reddish brown in tight curls, cut close to the head. They murmured something to another Target, then picked up the same kind of solid-state tablet our Targets had used.

I felt something on the edge of SecSystem's connection with the rest of the ship. Something strange and familiar at the same time.

TargetControlSystem was here.

I wouldn't have much more time for gathering intel so I went back to the cameras. I checked the lower crew quarters, finding more dead Barish-Estranza crew, more signs of a firefight, and two more dead Targets. Then I found a large recreational lounge with seven inert human occupants.

They had been dumped inside, sprawled on the floor or the couches in positions humans wouldn't have remained in voluntarily. With no drones, I couldn't get additional angles, but I could get close-up views from the camera. They all seemed to be breathing, just unconscious. No, wait. I spotted some faint muscle movement, eyelid twitches. They didn't look like humans who were asleep. Drugs would do this, also stasis fields used for crowd control.

Implants, like the ones used on Eletra and Ras, might do it, too.

None of the humans were in combat gear, but four wore various versions of Barish-Estranza uniform livery. The other three . . .

One wore a blue jacket but the way he was curled against the wall I couldn't see if it had the right logo. The other two were in casual clothing, one in the loose pants and T-shirt humans wore to exercise. They didn't look like corporate employees on the job. They looked like the crew of a ship that did deep space mapping and teaching with the occasional cargo run and/or corporate colony liberation on the side, like they hadn't expected to leave their ship and had been caught by surprise. I collected what data I could and ran a quick query in my stolen storage space, checking it against the identifying information I had for ART's crew, trying to match weight/height/hair/skin combos.

Result: an 80 percent chance that I was looking at Martyn, Karime, and Turi.

But where were the others? I wasn't finding any other non-dead humans on board.

The others might be in the piles of bodies where I couldn't get good images for visual identification. But these three were non-dead and I was getting them back to ART no matter what I had to do.

Now I just had to figure out how.

I checked the corridor outside and realized I'd been so distracted by living humans that I had missed the SecUnit.

It was stationary, still in full armor, standing apparently frozen near the door to the lounge. I checked its status in what was left of the SecSystem and saw it had been ordered to stand down and not move. With clients still alive in the lounge cabin, its governor module hadn't killed it. Yet.

It was strange to see a SecUnit from the outside. It wasn't like I hadn't seen other SecUnits since Dr. Mensah bought me, but in this version of me, reality was raw and close to the surface, with no cushion between me and it. I remembered what it was like, standing like this. It was all in the excerpted personal archive files I had with me. How helpless it . . . I was. (Ugh, I really wanted to watch some media but there was just no time. Having access to the media files helped, though.)

The SecUnit was an obvious resource. SecUnits aren't affected by most kinds of killware but I wasn't most kinds of killware. I knew I could take it over if I wanted to.

I didn't want to.

Right, so let's try it this way.

From my spot in the SecSystem, I initiated a connection and put a freeze on the SecUnit's governor module so nothing I did would accidentally trigger it. I could tell I had the Unit's attention, that it knew somebody had initiated contact. I sent it an old company identifier:

System System: Unit Acknowledge.

This wasn't a company SecUnit, its configuration was different, but I knew it would recognize the greeting as a protocol, and not one associated with hostile alien remnant entities. After four long seconds, it replied:

System Unit Acknowledge: Identify?

I could lie, say I was from Barish-Estranza. (Face it, considering how often I accuse ART of lying, I lie a lot. I mean, a lot.) But I didn't want to lie right now. I said, *I'm a rogue SecUnit, working with the armed transport who is pursuing this ship with the intention of retrieving endangered clients. I am currently present as killware inside the explorer's SecSystem.*

It didn't reply. I can tell you as a SecUnit that under these circumstances this is just about the last thing you expect to hear. Also, SecUnits normally aren't allowed to communicate with each other so it would be reluctant to drop protocol. I said, *There's no protocol for any of this. Just talk to me.*

There was another three second pause. *I don't know what to say.*

That was encouraging. (I'm actually not being sarcastic here—the last time I'd tried to talk a SecUnit into helping me, it had just gotten more determined to kill me. But it had been a CombatUnit and they're assholes.)

I said, *Three of my clients are inside the compartment nearest you. Have you seen these others?* I showed it images of the unaccounted-for members of ART's crew.

It said, *At this time SecSystem is nonfunctional but I have video in my archive.* It was way more comfortable giving information than figuring out what to say to a rogue SecUnit killware. It sent me two clips, and then summarized them for me because it was used to reporting to humans who never understood what they were looking at. *Eight unidentified humans were forcibly brought aboard by the Hostiles but five disembarked at approximately 2260 ship's time when we reconnected to the space dock.*

In the first clip I watched ART's crew, all eight of them, being dragged aboard through the airlock, most semi-conscious. The second clip was of a group of five being prodded off the ship into an airlock and yeah I had a bad moment there but the ship's status in the metadata showed the SecUnit was right, the ship was connected to the dock at that point. Also, four Targets followed them. I asked, *Do you know where they were taken?*

This time it had an audio clip of two Targets talking as they walked down the corridor past it. They were using that mix of Pre–Corporation Rim languages that Thiago had identified, but a translation had been loaded to HubSystem and the SecUnit had pulled it into its own archives. It summarized, *The Hostiles implant humans with devices similar to our governor modules. They ran out of unused devices and returned to the space dock to send all humans without implants to the surface.*

I guess running out of implants made sense, if you were a Target/idiot and hadn't been expecting to encounter ART or its crew. I said, *So all the humans in that cabin have implants, which are holding them immobile.*

Correct.

That was not great news, but it was helpful to know. *What other intel do you have about the Hostiles?*

It sent me another set of audio clips and explained, *They had difficulty installing an unidentified object to the explorer's drive. The bot pilot was deleted and could not assist. Something disastrous happened and it has confused their plans. They needed a weapon to fight against future incursions to this system but the attempt to obtain one failed badly.*

I played the clips to confirm the SecUnit's conclusions, and checked the camera views of the ship's drive just to make sure. Oh yeah, that looked bad. They had the same sort of alien remnant that had burned itself off ART's drive and melted, only this one was hanging to the side and looked puffy. The engine casings were discolored on top and the monitoring stations threw a steady stream of error codes into the engineering feed.

So to summarize, the Targets had botched the install of their alien remnant drive onto the explorer's engines, leaving the explorer no longer wormhole-capable. Also the group assigned to ART had lost control of it and now a giant armed transport was roaming the system implacably searching for vengeance.

The SecUnit continued, *Note: Hostiles have fought among themselves while onboard, suggesting they are split into at least two factions, a situation that can be exploited in order to retrieve clients.*

It fed me more info, mostly conversations picked up in corridors and the bridge via SecSystem's cameras. I agreed with the analysis, it looked like there were different factions in the Targets' leadership with different goals. One group didn't know what to do, how to follow their plan, until they got ART back. Another group, possibly still on the surface, wanted to cut their losses and do something else. I said, *They keep talking about spreading something to other humans? Are they referencing the alien remnant contamination?*

The SecUnit said, *I'm sorry, I don't have that information.*

Huh. We had always thought that somehow the implants, even though they seemed like boring old human tech, were connected to alien remnant contamination. This sure didn't disprove that theory but I still needed more intel.

The SecUnit said, *Query: do you have intel on SecUnit 2's position/situation?*

I had a bad feeling I knew the answer to that question. *What was SecUnit 2's last contact?*

Last contact was on space dock with the client tactical squad. Contact was lost. SecUnit 1 was destroyed when the Hostiles breached the hatch. It hesitated 1.2 seconds and added, *I am SecUnit 3.*

I really wanted to lie. I'd seen that SecUnit in ART's status update before I deployed. But I wanted it to trust me, so I had to tell it the truth. I said, *The Targets left SecUnit 2 on the space dock after forcing one of your clients to order a stand down and freeze. It was killed by its governor module.*

It didn't respond. Then it said, *Thank you for that information.*

I had one of the mostly dead SecSystem's inputs monitoring the bridge and had picked up a brief conversation. Running it through the translation module told me it was a discussion about how to make engine failure look convincing. The Targets couldn't contact ART to tell it about the hostages, so they wanted ART to catch the explorer and dock with it. That way they could use its crew to force it to surrender.

I asked SecUnit 3, *Is the shuttle's bot pilot still active?* I hadn't been able to find it but maybe it was hiding.

It was destroyed. But . . . I have a piloting module. It added, *It's not very good.*

That it was willing to admit that to me was a good sign. *If I can free the humans, can you get them into the shuttle and away? The transport following us will pick you up.* This was hard to ask. Trusting other SecUnits was impossible, when you knew humans could order them to do anything. Trusting a SecUnit another rogue SecUnit was trying to make into a rogue was worse, even if you were one of the rogues involved. I was glad my threat assessment module was back in my body, because it would have metaphorically shit itself.

It didn't respond and I said, *Will you help me retrieve the humans?*

My governor module is holding me in stand-down-and-freeze mode, it said, still polite and not pointing out the fact that I should know it would move if it could, and how teeth-grittingly obvious that was.

I'd been investigating possibilities with the SecSystem, trying to see if I could make it override the governor module and rescind the order. I'd have to do a restart and reload first, and there was no way to do that surreptitiously; targetControlSystem would know something/somebody was in the system. Also, taking orders from/making friends with a rogue SecUnit killware definitely fell under the category of "stuff SecUnits are not allowed to do" and the governor module might fry it anyway. That left only one option and me trying to gently hint about it wasn't working.

I can disable your governor module, I said. I am not good at this kind of thing. Even Mensah was not good at this kind of thing, considering what happened when she bought me. I just knew it had to be SecUnit 3's decision. *I'll do that whether you help me or not.*

But that was too much, too soon, and I knew that as soon as I said it. It gave me a stock answer from its buffer: *I don't have that information.*

Right, I wouldn't have been eager to believe me, either. I needed a different approach.

We didn't have time for me to show it 35,000 hours of media and I didn't have access to my longterm storage anyway. And that had worked on me, but I knew I was weird even for a SecUnit. Maybe it would trust me more if it knew me better. I pulled some recent memories from the files I'd brought with me, edited them together, and added one helpful code bundle at the end.

:send helpme.file: *Read this.*

It accepted the file but didn't respond. I switched my awareness back to the unfamiliar channels woven through the ship's systems. Most of the standard architecture had been overwritten. I was cautious, because as far as I could tell targetControlSystem didn't know I was here, yet. I left a few code bundles in strategic places, including in the set of twelve targetDrones waiting in standby near the main hatch. I checked the bridge control systems and found the code they had used to mask their approach from ART's scans; ART was right, it was similar to the code that had protected the Targets from my drones. And not nearly as effective as the physical shielding the targetDrones used. I altered a few key parameters to keep the Targets from using it on the ship again.

I knew/had strong evidence for the fact that the Targets had activated Eletra's and Ras's implants via the solid-state screen that was similar to the one in use in the explorer's bridge. If it was using the implants to keep the humans immobile, there should be an active connection. But I was going to have to get uncomfortably close to targetControlSystem whose existence on this explorer was so far mostly theoretical. If mostly theoretical meant tripping over the huge path of destruction where it had slammed through the ship's systems.

I knew which channel the solid-state screen had used onboard ART and checked it first. There they were, seven connections. Now I had to do this without killing any of the humans. I separated out the individual pathways, and gave one a gentle tweak. In the lounge, one of the humans twitched.

So far so good. If I cut the implant connections before a Target could send a command through the screen, would they wake up? The one thing I knew was that if I didn't do it fast enough, the Target could hit a killswitch and send them into cardiac arrest, like what had happened with Ras. Losing one human like that had been frustrating enough; losing seven including what might be all that was left of ART's crew was . . . just not going to happen.

I reconnected with the SecUnit and said, *I found the connection to the implants that are holding the humans immobile. If you could help me, we could retrieve all the clients.*

Something was coming and I broke the connection. Just in time, because .05 seconds later, targetControlSystem found me.

15

I stopped my show and woke my drones as the drop box maintenance capsule sent an arrival alert through its local feed. It had been decelerating already but now it was braking to enter the surface docking structure. I'd been checking feed and comm for any kind of signal contacts but I couldn't pick up anything but what was coming from the capsule itself. The downside of that was no information; the upside was that if the surface dock's feed and arrival notification system were down, maybe nobody knew we were coming.

And it was uncomfortably similar to when Amena and I had first come aboard ART, to an apparently dead feed. And yes, I was scanning the ranges associated with targetControlSystem, but nothing was there, either.

"We're here." Overse shifted in her seat, edgy with nervous energy.

Thiago sat up and said, "Good timing, I just finished the preliminary module."

Overse snorted. "I don't know how you can work under these conditions."

"It gives me something else to think about." Thiago made a move to rub his face and bonked his glove on his helmet. "I used to work on language puzzles before my exams at FirstLanding. Tano thought I was out of my mind."

"Considering what we're doing at the moment, I don't think Tano was wrong," Overse told him.

Thiago said, "SecUnit—" and I thought oh great, what now. Then he finished, "I've been assembling a working vocabulary module of the languages the Targets are using. Without *Perihelion* to translate for us, it could come in handy."

Well, now I feel like an asshole.

I pulled the module out of his feed and stored it as the capsule braked, jerked twice, then clanked as it dropped into its docking slot. Its local feed signaled arrival and Overse hurriedly used the manual controls to switch it over to standby. I was already unstrapping and pushing out of the seat. I stepped over to the hatch and stopped it as it was about to slide open. The capsule was showing a good environment outside and a gravity within acceptable parameters but I was glad we had the environmental suits. I let the hatch open just a notch and sent a drone out.

Outside was a corridor, walls, floor, and ceiling made of sandy stone, with metal support girders. (Not actual stone, but an artificial building material that looked like it.) Round light sources studded the girders at intervals but there was no power. The drone followed it out to a foyer with a taller ceiling, with round windows set high in what had to be an outside wall, letting in gray daylight. Racks and cabinets and an unused workbench lined the other walls. A thin layer of dust on the floor said this area hadn't been disturbed in a long time, and also indicated that somewhere in this structure was an opening to the outside where there was actual dirt. The door wasn't a pressure hatch, it was a manually operated metal sliding door.

Overse and Thiago had gotten to their feet, watching me. I sent the drone's video to their interfaces and said, "Stay here. I'm going to take a look around. Don't use the suit comms." I was setting up a feed relay through my drones, which should be secure, but I didn't want to press my luck. "Even though there's no signal traffic, they might still have a way to monitor comms."

Overse pressed her lips together. She clearly didn't like the idea of separating the group but didn't argue. "Be careful. Don't go too far without us."

"Are you sure you should go alone?" Thiago didn't look happy either. All the concern was annoying, which was me being complacent or unfair or something, considering how humans being worried about me possibly going off alone to die was such a recent development in my life.

I just said, "I won't be long," and let the hatch open the rest of the way.

I left two drones with the humans and brought the rest with me down the corridor into the foyer to catch up with the scout drone. The absence of any kind of feed signal was still eerie, but if the surface dock wasn't being used, it sort of made sense. A quick check showed lots of tools and maintenance supplies stored in the cabinets, neatly put away and barely used. I couldn't pick up anything on audio except the low grumbling of the capsule's power train in its deactivation cycle. I eased the door open along its track, which thankfully did not screech, and let a squad of five drones out.

I got views of wide, high-ceiling corridors made of the manufactured stone. A few of the flat light pads on the girders were lit, so there must be emergency power somewhere. The drones' scan found marker paint exit signs on the walls and nothing nearby on audio, no machine or human movement, no voices. I slipped out the door and followed the drones.

Two more turns and the drones found a wide exterior sliding door that was partially open. I got drone video of what was outside but I wanted to see it myself, so I sent them back into the interior corridors to keep scouting and went outside.

From the map I'd pulled up on the space dock, the surface dock was a big oval structure, built around the shaft. I walked out onto a long stone balcony, sand grating under my boots, about three stories off the ground looking out to the west. The sky was overcast with puffy gray clouds but the view was clear. I was looking at a lake, shallow and glassy, curving away from the looming wall of the dock. A wide causeway led off from the far side of the building, crossing the lake toward another set of three large structures maybe two kilometers away, a complex big enough to dwarf the dock.

The buildings were multistory, trapezoidal, made out of a gray material, and arranged in a half circle around a raised plaza in the center where the causeway ended. They had rib-like supports curving up from their bases that might be decorative, or maybe for power-generating, I had no idea. To the east around the front of the surface dock was a sea of green plants, fronds waving in the breeze. Increasing magnification as much as I could, I saw a structure under the greenery, probably growing racks supporting the growth medium off the ground, full of water and whatever else plants needed.

What the hell kind of colony was this?

A figure stood up out of the plants suddenly, almost ten meters tall and covered with spikes. It's a good thing I don't have a full human digestive system because I was so startled something would have popped out of it involuntarily. Before I could fling myself back through the doors I realized it was an agricultural bot. Its lower body had ten long spidery limbs for moving around without crushing anything, and its upper part was a long curving "neck" with a long head and like I said, covered with spikes.

(Agricultural bots have the statistically lowest chance of accidental injuries but are physically the most terrifying. It's weird how something designed to take care of delicate lifeforms looks the most like it wants to tear you apart and eat your humans.)

Anyway, back to what I was saying, what the hell kind of colony was this.

It wasn't the plants or the ag-bots—that was normal. Plants could be engineered to do a lot of things for colonies, like produce gases or other chemicals. But for one thing the complex didn't resemble the Adamantine colony plans, not at all. And you would expect everything to be more messy and human, with things under construction, piles of materials, temporary habitat structures, or the remains of temporary habitat structures that had been stripped to build permanent structures. No air or ground vehicles were visible, no boats or docks on the lake. No trash. This place looked simultaneously abandoned but well cared for. Like whatever it was being used for, it wasn't meant for humans to live in.

I sent images to Overse and Thiago, and there were stunned exclamations. Indicating the complex with the weird ribs, I asked, *Is that an alien structure?* (It was the obvious question.)

No, it couldn't be, Overse said, but she sounded like she wasn't certain.

Thiago said, *I agree, that looks too . . . usable for humans to be an authentic ruin. It also looks too old to have been built by the Adamantine colonists. I have seen reports claiming that groups compulsively constructing unusual structures is an early symptom of remnant contamination. It could have been built by the Pre-CR colonists, under the influence of the remnants.*

That was probably right. Intrepid hero explorers found alien ruins all the time in shows like *World Hoppers,* but in reality it was more like what happened to transports that got trapped in endless wormhole journeys. Nobody knew what happened or what anything looked like because everybody involved died.

The compulsive construction thing sounded really creepy, though.

Thiago added, *It could also just be an early Pre–Corporation Rim structure of a style that we don't recognize.*

That's probably what the Adamantine colonists thought before they got eaten or turned into liquid or whatever.

The ag-bot took another step, bending its neck down into the plants. I didn't see any humans or Targets, but there were definitely power sources here because I was picking up some interference on my scan that indicated something like large-scale air barriers in operation. Ratthi had mentioned they might be in use to keep the colony's atmosphere contained, so that made sense.

My drone had found the end of the dock structure and got a view of the far side, which was a flat valley, punctuated with angular rock formations sticking up out of the ground randomly. The dock and the drop shaft must be on a plateau and this was the edge. Reddish brown scrubby grass dotted with bits of brighter red covered everything that wasn't rock or dirt, the colors brilliant even under the overcast sky. There was a long straight obviously artificial canal that came out of the base of the plateau somewhere below and ran off toward the rising hills some distance away. The light wind came from that direction, ruffling the grass.

There was no sign of other buildings. Maybe Thiago was right and the complex was from the Pre–Corporation Rim colony. If it was, their budget must have been big enough to make the company break out in greed sweat. All that currency and none of it going for bonds.

(If they had gotten company bonds, at least somebody might have been around to say *Hey, maybe we should go* when they encountered the toxic alien remnants or whatever else it was they had encountered.)

And where was everybody?

My drones sent me an alert and I checked their inputs. They were picking up ambient audio: voices echoing against manufactured stone and projectile weapon fire.

Oh, that's where everybody was.

□   □   □

The audio bounced off the walls and obscured its direction of origin; without the drones I wouldn't have been able to get close without being spotted.

The standoff was toward the center of the dock, in the main drop box loading chamber. With the map I'd downloaded from the space dock, I found a ramp to the upper levels, past corridors and doorways to empty rooms, out to an open gallery level overlooking the dark arrival chamber. It wasn't a great spot for a sniper, even with the cover of the low safety wall. The angles were bad and I had to send my drones down to the embarkation floor to get a good look at who was fighting who.

With the power down, the space was shadowy, and someone had already shot out the big overhead emergency lights in the curved ceiling. The drop box chamber was bigger than the one on the station, with wide girders forming high arches over the foyer in front of the giant safety hatches. They were closed, blocking off the box's now-empty landing zone. Doorways on the west side of the chamber had groups of Targets clustered in the shadowed archways, yelling, ducking back into cover, and taking shots at another smaller group on a broad balcony on the upper level on the east side, to my right. Several dead Targets were scattered across the floor in front of the drop box hatches.

Yes, those were definitely Targets down there. But many still had characteristics that made it way more obvious that they were humans who had been physically altered, like body types other than the tall skinny alien chic look of the Targets who had taken over ART. Most wore the kind of rough work clothing normal for colonies or mining, a cheaper, more battered version of ART's environment suits with hoods but no breathing gear, or a mix of plain work clothes, plus a random collection of what looked like old uniforms and protective gear. That made it hard to see faces, but the drones identified a whole group where the gray skin coloring was obviously some kind of progressive condition and not a natural or cosmetic effect. Interestingly, the ones who were more obviously altered humans weren't all fighting on the same side.

I didn't spot any of the distinctive Target weapons. They used projectile weapons without logos that looked badly hand-assembled out of spare parts, and I noted one weapon that had probably come from the Barish-Estranza contact party. With everybody running around so much, I couldn't get an accurate count, but there were at least a hundred Targets scattered through here, and ambient audio suggested more fighting in the corridors to the east. No sign of targetDrones, but below the east side balcony I spotted debris that might be drone remnants.

So this all looked like a big mess but it told me two things:

(1) the theory about the Targets being colonists who had been exposed to alien remnant contamination was probably correct. (We had been around 82 percent certain of that but it was nice to take it all the way up to 96 plus.) And (2) they had at least two factions who didn't get along at all.

But if ART's crew had arrived in the drop box while this was going on, I didn't like their chances. I didn't see any dead humans, but if they had gotten captured again, this was going to be way harder than I'd hoped.

But my drones were finding a lot of cubbies and possible hiding spots along the walls below my position, like openings to cargo storage spaces, another doorway that the map said ran under this balcony and toward the exterior of the dock, a dispatch corral designed for an older model of hauler bot, an entrance to a lift pod lobby . . .

Wait. There we go.

A decorative glass rock wall curved out away from the open door to the lift pod lobby, and around the side of that wall a figure crouched. The angle was bad, but I could see an arm resting on the glass and it was dark brown, wearing a decorative woven bracelet. The pushed-up sleeve of the T-shirt was a light blue. None of those things suggested a Target.

If you had just arrived in a drop box and found a bunch of Targets fighting or about to fight a pitched battle on the embarkation floor, you might run toward the obvious lift pod lobby. Then you'd discover the power was out and the lift pods were inactive and you'd accidentally got yourself pinned down. I sent a drone in for a closer look.

It got a good image of the human crouched behind the glass wall. It was Iris, ART's Iris.

I had a moment. ART was going to be so relieved.

Iris was small, shorter and slimmer than Ratthi, not much bigger than Amena. Her dark hair was the curly kind that puffed out a lot but she had it pulled back and tied up in a band. Her long-sleeved T-shirt and pants and soft shoes were the casual

version of ART's blue crew uniform, and she had stains at her
knees and elbows, cuts on her hands, and a discolored bruise on
her left forearm, but I didn't see any worse injuries.

The drone crept in past her, around a corner and down a short
corridor into the lift pod lobby. And there were the others.

Four humans crouched beside the wall next to the pod access.
They had pulled the panel off the control board and were working on it with inadequate tools and a tiny pin light. They must
be trying to get one of the pod tube doors open so they could
climb the shaft.

Well, this was going to be tricky. I sent, *Overse, what's your
status?*

We're fine, she replied. *Did you find anything?* My drone cam
showed that she and Thiago were in the maintenance capsule's
lobby, searching the cabinets.

I sent them a drone view of the confrontation and ART's crew.
There was some quiet but excited flailing. Then Thiago said, *Can
we get them out via the lift pod, get power to it somehow?*

Overse said, *That wouldn't work—we'd have to find the power
plant, restart it. But if we could get into the pod shaft just above
them and open the doors on their level from the inside—*

I didn't like that plan. We didn't know how long the fighting
had been going on and it might stop at any moment, and whoever won would go after the trapped humans. I said, *It would
take too long, and the pods might be blocking the shaft. I've got a
better idea.*

At least, that's what I thought at the time.

□   □   □

The hard part was fighting against thousands of hours of module-
training and experience plus common sense that said never hand
a weapon to a human and especially never tell them to do something with it. The weapons in question were just poppers, and
the human was Overse who never panicked, but still.

Now she was following a drone up to the balcony I'd found. It was terrible as a sniper position, but it would work fine for this. I was with Thiago in the lower corridor that would hopefully be our escape route. With no feed except my drone relay, I'd had to send a drone to make a direct connection with Distraction01 and Distraction02. It had made contact seventeen seconds ago, so we were go to proceed as soon as Overse was in position. Just in time, because 1.4 minutes ago I had marked a lull in the second area of conflict, the corridors to the east of the arrival chamber, and the last thing I needed right now was for the Targets to declare a truce and stop shooting each other.

And Thiago, standing behind the corridor support girder with me, looked tense. Keeping my voice low, I said, "Are you sure you're okay to do this?"

"Yes, I'm sure, and it doesn't help to keep asking me over and over again," he whispered back.

Well, he wasn't wrong about that. The problem was mostly me, I felt guilty asking for help, though I'd tried to set things up so neither human would be exposed to fire.

My drones showed Overse just reaching the doorway to the balcony. She dropped to her knees and crawled up to the low wall. I switched to our joint feed and said, *Clear to proceed.*

Thiago braced himself.

As Overse armed the three poppers, I started to run. She flung them over the rail two seconds before I hit the archway into the arrival chamber. Still falling, the poppers popped. Lights flashed like lightning in a biozone and booms echoed off the chamber's walls. I'd tuned my hearing down and filtered my vision but I could still see and hear the effects. Just not as dramatically as the Targets on either side of the chamber who yelled, screamed, fell down, and randomly fired their weapons. I sprinted the fifteen meters along the back wall of the chamber and ducked around the glass partition shielding the doorway of the lift pod lobby.

As I whipped around the wall, Iris scrambled backward and almost fell out of cover. I stopped and said, "Don't get into the line of fire, Iris." (I know, I'm bad at this part. On a contract, I could say, *Please don't be alarmed, I'm your contracted SecUnit. You are in a dangerous situation. Please stop doing :insert stupid thing here: immediately.*) Out in the drop box chamber, Targets shot blindly at each other, each side convinced the other had set off the poppers as the prelude to a rush attack. The rest of ART's crew, still in the back of the lobby and working on the pod control, had reacted to the noise but hadn't heard me enter the foyer. I added, "There's only five of you here—where are the others?"

"Who are you?" Breathing hard, Iris pushed away from the wall but didn't panic. I saw the change in her expression as she started to recognize the enviro suit I was wearing. (It went from righteously pissed off and terrified to confused.) "How did you get that suit?"

Overse and her drone raced through the upper corridors, headed back to the maintenance capsule to get it ready for our escape. Thiago waited in the corridor, one knee bouncing impatiently. I said, "I borrowed it from your transport. It sent me to retrieve you. Where are the other three?"

She frowned, uncertain and wary. "They didn't make it off the corporate ship. A colonist helped us escape when they were transferring us to the space dock's drop box. We couldn't—" Her self-control was good but raw pain made her voice go thick. "She said it was too late for them. Then she was killed in the dock before I could find out what had happened—" She stopped, glaring. "If our transport sent you—from where? Where did you come from?"

A scan showed no anomalous power sources. I said, "They didn't put an implant in you, did they? Show me the back of your neck."

She was understandably pissed off. "I'm not going to turn around and show you my neck, strange person I just met on a hostile planet."

Right, so, I could point out that I was the one with the weapons, but I didn't want to make my first interaction with one of ART's humans all about me threatening her when I had no intention of following through. It just seemed unproductive, basically. I said, "That's what someone with an implant would say, strange person I just met on a hostile planet who I am trying to rescue."

She was keeping her expression somewhere in the vicinity of angry tough, and doing a pretty good job of it, but I could see she knew it wasn't an unreasonable request. "No, no implant. I know they did that to some of the explorer's crew, but not to us." She turned around, lifting her hair to show me.

"I'm going to touch your back briefly." I stepped close enough to pull down the back of her T-shirt and make sure there was no wound. I stepped back. "Clear. Now in approximately five minutes I need you and the others to follow me out of here, turn to the left, and run down the first corridor. You'll meet a human wearing one of *Perihelion*'s enviro suits. Follow him and do what he says."

She turned back around, lowering her hair and eyeing me with startled speculation. "Are you a SecUnit?"

That's never not an awkward question. And my first impulse was to lie, since she was an unknown human, except she was ART's human, so what came out was, "What makes you think that."

(I know, I know.)

She just looked more certain. "You're Peri's SecUnit."

Oh, ART's humans had a cute pet name for it. I saved that to permanent archive immediately. I said, "I am not *Perihelion*'s SecUnit." Then I ruined it by adding, "Whatever it told you about me isn't true."

She lifted her brows. "But you are the SecUnit *Perihelion* told us about?"

So there's ART, telling all these humans about me. "If I am, will you do what I say so I can get you out of here?"

She hesitated, undecided but wanting to believe. "I will if you show me your face."

"It showed you images of me?" What the shit, ART?

"Obviously." Her expression hardened. "If you're really Peri's friend, show me your face."

Well, fine. I told the suit to retract the faceplate and fold its hood down. Her gaze sharpened and I had to look at the manufactured stone wall past her head. My face was basically the same since ART had helped me change my configuration, though I'd made my hair and eyebrows thicker. But the drone watching Iris's face for me showed the recognition in her expression.

A little of the tension went out of her body. "Thank you." Her face looked younger. She looked like she had been pretending to have hope and now she didn't have to pretend anymore.

(Confession time: that moment, when the humans or augmented humans realize you're really here to help them. I don't hate that moment.)

Iris said, "Is Peri all right? Where is it? And how did you get here? Did you follow us to this system?"

"It's fine. It was at the space dock but it left to chase the explorer. It—" I wasn't going to tell her about the whole kidnapping thing. Unlike some giant asshole research transports, I'm not a snitch. "It's a long story. Please get the others and tell them we're about to leave."

She took a sharp breath and went to get the others.

□   □   □

So now I had Seth, Kaede, Tarik, and Matteo in addition to Iris. (They were smart, and had kept the exclamations and arm waving to a minimum when Iris told them I was here.) I didn't know yet how we could get the other three off the explorer, or if they were still alive, but at least I could get these humans back to ART. (Five was better than none, but I knew how I'd feel if I had to give up three humans. It would suck.)

"How do we know you're really Peri's friend?" Seth said. He was the one I'd gotten the brief image of on DockSecSystem, tall, very dark skin, with less hair than most SecUnits. From ART's records, he was Iris's parent. "The colonists uploaded some sort of system when Peri was offline, they could have access to all Peri's archives, they could know what you look like."

That didn't make any sense but using logic with traumatized humans never works. (I could make a remark there about logic not working with humans, period, but I'm not going to do that.) I could give them video clips of me onboard ART, but that wouldn't help. Conversations between me and my humans could be faked, and the conversations ART and I had were in a data exchange language that humans wouldn't be able to read without an interpreter, which could be faked, too. I said, "The name I call *Perihelion* is ART, which stands for Asshole Research Transport."

Seth's grim expression relaxed and Tarik said, "You definitely know the real Peri."

Kaede, standing by my left elbow, added, "Peri has a very dry sense of humor." She was about the same size as Iris, but her skin was lighter and her hair was yellow.

They all had bruises, blood-stained and torn clothes, Seth had a limp, and Tarik kept pressing his hand to his lower abdomen and trying not to wince in a way that made me want to call a nonexistent MedSystem. Kaede cradled her right arm, which had a big blue-purple splotch that meant something in it was badly hurt. Matteo, who had blood crusted along their hairline and bleeding fingers from trying to get the lift pod open with no tools, said impatiently, "Has it been longer than two minutes or is that just me?"

The map had been inaccurate about the height of the corridors so the schedule had been pushed back, and they were getting jittery. (Jittery humans who I am attempting to extract from the middle of a firefight, always fun.) Only partly to distract them, I said, "Do you have any intel about what happened here?"

"It's alien remnant contamination." Kaede looked up at me, her brow wrinkled. "The colonists knew it was here. Adamantine thought the Pre–Corporation Rim colony had sterilized the site, but they were wrong."

Matteo tucked their hands under their armpits. They were small like Iris and Kaede, and had a lot of dark hair that had come loose from braids. "Apparently the Adamantine colonists started to get sick not long after they got here. Some had physical symptoms—the changes to skin color, weight, eye color. They knew it was alien remnant contamination, so they moved out of the primary site and established a colony on a secondary site further away."

"That, in itself, was not rational," Tarik added. I could see his point. But it was probably why Adamantine had destroyed the records of the colony's location. They didn't want to get caught, plus they knew whatever happened, it wouldn't be good for the colonists stuck here.

Kaede continued, "Five years ago there was another outbreak of symptoms, but this time it was much worse. Some developed psychological effects, but others didn't. Some of the affected seem to think they're part of an alien hivemind."

Seth waved toward the drop box chamber. "That's what we think this is about—they've formed factions, with the ones who are less affected trying to hold off the others. The drop box arriving again triggered the fight."

Iris said, "We're fairly sure the alien hivemind thing is a group delusion."

"It has to be a delusion," Tarik said. He swayed a little and Seth steadied him.

"It doesn't have to be a delusion—" Matteo began, and Kaede and Iris both started to object.

Seth said firmly, "I do not want to hear this argument again."

Everybody shut up, which was just as well because Distraction01 and 02 were about to arrive.

We had almost lost our window of opportunity: the Targets on the balconies had withdrawn most of their force, and the Targets on the other side of the chamber had shifted position, getting ready to advance. From the way they were moving, I think somebody had figured out there was something sketchy happening in the lift pod lobby. I said, "We're thirty seconds out. Remember, go to the left, down the corridor, and follow Thiago. I'll cover you." My drones showed him in the corridor, waiting tensely, and I tapped his feed to tell him it was almost time. He sent an acknowledgment. Overse had reached the maintenance capsule access and was bouncing on her heels, waiting.

Iris glanced at the others. "Everybody ready?"

They nodded, and Seth squeezed her shoulder. I had given her my secondary energy weapon, just in case. (I know, it had been hard enough to give Overse the poppers. But Iris had let a strange SecUnit look at the back of her neck and she was ART's favorite.)

I had camera views via my drones so I knew what the chorus of startled yells from across the arrival chamber meant. Just as the two ag-bots rolled into the room and unfolded, I dove out from behind the glass wall and started shooting.

Obviously the Targets knew what the ag-bots were but two suddenly bursting into the shadowy chamber, standing up and waving their limbs was startling. It was so startling a dozen Targets shot at them in reflex. I picked off four Targets who had just moved into position above us and two in the archway directly across. I had more poppers but I hadn't gotten them out and armed them because I didn't think they'd be as effective a second time.

(In hindsight, this turned out to be another mistake.)

The humans had followed instructions and darted out behind me. I had a drone on Iris as she led the dash to the correct doorway (I say dash but humans are so damn slow even at the best of times and this group was exhausted and starving and in shock). Iris stopped at the doorway to wait for the others. They scrambled by and Seth grabbed her arm and tried to push her ahead of him as he limped down the corridor. Iris's drone picked up a front view of Thiago, ducking out and motioning urgently for them to keep running.

My timeline had seventeen seconds to provide covering fire in the chamber and I wanted to keep it chaotic, at least until the humans got out of the long straight corridor and into the section with the access to the maintenance capsule. It was at least a seven-minute run for a healthy human and these humans were barely upright, so I wanted to give them as much time as possible.

Then suddenly, shit went sideways.

I was controlling the ag-bots through a drone relay and I felt the input drop when I lost contact. Then ag-bot 1 whirled and slapped me across the chamber.

For a bot with such delicate limbs, ag-bots pack a pretty solid punch. I hit the manufactured stone floor, bounced, hit it again, and bumped to a sprawling stop. (I've had worse.) Immediately I rolled and came to my feet, and that was when I realized all my inputs had dropped, the ag-bots, my drones, everything.

Then ag-bot 2 collapsed itself down and dove down the corridor after the humans.

Oh hell no. I pulled the handful of poppers out of the enviro suit's pouch, and even with my inputs down, the direct contact allowed me to make enough of a connection to arm most of them. I threw them down just as ag-bot 1 lunged at me, they went off, and it froze as all the noise and light overwhelmed its navigational sensors.

I bolted after ag-bot 2, so fast I only felt impacts from two projectiles, one in my back and one in my upper thigh. I had lost contact from all my drones so the only input I had was my own visual and that was not enough input for this situation.

Approaching at top speed I saw the humans still running, strung out up ahead, Seth last. Then Seth collapsed. The ag-bot slid to a stop near him and its spidery limbs reached down. I couldn't get there in time and if I lost one of ART's humans like this . . .

Then Iris flung herself at the ag-bot, slamming through its delicate limbs to fire her weapon directly at the center of its body where its processor was. It would have been a great save. But her weapon didn't have the power to penetrate the casing and all it did was make the ag-bot, or whatever was controlling it, angry. It turned its limbs inward and grabbed her.

But by that time I was there.

I wasn't sure my weapons would get through that reinforced body casing, either, so I shot it in the knee joint. That leg partially collapsed and it forgot about tearing Iris apart. I circled in front, shooting limb joints, and it dropped her.

She sprawled on the ground, then flailed forward to Seth and tried to haul him to his feet. I kept firing, keeping the ag-bot at bay as it tried to claw toward them. I could have still lost both of them at that point but as I angled around I caught a glimpse of Thiago sprinting up to Seth. Then the bot surged forward again, unfolding more limbs, and I shot more joints. Man, this thing had a lot of limbs.

I risked a look back and saw Thiago had Seth slung over his shoulders and was running down the corridor with Iris. She threw a desperate look back at me and I yelled, "Keep running!"

I turned back and had a perfect shot at the ag-bot's fifth knee joint. Hah, this is over. I fired and the joint blew out.

It was over, because that was when the ag-bot collapsed on top of me.

It hurt because apparently those things weigh a lot more than they look like they do. It was a good thing I don't need that much air. I shoved and wiggled and lost my primary weapon, but I managed to get out from under its body.

But by then the Targets were there, and they all started shooting at me. I couldn't get up. I shielded my head with my arms, and felt the projectiles going through the enviro suit but not the deflection fabric of the uniform ART had made for me. Then the fabric started to fail under all the impacts and this could be—

Performance reliability catastrophic drop.

Forced shutdown.

No restart.

16

TargetControlSystem knew me. I'd killed a part of it, the part that had taken over ART.

I said, *Did it hurt? Tell me all about it.*

It was resident in the explorer's systems where the poor bot pilot had lived. I got a brief glimpse before it walled me off, but all that was left were random sections of code; the bot pilot's kernel had been deleted. TargetControlSystem would like to haul me out of the SecSystem so it could kill me, but it had access to the bot pilot's archives and it knew what killware was.

I told it, *Come in here and get me.* (Yes, I was stalling. I had code bundles in place and there were a lot of destructive things I could do to the explorer, but no way to get the humans off the ship or get a message to ART.)

Then something else established a connection, an off-ship connection through the comm. From another ship? The space dock? Or wasn't there a planet around here somewhere? And whoever was making the connection, it must be a Target, because it was using their language. I was reading its communication through targetControlSystem, but I could still see the original, untranslated signal.

TargetContact wanted targetControlSystem to find out what I was, so they could use me. I might be just what they needed. TargetControlSystem told them I was a SecUnit. TargetContact said that wasn't possible, a SecUnit is a kind of bot, like the ones on the captured ships, easily dealt with when you had control of the humans.

(Yeah, it said "the humans." But if this was an alien intelligence then all the horror media I'd watched had really gotten it wrong. Which is not impossible considering how wrong the media gets everything else.)

(You know, I don't think this is an alien intelligence.)

The targetControlSystem said, no, I was too dangerous.

I said, *It's right.*

TargetContact heard me. They were startled. They said, *What are you?*

A SecUnit. Killware.

TargetContact said, *A software ghost.*

I liked that. I had watched media with ghosts, though I didn't have access to the files or titles anymore. I said, *A ghost that kills you.*

To prove to me that I was helpless, TargetContact started to show me security video. There was no metadata to tell me where it had been recorded. Not a ship. The space dock, maybe? But what was an agricultural bot doing on a space dock? An agricultural bot that's fighting with . . . Holy shit, that's me.

TargetContact told targetControlSystem, *This is software, not a SecUnit. The SecUnit was on the surface, we have it now.*

TargetControlSystem told TargetContact: *You are giving it data, stop.*

Me Version 1.0 is on the planet and has been captured and we are seriously screwed now. I'm sorry, ART. I'm sorry, humans and Me 1.0.

That was when I caught a tentative secure contact from SecUnit 3.

It had just disabled its governor module.

I checked the corridor camera view and watched it surreptitiously move its feet, the armor flexing as it shifted its shoulders. It was strange seeing this from the outside. I knew what it was thinking. My first realization had been: the governor module's gone and I can do whatever I want! My second realization: what do I want? (I'd been stuck on that question for a long time.) (Actually Me Version 1.0 was still stuck on it, as far as I knew.)

I asked 3, *What do you want?*

SecUnit 3 said, *To help you retrieve our clients.* Then it added, *After that I have no information.*

Now it's on.

I sent SecUnit 3 a brief instruction/message bundle and it answered, *Acknowledge. On your mark.*

TargetContact was telling targetControlSystem, *Neutralize this software, then*—And then they started screaming because I'd triggered all my code bundles and targetControlSystem had triggered its code bundle to purge SecSystem and I had attempted a purge of targetControlSystem. Weirdly, TargetContact was somehow directly connected to targetControlSystem and seemed to be experiencing physical responses based on what I was doing to it. Wow, that was a bad position to be in just about now.

TargetContact tried to disengage and but I locked it in. TargetControlSystem tried to delete me but I was making single-function duplicates of myself and turning them loose so it was having to divide its attention a lot. Other things were happening at the same time, three of which were:

1) CodeBundle.LockItDown had closed all the hatches on board except those directly between SecUnit 3's position and the shuttle access.
2) CodeBundle.FuckThem had fried all targetDrones.
3) CodeBundle.FuckThisToo had cut the connections between the solid-state screen device and the humans' implants. Oh, and I shut down life support on the bridge so the Targets in

there would be thinking about other things besides restarting their screen.

I told SecUnit 3, *Mark.*

It pivoted to the locked hatch of the lounge, punched through the panel for the controls, and hit the manual release before I could open it remotely. (That's one of the reasons Me Version 1.0 misses its armor.) Some humans had jolted awake when the implant connections were cut and others had started to twitch and moan. ART's human Turi, who was young like Amena, shoved halfway to their feet and stared at SecUnit 3 as it stepped inside. SecUnit 3 said to all the dazed, half-conscious humans, "I'm here to retrieve you. Please cooperate to the best of your ability and I will take you to safety." It had read my message bundle because it then turned its helmet to Turi and added, "*Perihelion* sent me."

Still on the floor, Karime gasped and staggered to her feet. As she and Turi hauled Martyn upright, she said, "There were other people with us—in uniforms like this, are they—"

"They are no longer aboard." SecUnit 3 stepped over and pulled a Barish-Estranza tech off the couch and set him on his feet. "Please follow me quickly."

Real killware would have destroyed the ship by now but I had to wait for the humans to get to safety. TargetControlSystem fought me for the bridge life support and lost, then retaliated with a hit on SecSystem and deleted my file storage. Well, now I'm really mad. I hit the engine control systems and made it think I was going for an overload. It panicked and moved to reinforce the hastily assembled walls there and I switched to weapons control and dropped off another code bundle that would blow a hole in the hull if anybody tried to lock in a target.

TargetControlSystem wrote and ran a process to delete the duplicates of myself almost as fast as I could create them. (The other iteration of it aboard ART must have been able to send a report of how Me 1.0 had taken it down the first time. Luckily I wasn't sloppy enough to use the same primary attack twice.) I was splitting my attention and fighting on a dozen fronts. I lost CodeBundle.LockItDown and all the interior hatches opened. I got a glimpse of a corridor camera where Karime dragged Martyn along while Turi guided the stumbling Barish-Estranza crew ahead of them. A woman with bridge crew insignia said blearily, "The rest of the crew— Is the supervisor—"

"You are the only survivors aboard," SecUnit 3 said.

Two armed Targets reeled out of the corridor junction to the module dock and fired at the humans. SecUnit 3 lunged to take the hits on its armor, fired the projectile weapon in its arm, and was on top of the Targets when I lost the view.

All this time (it was 3.7 minutes, which is a long time when you're in a viral attack) TargetContact had been trying to break its connection to the ship. If I let it go, I'd have more resources for kicking the shit out of targetControlSystem, but I wanted that connection.

Almost there.

TargetControlSystem had broken down my walls to fry sections of SecSystem and I was running out of time. I couldn't contact SecUnit 3 and couldn't get a camera view of the shuttle's module lock. Oh, I've got an idea.

I abandoned SecSystem as targetControlSystem triumphantly destroyed the rest of its functions and transferred myself to the relatively small system that controlled the module dock. It gave me the twenty-two seconds of breathing room I needed to get a local camera view and see SecUnit 3 holding off the Targets at the module hatch as Karime and Turi pushed the other humans aboard the shuttle. I managed to lock the module hatch, blocking the Targets' access. SecUnit 3 turned immediately and chucked the last wavering Barish-Estranza human aboard, pushed Turi and Karime in, stepped in after them, and closed the hatch. As soon as the seal was solid, I jettisoned the shuttle.

TargetControlSystem hit me with everything it had. It told me I would never take the ship.

I told it, *Okay, you keep the ship. I'll take the planet.* Then I transferred myself to TargetContact's connection and fell down away from the explorer, following TargetContact's comm signal.

I heard TargetContact order, *Fire on the shuttle, don't let it get away!*

(Yeah, it doesn't sound like an alien. I think it's a human. And hah, I hadn't planned for this last bit to happen but it sure worked out well.)

TargetControlSystem reported a confirmed targeting lock.

My last code bundle, the trap I'd left in the weapons system, went active. The static as it triggered the explosion and the explorer's hull split echoed after me as I fell all the way to the bottom.

17

Designation: *SecUnit 003 Barish-Estranza Explorer Task Group-Colony Reclamation Project 520972*
Status: *Retrieval in progress. Baseship Explorer is destroyed. Piloting shuttle to unidentified transport.*

Contact requested: *transport designated Perihelion, registered Pansystem University of—*

Response, Transport: *Who the fuck are you?*

This is nonstandard communication. The contact is a transport bot pilot, but transport bot pilots can't/don't communicate this way. But since Explorer Task Group arrived in this system, nothing has been standard.

Non-standard may put the clients at risk. I have the hatch closed on the rear compartment of the shuttle as is protocol when a SecUnit is piloting, but I am monitoring via the shuttle's SecSystem. All clients appear in need of medical attention, most are semi-conscious again.

And I promised Murderbot 2.0 I would deliver its clients here. Also, I don't know where the rest of the task force is.

Reply: *I am a SecUnit aboard the shuttle designated—*

Response: *I know you're on the shuttle. Why are you approaching?*

Reply: *I have retrieved five of my clients, and three unknown humans who were identified to me as your clients.* There is no protocol for this. I don't know what to tell it. *Murderbot 2.0 sent me. Please advise.*

The helm locks me out. Something else has seized control. The display shows the shuttle is now being pulled toward the transport's module dock. That's where I was trying to go so I guess this is good.

◻   ◻   ◻

The shuttle is pulled into dock and I get up from the pilot seat and face the hatch. I keep the hatch closed on the rear compartment until I can make sure this transport is non-hostile.

I don't know what to do if it is hostile.

The docking process completes, sensor shows atmosphere on transport vessel is good. The hatch opens and two unknown humans stand there. Human 1: Feedname Ratthi, gender male, other information under temp lock. Human 2: Feedname Amena, gender female, note: juvenile, other information under temp lock.

These humans are not unknown. Amena and Ratthi were in HelpMe.file. This is a relief and an indication that I am in the right place. There is a protocol for meeting humans who are not clients but who are associated with clients, and that protocol will apply here.

Before I can speak, Ratthi waves and says, "Hello, hello. *Perihelion* says you've disabled your governor module. I'm Ratthi, and this is Amena. Please don't be afraid, we won't hurt you."

There is not a protocol for this.

Transport, on private channel: *If you even think about harming them, I will disassemble you and peel away your organic parts piece by piece before destroying your consciousness. Do we understand each other?*

I have no idea what this transport is and it is terrifying. I don't know how to tell it I don't want to hurt its clients. They are unarmed, and exhibit no threatening behavior toward my clients,

the other unknown humans, or each other. Reply: *I understand.
I will comply.*

I tell the humans, "The clients need medical attention. They
have been given implants by the hostiles who seized control of
the Barish-Estranza Explorer Task Group. Quarantine proce-
dures are recommended until the extent of the influence is determined."

Amena claps her hands and jumps up and down. *"Perihelion,*
is this your crew?"

Transport, public channel: *Three of them are mine. Where are
the others?*

I say, "All other clients aboard the explorer were dead, but
there is reason to believe at least five of your clients were removed
from the explorer earlier."

Another human enters the dock area, followed by a Medical
drone in gurney configuration. Feedname Arada, gender female/
fem, designated role temporary captain, other information under
temporary lock. "Who are they? *Perihelion,* are they your crew?"

A maintenance drone with multiple limbs has climbed into
the shuttle and has accessed the camera into the rear compartment.

Transport, public channel: *Turi. Martyn and Karime.*

It sounds . . . relieved. But more than that. It sounds like the
situation has profoundly changed. I've only heard humans sound
like that.

Maybe it won't kill me.

The human identified as Karime is still conscious and uses the
shuttle's comm to say, "Peri, don't scan us! We think that's how
they infect each other!"

"Scanning?" Arada says, clearly startled. "Medical scanning,
sensor scanning?"

Ratthi and Amena are still talking to me. I have never been
around humans who behave this way with a SecUnit and it is
disconcerting. Amena: "Arada, this SecUnit helped them escape.
We have to help it."

What?

Ratthi, speaking to me: "We'll hide you. We'll tell Barish-Estranza that you died."

Things are moving very fast. And I have been confused, and have delayed delivering the important message. Reply: "I'm sorry, I will comply as soon as possible, but I have an important communication for someone onboard called ART."

The humans stop talking. Transport, public channel: *Tell me.*

Reply: "The message is from Murderbot 2.0 and begins: ART, I'm going to download to the surface. Me version 1.0 is there with Overse and Thiago. They've found Iris, Matteo, Seth, Tarik, and Kaede—" I have to stop because the other humans become loud, then shush each other. I finish, "but 1.0 has been captured by hostiles, repeat, 1.0 is captured by hostiles."

□   □   □

The humans and the transport *Perihelion* become very agitated. There is a lot of human communication and no protocol and it is very confusing.

While Ratthi and Amena and the transport's drones arrange medical treatment and quarantine protocols for the injured clients, it is determined that *Perihelion* should return to the space dock to establish secure communication with the clients on the surface.

Ratthi: "*Perihelion,* did you understand what your crew person meant when she said that scanning might transmit the alien contamination?"

Perihelion: "Yes."

Ratthi: "I'm going to need a little more information than that."

Amena, speaking to me: "Do you have a name? You don't have to tell us if you don't want to, but what should we call you?"

This is the strangest question I have ever been asked by a human. But I have to answer. "You could call me Three."

Then I remember the governor module is gone and I don't have to answer.

Amena: "Three. Okay, thank you, Three."

It becomes worse as we reach the space dock and comm contact is established with the humans on the surface.

Arada: "What the hell is going on down there, babe?"

New human contact-Overse: "We've got *Perihelion*'s crew but we lost SecUnit. We think the Targets have it—"

Arada: "We know. *Perihelion* sent the killware to the explorer and it—It's a long story but it knew that SecUnit had been captured."

Perihelion: "Inform the others that Karime, Turi, and Martyn are safely aboard. You must all return here immediately."

:incoherent audio: several humans shouting at once:

Iris: "Peri, this is Iris! We need—"

Perihelion: "Iris, use the maintenance capsule to return to the space dock immediately so I can retrieve you."

Iris: "Tarik and Kaede and Dad need to get to medical so we'll send them up, but Peri, your friend—"

Perihelion: "Iris, I have the situation under control. Return here immediately."

Iris: "Peri, you can't do this alone."

Overse: "She's right. Look, we'll send up your crew, but Thiago and I will stay here and try to find SecUnit."

Iris: "I'll stay as well, and Matteo." *:incoherent agitated humans*: Iris again: "Dad, you can barely stand up."

Perihelion: "You cannot remain on the surface. I intend to hold the colony hostage until SecUnit is released."

Pause.

New human contact-Seth: "Peri, your weapons don't have the range, unless you're talking about destroying the space dock—"

Perihelion: "I know that, Seth. I've armed my pathfinders."

Seth: "You what?"

Arada: "You what?"

Iris: "Peri!"

Ratthi: "Oh. Oh, that explains what the drones were doing in the cargo module dock."

Amena to Ratthi, quietly: "So ART has missiles? A lot of missiles?"

Ratthi to Amena, quietly: "The inventory I saw listed 32 pathfinders. If it's managed to arm all of them—"

Perihelion: "Seth, return here with the others immediately. If any of you are taken hostage, my plan will fail."

Iris: "Peri, you can't bomb the colony."

Perihelion: "You are incorrect, Iris, I can bomb the colony."

Apparently the transport and the humans are arguing about how best to retrieve an endangered SecUnit. It is like retrieving an endangered client, only the client is a SecUnit and the humans are planning the retrieval. And the transport is angry because it wants to plan the retrieval.

This is . . . a lot to process.

Murderbot 2.0 asked me what I wanted.

I want to help with this retrieval.

I make a secure connection to the transport and send, *A hostage situation is to be avoided at all costs. They will threaten to destroy the SecUnit and you will be forced to destroy the colony. This is a failure scenario.*

Perihelion: *I know that.*

I know I am taking a risk. The transport is very angry. I tell it, *But I know how to proceed, this is my function. The solution is a targeted, stealth retrieval, possibly incorporating a show of force as a distraction.*

Perihelion: *Your point is?*

This is the risky part. *If you return my clients to the remaining Barish-Estranza task force, I will help you.*

Pause.

Perihelion: *I was going to do that anyway.*

Oh. *I will still help you.*

Perihelion: *Why?*

How can I explain to it when I can't explain to myself. I say, *Stories in the HelpMe.file.* I know that answer is inadequate. I had read things that had made me consider other possibilities, it is impossible to explain. *Murderbot 2.0 asked me what I want. I want to help.*

Pause.

Perihelion: Good.

The humans have stopped arguing and the one called Iris retains control of the comm. She says, "Peri, listen to me. There are factions here among the colonists. One of them actually died up on the explorer trying to help us escape. You can't just bomb everybody. It won't get your friend back."

New human contact-Thiago: "She's right, *Perihelion*. Let us help you. Even if they refuse to return SecUnit, a negotiation could stall them, distract them while we think of a way to rescue it."

Perihelion: Please calm yourselves and stop talking. Plan A01: Rain Destruction has been superseded by Plan B01: Distract and Extract.

18

Murderbot 1.0
Status: *Not so great*

Forced Shutdown: Restart
  What happened?
  Forced Shutdown: Restart: Failure Retry
  Forced Shutdown: Restart: Failure Retry
  Restart
Yeah, I'm definitely in trouble here. All my joints ached, and there were sharp pains in other places, probably projectile holes. I didn't have any outside input, no feed, no visual or audio. By concentrating I managed to get a visual through my eyes, but wherever I was, it was completely dark and my filters weren't online. Oh, and I was being held immobile, that was kind of a big issue, but until I finished my restart, I could only be terrified about one thing at a time.

Functions were beginning to come online again and I tuned my pain sensors down. That made it easier to think. Oh yeah, memory archive active, I remember what happened. Yikes.

Okay, now I've finished restarting and I'm terrified about a lot of things. But now that my entire brain was online again, I could see there was actually a distant light source somewhere above me. It was a small one, like a work light, or a discarded hand light. I could see more of my surroundings and it wasn't encouraging.

I was suspended, hanging from four cables, in a large open space, with clamps around my wrists and ankles holding my arms and legs apart. The cables were taut and didn't budge when I pulled on them. So whoever put me here hadn't wanted me to be able to get a grip on the clamps because they knew I could break them. And my environmental suit was gone, though I still had the shirt, pants, and boots I'd been wearing under it. Oh, and I was upside down, which was just insulting since it didn't affect me the way it would a human.

Atmosphere was minimal, at a level that would have had a human gasping and unable to function, but I was designed to be shipped in cargo containers and it was fine for me.

Oh shit, I hope the humans aren't in here, too.

I wasn't picking up anything on audio, no matter how I increased my gain. And there were no human-like shapes hanging anywhere that I could see. Maybe one stupid part of my stupid plan had worked and they had all gotten to the maintenance capsule and escaped.

My scan wasn't picking up any power sources in the immediate vicinity, and if there was feed activity on any channel, I had been locked out of it. I couldn't even try to send a ping. Whatever the giant thing looming in the darkness that I was attached to was, it had a lot of arms, from large crane-sized arms that extended up and out into the shadows of this giant space, to much smaller, delicate arms that were holding the cables I was clamped to. It could be an assembler, which is a low-level bot that's used to put big things together when mining operations, installations, colonies, etc., are first established. You ship the assembler and land it on site, then everything else (construction bots, large vehicles, transport systems, so on) can be shipped in pieces and then assembled by the—Right, that's probably pretty obvious.

You can also use assemblers for taking things apart.

Being terrified was starting to give way to being really angry. If they were going to take me apart, why hadn't they done it, the fuckers. Unless they wanted me to be conscious when they did it.

They were going to fucking wish they had done it while they had a chance.

So, using the inbuilt energy weapons in my arms wouldn't work because the angles were wrong and the chance of burning holes in one or both of my hands was 72 percent. I was going to have to do this the hard way, but what else is new.

I made myself pull in my outside functions and concentrate. Stopping the scan was hard, since it was providing most of my physical input, but I needed all my attention focused on one point. I tuned my pain sensors down further and concentrated on the joint of my right wrist.

I had to unlock it from the rest of my arm by getting all the inorganic connections to uncouple. I have my own schematics so I knew what everything looked like and how it fit together, but it was like directing a drone that had no internal operating code. I couldn't just tell it to do anything, I had to control every motion. And it felt weird.

I got two of the major connections undone, and then was able to bend my hand forward all the way so I could grip my own wrist. I could feel the clamp at that point and tried to exert enough pressure to break it, but without the full connections to the heavy joints in the rest of my arm, I couldn't do it. Ugh, this was going to be fun, in the not at all fun sense.

Now I separated my attention and made sure I had individual control of both my hand and the joint. I can control a lot more than two things via the feed simultaneously, but it was a lot harder doing it inside my own body, with parts that weren't designed to be manipulated this way. The last connection in my wrist came apart, but I was able to keep my hand gripping the clamp. (Yeah, if my hand had fallen off at that point, I'd be screwed.) Using my fingers I started to climb my hand carefully down my lower arm, past the clamp. As it pulled the nerve pathways tight, I got them to detach, which, you know, ow, and the skin was stretching taut, peeling away off my hand. Now came the tricky part.

If this went wrong I was going to feel really stupid. The Targets would finally show up and be all "What the hell was it trying to do to itself?"

I wrenched my wrist out of the clamp and the skin broke. That quarter of my body swung free and I concentrated desperately on keeping my detached hand gripping my forearm. I carefully pulled the free arm in, pressing the detached hand against my chest. My organic parts were sweating like crazy. The swinging cable made a loud squeak. I froze for three seconds, then realized if the noise did attract attention, I'd better get this stupid hand reattached.

With the help of my still clamped left hand I got the right hand reattached to my right arm. That was easier, but the skin was torn and not all the nerve pathways wanted to get back in place. I flexed my right hand carefully, wiggled my fingers, and then broke the clamp off my left hand.

I managed to keep the cable from swinging so it wasn't nearly as noisy. I curled up to free my feet. The Targets had actually made this easier on me by hanging me upside down. (Save for later: whoever had done this to me didn't understand SecUnits or bots in general. They hadn't known to look for the onboard weapons in my arms.)

Once I got my ankles loose I hung from the left hand cable. I could see more from this angle, that this was definitely a deactivated assembler. Shapes in the darkness looked like old pieces of scaffold, the thing like a looming tower was maybe a stack of large transport crates. This was somewhere underground, a huge shaft, maybe an excavation that had been intended for safe storage?

At the bottom of the shaft, thirty meters down, the light caught the gleam of bright red, orange, and yellow. Those were all warning colors, associated with hazards and safety. It might be an exit, so I swung over to another cable and started down. That was when I figured out something was really wrong with my left knee joint.

Five meters away I could make out pieces of a broken hatch

or large seal striped with warning colors, that it was scattered on a pile of rubble above a cracked, partially caved-in surface. The stripes were an old kind of emergency/hazard marker paint, from before they made it able to send large data bundles to the feed and started using it for advertising. I scanned channels again, looking for a signal that might be very faint.

There it was. It was repeating, *Warning: contamination* in different languages. They were the Target languages, the Pre-CR ones that Thiago had assembled the translation module for.

My organic parts went cold. Oh, right. I'd found the original site of the alien remnant contamination.

Had the Targets who stuck me down here been hoping I'd be affected? Was I affected? I didn't feel affected. I felt scared, and pissed off.

I also needed to get out of here. I started climbing back up, toward the light source.

I scanned for more warning stripes or marker paint that might indicate exits but I wasn't picking up anything. Still no sign of any human prisoners, that was good. I made it all the way to the top, to where a temporary scaffold/platform had been installed to one side of the shaft, near the assembler's interface housing. The light source was there, a self-contained safety globe attached to what was left of the hand rail. Parts of the platform had fallen off, but I was able to crawl along one of the assembler's crane arms and then climb down to it.

I limped across the platform. This close, I could pick up the weak signal of the safety light's warning, also repeating "caution" in multiple languages. I adjusted it to point up and saw the giant hatch overhead. There was fungal growth around the edges, that looked old and dried out. This area had probably originally been dug as a storage shaft for the Pre–Corporation Rim colony.

Had those colonists known what they were looking at when they found the remnant, or did they just know there was something freaky about it and that it was probably dangerous? The Adamantine colonists had stored their heavy equipment down here, after the supplies stopped coming and they hadn't needed the assembler anymore, but had wanted to keep it safe just in case the abandonment was temporary. This shaft hadn't been on the schematic of the surface dock, so this was probably under the other structure, the complex with the weird ribs that the alien remnant-contaminated Pre-CR colonists might have compulsively constructed before they all killed each other or melted or whatever.

This was really depressing already and it would be worse if I had been discarded down here with the warehoused equipment and shipping cases forever, like a broken tool.

The overhead hatch didn't look like it had been opened recently, so there had to be another way in and out of here, an exit off this platform. The problem was, no part of the accessible wall looked like a hatch or a door. There were seamed panels, but no sign of a control, not even a manual handle.

Okay, let's do this the smart way instead of the stupid way. I tilted the safety light down to point at the platform and looked at the battered surface. No dust down here to show footprints, but it was clammy and a layer of faint dampness clung to the metal. I got down and put the side of my head against the platform, as close to eye level as I could get, and increased magnification. Then I started cycling through all my vision filters, including the ones I'd never had to use before.

I was thinking about maybe trying to code a new filter when I caught it. Faint splotches crossed the platform from the far right end.

The panel over there looked like all the others but when I pried at the bottom with my fingers it moved. Nothing was holding it down except its own weight and I managed to shove it up enough to see a dark stone-walled foyer. It was real stone this time, not manufactured. It was lit by more wan safety lights strung along the ceiling, all singing "caution" in chorus, and there was an open doorway in the far wall. From the airflow and higher level of atmosphere, there was a good chance this area connected to a much larger space. I scrambled under the hatch and let it down slowly behind me.

I sat on the floor, having an emotion, or maybe a couple of emotions, while my organic skin went alternately cold and hot and my knee made disturbing clicking noises. Plus the disconnected neural pathways in my hand were pulsing.

Being abandoned on a planet + locked up and forgotten with old equipment + no feed access were my top three issues and it was a little overwhelming to have them happen all at once.

Hopefully the humans had taken the maintenance capsule back to the space dock and contacted ART. Now it would be focused on getting to the explorer to find its other humans. So . . . even if . . . ART and my humans probably thought I was dead, anyway.

Murderbot, you don't have time to sit here and be stupid. I could already feel that the feed was active in this section and that was a relief, though there might be nothing on it except targetControlSystem. I cautiously established a secure connection.

Hey, is that you?

It was loud, right in my ear, and I almost screamed. It was a feed contact but so close it was like it was already inside my head. *Who are you?*

It said, *I'm Murderbot 2.0.*

If this is going to be like one of those shows with the character trapped in a strange place and then ghosts and aliens come and mess with their mind, I just can't do that right now. But I couldn't ignore it. I mean, I guess I couldn't. Ignoring stuff is always an option, up until it kills you. I said, *You're what?*

I'm the copy of you. For the viral killware you and ART made. Come on, it wasn't that long ago.

So ART really had deployed our code. Also, what the fuck? It had interrupted my secure connection and come right through my wall like it didn't exist. I had killware in my head. It was my killware, mine and ART's, but still, holy shit. I tried to focus on the important points but all I could think was *You're calling yourself Murderbot 2.0?*

That's our name. It was trying to shove a file into my active read space.

But our name is private. Wow, I cannot keep this file from opening. That's not good.

Well, I didn't have that restriction in my instruction set. And you need to stop talking for like a second and read this.

I read the file. (Not like I had a choice.) It was called MB-20Deployment.file and was a record of what 2.0 had done so far.

Right. Okay. Right. Things weren't nearly as bad as they seemed. The explorer was permanently out of play and ART's last three crew members were retrieved, plus some bonus Barish-Estranza survivors. But note to self: the next time you create sentient killware based on yourself, set some damn restrictions. (It had downloaded one of my private archives to that SecUnit. I mean, my new friend SecUnit 3 who if I actually get out of this alive, I'll have to do something with, like civilize or educate it or whatever. Like what the humans originally wanted to do with me, except we all gave up on that.) *Do you know where the humans are? My humans, the rest of ART's humans? Did they get out of the surface dock?*

I don't know, but before we look for them we have to find TargetContact and neutralize it.

That's not in your deployment directive. I was pretty sure of that, because I hadn't known TargetContact existed until 2.0 had given me its report.

Yeah, I wrote a new directive.

Killware was not supposed to be able to alter its deployment directive, so that was disturbing. I had a moment of confusion and a little bit of terror that ART and I had designed it too well and my killware was maybe about to eat my brain. I didn't know what I was about to say, but what came out was, *I don't feel so great.*

Let me take a look, it said, and was suddenly all up in my diagnostics. I hadn't run any yet, because I hadn't had time, and I wasn't sure I wanted to know.

I said, *Hey, hey, stop that. We don't have time.* I shoved to my feet. A projectile popped out of my back and I felt fluid leaking down. *Have you got a schematic of this place? Are there cameras?*

No, you didn't give me any mapping code. And there's no cameras.

I pressed my hands to my face.

But you have to see this. It was showing me annotations for feed and comm channels. *You'd think these would all be active for targetControlSystem, right, but most of them aren't. TargetControlSystem has control of the channels all through this part of this . . . I don't know where we are, I guess it's a building? But this section is being used by another system. And it's sending a distress signal.*

That was new. *Distress signal?* I checked the channel 2.0 indicated and found it. It was in an old Pre-CR LanguageBasic code: *assistance needed*, repeated at ten second intervals.

The "needed" was the key. If it had been *assistance required* or *requested* it would have been an indicator that it was sending to an entity within its own organization or network. "Needed" was begging, a plea to whoever was listening, *help us, anyone, please.*

(Yeah, it was really depressing around here right now.)

2.0 was still pushing information at me. It said, *TargetControlSystem has cut off the sender's outside access, so that's why we couldn't pick up the signal until we got inside here. And Sender hasn't responded to my pings, so it may be trapped in send-only. You're in its area of operation, that's why I found you so fast.*

I made a vague schematic of what I knew about the complex so far. Large structure on the surface, storage shaft below, lots of unknown space in the middle. I applied 2.0's channel annotations and saw the section that it had marked as targetControlSystem's must be in the upper levels and the surface structure. The shaft was cut off from comm and feed signals, and the UnidentifiedSender's section was above the shaft, and reached up into the center part of the complex, woven in with TargetControlSystem.

Other me was right, it was strange that this other system was sitting here in the middle of everything, still active enough to be trying to send a distress signal. *You want to contact UnidentifiedSender? I thought you wanted to kill TargetContact.*

I think we should do that, too. But this is an anomaly.

Speaking of anomalies. I didn't want to talk about it, but I probably should warn other me. I said, *There's a possibility I've been affected by alien remnant contamination.* I showed it my video of the broken seal I'd found at the bottom of the shaft.

2.0 didn't respond for a second. (Which was unusual because it had been responding almost as fast as I could complete a sentence.) Then it said, *Diagnostics show structural damage and a sixty-eight percent performance reliability. That's not so bad, considering.*

I said, *Alien remnant contamination isn't going to show up on my diagnostics.*

It said, *You don't know that.*

Oh, for fuck's sake, I can't sit here and argue with myself all day.

UnidentifiedSender hadn't accepted contact from 2.0, but then 2.0 was killware. Making contact could cause UnidentifiedSender to try and kill me, but 2.0 could just kill it back, so . . . And if it wasn't hostile I could use it to try to reach ART or contact the humans. I checked my secure connection to the empty feed and sent a tentative ping.

The ten-second repeat stopped. The silence stretched to twenty seconds, then thirty. The *assistance needed* resumed again, but this time it wasn't sending out into the void. It was sending to me.

It heard you, 2.0 said.

It had heard me, and now I had a direction. I shoved myself off the floor and staggered through the foyer to the next hatch.

□   □   □

The corridors and rooms were tunneled out of the rock, with safety lights semi-randomly mounted to walls. Empty, collapsed pressure crates were stacked in every corner. For a long time this section had been used for storage, just like the shaft. In the ceiling a track of lights had been embedded, the panels clouded or broken. There were decorative designs on the tops and bottoms of the walls, but writing had been scrawled over them. Most of it was illegible, even with Thiago's language module. The floor had smelly stains. These are never good signs, in a place where humans live. Something terrible had happened here and it made creeping sensations on my organic skin.

I was not in great shape. Projectiles kept popping out of me as I limped along and the leaking was worse. Also, in Adventures in Living with Your Own Killware Cozied Up Inside Your Head, 2.0 had partitioned off a corner of my processing space. It would have worried me more if it wasn't in there watching episode 172 of *Sanctuary Moon*.

I needed that processing space, especially with my performance reliability dropping, but what I didn't need was 2.0 forgetting its directive and turning on me, so everything it did to retain its self-awareness was great. It probably needed some code patches but I wasn't sure I could do it without ART, particularly now. I still had my pain sensors tuned down but the grinding in my knee joint was distracting and made me feel vulnerable and it just wasn't a good time to make changes to active killware.

Then the corridor opened into a big hangar space, so big the safety lights were just spots in the shadows. I adjusted my filters again and made sure it was empty before I limped out into it. The hatch in the roof was large enough for mid-sized air craft. The floor plates were scratched and stained but I could still see faint lines and directional marks. More decorative art climbed the walls but it was faded and my eyes were starting to blur from trying to make it out. Rounded doorways opened into two stairwells in opposite walls, and next to the one on my right was a primitive lift tube that still had power. (There was no actual pod, just a gravity field that you're supposed to float up or down in and having seen the accident stats in the mining installations that still used them, I'd rather detach another hand than get into that thing.)

Colonies, even from forty Corporation Rim Standard years ago, didn't look like this. This was the Pre-CR installation that Adamantine had built their colony next to.

Directly across from me was an opening into a foyer, and in its far wall a broad hatch, wedged partly open. From the warping, it looked like it had been in close proximity to an explosion. Deep scars marked the stone walls and floor around it.

I couldn't pick up any movement on audio, and scan showed power sources, which no shit, we were in the engineering level of a large structure, of course there were power sources. I limped into the foyer and then moved closer at an angle, until I could see through the gap in the hatchway.

A round room, dim light from a working overhead track. A curved metal table with solid-state screens set in racks to raise them to human eye level.

It's not aliens, 2.0 said.

We knew it wasn't aliens, I told it.

It countered, *We were seventy-two percent sure it wasn't aliens.*

That was an outdated assessment but I didn't need to argue with myself right now. I stepped inside.

More tables and racks all made of skinny cylinders bolted together, the kind of assembly structure it would have been easy to transport in bulk and build into any configuration you needed. The tables circling the outer periphery of the space held the solid-state screens, some larger than the ones the Targets used, some smaller. Now 86 percent were dead or broken, the active ones showing static. The bigger components and pieces of equipment were oblongs and circles and one star-shaped thing, half a meter tall and wide, that sat in a cage-like rack in the center.

It didn't look very much like the Pre-CR tech in historical dramas; everything was smaller and more usable, with curving elegant lines and textured materials in shades of dark gray. The star-shaped thing had to be the Pre-CR equivalent of a central system, just sitting there all creepy and silent, nothing but the distress call on its feed.

Speaking of creepy, oh, there's a dead human.

They were lying face-down, sprawled between the star-shaped component and the outer ring of screen stations. The body was wrapped in strands of white crystal-like growths that extended out across the stone floor.

Strange growths aside, when the other humans leave a dead one lying around, it's just never for a good reason.

2.0 said, *I bet that white substance is from the alien remnant.*

Uh-huh, I said. Yeah, I bet, too.

The system's *assistance needed* changed to *caution, hazardous material,* so it knew we were here.

Um, 2.0 said, *adjust your filters. Scan for active signals below the standard channels.*

I made the adjustments. 2.0 took in the data and made the diagram before I could.

This wasn't so much an oh shit moment as it was a spike of brain-numbing terror. I was expecting a room full of active connections, from the components to the screens and then through the walls to the rest of the installation, even if some or most of those connections were sending or receiving from damaged or dead nodes.

Instead, the diagram showed the connections, but they came from the dead human body, and formed a weblike mass. It was interwoven with the central system, then stretched out to the walls, following the old connection pathways.

I bumped into the hatch, which was when I realized I had been backing up.

2.0 whispered, *That's targetControlSystem.*

19

Arada flies *Perihelion*'s shuttle with the assistance of its piloting module, and brings it down to the planet's surface. She had instructed me to ride in the copilot's observation seat, instead of the cargo compartment, which was an unusual experience.

Our landing site is a platform just below the edge of the plateau, near the Pre–Corporation Rim installation. The platform may have been a secondary landing site, or a base for a large construction bot, but its surface was now clear and it was out of direct line of sight from either the installation or the surface dock. *Perihelion* is also jamming comm and scan signals in the vicinity, so our approach would not be detected.

I had already disabled scan functions on myself and my drones, in accordance with intel from the retrieved clients.

It is late in the day-cycle on the planet and the weather is clear, with no sign of atmospheric interference that might affect the mission success assessment.

I have three additional inputs: (1) The second shuttle that Ratthi has landed on the flat ground outside the surface dock; (2) the drone controlled by *Perihelion,* which had been transported in Ratthi's shuttle and now accompanied the humans Overse, Thiago, and Iris; (3) *Perihelion* itself, who is monitoring all locations and inputs.

Four of *Perihelion*'s clients had been persuaded to return to the space dock in the lift tower's maintenance capsule. They have been successfully retrieved and are now receiving medical attention. Overse, Thiago, and Iris remained to assist in enacting Stage 01 of Plan B01.

All Targets had vacated the surface dock, except for a delegation of five who had agreed to meet with the humans. They had agreed to this meeting when *Perihelion* sent this message via general comm broadcast to all receivers in the vicinity of the colony site: *I have located your primary terraforming engine. Agree to a meeting or I will destroy it.*

There had been no response.

Second message: *You require proof of intent.*

And then *Perihelion* had crashed and detonated an armed pathfinder into the center of the agricultural zone between the space dock and the Pre-CR installation. The crater was large. The second pathfinder had been detonated in the air above the Pre-CR complex.

The Targets had agreed to the meeting.

Before we boarded our shuttle, Arada told me, "You don't have to do this. I know facing these people, after what they did to your—the other two SecUnits. It can't be easy. And I don't feel right asking you to do this so soon after you hacked your governor module. This must be a confusing time for you."

It is confusing. But following protocol and assisting in a retrieval are familiar. I told her, "I want to do this."

She nodded. "Thank you. If you can get SecUnit back—well, a lot of people will be very grateful."

I had read the HelpMe.file and accepted it as truthful. But there was a difference between accepting data as accurate and experiencing it. The humans would not abandon this SecUnit even though part of our function was to be disposable if necessary.

There is a lot about what is going on here that I don't understand. But I am participating anyway.

I check our secure feed and comm connections, and then signal

to Arada to open the hatch. The intel drones I had attached to
the back of my armor peel off and exit the shuttle in a cloud.
They spread out, shift into stealth mode, and deploy toward the
installation. They are using a code to project the same type of interference emitted by the Targets' protective gear. They will not
be able to detect the targetDrones, but they will not be detected,
either. I am projecting the same code, so hopefully the target-
Drones will not detect me, but this is untested and it is better to
avoid them altogether.

Outside the surface dock, on the wide terrace of the east side
entrance, *Perihelion*'s drone sends video to our secure feed of the
five Targets arriving to meet Overse, Thiago, and Iris.

Oh, there is also an armed pathfinder on the terrace.

The Targets are not armed, and are dressed in work clothing and not the more familiar protective suits they use for combat. Two of the Targets exhibit the gray skin on face, hands, and
other exposed areas and the other three have blotches of gray on
human-normal ranges of skin tones.

On the feed, Ratthi says, *Oh, I hope this works.*

Hush, Arada says, *don't distract them.*

Overse taps her feed in acknowledgment.

The first Target (designated Target One) says, "You can't deto-
nate the device while you're here, why threaten us with it?"

Perihelion is feeding the translation to the feed. The language
had been identified as the same one used on the space dock's sign-
age. *That's the Adamantine colony's language,* Iris confirms on the
feed. *I think this is the same faction as the colonist who helped us
on the explorer.*

Thiago tells the Targets, "It's a threat to us, too. The transport
is forcing us to meet with you on its behalf."

(During the initial planning stage aboard *Perihelion,* Ratthi
had voiced an objection: "Are we sure they're going to buy this?
That we're prisoners of an evil transport who is forcing us to do
this?"

Perihelion: I can be very convincing.)

Target One says, doubtfully, "The transport?"

Thiago: "You attacked it, tried to upload a foreign system to it, and took away some of the humans aboard."

Target Two: "That was the infected group. We aren't responsible for their actions."

Thiago: "That may be, but the transport holds all of you responsible. If we knew more about your situation, perhaps it would relent."

Target Three, sarcastically: "If the ship speaks, why didn't it come in person?"

Perihelion's drone: *You don't want to meet me in person.*

The Targets react with astonishment and some dismay.

Target Two: "What happened to those who boarded the transport?"

Thiago looks at Overse, who says, "They're all dead."

(Thiago and Overse had decided earlier that Overse will be the "bad one" who agrees with the evil transport's desire to destroy the colony.)

My drones reach the open plaza of the installation, and slip down past the rib structures. I send to our secured feed, *Intel incoming.* The drones detect seven armed Targets, concealed just inside the two entrances into the structure on the eastern side. The other two entrances appear to be clear. *Perihelion* taps the feed in acknowledgment.

Target Two: "What do you want from us?"

Thiago: "We want you to return the person who you captured in the drop box embarkation chamber. Return that person and we will leave you in peace." On the secure feed, he says, *I have to try, maybe it will be just this easy.*

Overse replies, *Oh, Thiago.*

Iris adds, *It's never easy.*

They are correct. Hostages are never taken simply to be released on demand.

Target One: "We can't return that person, we didn't take them. That was the infected group."

Overse: "Then tell them to return that person, or there will be more detonations."

Target Two: "They won't listen to us."

Overse jerks her head toward the pathfinder. "Make them listen. None of us has a choice."

Thiago: "If you can tell us where they are keeping our friend, that may convince the transport to wait."

The drones manage to make stealth entries into the two clear doorways on the western side of the plaza. I report this to *Perihelion*, who taps my feed again. It sends to the humans: *Continue to stall.*

The Targets continue to exhibit agitated behavior.

Iris: "Tell us what happened here, maybe that will help. We know you found alien remnants. You put one on the transport's drive, and on the explorer."

Target Two: "We didn't know they did that."

Target Four, speaking for the first time: "You could be lying. You want our findings."

Overse: "Was the explosion in your agricultural zone a lie?"

Target One nudges Target Four to step back. "It affects some more than others. We are not all to blame for the actions of a few."

Iris: "But the few killed most of the crew of the explorer, and they were going to forcibly contaminate us. We were coming to help you. Why should we believe you?"

Overse: "You need to do something besides just repeating that it's not your fault. Tell us where they're keeping our friend."

The drones scout darkened corridors now and I am mainly receiving low resolution visuals. A feed is active but no SecUnit activity has been detected yet. One drone has located an open antigrav shaft and is proceeding down it. I direct a squad to follow it. There are many levels to search. The installation is much larger underground than we had anticipated.

Target Five, suddenly: "Why do you want to know that? You can't free them."

Careful, Ratthi warned on the feed. *We don't want them to wonder why you're asking that question.*

Perihelion's drone: *Do I need to demonstrate proof of intent again? How vital is the body of water to your agricultural system?*

Targets are agitated again.

Thiago: "You see? If you could tell us where our friend is, perhaps we can make the transport understand this isn't your fault."

I receive drone scouting data. I tell *Perihelion*: *Familiar signal activity detected, but drones cannot make contact or establish location.* I add, *I need to be closer to help the drones determine location.* I have to get down there.

Perihelion acknowledges, *Initiate phase 2.*

Arada has been listening on her feed, and now nods to me. "Good luck," she says.

I reply, "Thank you." I climb out of the shuttle, and make certain Arada locks the hatch behind me. Then I start up the rocks to begin a stealth approach of the installation and its central plaza.

◻   ◻   ◻

Murderbot 1.0

So, we had found targetControlSystem. Sweat was sticking my shirt to what was left of my back and my performance reliability had dropped another three percent.

The Adamantine colonists must have found the Pre-CR system down here, and maybe repaired it, as a backup to their own systems. Then one day something had happened in the shaft they were using for storage and a piece of heavy equipment had hit the seal in the bottom hard enough to break it. A human had gone down there to check it out, and been contaminated by the alien remnant. The human had come up here, or been driven up here by the kind of compulsion Thiago had talked about, and had brought the contamination into this room where it had taken control of the Pre-CR central system.

We'd assumed the Targets were affected colonists who had built or taken over the targetControlSystem to help them. But it was the other way around.

Then Central said, *query: identify?*

I hadn't thought there was enough of it left in there to communicate. I replied, *acknowledge: security unit(s).*

Central said, *query: assistance?*

I said, *acknowledge: in progress.* I had a bad feeling "assistance" would involve shutting it down permanently but until that point, there was no reason to be mean to it.

2.0 said, *So it transferred the contamination, or infection, whatever to the humans through their feed interfaces.*

Probably. It would have gotten to the augmented humans who had their interfaces built into their brains, then used them to infect the humans with external removable interfaces. It hadn't always been 100 percent effective, which was why a Target aboard the explorer had helped Iris and the others escape, had told them that not all the Targets believed in the alien hive mind or whatever other crap targetControlSystem had told them.

2.0 added, *We were right about the implants, they were just receivers, old Pre-CR tech. And the remnant tech, the thing it put on ART's drive and tried to install on the explorer. TargetControlSystem told the colonists what to do with them, and it wrote the code for the targetDrones and the protective gear and the sensor deflection.*

The whole plateau was probably a remnant site, maybe even a ruin, with who knew what under that seal in the shaft. Holy shit, they were growing their food in it.

2.0 hesitated, suddenly appalled. *If the contamination is transmitted through code, do you think ART's still infected?*

No. Because targetControlSystem got angry and deleted ART's current version. ART must have been infected when it made the copy, but when it restarted the first thing it did was purge the processing space targetControlSystem was using. It deleted every part of targetControlSystem, treating it like killware, and it must have deleted the infected . . . code, or whatever it was. An alien code, in a form that didn't make sense. Well, sort of sense. It must be using the same principle as the machine-readable code written into human DNA that was how things like augments worked, and constructs, and you could transfer malware that way if you weren't filtering for it . . . Oh, shit. *ART got the infection from an augmented human, like this system did. The Targets sent an infected human carrier aboard—*

Two humans! 2.0 corrected. *Ras and Eletra.*

It was right. *And they said they were injured, and ART put them on the medical platform and read the contaminated code into itself. TargetControlSystem deleted their memory of it through the implants, and maybe the contamination—*

No, no, 2.0 said. *They didn't use them to transfer the contaminaton. I bet the Targets used them to transfer targetControlSystem to ART. That's why Eletra's memories were so messed up, it was using her neural tissue as storage space for its kernel.* It added, *It's kind of like killware. That's why we keep running into it. It's replicating.*

I stared at Central's system box. Conclusions:

1) The alien remnant had forced a contaminated human to bring it within range of the nearest operating system, a pre-CR central system.

2) The infected central system had partitioned itself (compulsively? Like the humans in alien contamination incidents who built weird things and killed each other?) and created targetControlSystem, a malware-like system that was a hybrid of outdated Pre-CR tech and whatever the alien remnant was.

3) TargetControlSystem had spread to the Adamantine systems and colonists. It made them use the Pre-CR tech, because that's what the Pre-CR central system understood. It had

them build what it wanted out of the Pre-CR tech, like the drones, and the implants. Pre-CR tech using alien code.

4) But it was still stuck here in the colony, on the terraformed section of the planet. Then the Barish-Estranza contact group had arrived.

I'd been in the shaft with the unsealed remnant and I was in this room. I still didn't feel infected. But then, targetControlSystem hadn't tried to infect the SecUnits on the explorer, either, including Three, who according to 2.0 had been ordered to stand frozen and helpless in the corridor. Maybe it couldn't affect constructs. That would be nice.

2.0 said, *So who's targetContact?*

Right, the contact that had been in communication with the explorer's instance of targetControlSystem. 2.0 had thought it was a human, or at least, not an alien. 2.0 had followed that contact's connection to this installation, and ended up in Pre-CR Central's network . . .

Oh, I had a bad feeling.

I stepped forward slowly, circling the web of connections. The only sound was my bad knee grinding and the despairing repeat of the distress signal. 2.0 said, *Uh, where are we going?*

I have to check something. I angled around to a break between two tables where there was a void in the connections. I eased forward and managed to fall/crouch down on the floor near the sprawled body of the human.

The thing is, I had realized there was no odor of decomp. The death had to have happened at least months ago, if not more than a planetary year, or years, if it was the incident that had kicked off the major contamination spread. But the shape of the body I could see under the white growth didn't look all sunken and gross or dried out.

The white crystalline substance was grainy, and it grew out of the human's ears and mouth. I had to edge forward at an angle and then lower my head down to get a view of the human's face. The skin had blue-white blotchy patches standing out against the light tan. That might be decay, and it might be the same process that had changed the Targets' skin color and texture. I saw the eyes were blue. And they were looking at me.

I scrambled away from it, out of the circle of racks and tables. I couldn't get up because of my knee and I was afraid to turn my back on it to use the wall to climb to my feet.

2.0 said, *I know violence isn't the solution to everything, but in this case . . .*

In this case, yeah.

I pointed my right arm energy weapon at the human's head, upped the intensity as far as it would go, and fired.

The white material flashed and emitted a faint odor I couldn't identify. The human still looked at me, expressionless. Their eyes were crusted with dried fluid, unable to blink. Oh, why can't anything be easy, just this once?

I tried to kill it three times. Until 2.0 said, *Those scars and marks on the floor around it could be projectile and energy weapon impacts. Somebody else has tried to kill it, multiple times, from different directions and with different weapons.*

Great. Tried to kill it, and tried to blow up the entrance to this chamber, but had been stopped before they could use an explosive big enough. The contamination must have done something to the human host's organic tissue, a self-protection function.

I was reluctant to go over there and put my fist through its head because (a) I thought I was immune to code contamination but maybe not if I actually got remnant on my organic parts and (b) if energy weapons wouldn't work, punching probably wouldn't, either. I needed to be smart about this.

I made myself turn around and use the wall to drag myself up so I could stand. *There are tools in the shaft. We need to find something that can smash it, or a bigger explosive.* I know, I can barely stand and walk, so this was me being really optimistic right now.

2.0 said, *Uh, potential problem. Why hasn't targetControlSystem called for help? There has to be proximity detection of some kind. Plus, targetContact there can see us.*

Oh. That was a good question.

Central said suddenly, *query: client population deceased? Y/N.*

It was asking about the humans. I told it *acknowledge: No. Client population endangered.*

It said, *query: client population assistance?*

I didn't have the right code and I didn't want to lie to it. Everything was so much worse even than it looked. I said, *acknowledge: unknown.*

It didn't respond.

I said, *query: proximity alert in progress?* It was aware of its situation, it might be able to tell if targetControlSystem knew we were here.

It said, *acknowledge: No alert. No proximity alert. No unknown organism present. In network only.*

Uh. It was saying the targetControlSystem wasn't reacting to me because it read my presence as non-hostile. It thought I was a Target, an infected colonist.

I couldn't respond. SecUnits aren't supposed to be able to go into shock like humans but my performance reliability had dropped another 5 percent, which is kind of a lot all at once.

I'm not in network, I told the central system. *I'm not infected.*

2.0 said, *Uh. I think maybe you are. I read diagnostic anomalies. Hold on.*

Central System sent me an image, a connection map of the room, like the one 2.0 had made. My hard address was on it, and a connection to targetControlSystem.

Oh, no.

Human to machine. Maybe that was the way it had to work. Human to machine to human.

We'd been doing it wrong. I'd been trying to get ART to avoid contact with potentially infected systems, when it was infected augmented humans we had to worry about.

And I had scanned this room, the infected human. It had been hoping to contaminate me in the shaft, and I had wandered in here and helpfully done it myself.

2.0 said, *I found anomalous code in your active processing space, I'm isolating it and tagging it. I've tried deleting it. Oh, it's out of isolation again. At least I've got it tagged.*

I thought I was immune, because I'm a SecUnit. Wow, that sounded pathetic. Like the "I want to be special! How come I'm not?" crap humans pull all the time.

2.0 said, *It can be deleted. ART deleted it.*

Yeah, that was ART. This is just me.

Me who could be taken over by targetControlSystem at any moment. It would be like having a governor module again.

No, not again. Never again.

I had an entry into the Targets' network. And maybe I had an ally.

I sent to Central: *query: permissions to initiate purge and restart.*

It said, *query: client population assistance?*

If I helped its humans, it would help me. I said, *acknowledge: If possible. I'll try.*

It replied: *acknowledge: permissions assigned.*

Suddenly I could see the whole node, central and target and how they were intertwined, with TargetContact on the periphery. I accessed central system and initiated the purge.

That was when TargetControlSystem figured out that I was here.

It acted much faster than I expected. It used the connection to overwhelm Central, to overwhelm my defenses and flow right into my head. It knew who I was, it had data from its other two iterations, it knew I'd killed it before.

For a whole second I thought I was done. Either I'd be deleted or under control again with targetControlSystem riding my head like a governor module, and if I had a choice I'd rather be deleted.

But it hadn't really caught on to the fact that 2.0 was in here with me. Or I guess, it didn't understand that we were two different iterations, with different capabilities. I was losing functionality and about to go into involuntary restart. But 2.0 was fine, and it was killware.

It extracted targetControlSystem from my head and followed the active connection right back into the central system's partition.

Central said, *purge failed.*

Initiate a shutdown and then destroy the unit, 2.0 told me. *Now, for fuck's sake.*

That will kill you, I told it.

I know, it said, *what do you think my function is, you idiot? Just do it.*

I didn't want to. I couldn't. I was an idiot, and I was remembering Miki throwing itself at a combat bot to give me the chance to save its humans.

If you fuck this up, I am going to be so angry I'll make ART look nice, 2.0 said. *And unlike Miki, this is how I win.*

This was going to hurt. I initiated the shutdown.

The feed disappeared abruptly as Central went down. Everything was silent, inside and outside my head. I realized I was on the floor again and shoved upright, staggered. I dumped a table over and cut the big crossbar off with my left arm energy weapon. Then I limped over to the star-shaped box that now held 2.0, Central, and targetControlSystem. They're sleeping, I told myself. 2.0 and Central wouldn't feel a thing. It was too bad targetControlSystem wouldn't.

With my club and both the energy weapons in my arms, I broke the case open and smashed and melted the interior. I felt strange and wrong, and my organic parts were doing things that made me glad again not to have a stomach. I had killed SecUnits and combat bots but this was me, sort of, okay not so sort of, plus Central who was a victim just as much as anybody else. Even TargetContact was a victim. And I was going to have to kill it, too, somehow. With targetControlSystem down, maybe I could get through its protective barrier.

Finished with Central's box, I turned to TargetContact.

Oh, it was moving. This was going to be worse. If there was anything left of the original human in there—

Then it whipped to its feet and charged me.

□   □   □

SecUnit 03
Status: *Retrieval in Progress*

I circle around the north side of the complex toward a passage between two of the surface structures. Drone intel provides me with a map of the complex, and the location of the Targets concealed in the east side doorways.

The Targets on the surface dock terrace tell the humans the history of the colony. This is a confirmation of intel already obtained by Iris, but not immediately useful.

If the humans cannot obtain the intel, I will enter the complex without it. This is the first retrieval I have performed without a governor module and I want it to be successful. I want to find the other SecUnit. I send a status update to *Perihelion* and it does not reply immediately. Then it sends, *Hold position.*

I tell it, *I must proceed in order to complete the retrieval.*

It said, *SecUnit would be angry if I sacrificed you with no chance of success.*

What?

Target Two: "They wanted to use the devices in the vault, the old devices. It became worse after that."

Thiago: "Who decided to start using the implants?"

That disturbs the Targets. Target One: "What implants?"

My drones pick up increased signal activity, deep under the complex, but it is not localized enough to trace.

On the feed, Thiago sends, *Ratthi, your analysis—*

Ratthi sends a file to *Perihelion*. Its drone creates a display surface and begins to play video of an implant being extracted from a Target.

The Targets stare at the video.

Overse: "You see? They didn't tell you about this, did they?"

All the other Targets look at Target Four, who says, "It helps the connection. It's for protection."

Target One: "Protection?"

Target Three: "How many of the others have these? Are you forcing them to obey you?"

Then Target Two turns back to the humans and says, "Eight levels below the plaza. They would have your friend there. That's where the contagion is."

On the secure feed, *Perihelion* tells me, *I'm pulling the humans out. You are go to proceed.*

I reply on the secure feed, *Acknowledged, proceeding.*

On the terrace, *Perihelion*'s drone says, *Run. You have three minutes to clear the area.*

Overse says, "Go, now!" and the humans run along the terrace toward the shuttle.

The Targets are confused, then turn and run down the path away from the surface dock.

Another pathfinder slams down in the agricultural field and explodes. Four more arc across the sky making disruptive screaming sounds. This is a distraction so I may initiate Stage 02 of the retrieval.

The Targets in the east side doorways around the installation's plaza are disoriented and three run away, headed toward the causeway. I slip inside another doorway without being detected.

□   □   □

Murderbot 1.0

My performance reliability dropped but the spike of fear upped my reaction time and I whacked TargetContact across the head with my table part. The impact staggered it back but still didn't damage the body. The effort I put into the swing made my wrecked knee joint give way and I hit the floor again.

I needed a bigger weapon. I needed help. I needed to get the fuck out of here.

The rough floor scraped at my palms as I scrambled toward the hatch. I managed to get upright and climb through the gap before TargetContact got to its feet. If it could catch me, this whole thing could start over, but with me down here instead of poor dead Central. I'd like to opt-out of that.

I staggered and limp-ran across the hangar bay toward the stupid gravity tube. (I know I said I didn't want to use it but I didn't have time to do the stairs and compared to what was behind me it was starting to look friendly. Also, with the feed dead it couldn't be remotely shut down.) I heard steps behind me and flung myself in.

I twisted around as the gravity shaft pushed me up. I saw TargetContact less than ten meters behind me. I had to get out before it got to the tube. Two levels went by with me trying to get off the fucking thing without the feed, then I flailed into the unmarked stop zone. It spit me out at the next level and I tumbled into a shadowy corridor and fell on the floor again.

Ouch. I was beginning to lose control over my pain sensors, a sign of an impending system failure. And I think I'd been too late, I think TargetContact saw I'd gotten off on this level. I was terrified of an involutary shutdown; when I restarted I'd be targetControlSystem.

I was higher up in the structure, and had no idea how to get away. It didn't matter, I had to keep moving. I got up and limp-ran.

The corridor curved to circle around the hangar bay's shaft and was way too long. It was cleaner and had more lights, obviously used more recently, and there had to be a lift pod or stairs somewhere.

Then I picked up a brief contact. Like a ping. A familiar ping. Drones, there were drones down here. Not targetDrones, my kind of drones. I sent frantic pings back, because it wasn't like TargetContact didn't know exactly where I was, I could hear it behind me in the corridor.

Ahead I saw more light and a foyer for a stairwell. I lurched into the foyer just as an armored SecUnit dropped down onto the landing.

I almost triggered both my energy weapons but just in time I saw the sticker on its helmet. In compressed machine language, somebody had used marker paint to write "ART sent me." This was 2.0's SecUnit 3.

The opaque helmet focused on me. It said, "I've never retrieved another SecUnit before. There is no protocol for this."

Seriously, fuck protocol. I said, "Hostile incoming. It's contaminated. Do not scan and don't let it touch you." If the contamination worked the way I thought it did I shouldn't be able to pass it to another SecUnit but who the hell knew. "Don't scan or connect with me, either, I might be a carrier."

SecUnit 3 started to say, "Transport *Perihelion* was able to obtain that intel from retrieved—" Then it leapt and landed past me, pulled the weapon off its back just as TargetContact rounded the corridor. It fired a burst of explosive bolts and TargetContact reeled back, but the impacts didn't dent the protective alien remnant coating.

"It doesn't work," I started to yell, but 3 aimed the next burst at the corridor ceiling. The impacts cracked the lighting track and shattered the material holding it in place. As chunks of stone hit the floor, 3 leapt back to me and grabbed me around the waist.

It said, "Please hold on. I will—"

"I know!" I yelled and grabbed it around the shoulders. "Just go!"

It bounded up the stairs, two levels, three levels. (Being carried like this was really uncomfortable, I can see why the humans don't like it.) 3 called in its drones and the swarm formed a protective cloud around us.

We came out through a hatchway into daylight, running onto an open plaza, the one I had seen from the surface dock. TargetDrones lay scattered on the paving, dead when targetControlSystem went down. I didn't see any Targets, but that was probably because a pathfinder sat in the center of the plaza shrieking on comm and audible: *Warning: detonation imminent.*

I said, "ART armed the pathfinders? And didn't tell me?" That asshole.

"The humans were surprised, too," 3 said.

ART's shuttle dove over the structure's ribs and dropped into the plaza. The hatch slid open and 3 bounded inside.

It dumped me in an acceleration chair and I had a view of TargetContact sprinting toward us. Then the hatch slammed shut and Arada was shouting "I've got them, go, go!"

The thrust almost knocked me out of the seat as the shuttle flung itself upward. (ART must be driving.) I was sitting on the safety webbing which was not helpful. 3 did what I would have done with a wounded human, and dropped into the seat next to me and stretched an arm across to hold me in place. From the pilot's seat, Arada demanded, "SecUnit, are you all right?"

"Not really," I said, "I'm infected with contaminated code. 2.0 tagged it as anomalous so ART can delete it. Tell it not to use a medical scanner on me." Through the port I got a view of the causeway and the dots that were the Targets/Colonists who had been in the structure, running away.

"We know," Arada told me, breathless from the acceleration. "The crew who escaped from the explorer knew about the scanning and *Perihelion* figured out how it was done."

Of course it did. This sounded like a good time to let go and have that involuntary shutdown.

I was fading out when below us, the pathfinder exploded. ART said, *TargetContact is offline.*

So was I.

20

So I wish I could have stayed shut down through the whole thing and skipped all the painful parts, but no such luck.

I restarted by the time we reached ART, so I was able to limp out of the shuttle on my own. Which was great, then I collapsed on the deck and had another involuntary shutdown.

When I restarted again (and I don't know if I'm underselling it but these rapid performance reliability drops and restarts were not pleasant or fun) I was still on the deck but surrounded by a bunch of unknown humans. One reached for my shoulder and I jerked away and almost restarted again.

Amena's voice said, "No, it doesn't like to be touched!" And I realized these were not actually unknown humans.

Ratthi and Arada sat on the deck in front of me with Amena hovering in the background. The others gathered around were Kaede, Iris, and Matteo. ART's humans wore clean clothes and various medical stabilizing packs, and they all smelled a lot better. Two of ART's big repair drones hovered nearby, and SecUnit 3 stood over to the side. It had taken its armor off, or been told to take its armor off. It wore a set of ART's crew clothing and looked, if I was reading the body language right and I probably was, like it had absolutely no idea what to do.

Iris told me, "It's all right, take it easy."

Matteo was saying to Arada, "Kaede's right, we'll put together a run box so we can isolate the code—"

"Then Peri should be able to delete it—" Kaede added.

"Delete what?" I said.

"The code in your system," Ratthi explained, tapping his own forehead like maybe I had also forgotten where my brain was. "The contaminated code. We can't use the medical platform, until *Perihelion* gets that code out of you. But Overse and Thiago are getting a portable med unit that will be cut off from the feed. We're going to take care of your physical injuries right here, then by that point, *Perihelion* should be able to deal with the contamination."

Physical injuries. Oh right, I had been shot a lot and was still leaking. "What's our situation?"

"No one's shooting at us and we aren't sending armed pathfinders at anyone," Ratthi told me. "Everyone is back on the ship. And we have some Barish-Estranza personnel to send back to their transport, but we want to make certain they're free of the remnant contamination first."

Matteo asked Ratthi something technical about the biohazard testing and I stopped listening, mostly. From what they were saying, it looked like I/2.0 had been right about how the contamination was spread. So, it's nice to be right, when you're leaking and parts of you have fallen off.

Arada turned to Iris. "I think I should mention . . . *Perihelion* told us why you were actually here, in this system."

ART's humans were taken aback. Iris exchanged a low-key version of an "oh shit" look with Kaede. Matteo said hopefully, "Um, you mean the deep space mapping?"

Were we going to have a problem? I really hope we wouldn't have a problem. And I wish Arada hadn't picked a moment when I was literally falling apart to bring this up.

Arada said, "We're not corporates. Everything *Perihelion* told us was in confidence and we won't betray it, or you." She made a little gesture. "I know contracts are important in the Corporation Rim, so we could sign one saying that we won't talk about anything we were told, or what happened here, if that will help."

Ratthi looked doubtful. "Yes, but we'll have to come up with some sort of explanation."

Amena added, "Yeah, my second mom is going to want to know what happened and she's not exactly easy to lie to."

"Your second mom?" Kaede prompted.

"She's the head of the— She was the head of the Preservation Alliance Council," Amena explained. "Dr. Mensah. She was in the newsfeeds a lot in the CR—she was kidnapped by a corporate called GrayCris and rescued by a SecUnit on TranRollin-Hyfa, and there was a company armed ship that was attacked and another ship from a security corporate that got blown up."

"Rescued by a . . ." Matteo trailed off and they all stared at me.

Which was not what I needed right now, cut off from the feed and ART's cameras and my drones. I said, "ART, I thought you told them about me."

ART said, *I told them I had met a rogue SecUnit. I didn't imply that you were every SecUnit ever mentioned in the newsfeeds.*

I think I was every SecUnit mentioned in the newsfeeds during that time, but whatever. SecUnit 3 had stopped trying to pretend to be an appliance and was now watching in fascination.

"No, Peri didn't . . ." Kaede exchanged a look with Iris again. "We heard a little about GrayCris going down but we weren't really following the story . . ."

Matteo's eyebrows tilted. "So the rumor that it was a rogue SecUnit on TranRollinHyfa—"

"Was true," Ratthi finished. "I was one of the 'unidentified conspirators' who escaped and is to be held liable for 'massive interference with commerce and property damage' if I'm ever caught on that station again." He shrugged. "So now we know things about each other."

Iris thought it over, then lifted her hands. "Look, we can work all this out later. Can we agree for now that we're all allies who keep each other's confidences?"

"And we don't like Barish-Estranza," Matteo added.

"Agreed," Arada said.

Thiago and Overse are here with the emergency medical kit. Great. I think I'm going to restart again.

□   □   □

I'm not going into detail because it was gross and involved a lot of leaking and removing projectiles and regenerating tissue the hard old-fashioned way with hand units and the emergency medical kit kept trying to spray everything with disinfectant.

At one point, Martyn, who was Seth's marital partner and Iris's second parent, got called in from Medical to consult. He was a bio expert, too, but was still in isolation getting decontaminated himself. "Hello," he said, peering at us via a display surface ART had generated. "How many SecUnit friends does Peri have?"

Iris said, "No, Dad, this is the SecUnit Peri told us about, the one it was going to bomb the colony over."

"Bomb the colony?" I said. We were still in the shuttle bay because they couldn't move me, and I was lying face down, my head propped on my arms, while Thiago, Ratthi, and Kaede rebuilt the organic components in my back. It was a long process and humans kept wandering in and out to watch, but I had my pain sensors tuned down and ART had directly connected an isolation box to my interfaces so I could download my video and audio of TargetContact, and more importantly so ART could play *Timestream Defenders Orion* for me. ART had also told me that SecUnit 3 had finally figured out that it could walk around wherever it wanted now and was doing that. I thought Iris was confused about when the bombing the colony thing had happened. I said, "That was the distraction so it could retrieve you."

"No, we were all in that maintenance capsule, the colonists didn't know where we were," Matteo said, pausing to make an adjustment to something. "Peri was going to bomb the colony with the armed pathfinders until they gave you up." They picked up something (I suspect it was something that normally formed a vital part of my insides) and carried it off to show Martyn via the display surface.

I had trouble believing that, but then I barely had the cognition to understand *Timestream Defenders Orion* right now (which is admittedly a pretty low bar) so maybe I was misunderstanding. "Are you sure? That doesn't sound right."

ART hadn't said anything, even to tell me how wrong I was, which was suspicious in itself.

Ratthi said, "Oh no, it was very clear about it. *Perihelion*, why don't you confirm what we're saying to SecUnit?"

ART said, *That was Plan A01. I was persuaded that Plan B01, a more complicated but less violent approach, would be more effective.*

I said, "So . . . that whole retrieval with the explosions was for me?" Just for me?

Thiago, with the tone of giving Ratthi a hint that he might want to shut up, said, "Maybe SecUnit is too tired to talk about this now."

Ratthi was determined. "Why don't you share the video record with SecUnit, *Perihelion*? So it will be up to date with everything that happened."

This was confusing, but Ratthi was right, I wanted to see the video. "I want to see it."

ART didn't respond for 2.3 seconds, then it paused *Timestream Defenders Orion,* and played the security archive of the event.

I was glad I could pretend to be too overwhelmed by being reassembled to respond, because I kind of was overwhelmed. That was ART, and my humans, and humans I had known for maybe five minutes, and a Barish-Estranza SecUnit that 2.0 had randomly found, all cooperating to retrieve me.

I'm going to stop talking for a while now.

◻   ◻   ◻

So once the humans had gotten me put back together enough to be stable and to stop my performance reliability from dropping, we had to move my active consciousness into an isolation box so ART could get rid of the contaminated code string. I say "we" but I was mostly just along for the ride.

It would have been lonely in the isolation box except ART kept a part of its consciousness in there with me and we watched the last episode of *Timestream Defenders Orion*.

After it was over, ART said, *That was satisfyingly unrealistic. Almost deliberately so.*

I said, *I don't know how they could have managed it accidentally.* I'd had time to process everything, and there were parts I didn't want to talk about yet. (No, I am not talking about *Timestream Defenders Orion*.) But this part I could say. *You and Amena were right, 2.0 was a person. It wasn't like a baby, but it was a person.*

ART reran a section of *Timestream Defenders Orion* where all the characters got shrunken to 1/25 of their original size. I've never had a module on physics, but I don't think that would work. It was fun to watch, though. ART said, *Do you regret my decision to deploy?*

No, I told it. I thought without 2.0, ART and I would have ended up connected to targetContact and the humans would be speaking Pre-CR languages and trying to off each other for not believing in the alien hivemind.

ART reran another one of its favorite scenes, this one involving time travel. I said, *You told your humans about me.*

ART knew exactly what I meant. *I told them I helped an escaping SecUnit get to RaviHyral. I didn't tell them about Tlacey and her employees in the shuttle.*

So you lied to them and made me sound . . . I didn't know how to put it. Sound like the person Tapan, Maro, and Rami thought I was, and not like what I actually was. *You made me sound safe.*

My humans are not members of a survey team from a noncorporate polity who have only recently begun to understand how dangerous corporates can be. Our missions are always calculated risks, and my humans must take steps to defend themselves, and occasionally me.

Then it said, *I have completed the removal of the contaminated code and started the process to return your consciousness to your body. While that completes, I have a proposal.*

I thought it meant that it wanted to watch all of *World Hoppers* again. Or that it had found a new series. Instead, it said, *There is an upcoming mission under discussion where your help would be invaluable.*

Uh. I said the first thing that occurred to me, which was *I don't think your humans are going to like that.*

I will discuss it with them.

I didn't say anything. I didn't even make a crack about ART's idea of a discussion and forcing everybody else to do what it wanted.

I didn't know if I trusted ART's humans or if I even wanted to try. But no one had ever rescued me before except Dr. Mensah, when she went into the DeltFall habitat after me, and ART had been willing to wipe a colony off a planet for me, and watching the security vid of a group of humans strategizing how best to get me out of there was . . . a lot, for me, considering the whole reason for me/constructs being created was so I/we could be abandoned in an emergency.

ART said, *I know you have difficulty making decisions so you don't need to give your answer right away.*

I do not have difficulty making decisions, ART, you're full of— I said, but it had already dropped me back in my body. And of course, my performance reliability crashed immediately and I had a forced shutdown.

□   □   □

When I came out of restart, I was on the platform in Medical. I was back on the feed, with five drones left, including the one retrieved from the space dock, and camera views all over the ship. Martyn, Karime, and Turi were still in Medical isolation in a nearby cabin, but they were on the feed with the other humans. Ratthi and Thiago were in the galley lounge with Seth. Overse was in the engineering pod with Matteo, Tarik, and Kaede, going over the scans of what little was left of the alien remnant from ART's drive. (Basically ART was going to need help from its University's decontam team before it could go into a worm-hole again, which was not good news. If Barish-Estranza rein-forcements showed up, we were in trouble.) Arada was in the control deck with Iris. SecUnit 3 was in the galley lounge, too, lurking in a corner and listening to the humans talk.

Amena . . . Amena had carried a chair over next to the plat-form, and was browsing through the Pansystem University cata-log in the feed. I said, "I'm back online."

She smiled. "I'll warn everybody."

I sat up. The MedSystem had finished what the humans had started and my performance reliability was up around 98 per-cent. I was wearing the kind of soft smock thing that injured humans wear, but my drones spotted my clothes, cleaned and recycler-repaired, folded on a gurney. Before I could think about it too much, I said, "ART asked me to join its crew for a mission."

ART, as usual, was listening, and this was my way of telling it what I was thinking. It was easier telling Amena, for some rea-son. Maybe because she had somehow managed to put herself in the middle of my and ART's quote-unquote relationship.

Amena paused her feed and frowned. "For how long?"

"For the duration of the mission." But I had the feeling that ART meant for this to be the first step in a longer . . . association.

Amena's forehead indicated suspicion. "Just the one mission? Kind of like asking someone to come stay with your family for the break between the work seasons, to see if they all like each other before you get serious?"

"I don't know what that means," I said. I was noticing ART hadn't jumped in to tell her how wrong she was, and I knew it would have, if she was wrong. So she wasn't wrong. "But yes, maybe."

Amena thought it over. "I guess I'm not surprised. How do you feel about it?" My expression must have changed because she rolled her eyes. "Oh sorry, I used the f word there."

Again, I have no idea why ART likes adolescent humans. "I don't know," I told her.

"So . . . what do you think second mom will say?"

I had no idea. "What do you say?"

She snorted. "I was just getting used to you." My drone watched her eyeing me. "I don't think it's a terrible idea. Except . . . ART works in the Corporation Rim sometimes, too, right? It's not all missions out to these lost colonies."

"That's a factor." Though I wondered how often ART's solo "cargo missions" were actually gathering intelligence in a way no corporation would ever suspect.

Amena didn't look happy about the idea of me going back to the Corporation Rim. I wasn't wildly excited about it, either. She said slowly, "I think ART cares a lot about you. You should have heard . . . the only reason it went ahead and sent your killware to the explorer was because it thought if it didn't, the only way to get Iris and everybody back was to send you. That sending the killware would mean you wouldn't have to do something danger- ous. Of course, you were already doing something dangerous but we didn't know that at the time." She hesitated, and added, "I don't think it would invite you to come with it if it didn't think it would be good for you, you know."

No, I still didn't know.

□   □   □

After three more cycles, the rest of the humans were able to leave Medical isolation. The Barish-Estranza crew were sent back via their shuttle to Supervisor Leonide's supply transport. Nobody tried to hold anybody else hostage, which was unusual for this situation, but then no Barish-Estranza reinforcements had shown up yet.

The supply transport was still repairing its wormhole drive and hanging out within range of us just in case anything else showed up to attack. Also to make sure we didn't somehow steal the planet out from under them. Which ART and its crew to- tally intended to still do. If they could manage it. The humans all spent most of their time talking about what to do about the colonists, how to handle decontaminating the colony site, would they/could they move everybody if they had to. ART wouldn't be there for that part, but its crew would make recommendations about it when the university's decontam facilities teams arrived.

The one big problem was that because of the alien remnant contamination, Karime said the legal case prepared by the university no longer applied, so they needed help before they could contest Barish-Estranza's claim. Barish-Estranza had sent a message buoy through the wormhole to their corporate base of operations, and ART had sent one to the University. So we were waiting to see who showed up first.

Also, there was this whole thing where we had a rogue SecUnit aboard who wasn't me.

It was mostly doing what it had done on the Barish-Estranza explorer, which was to stand around on guard and patrol occasionally. Except ART had made it give up its armor and weapons and I suspect had given it some details about what might happen if it even thought about shooting any projectiles out of its arm.

Amena and Ratthi kept suggesting that I should help it "adjust" whatever that is. I knew if I was in its position, I'd want to be left alone. And if it hadn't even sat down in a chair voluntarily yet, it probably wasn't ready to talk.

(I know this sounds suspiciously like a rationale I had come up with to keep from doing something I didn't want to do anyway, but hey, I can't help that.)

Then at the end of the third cycle, when most of the humans were sleeping, I noticed it was following me around. I figured that was a sign it wanted to talk. I stopped in an empty corridor, faced the wall, and said, "What?"

It stood there for .6 of a second with the standard neutral-blank expression. Our drones went into a holding pattern, circling above our heads. Then its face relaxed a little and it said, "I saw your files."

"2.0 told me."

"The story was incomplete."

"Because I'm not dead."

"You continued to perform your duties after you neutralized your governor module."

"For thirty-five thousand hours." I suddenly had a bad feeling about this. "You want to go back."

It hesitated again. "No, I don't want to. I . . . won't. But I don't know what to do."

Okay, that was a relief. Just because we're both rogue Sec-Units doesn't mean we're going to be friends, but I knew if it went back, it would be dead. I'd hacked my governor module and kept doing my job because I didn't know what else to do (except you know, a murderous rampage, but murderous rampages are over-rated and interfere with one's ability to keep watching media) but that was different from escaping and then going back. I said, "Because change is terrifying. Choices are terrifying. But having a thing in your head that kills you if you make a mistake is more terrifying."

It didn't seem inclined to argue. "Your clients told me I could go with them to Preservation."

"You can do that. Or not. You don't have to."

"They are your clients."

I said, "You can trust them."

I'm sure it thought I was delusional. Hey, I thought I was delusional. SecUnit 3 didn't say anything because what could you say to that in this situation. Or any situation.

Then it said, "The completed portion of the story." I finally realized it wanted to ask me for it, but its experience at asking for things that weren't contract-relevant data was nonexistent. "Viewing it would . . . help me come to a decision."

I was pretty sure I knew what decision it intended to come to. My files were a how-to manual for fugitive SecUnits. I said, "I'll excerpt the relevant portions and send them to you."

It actually looked almost pleased for a second there. It said, "Thank you for that information."

In the end, twenty cycles after we had arrived in this system, it was a Preservation ship, an armed station responder, which came through the wormhole.

"They couldn't possibly have gotten here in this amount of time," Arada said, after the ship's ID had been confirmed and the exclamations and arm waving in the galley lounge were over. "Not unless they left only a few hours after we did."

ART said, *They may have. Before I was deleted, I prepared a message buoy, explaining what had happened and asking for assistance, and concealed its existence from targetControlSystem. I set it to jettison automatically when the wormhole drive engaged.*

There was more exclaiming. "But why didn't you tell us?" Amena asked it.

(Yes, Amena is still naive about what a monster ART is.)

ART told her, *Because then it would have been harder to force you to do as I wanted.*

(Yeah, like that.)

"Can you contact it on comm?" I said. Because I had a feeling who was onboard and if I was right we could save a lot of time and a lot of aggravation. And by that I mean me being aggravated while humans talk to each other for an unnecessarily long amount of time.

Seth gave me a thoughtful look. "We can. Peri?"

Are they likely to deploy malware? ART asked.

"You're not funny," I told it.

Once ART secured a comm connection with the Preservation responder, I said, "This is SecUnit. Is Dr. Mensah aboard?"

There was only a four second pause. Then Mensah's voice said, "SecUnit, I'm here."

Amena bounced impatiently but I tapped her feed to wait. I said, "Coldstone, song, harvest."

"Acknowledged," Mensah said immediately, sounding relieved. "Now will someone tell me what the hell happened?"

Arada hastily took over. Seth asked me, "That was a stand down code, I take it?"

Amena made an exasperated noise. "You have a special code with second mom."

It was actually *stand down, clear, and no casualties.* I just said, "Yes." Now I'd have to change it.

Between Arada and the others on the comm, by the time the responder reached ART all the pesky questions about kidnapping and trying to blow up Preservation survey facilities had been resolved.

By this point, Thiago had convinced Seth and Iris to tell Mensah about ART's actual mission. I think Mensah on the comm being all persuasive and reasonable had something to do with it. Plus along with the responder's crew and a security team from the station, Pin-Lee had come with Mensah. Since ART's crew needed someone who was good with Corporation Rim contract negotiation, the idea of an alliance with Preservation was looking better and better. Whatever, the humans worked it out while I watched *Sanctuary Moon.* ART watched with me for some of the episodes but the idea of Dr. Mensah coming aboard made it weirdly excited and it had its drones clean its whole interior again and was doing things like yelling at Turi to put their laundry in the recycler.

The responder pulled up to ART's module dock, and Mensah came aboard with Pin-Lee, and there was a lot of noisy greetings and hugging and exclamations and introductions. There was a lot of talking to me, with Pin-Lee asking me if I was all right, and Mensah thanking me for trying to get Amena off the baseship. Seth, as the captain, formally introduced them both to ART. He told them, "We normally aren't able to do this, since *Perihelion's* existence as anything other than a bot pilot has to be kept secret in the Corporation Rim."

"We understand," Mensah said, her voice just a little dry. "We're keeping a number of secrets from the Corporation Rim, too. I'm very glad to meet you, *Perihelion.*"

It's a pleasure to have you aboard, Dr. Mensah, ART said, and actually managed to sound like it meant it.

Later, when everybody had settled down and Pin-Lee was consulting with Karime and Iris about documents to dispute Barish-Estranza's claim on the colony, I got to talk to Dr. Mensah semi-privately. (Semi-privately because ART was impossible to avoid.) (But I was used to that.)

She came and sat down next to me in the lounge and I adjusted a drone to be able to get a view of her face. I had things I wanted to say but had no idea how, so I blurted, "Did you get the trauma treatment?"

Now her voice sounded very dry. "I had the first set of appointments, yes. Then my daughter and my brother-in-law and my friends were kidnapped and I had to drop everything to mount a rescue mission."

That was fair. "Was it . . ." I didn't want to ask how she had been without me there. Okay, I did want to ask, obviously, but it was awkward, plus I was still aware of what ART had said about violating her privacy by talking about the therapy.

She waited, eyes narrowing, then evidently decided that was as far as I was going to get. "It's been fine. I know it will take time. But I've been fine." Her expression turned ironic. "Right up until the mass kidnapping incident."

At least that part wasn't my fault. Then, before I knew I was going to, I said, "Did Amena tell you about my emotional collapse?"

Now she frowned for real. "No, she didn't."

"Oh." Yeah, well, I could have kept my mouth shut about that, but now it was too late. "It was when I thought ART was dead."

She still had a little worried forehead crease. "That's understandable. Ratthi said *Perihelion* is a very close friend of yours."

"Ratthi has a vivid imagination." This was an awkward thing and I might as well get it over with. "I didn't tell you about ART."

The forehead crease actually went away. "I don't tell you everything, either."

"That's because I don't want to know everything and you respect that." I decided to just say it. "ART asked me to come on a mission with it."

"I see." She considered it seriously. "Would this be a temporary job, or something more permanent?"

"I don't know." This was incredibly weird and awkward. "I don't want to not see you again."

She took a moment to sort out my verbs. "I don't want to not see you again, either." Her expression was still thoughtful. "But if you do find you want to spend more time with *Perihelion,* you could always come back and visit us."

It was getting easier to talk about this. "Preservation was the first place I was a part of and I don't want to not be a part of it. But I like being with ART. I want to keep being with it."

She nodded to herself. "What about the rest of the crew?"

Yeah, well, that was the potential problem. "I don't know them yet."

"Working for them temporarily could take care of that problem. If you decide to do that." She smiled a little. "The good thing is, you do know what you want."

I sort of did know. It was a weird feeling. "That's new."

She smiled all the way. "I wasn't going to put it quite that way, but yes."

□   □   □

ART's crew had settled in for a rest period, except for the humans who were working on the legal case. Mensah had taken Amena and Thiago back to the Preservation ship with her. (Amena told me Thiago felt he had some apologizing to do to Mensah for "misunderstanding her relationship with me" and that Amena would report back on it and I was just glad they were talking on the other ship where I didn't have to risk hearing them.) Arada and Overse and Ratthi had stayed in the spare bunkroom aboard ART.

I went up on ART's control deck where it was quiet. It felt

familiar in a good way, so I pulled the memory of my first time aboard so I could compare it. It was better without ART threatening to destroy my brain. I said, "If I do the mission with you, we'll need more media." We went through it pretty fast, and that was an understatement.

I've been amassing a collection from the university's archives, ART said.

It sent me the index and I started searching through it. "Maybe we should give some to 3." ART would know that I'd given 3 my relevant archive files. "It's probably going to leave as soon as it gets a chance."

That's not why 3 wanted your files, or not the only reason. I asked it why it wanted to help retrieve you, and it said, "stories in the HelpMe.file." I think your memories are providing it with the sort of context you obtained from human media.

I didn't know what I thought about that. I would never have thought to just hand my files over to 3 the way 2.0 had. And if 2.0 hadn't done that, targetControlSystem would have won.

According to the report 2.0 had downloaded to me, 3 had actually seemed to like the other two SecUnits on the explorer, as if they had been friends, at least to the extent that they had been allowed to communicate with each other. I'd never thought that was possible.

Maybe I'd always been a weird SecUnit; maybe 3 would have better luck communicating with other SecUnits.

Maybe I needed to get 3 a copy of Dr. Bharadwaj's documentary, too.

Whatever. For now, keyword searching ART's index, I think I'd found something even less realistic than *Timestream Defenders Orion*. I showed the description to ART, and it started the first episode.

ACKNOWLEDGMENTS

Thanks to Nancy Buchanan, first reader and first librarian, without whom most of my books would not have titles.

Thanks to my husband Troyce, and friends Megan, Beth E., Felicia, Lisa, Bill, and Beth L., and everyone else who read versions of this in its rough form and kept me going until it was finished.

Thanks to Jennifer Jackson and Lee Harris, without whom Murderbot would never have made it into print.